What Readers Are Saying About Sharlene MacLaren and *Her Rebel Heart*

I haven't missed a single Sharlene MacLaren book because I find that every new release is better than the one before!

—*Renee*, Kentucky

MacLaren writes in a way that pulls her readers in from the very first word! My favorite was the Tennessee Dreams series. I think I cried at the end of every one of those books.

—*Karen*, Ohio

What can I say? Sharlene MacLaren's writing style is the best! Whenever I hear about another of her books coming, I race to the pre-order section online because I want to be first to get it in my hands.

—*Cathy*, Florida

MacLaren's novels are heartwarming, but also fraught with emotional drama. I can hardly get through one of her books without crying at some point. I've learned to keep a box of tissues handy.

—*Marsha*, Michigan

Every time I read one of MacLaren's books, I know I'm going to be missing a lot of sleep because I can't put them down until I finish. I usually read them in one or two sittings.

—*Shelley*, Oklahoma

A Love to Behold was my favorite book by Sharlene MacLaren. She gave me an excellent historical perspective into what life was like in the Reconstruction of the South after the American Civil War. The beautiful romance that developed was just the icing.

—*Ann*, Illinois

The only problem with Sharlene MacLaren books is that they are too far apart. I wrote to her and asked her to write faster!

—*Millie*, Texas

I live in Australia, so I have to wait a little longer for her books to reach me, but they are always worth the wait!

—*Janet*, Australia

A NOVEL BY SHARLENE
MACLAREN

HER Rebel HEART

WHITAKER
HOUSE

Publisher's Note:
This novel is a work of fiction. References to real events, organizations, or places are used in a fictional context. Any resemblances to actual persons, living or dead, are entirely coincidental.

All Scripture quotations are taken from the King James Version of the Holy Bible.

HER REBEL HEART

Sharlene MacLaren
www.sharlenemaclaren.com
sharlenemaclaren@yahoo.com

ISBN: 978-1-64123-384-2
eBook ISBN: 978-1-64123-385-9
Printed in the United States of America
© 2020 by Sharlene MacLaren

Whitaker House
1030 Hunt Valley Circle
New Kensington, PA 15068
www.whitakerhouse.com

Library of Congress Control Number:2019955054

1 2 3 4 5 6 7 8 9 10 11 **WH** 27 26 25 24 23 22 21 20

DEDICATION

To all my wonderful sisters-in-law,
whom I've come to dearly love:
Charity, Lillian, Shirlee, Gayle, Mary, Debbie, and Penny.
I cherish you.

1

June 1863 · Ripley, West Virginia

Cristina Stiles fell hard against the wooden table and flinched when the soldier in blue yanked her up by one of her long braids, hauling her so close that, even with the bandanna covering his face, she smelled his foul breath. She screeched from the terrible pain but fought with everything in her, thinking only of her two children, out in the barn, and hoping they would stay concealed and quiet, as she'd urgently instructed them.

The soldier slapped her hard across the cheek, this time knocking her against a high-back chair. The chair toppled, and she nearly went down with it, but he snatched her upright again and spewed hideous words into her ear, words about what he would do with her the next time he and his repulsive cohort paid a call. Despite her racing heart and bruised innards, she whipped around, yanked down the bandanna, and spat in the fellow's dirty face. Her spittle traced a path down an ugly scar that started under his left eye and ended at his cheekbone. She managed to free her hand from his grasp and quickly clawed at his left eye, just over the scar.

"Why, you little...." He growled like a bear as blood trickled along his face. "You're a she-devil, ain't y'? Somebody's gotta teach you a lesson."

He swiped at his bleeding eye, then spun her around and grasped her tight, pressing her back against his flabby chest. His lips tickled her earlobe in a sickening way as he whispered, "You need t' learn some respect." Then he let out a wicked chortle.

"We better get outta here," the other soldier sputtered from the window, rifle in hand. "Somebody's ridin' in. Cain't tell if it's a man 'r a woman."

The soldier adjusted his hold on her, and she found an opportunity to bite his hand.

"Ouch!" he squawked, yanking his hand away. "Y' little witch!" He jerked her around to face him and then punched her in the gut, this time letting her fall to the floor in a heap. She curled herself into a ball, trying with everything in her not to cry out, for fear he would blast her with his boot. Little good her efforts did, for he kicked her anyway and the sound of cracking ribs rent the air. Pain ripped through her. A bitter blend of saliva and blood pooled in her mouth. Had she lost a tooth? She lay there swallowing her fear, trying to breathe gingerly past her tender, aching ribs.

"Come on," the fellow at the window said.

"What's yer name, huh?" the other demanded.

Cristina bit her lip. Would answering make her situation better—or worse?

"I asked yer name," he growled.

"Cristina," she said finally, angry with herself for giving in, but also not wanting to suffer another blow. "Cristina Stiles."

The fellow stood over her. "And where's yer man?"

She pursed her lips and swallowed blood. Every ragged breath she took hurt her chest.

The one by the window said, "We gotta leave. Now."

The other bent down and lifted her head by the hair. "I bet yer man's a Reb, ain't 'e?"

"Yes, and we're proud of it," she said through swollen lips.

He let go of her hair so that her head dropped like a rock. "Well, you're in Union territory now. You best start thinkin' like a Yank if'n ya know what's good fer ya."

Blood dripped out the side of her mouth, but that didn't keep her from muttering, "Now, get…off…my…property."

"Oh, we're goin', but we'll see you soon, Missus Stiles. Don't go waitin' up fer us, though, 'cause y' never know when we'll be back. Oh, and I'd keep my mouth shut about our visit if I was you. We know you got little ones. We seen 'em run out to the barn." He leaned down close to her face so that his breath reached her ear again. "You wouldn't want anythin' happenin' to them, now, would y'?" Seconds slipped by. "Would you?" he screamed.

She gave her head several fast shakes, somehow keeping herself from moaning at the pain.

"Didn't think so."

"Come on," the other said.

Cristina got another boot in the side, and she couldn't contain the anguished cry that came up from her depths.

"I had to do that for good measure, y' understand. Wouldn't want you t' forget us."

Out the corner of her swollen eye, she tried to get a good look at both men. Stupid Yanks. They had no scruples. To them, she was nothing but a Rebel woman whose husband fought for the South. Even if she did report them, no one would take her seriously.

If only she'd had her gun nearby when they'd exploded through her door. She could've downed them both before they ever took a step inside. But she hadn't heard them coming. Hadn't heard as much as a horse's bluster. She hoped her children were safe.

Lying as still as a dead bird, she listened as the men crammed a sack full of food she had intended for her children. The wretched pair stepped over her body as they made for the door, which they opened and then shut with a loud bang. She finally gave herself permission to take a shallow breath as their footfalls thudded across her rickety little porch. Next thing she heard was a loud "Gidd'up" and the rumble of horses' hooves. That's when she allowed a single tear to fall off her cheek. They were gone, and she had survived. Grabbing hold of a chair leg, she dragged herself over to the table, then inhaled a breath and immediately exhaled a painful cry. *Elias, Catherina.* Her only thoughts now were for her children, but how to reach them?

"Cristina!" called a familiar voice. There was a shuffle of hoofbeats outside, and then a "Whoa!"

The voice belonged to her friend and neighbor Clara Woodrum. In her early seventies, the woman was still as spry as a calf. Cristina heard the click-clack of boots and then the groan of the door as it opened.

Her neighbor rushed across the room to Cristina and crouched down beside her, her knees making a noisy protest. "What in the name o' goodness happened to you? And who were those men ridin' off in a flurry o' dust?"

"Yanks, Clara. Mean ones. What...?" The strain of speaking weighed on Cristina. "What're you doin' here?"

"I just came by t' visit, and I'm sure glad I did. What'd them dumb Yanks do t' you? Wait, they didn't...? Oh, good gracious, if they did somethin' ungodly t' you—"

"They didn't, but they hinted they'd come back. They're prob'ly from that Union camp outside o' town, which, I was told, was charged with protectin' us citizens." Cristina scoffed.

"Where're yer youngins?"

"Hidin' in the barn."

"Once I've tended to you an' the kids, I'll run into town an' report them rotten chumps."

"No!" Cristina rolled to her side with a great deal of effort, wincing all the while. "We can't tell the—the law."

Clara tipped back on her heels. "What d' you mean, we can't tell the law? We've gotta report them no-good apes. A crime's been committed."

"They threatened t' hurt my children if I told anyone. I'm scared for them. Speakin' of, I've gotta get out there an' make sure they're okay. Help me up, please?"

"You ain't gettin' up, blossom. Not jes' yet, anyway. I'll go fetch 'em."

The taste of blood made Cristina's stomach roil. "Hurry. Please."

"Y' stay right here. When I come back, I'll help you to yer bed—and then we'll talk." Clara rose to her feet, her knees creaking. "Them blamed Yankees. I hate 'em clear t' kingdom come. They ain't caused nothin' but trouble ever since our side o' Virginia went blue. You'd think they'd treat us better now that we're officially Yanks ourselves."

While Clara went to the barn, Cristina forced herself to get up from the plank flooring. No sense in letting her children see her in this state, never mind that they would immediately notice the bruises and blood on her face. With great effort, she managed to sit.

Soon the door squeaked open once more. "Mama, Mama," her two children chanted anxiously as they ran to her.

"We stayed in the hayloft, jes' like you said to," ten-year-old Elias told her while Catherina, who was not yet six, merely whimpered. "Only we di'n't like it one bit. We was pure scared."

Cristina winced as she reached up and gently stroked her daughter's smudged face.

"Maw, you're hurt bad," said Elias.

"I'll be fine," Cristina assured him. "I'm just glad you stayed safe in the barn."

The children must've buried themselves in the hay, just as Cristina had taught them. Spikes of straw stuck out in every direction from Catherina's dark hair. "You did good, both o' you. Now, help me stand so I can put this house back t' rights."

"You'll be doin' no such thing," Clara insisted. "I'm here now. I'll tidy up the place, rustle up some food fer yer evenin' meal, an' help these younglings get ready fer bed. Here, put yer arm 'round my neck so's I can help you to the bed."

"I'll help," said Elias.

"Me, too," Catherina echoed.

Cristina was sorer than she'd expected to be, which told her tomorrow would be even worse. She gave her side a gentle rub as she got to her feet.

Clara shook her head as she watched. "Blasted, no good—"

"Clara…" Cristina wanted to limit her children's exposure to her friend's wrathful words. While Cristina was no saint herself, she did take extra care when it came to her language—not because she held to any strict religious code but because she wished to teach her children proper English. With it being summertime, the local school was closed, so Cristina worked as often as she could with her children, tutoring them in cyphering, reading, and writing. They devoured literature, which she attributed to her own love of the written word. The family owned few books due to limited finances, but they took advantage of Ripley's tiny library. Cristina had read nearly every book on its shelves, multiple times. Orville used to read to the children, but he often faltered at a word, so most of the reading fell to Cristina. Sadly, they hadn't seen Orville since last January, and his latest letters spoke of the awful things the war had done to him—how every day seemed darker than the one before. Cristina worried that his state of mind had declined. He never acknowledged any of her questions or concerns regarding his well-being.

"Here, sit y'rself down," Clara said, breaking into her sullen thoughts. They'd reached the edge of the bed, and so, with assistance, Cristina turned around, then lowered herself to the old, flimsy mattress. "Elias, you go fetch yer maw a cup o' water," Clara directed. "Catherina, you help me fill a basin with the water that's heatin' over the fireplace so's we can wash yer maw's face. It's gonna be a bit black an' blue, if I was t' guess."

As the threesome went about their duties, Cristina gingerly touched her jaw and felt the bulge there, then ran her tongue along her upper lip. The sensations made her shudder. Every breath pained her something fierce. She gave a light cough and flinched at the sharp jab. Tears threatened, but she wiped them away. The single tear she'd already shed had been enough. She didn't want her children feeling sorry for her or sensing her fear. They borrowed daily from her strength—and she would not fail them now.

"Everything's gonna be jes' fine," Clara whispered as she began cleaning Cristina's face with a warm, damp cloth. Her gentle ministrations calmed Cristina's wracked nerves.

"Here, Maw," said Elias, handing her a cup. "Take a good drink."

Cristina gave her son a small smile, ignoring the pain it caused her, as she took the offered cup. "Thank you, Elias." She sipped slowly, savoring the cool liquid.

"Maybe I oughtta stay here fer a couple o' days," Clara mused aloud.

Cristina gazed into her daughter's watery eyes as she considered the offer. "Thank you, Clara, but we should be fine. I don't think those soldiers'll return anytime soon. It's just a hunch. To be safe, though, I plan t' sleep with my rifle by my side. Anyway, you have animals t' tend."

"That's no problem. I can always ride back an' forth a couple o' times a day."

"That's not necessary, but I do thank y' fer the offer."

"Who was them mean people that hurt you, anyway?" asked Elias. "We were pullin' weeds when we seen 'em comin' over the ridge. Ran like foxes to the barn, jes' like you tol' us to, so I didn't get a good look at 'em."

"They was Yankee soldiers, Elias," answered Clara. "Mean ol' brutes, they are. Ain't an ounce o' good in 'em. Don't never trust 'em, you hear me, boy?"

Elias pursed his mouth, raised his chin, and pulled his narrow shoulders as straight as pins. Cristina worried her son was maturing faster than a ten-year-old boy ought to. "I hate 'em, every last one of 'em. If they come back, I'll kill 'em."

"I hates 'em, too," said Catherina with a crack in her voice.

Cristina frowned. "Don't talk like that, either o' you. No point in causin' more reason fer frettin'. And you'll not be killin' anybody, Elias Eduardo."

"With Paw gone, I'm the man around here. It's my duty t'—"

"It's yer duty t' watch after yer sister, not protect me or this house, y' hear? I won't have you grabbin' a gun unless it's fer huntin' purposes."

"He should learn how to defend 'imself," Clara put in.

"Clara, don't encourage 'im, please."

"I hear-tell there's some boys fightin' in the war who's my age, Maw," Elias persisted. "Paw shoulda took me with 'im."

"Don't ever say such a thing again. You're a mere boy."

Elias stretched himself as tall as possible. "I'm older 'n I look."

"Well, we aren't discussin' such nonsense any further." She gingerly took a few more sips of water. Every part of her body throbbed with pain.

"Why don't y' lay y'rself down on the bed?" Clara asked as she bent to lift an upturned chair. She pushed it to the rough-hewn pine table Cristina's husband had inherited from his grandfather just after their marriage, some eleven years ago. "I'll look through your cupboard and the lean-to for somethin' t' make fer supper."

"I'm not sure what you'll find. 'Fraid the soldiers stole a good deal of our provisions."

"Well then, I'll check the springhouse. Surely, I'll find somethin' out there. I ain't worried. I been known t' rub two sticks together t' make a meal."

"I don't like sticks," Catherina said, her face scrunched into a big frown as she sat beside Cristina on the bed.

Clara's eyes twinkled. "Y' ain't tried mine yet. Sprinkled with the right amount o' seasonin', sticks can be quite tasty. Might even add some sugar."

Catherina fretted and looked to her mother for comfort. Unfortunately, Cristina couldn't think of much to say to ease her daughter's mind. Instead, she patted her arm. "You'll eat whatever Miss Clara fixes an' not complain."

The child hung her head, giving it a tiny nod. "Okay. If I have to."

Cristina managed a smile, ignoring the pain it triggered. "Don't you worry, Catherina. Miss Clara makes a fine stick soup."

Across the room, Clara chuckled.

2

At dusk, after their meal of fried eggs and bread, Clara cleaned the cabin's makeshift kitchen, washed the dishes, and swept the floor before turning to Cristina with a worried look. "You sure you'll be all right?"

"I'm not worried," Cristina lied. "The children and I will walk you out. We still need to feed the animals." Besides their horses, Starlight and Thunder, the family kept a small group of livestock. Rita the cow provided milk, as did the nanny goats Darlin' and Sally. Billy goat Fred kept them in line and Gopher the donkey brayed out a warning whenever coyotes came near. Pete the hog was still too young and small to eat, so Cristina relied on a number of mostly nameless chickens for eggs or meat.

"We already done fed an' watered the goats and pig," said Clara. "Did it before fixin' supper whilst you was nappin'."

Cristina shook her head, overwhelmed by her friend's kindness. "Thank you, Clara. You've done more than enough. You best get home before it's too dark t' see."

"I'll come back in the mornin'."

"No need."

"Of course, there's need. I'll bring y' some supplies. Them rapscallions done took most all yer grub. You'll need rations t' tide you over till you feel up t' makin' a trip into Ripley."

"Thank you again, Clara. You're as dear a friend as anybody could have."

Clara nodded. "Orville'd be proud o' you. Brave mama, you are. Y'all sleep tight, y' hear?"

Left alone with her children, Cristina tousled Elias's crop of light brown hair. "Do you mind climbin' the ladder to the attic by yerself tonight? I'm afraid my body's a bit too sore fer me t' get up there an' tuck you in."

"I'll just say good night. I'm gettin' too old fer tuckin' in anyway, Maw. Did y' lock the doors?"

"Yes, I bolted both doors. We're safe."

Catherina looked up at her with weary eyes. "They ain't comin' back, are they, Mama?"

"Not tonight. And don't say 'ain't.'"

"Are they gonna come back sometime, though?"

"I don't know, but you aren't t' worry about such things." Sadly, she couldn't promise that the soldiers wouldn't return. She bent, flinching at the pain, and placed a soft kiss on her daughter's forehead.

"Does it hurt, Mama?" the child asked.

"Just a little."

"Them men was mean."

"They were, but we don't need t' give 'em any more thought."

"It's hard not to," said Elias, propping one foot on the bottom of the ladder leading to his attic room.

Cristina gave a soft sigh. "O' course, it's hard. It's still so fresh in yer minds. You'll be feelin' better by tomorrow."

"Don't forget to keep yer rifle handy."

After bidding Elias a good night and watching him climb the ladder, she turned down the lamps, then got Catherina settled in her trundle bed. Soon the girl's soft breathing reached Cristina's ears, a welcome sound that told of her daughter's trusting heart.

But sleep would not come easy to Cristina. With her rifle beside her, she rolled over on the mattress, wincing with pain, then squeezed her eyes shut and tried to keep her mind from wandering to those wicked men. Eventually, she drifted into a restless slumber.

⁓

Clive Horton stretched out his legs in front of the fading camp-fire, feeling quite satisfied with the day's events. After beating the day-lights out of that little Rebel woman and then taking what grub they could find that looked appealing, they'd ransacked a farmhouse after knocking the old farmer out cold—not intentionally, but in self-defense when he came at them with a gun—coming away with a leather pouch of gold coins, as well as some fine jewelry. The four or five weeks they'd been posted in Ripley had proved lucrative indeed, especially with no real orders except to keep the peace along the border between Ohio and West Virginia. Their previous assignment, providing relief in the Battle of Banks' Ford in Spotsylvania, hadn't been too difficult either.

So far, Clive had lucked out in his life as a soldier. With the help of Mike Farmer, willing yet somewhat dim-witted, he'd robbed at least eight homes. Most of them had been vacant, except for today when they'd come upon that Mexican woman Cristina and then, later, the old codger with the gold. They'd had no choice but to hit him, and the woman…well, she made Clive plain mad when she mouthed off at him. To add insult to injury, she'd had the audacity to pull down his ban-danna and then spit right in his face before nearly scratching out his eye. He was downright lucky he could still see.

"You still think our stash is safe?" Mike whispered from his seat next to Clive.

"'Course, I'm sure," Clive answered quietly. "Nobody's gonna go lookin' in that deserted ol' barn on that godforsaken land. And the stuff we took today is tucked safe in the hidden pocket o' my haversack till we get a chance to go back out there. On our next day off, we'll ride up to Ravenswood and cash in our loot." Of course, he would never tell Mike about his own private stash elsewhere in the barn. Every so often, he'd sneak away in the middle of the night, take some of the loot out of the bag under the board and move it to his own hiding place. Clive had no problem taking advantage of Mike's feeble-mindedness. Mike would never know the difference.

"You ha'n't better cross me."

"Cross you? How many times I gotta tell you t' trust me?"

Mike huffed. "Yeah, yeah. I trust you, all right. Just don't go losin' any of our stuff."

"I ain't gonna lose nothin', so stop yer yappin'."

Mike picked up a small branch, broke it in two, and tossed both pieces on the dwindling embers. Fresh flames rose. "I hope our luck don't run out. We forgot t' take off our Army jackets today. What was we thinkin'?"

"Don't worry. That ornery gal will keep 'er mouth shut. As for that ol' man, we never gave him much of a chance to look us over 'fore I smacked him a good one."

Mike sighed loudly. "Hope you're right."

"Shut up an' stop worryin'."

Neither spoke another word. After a while, they stood and stretched, threw some dirt on the fire, and moseyed back to their tents.

3

July 19, 1863 · Buffington Island, Meigs County, Ohio

Rain fell on the muddy face of the dying Confederate soldier, mixing with the blood that flowed from his nose and mouth. His eyes, though they were glossing over, hinted at a desperate need, and his lips twitched as they emitted a faint sound. Lieutenant Jack Fuller hunkered down, dismayed, beside this fallen soldier he'd felt forced to shoot. Only two hours into the battle that morning at Buffington Island, Jack's Union gunboat had cornered a Confederate gunboat trying to cross the Ohio River. It had been an undisputed victory for the Unionists, who had gone on to capture 600 Confederates as they fled the field. Only this soldier, this dying man, had not run away. In fact, he'd aimed his rifle at Jack as if he meant to kill him. Hence Jack's decision to fire upon the Reb. The soldier had seemed to hesitate before turning his weapon aside...too late. Why hadn't the fellow retreated with the rest of his unit? It was almost as if he'd *wanted* to die.

"Why'd you do it, Reb?" Jack wondered aloud, not expecting the man to hear him, much less answer. "Why'd you stand right in my line of fire? Why'd you cock your rifle if you didn't intend to kill me? Why didn't you withdraw with the rest of your unit?"

"P-pocket," the soldier muttered.

"Pocket?" Jack frowned. "What do you need, soldier? Do you want me to get you something?"

The fellow began to choke on his blood. To ease his discomfort, Jack reached an arm under his shoulders and head and attempted to prop him up. "I'm sorry, Reb. You shouldn't have come up on me like that. Why didn't you leave with the rest of your camp?"

"Take it. Please."

"What's that you said?"

"R-reach…in…my pocket. Take…it." His voice had turned low and raspy. "The…letter." A hint of irritation laced his tone.

Gingerly, Jack slipped a hand into the soldier's jacket pocket and retrieved a wrinkled, filthy missive that was still sealed. More choking ensued. When the fellow managed to gain some measure of control, he muttered, "Make sure she…*Cristina*…gets it. Tell her I…." In desperation, the fellow reached up and snagged hold of Jack's collar, pulling Jack down with surprising force. "Please, tell her."

"I don't— What's your name, soldier? Where do you live?"

"Orville…Stiles. Ripley." He released his hold and let his arm fall across his bloody chest.

Ripley? That was just across the river and the state border, probably no more than 20 miles south. The man could have easily deserted. "Is Cristina your wife?"

The Reb closed his eyes and gave a slow nod before going still. For a few moments, Jack thought he'd passed on. But then he revived long enough to spit out his last words: "Tell her I…love her. Please…give her…the letter."

"Where in Ripley does she live?"

Jack waited several seconds for a reply.

"Farm…in…in the country," the soldier whispered hoarsely.

He looked at the insignia on the soldier's lapel. The bloody splotch on the front of his soiled jacket grew larger by the minute. Private Orville Stiles closed his eyes again.

"Oh, Lord, help this fellow into eternity," Jack muttered quietly. "I pray he knows You, God."

The man struggled with his final breaths. His eyelids fluttered faintly a few times until all movement ceased, and he crossed from one world into the next.

"I'm sorry, Reb." Jack removed his cap and placed it over his own beating heart as he stared down at the man. Why hadn't this fellow escaped with his troop? The question haunted him. Had he wished to end his life and saw getting himself shot as the best way?

This war was a horrific thing, albeit necessary. Jack swiped away the tears that had gathered in the corners of his eyes. "I hate this," he said to no one in particular.

"Do you need help there, Lieutenant?"

Jack turned at the voice. Private Darrell Rhoades, one of the fellows he oversaw in his unit, approached. All day long, he and every other available soldier had been hauling the wounded to medic stations, guarding prisoners, or helping transport men to the wagons that would carry them to Camp Chase in Columbus.

Jack tucked the letter into his jacket pocket, deciding to keep it, and his conversation with the Reb, to himself—at least for now. "Not more than ten minutes ago, this soldier here stepped in my line of fire. He cocked his rifle but missed me by a mile. It was almost as if he wanted to get shot. From what I could see, he didn't even try to escape with the rest of his unit." Jack shook his head.

Rhoades shrugged. "Weren't your fault, Lieutenant."

His words provided little comfort.

Around two in the morning, Jack lay shivering in his tent, and not because of any chill in the air. If anything, the temperature was stifling, an all-too-typical humid, midsummer night. Still, his body quivered as his mind wrestled with the sights he'd seen and deeds he'd done that day, the most bothersome of all being the Reb who'd cocked his rifle at him, pretending that he was going to fire it. This was *war*, after all, and Jack had signed on for three years. But today marked the first time he knew for certain that he was responsible for another man's death. The reality hit him hard in the gut, producing a bitter taste he couldn't seem to swallow.

If there was one thing he knew, after pondering the matter, it was this: he had to fulfill the dying wish of that Rebel soldier. He had to deliver that letter to the man's widow, no matter how difficult a task that might be. There wouldn't be any Confederates knocking on her door to deliver the news. The Confederate Army wouldn't know what had happened to him. As a matter of fact, when they discovered him missing from their unit, they'd no doubt assume he'd deserted. In a way, he had. Still, the man's wife deserved to know her husband's fate, and Jack's conscience wouldn't allow him to delegate the task to anyone else.

Earlier that evening, he'd borrowed a tattered old map from someone and located Ripley. It would be a good hike, but nothing compared to some of the tiresome treks he'd taken during his almost three-year stint in the Army. He could ride his horse and arrive in five or six hours, or he could use his own two legs and make it in eight. He'd spent the better share of his time walking from one battlefield to another and had actually come to favor traveling that way over riding. Should he come upon an adversary, he'd have an easier time of hiding on foot than on horseback. But riding would get him there sooner. He would have to think on this a bit before making a final decision. West Virginia had recently seceded from Virginia, but that didn't mean the entire state was Union-minded. No, plenty of West Virginians had opposed secession; to be sure, he would pass through pockets of hostile territory. Mind made up, he decided to bring the matter to Major Marsh the next day, after he'd completed all his duties.

When Cristina felt strong enough, she ventured into town with her children. They took the wagon so they could sell eggs to Mr. Greeley and purchase supplies from his store. On the outside, she had mostly healed, but inside, she still felt raw and anxious; her heart pounded at every unexpected noise or movement, and her nerves stood at high alert. Once they had parked the wagon and were making their way toward Greeley's Market, Cristina saw a sight that sent a horrid chill through her. Further up the street, speaking with several men, was the soldier who'd beaten her. His facial scar was unmistakable. Thankfully, she managed to keep her wits about her and quickly ushered her children past him unnoticed.

"Mama, can we have a peppermint at Greeley's Market?" Elias asked.

"Yes, yes, we can manage that," she hastily replied. "But first, let's go in here." She steered her children through the door of the first establishment they came to, Miss Harriet's Hat Shop.

At the sound of the bell tinkling above the door, the proprietress looked up from the cash register, where she stood ringing up a customer's order. She smiled. "Hello there, ma'am. I'll be right with you."

"Thank you." Cristina had had no interest in purchasing a hat. The beat-up straw one on her head had served her quite well for years. Fanciful hats like the ones Miss Harriet sold didn't fit in her budget or her plain lifestyle. While Miss Harriet finished up with her client, Cristina walked to the front window to watch the wicked soldier on the sidewalk.

"Are you buyin' a new hat, Maw?" Elias asked, coming up beside her.

"No," she whispered.

"Then what're we doin' in here?"

"Shh. I just…I thought…thought I would *look* at the hats. That's all."

"Then why are you starin' out the window?"

"I'm not." She set her basket of eggs on the floor and then, from a nearby display, picked up a lavish, feathered contraption. She removed her own straw hat and placed the feathered one on her head.

Elias immediately laughed. "Maw, you look awful funny."

"Humph." Cristina removed the hat and put it back where it belonged. "It's awfully heavy, too. Who wants t' walk around town with a giant bird on 'er head?"

"Mama," came the wee voice of Catherina. "Look at me. Do you like it?"

Catherina had donned a gigantic bonnet full of colorful dried flowers.

Elias giggled, and Cristina, in spite of her nerves, burst out laughing. "Please put it back, honey. That's a lady's hat."

Slowly and dutifully, Catherina returned the hat to its shelf.

Across the store, the cash register drawer closed with a loud clack, and Miss Harriet handed a large hatbox to her customer before bidding her good-bye. The customer nodded and made her exit, her elaborate hoopskirt swishing with every strut.

"Now then, what can I do for you?" The tall, slender woman fairly floated across the room in her lovely gown. Everything about her spoke of grace and poise, from the meticulously styled waves in her hair to her perfectly polished tan leather pumps. "Are we hat shopping today?"

"We're just lookin', thank you," said Cristina, casting another glance out the window. "We just came in to admire yer selection."

"We did?" asked Elias. "Not me."

Even Miss Harriet's laughter came off sounding quite proper, if not dainty. "I shouldn't blame you, young man. Few are the young men who visit my store." She bent at the waist and tapped Catherina on the nose. "Aren't you a pretty little thing?" She grinned up at Cristina. "I believe I've seen you about town, but we've never formally met." She stood upright once more and extended a hand. "I'm Harriet Haverstock."

Cristina put a smile on her face. "I'm Cristina Stiles. It's nice t' meet you." They shook hands, and she couldn't help but notice how smooth and feminine Miss Harriet's hand felt in comparison to her own rough and callused one. This refined lady surely never had need to dig in a garden, milk cows, or feed chickens. "You have a mighty nice store, ma'am. I regret I've only ever looked in through the window at the colorful hats an' ribbons an' bows an' such. Someday, I hope t' buy something—when I'm not busy furnishin' my children with bigger shoes and larger clothes."

The woman gave another merry laugh. "I understand. Most of my hats are imported, hence the considerable prices. But their quality is unparalleled."

"We don't gots enough money fer fancy things," Elias explained, "'cause our Paw's off fightin' in the war."

"Is he, now?" Miss Harriet eyed Elias with interest.

A feeling of uneasiness came over Cristina. "Elias—"

"Yeah. He's gonna defeat those dumb Yanks. Last week, a couple'a soldiers—"

"Shh, Elias, mind yer manners." Cristina turned to Miss Harriet. "I'm sorry. He gets these ideas in his head."

Miss Harriet stood a little taller, a little straighter. "It's quite all right. Our family is pro-Union, but everyone's entitled to his own opinion. Frankly, I'm glad to have the Yankee soldiers' presence in town. Gives me a real sense of security."

Cristina smiled politely as she craned her neck around for another look out the window. The scar-faced Union soldier crossed the street and met up with another uniformed man—was it the soldier who'd been with him at her house?—before the two walked away. Good. It was now safe to leave the store.

Cristina cleared her throat. "Well, thank you again, ma'am." She bent to pick up the basket of eggs. "Come on, Elias, Cath."

"But, Mama, why can't we buy a hat?" Catherina whined.

"Maybe another time, honey." Over her daughter's head, Cristina smiled at Miss Harriet. The woman waved, probably just as happy to see them go.

Outside, they headed toward Greeley's Market.

"Why we walkin' so fast?" Catherina groused.

"I've got a long list o' things t' do today. Just tryin' to get us home before too long."

That evening, as she lay in bed, Cristina heard a crackling sound outside her window that had her sitting bolt upright in seconds. She skittered off the mattress and crept to the window, her rifle clutched tightly in both hands. By the light of the summer moon, she spotted two foxes slinking by, their bushy tails poised. Nasty critters were hungry for chickens. Fortunately, she'd locked her entire flock in the henhouse and secured the gate. She didn't foresee those predators getting inside, so she went back to bed, tucking her rifle safely under the sheets beside her.

4

"With all due respect, Major Marsh, I feel duty bound to carry out the dying wish of that soldier." It was a hot, muggy evening and Jack swiped at his sweat-soaked brow. It had been another long day of burying bodies, the Battle of Buffington Island long over and the Confederates moving yet further south. Jack had not been successful in forgetting the dead Reb's final request for Jack to deliver the still-sealed letter that lay in the front pocket of his rucksack. "Somebody's got to take this letter to his widow."

"His comrades will go knocking on her door. Might be she already knows by now."

"Might be, but I doubt it. At any rate, I have in my possession the last piece of correspondence she'll ever have from him. Wouldn't you want someone to hand-deliver a letter you'd written to your wife if it was the last words she'd hear from you?"

His superior, older than Jack by more than 30 years and in ill health, adjusted his hefty frame by pulling back his shoulders. "I'd not have my enemy delivering any letter for me, that's for doggone sure. West Virginia's only been a Union state for a matter of weeks now, so you can be sure it's still swarmin' with solid Virginians who weren't in favor o' withdrawin', even if they do hail from the west side." He nodded his head eastward. "You cross over that line, and you're sure to run into trouble."

"I'll lie low, sir."

"Yeah, that's what they all say. And then we bury 'em."

"I'm determined, sir."

The major eyed him askance, his face tilted to the side. "I can see that." They'd been in discussion over the matter for the last 15 minutes. The major dropped his shoulders, then walked to a chair outside his tent and lowered himself into it. At times, Jack wondered why the man didn't resign and hand over his post to someone younger and perhaps a bit abler. "I suppose I could call in Captain Jack Timmer. He could handle two companies for a couple of days until you return."

Jack heaved a sigh of relief. "He would be more than capable."

"When will you leave?"

"At dawn, sir. I figure I'll stay one night in Ripley, maybe two, depending on what time I arrive there and then what time I finish talking to the widow."

"You should at least allow someone to accompany you."

"You know as well as I we can't spare anyone. It's enough that I'm leaving."

Major Marsh adjusted his position in the chair and squared his shoulders, gazing up. "You know the way?"

"I borrowed a map from someone. It's an average day's hike. I'm heading to a farm, but that's about all I know. The soldier was rather vague about the location, but then he was short on breath and time. I figure I'll get to the town and inquire. Small town like Ripley, somebody'll be sure to point me in the right direction. Once I find her location, I'll probably go back into town and spend a night in a hotel."

"Take a horse, at least."

"I'm still pondering whether it's better to walk or ride, sir. I'm used to walking and actually prefer it."

"You have an assigned horse, Lieutenant."

"I know, but if I come upon the enemy, it would be easier to jump into hiding if I were walking as opposed to riding."

"If you come upon the enemy, it's already too late to hide, Lieutenant Fuller. You're likely to get there quicker by horse."

Jack considered the older man's words and decided he was right. "I see your point. I'll take a horse then."

The major grunted. "Well, at least you find me right on one thing."

Jack chortled. "You're almost always right, sir."

The major wasn't one for niceties, but his mouth curved up slightly and he nodded. "Well then, return in one piece—if you can manage it."

"I'll do my best, sir. Like I said, it shouldn't take me more than a couple of days."

The two saluted, and in the hot, humid night, with sweat still dripping down his brow, Lieutenant Jack Fuller trudged back to his unit, serenaded by the song of crickets.

He'd barely slept a wink last night, but he had a feeling tonight would go better. He was going to Ripley in the morning, and now that the decision had been made and approved by the major, he could rest more easily. And rest he did! About the same time his body hit the hard ground and he drew his threadbare blanket over himself, sleep came, and he didn't awaken until the first light of dawn broke through the crack in his tent flap. He drew a deep breath and then slowly let it out before tossing his blanket aside, glad for the aroma of coffee wafting on the thick morning air. A few sips of the dark brew and a couple pieces of hardtack would give him enough energy for the first leg of his 20-mile jaunt.

He'd slept well, but now he lay still and stared at the roof of his small tent while visions of the man he'd killed two days ago marched across his mind. Added to those were various versions he considered of how to tell Orville Stiles's widow about her husband's death. It wouldn't be the first time he'd traveled a distance to inform a family of a soldier's passing, but until this point, the homes he'd visited had always belonged to Union soldiers. This would be his first visit to the household of a Rebel soldier, and he had no way of knowing what to expect—or what words to use, particularly since he'd been the one responsible for the man's death.

He whispered a hasty prayer, then stood and rolled up his bed, tying it with a leather string, as he did every day. He dressed, laced up his boots, and stuffed his hat atop his head of unruly dark brown hair. Then he grabbed his knapsack of paltry supplies, a couple of hardboiled eggs, hardtack, and a few more food items. It also contained his canteen, which he would need to refill along the way, a tiny washing towel, some soap, tooth powder, and, of course, his worn Bible. He never went anywhere without the Good Book. Lord knew he clung to the Word of God night and day. It was the one thing that kept him going. Running a hand down his whiskered face, he decided to skip his morning shave and wait until after his sweat-inducing journey to get cleaned up and make himself presentable.

With a sigh, he exited his tent, then proceeded to untie and take up the stakes so he could roll up his go-to shelter and jam it inside his sack. There was no telling where he would spend the night, whether in a hotel or somewhere out under the stars. Besides, a soldier never left camp without all his belongings in tow. In wartime, everyday life was full of uncertainties.

After a breakfast of two fried eggs, compliments of Private Lewis Arden, and two cups of coffee, Jack headed for the camp livery just as Second Lieutenant Wilbur Brownley sounded the cry for roll call. At the livery, Jack picked up his horse and exchanged a few words with the liveryman before mounting and setting off. He decided it best not to advertise the nature of his mission. Some would not understand it and might even turn against him. No, best to keep his plans to himself.

Jack made good time. He reached the banks of the Ohio around eight that morning and found a boatman willing to take him and his horse across for a small fee. They traveled on, maintaining a good pace despite the rising heat. When the sun peaked in the sky, he found a good shade tree next to a stream and sat down. While his horse grazed, he reached into his knapsack for several pieces of hardtack and one of the tomatoes he'd picked from a garden he'd passed. Before long, he finished his meal and guzzled the last of the water in his canteen. He would refill it now at the stream and hope to find a kindhearted farmer later who would let him use his well pump.

Not for the first time on his journey that day, Jack thought about the letter he carried for the widow named Cristina Stiles. How would Mrs. Stiles take the news of her loss? What would she say? What would *he* say, for that matter? "I know what it is to lose a spouse"? No, that wouldn't do, true though it was. He hadn't lost his wife Marilee to death. It had been three years since his sham of a marriage had ended and he'd made a pact with himself never to remarry. Women were more trouble than marrying them was worth.

Feeling reenergized after the rest and a bite to eat, he stood, brushed himself off, then retrieved his horse, fastened his knapsack and canteen to his saddlebags, and resumed his journey, taking care to stay alert. Barring any major setbacks, he figured he would reach Ripley by early afternoon. The trek had taken much longer than he'd anticipated due to uncharted paths, and rough, hilly terrain. So far, the worst thing he'd come across was a skunk that stopped and gawked at him from a distance of about 10 feet. They had a stare-down that lasted all of a minute before the skunk decided to scamper the rest of the way across the two-track path and into the woods. Jack had breathed a sigh of relief, thinking that he would just as soon as deal with a Reb as face the wrath of a smelly skunk.

The first thing he would do upon reaching Ripley was locate a bathhouse where he could get a shave and a haircut. Then he would take a meal at an eatery where, he hoped, he could inquire after the location of the Stiles farm. After spending the night at an inn of some sort, he would deliver the letter and the sad news the following morning, after which point he would turn himself around and begin the journey back to his camp on the other side of the Ohio, returning to his post sometime late tomorrow. To his great relief, he hadn't come across a single Confederate soldier. Sure, there were likely Rebs lurking in various places, but anyone who might have seen him must have deemed him a negligible threat, hence his failure to have been captured.

Jack raised his eyes to the cloudless blue heavens. "It's been an easy trip thus far, Lord," he said. "May the rest of my journey go just as well." Blowing out a breath, he urged his horse up the rugged path until he came to a winding dirt trail in which thousands of wagon wheels had carved out a semblance of a road that went uphill and down. Since it headed slightly south and then east, he chose to follow it. Birdsong cheered him along, as did the occasional tree frog's croak and cricket's chirp.

An hour later, he came upon a farmhouse with a visible water pump. He figured he couldn't be more than a few miles outside of Ripley. His canteen having run dry again, he decided to knock on the door and see about getting a refill. He had barely set foot on the property when an old fellow stepped out onto the rickety porch, his rifle pointed straight at Jack. "Don't think 'bout steppin' even one foot closer to my house, you ugly, egg-suckin' dawg. Sure as the sun's shinin', I'll shoot off yer head. I ain't got no use for Yanks, never mind that I'm standin' on West Virginia territory. I never asked nobody to change the name o' my state and I ain't no Yank, so jes' turn around and head back to where you come from."

Jack raised his hands in the air. "I mean you no harm, mister. I merely wanted to ask for the use of your well to refill my canteen so I can make it the rest of the way to Ripley. I'm parched, you see, and so is my horse."

The fellow eyed him with a look of hatred. "Ain't no Yank gonna drink from my well. I ain't takin' no chance on you pollutin' my water. You go keel over on somebody else's property, hear? I ain't in no mood to bury you on mine."

"And I'm in no mood to argue, sir, but if you'll just allow me to refill my canteen, I'll be on my way."

"I said for you to get!"

"Just a few drops. Please."

After that, everything seemed to happen in slow motion. The sound of gunfire exploding through the air…the strength beneath him giving way as his horse's legs buckled…. The poor beast collapsed and gave a terrible groan. Jack had kicked his feet out from the stirrups and jumped off the horse's back just in time to avoid being trapped under its body. Shocked and downright stupefied, he bent down to assess the animal's condition. Shot through the heart, the mount was already dead. Blood poured out of the gunshot wound and flies swarmed around it.

"Why, you no-good piece of— You just killed my horse!"

The farmer sneered and spat on the ground, keeping his rifle cocked and aimed. "And you'll be next if you don't make for that trail and move on."

"Without my horse?"

The man shrugged. "You wanna haul away a dead horse on your own, help yerself."

Jack had half a mind to pull out his revolver and pick off the hideous farmer, but his better sense told him to straighten his shoulders and move along. "At least give me time to gather my belongings."

"You got thirty seconds."

Without further thought, Jack grabbed his knapsack and empty canteen, and then, with one last look at the dead horse, he pivoted on his heel and walked away, taking care not to look back, lest, like Lot's wife, he turn into a pillar of salt.

Foolish man! It would take some time for Jack to forgive his despicable actions. War sure did strange things to a man's mind.

5

It was a couple of days after having spotted that wicked Union soldier on the sidewalk in Ripley and then, later, his dreadful cohort, that Cristina decided to pay a visit to Clara. She felt certain that once she'd told her friend about the matter, it would get her mind to thinking on a more even keel and also help her regain the confidence she needed to be the best mother she could be to her children. Lately, she'd been jumping at every little sound.

They arrived at Clara's farm around three in the afternoon. Clara had a fine little settlement nestled high in the hills on a flat patch of earth that spanned a few acres. In addition to her three-room house, her late husband, Melvin, had constructed three outbuildings for her horses, cow, chickens, rabbits, and several other critters. Cristina's intent was to stay an hour or so and then head home—if Clara didn't talk off her arm and leg and then insist they all stay for supper.

Clara's big, hairy black dog, Gus, greeted them with a hearty, woofing welcome, his tail wagging and his whole body swaying with excitement. Clara stepped out of the house, wiping her hands on her apron. "Well, grease my gizzard!" she exclaimed over Gus's shrill barking as she approached their wagon. "If it ain't the Stiles family come a'visitin'.

I been wishin' someone would stop by. What brings y' up the mountain—'sides that wagon and them two horses?"

Clara never had been short on her welcomes. Just seeing her made Cristina's anxious heart settle into a more comfortable rhythm.

"Hi there, Miss Clara!" Elias shouted. "Maw said it was time we come t' see you instead o' th' other way around." He jumped down just as soon as Cristina brought the wagon to a stop and set the brake lever. Gus jumped up to give Elias a wet kiss on the chin. Elias hugged him back and patted his head.

"Well, I'm mighty glad t' see you. You're just in time t' help me eat some fresh-baked apple pie."

"Can we really have some?" Catherina asked from atop the wagon.

"You bet yer bonnet you can."

Catherina frowned as she touched the top of her head. "But I ain't wearin' no bonnet, Miss Clara."

"Well, you should be. Sun's hotter than the devil's kitchen t'day!"

"Bonnets only make my head hotter," said Catherina. "'Sides, I like the wind blowin' my hair."

Cristina climbed down from the wagon, then turned and helped her daughter out before turning to her son. "Elias, would y' please take Starlight an' Thunder out back? Water 'em down an' give 'em a drink. Remember, not too much water at once, y' hear?"

"I know that, Maw. I been takin' care o' horses all my life."

"That you have, I suppose. I keep forgettin' that you're growin' up. Too fast, if y' ask me."

"Can I go with him, Mama?" Catherina asked "I wanna see the new kittens."

"Yes, but you two mind yerselves, and, as always, keep yer wits about y'."

Elias unhitched the horses, and soon he and Catherina disappeared around the side of the house.

"Jus' what sorta trouble y' think they are about to find in my backyard?" Clara asked with a skeptical face.

Cristina shrugged. "Nothin', I s'pose."

"Uh-huh." Clara put an arm around Cristina's shoulders. "All right now, my bosom-bird. You come on in the house and tell me the real reason you came up that mountain on this hotter-'n-Hades day."

Was it that obvious that Cristina was still on edge? She'd thought she had mostly regained her sense of confidence after the soldiers' attack, but after seeing the scar-faced soldier in town, she hadn't been able to shake the jitters.

Clara served her a tin cup of cold sweet tea and they sat down at her old wooden table. At the center sat a vase of fresh-cut flowers—sweet peas, lilies, and gardenias—and Cristina leaned forward to inhale their sweet aroma.

"Now, tell me what's on yer mind," Clara ordered.

Cristina shifted her position in the high-back chair. "I…I took the children into Ripley a couple o' days ago, and I…I saw him," she said quietly.

"Him?"

"The Union soldier who attacked me. The one with the scar."

Clara leaned across the table, eyes round. "You sure?"

"Positive. I would recognize him anywhere."

Clara nodded. "Well, are you goin' to the sheriff, or should I?"

"No! Neither. The soldier made it clear he'd hurt my children if I reported 'em. I jus' keep tellin' myself they won't come back, but I can't help worryin' they will."

"Well, I don't blame you none for worryin'. Them rotten nutcrackers beat you bad. That's why you gotta report 'em."

Cristina shook her head. "I'm not takin' any chances, Clara. I saw those soldiers' evil eyes, and I know what they are capable o' doin' if I don't play by their rules."

Clara gave a little shudder. "Well, I'll tell you what. If them two ever sets foot on yer property again, you tell me, an' I'll go after 'em myself. I'm a good shot, y' know."

Cristina gave a little laugh. "I don't doubt y' are. But you'll do no such thing. I don't want you gettin' involved an' bringin' any trouble on yourself."

"Better me 'n you. You's young. You've got a whole lotta life left t' live. Me, I be nearin' those pearly gates pretty soon anyways."

Cristina set down her cup and eyed her friend. "D' you really think there's somethin' waitin' for us when we die?" The realization that she wasn't sure where she would go when she died created a surprising sense of anxiety in her gut.

Clara shrugged. "Guess so. I mean, it's a comfortin' thought, ain't it? Got me through Melvin's death all those years ago."

"So, do you pray? To God?"

"I 'spect I do, from time t' time."

"An' He answers you?"

Clara scratched her head and then twirled the end of her long, white braid. "Maybe. Sometimes. I ain't ever sure. I used to read the Bible now an' again—ours belonged to Melvin's mother. I'd have to search awhile t' find it now, though."

"Let me know if you find it. I'd like t' see it sometime."

"I'll do that."

The two sat in reflective silence until the door opened and Catherina entered with two kittens cradled in her arms. "Mama, look at these li'l cats I found in the barn."

"Aw, aren't those cute?"

"We oughtta take 'em home with us."

Cristina sighed. "Mama's got too much on her mind at the moment to be takin' care o' more animals, honey."

Catherina pressed her lips into a classic pout.

"Those babies ain't ready t' leave their mama yet either, my moppet," Clara told her. "But if y' want t' go tell yer brother, pie's cool enough t' eat now."

Catherina brightened and quickly turned.

"You walk with them babies," Clara said.

Catherina nodded dutifully as she walked out, leaving the door open behind her.

Cristina went to close the door, but she needn't have bothered. The two children raced inside less than two minutes later, leaving the door open again. Catherina still held the kittens.

"Close the door," Cristina told Elias. He did as told.

"Can we have pie now?" Catherina asked.

Cristina frowned. "Cath, where're yer manners?"

"Please?" the girl added.

Clara laughed. "Tell you what. Why don't y'all stay for supper, and we'll have pie after?"

"Mama, can we stay for supper?" Catherina pleaded. "Then I'll have more time t' play with the kittens. Me an' Elias are havin' so much fun. Elias wants another goat. He just said so. Mama, Miss Clara has—"

"Catherina, slow down. And take the kittens back out to the barn. I'm sure Miss Clara doesn't want 'em in her house."

"Oh, mercy, I don't care. Most of 'em wrangle their way inside sooner or later, and then they wrangle their way into my heart soon after. But, as yer mama said, you need t' take them back out to the barn. It's prob'ly 'bout time fer their mama t' feed 'em."

Catherina started to turn, then stopped. "Are we stayin' for supper?"

"I—I don't want to impose," Cristina said, glancing at Clara.

"'Course, you're stayin'," the older woman declared.

Cristina wouldn't protest further.

6

J ack arrived in Ripley just past three o'clock, exhausted and hungry. At least he had quenched his thirst at a stream outside of town. He'd sprawled on his stomach and dipped his whole head in the refreshing water, drinking deeply.

He stopped at an outdoor market to ask where he might find a bathhouse and the worker pointed him up Main Street. "Go up to the first cross street and turn left. You'll see Nettie's Bathhouse. It'll cost y' a nickel, though, even if y' are a soldier. Nettie's a stingy one. Old woman's so cheap, she wouldn't pay one cent to see Jesus iff'n He was t' be in town."

Jack might have told him Jesus was indeed in town; in fact, His presence filled the place. But after his tiring journey, he hadn't the gumption to converse. He thanked the fellow and started up the street, relishing the mere idea of a good wash followed by a decent meal. It had been too long since he'd stood under a stream of clean water. Sure, his company had come across an occasional waterfall on their long hikes from one battlefield to another. But aside from those welcome sights, a few quick dunks in rivers or streams, and cooling heavy downpours of rain, he hadn't had a bath in months.

The folks he passed on the sidewalk either acknowledged him with half a nod or turned their heads away to avoid eye contact. He wasn't the only Union soldier in town, which perchance explained certain residents' disapproval of him. Whenever Unionists took over a town, their occupation was intended to hold the enemy at bay. Some folks appreciated the protection, while others resented it. He had no way of knowing where the majority of Ripley stood on the matter, aside from that rotten farmer who'd killed his horse.

He located Nettie's Bathhouse without incident. A rather gnarly-looking, rough-around-the-edges woman with scraggly white hair met him at the door to the wooden shack. She looked him up and down with a critical gaze, then wrinkled her nose and blew upward at several strands of hair that had fallen across her gray-green eyes. "You got a nickel on y', soldier? Y' look like you could use ten cents' worth, but I'll only charge y' five. Be sure t' get that smell off'n y' while you're at it. Y' got yer own soap n' dryin' cloth?"

"In my bag, ma'am."

"Good, then I won't have t' waste mine on y'."

Jack fetched a five-cent piece from his coin bag and handed it to her. As he returned the purse to the front pocket of his rucksack, his hand brushed against the letter to Cristina Stiles, and he found himself blurting out, "You wouldn't happen to know where the Stiles farm is located, would you?"

"The what?"

"Family of Orville Stiles owns a farm in these parts. I'm trying to locate it."

Her old eyes crinkled at the corners with a look of suspicion. "Cain't say I do. Why'd y' want t' know?"

"Official Army business. I'll inquire elsewhere after I've gotten cleaned up and had a good shave and a haircut. I did notice a barbershop on my way here but no eating establishments. Can you recommend a decent place for a fellow to eat? I'm also in need of a hotel. You wouldn't, by chance, happen to—"

"I ain't yer travel guide, soldier," she cut in.

"No, you certainly aren't. Well, much obliged for the shower." He started to move past her.

"Think the Stiles farm is somewheres west o' town," she muttered. "That Orville feller's off fightin' the war, though. His missus an' their two youngins are managin' the tiny farm, far as I know. As fer a place to' stay, you'll find yerself a hotel iffin' you walk on over t' North Street."

"Thank you, ma'am. Much obliged for the information." He gave her what he hoped was a friendly grin before entering the small bathing area.

There was a stall with three walls and a curtain, which he drew shut after stepping inside. On the floor was a wooden platform that allowed the water to drain into the ground. Over that hung a bucket attached to a pulley system that drew water from a well with a gentle tug of the rope. Jack disrobed and draped his clothes over one of the walls, glad for the clean undergarments and spare uniform he carried in his knapsack. The water felt cold but refreshing. His parched skin soaked it up like a sponge, and he longed for several more bucket loads to further drench himself. But, not wanting Miss Nettie drawing back the curtain to scold him for wasting her precious water, he decided to content himself with two full buckets to rinse off the grimy lather he'd worked up using dampened soap powder. He must have stood there for a solid fifteen minutes before he felt he'd cleaned himself sufficiently enough to get him through another week or two. After a final rinse, he dried off, quickly dressed, and went to the barber's for a shave and haircut.

The barber recommended Rosalyn's restaurant. The food was probably fair to middlin' to the average diner, but Jack—accustomed to sustaining himself on scanty rations of hardtack, dried meat, rare in-season fruit, and half-rotten vegetables he happened upon in the occasional field—felt the meal was a feast fit for a king. Sitting in back of the restaurant, he savored every bite of tender beef stew and buttery biscuits. It required great effort not to gulp down the cold water in his tin mug, which the woman waiting on him continually refilled. The only damper on his experience was the nagging notion that, come morning, he would have to tell a young woman that her husband had left her a widow. Whether he would divulge the role he had played in the wid-owing process remained unknown. He supposed he would wait and see how he felt when the time came.

The supper crowd at Rosalyn's had thinned since Jack's arrival, but several older gentlemen dressed in farm clothes didn't budge from the large round table they shared in the center of the restaurant. They looked to be regular customers, the way they jawed back and forth, smoking their cheroots and exchanging one laughable remark after another. They seemed to pay him no mind, other than the two who'd glanced his way at one point and muttered something under their breaths. Whether they approved of his presence in the restaurant, Jack couldn't say, but he determined not to engage them in conversation, just in case they didn't.

A wrinkled copy of the *Main Street Herald* lay on the vacant table next to his, and Jack reached over and took it, hoping that a bit of read-ing would take his mind off tomorrow's unpleasant task. Of course, he still had to locate the Stiles farm.

The barber had not been much help, telling him only that he knew the farm to be a short distance outside town, accessible by South Church Street and a number of smaller roads. The fellow had asked Jack what brought him, a Union soldier, to visit the Stiles farm. Jack hadn't been about to divulge the whole story, so he merely replied, "I'm to deliver a sealed message to the missus."

"Wull, that's mighty nice o' y', 'specially when you'd prob'ly rather be out there fightin' battles." He'd gone on clipping Jack's hair. "Hear-tell there was quite the fight up near Ravenswood. Buffington Island, I believe?"

"You heard right."

"Glad to see the Union farin' so well. Until Gettysburg, I was a mite worried. Widespread devastation, no matter how y' look at it."

At the dinging sound of the bell above the door, the barber had glanced over to see three patrons enter—all of whom seemed to be good friends from the way he engaged them in conversation for the remain-der of Jack's haircut and shave. Jack hadn't minded in the least. He was thankful to put aside talk and thoughts of war.

He skimmed a few newspaper articles as he finished his stew and polished off the last bite of biscuit. Setting down the paper and picking up his tin mug, he swallowed the rest of his water, his stomach satisfied at last.

"You want anything else, soldier?" asked the woman from behind the counter. The rosy glow of her cheeks and the sparkle of sweat on her brow indicated just how hard she worked. He wondered if she owned the place, and imagined her pinching pennies like everyone else, desperate to make ends meet. Might be she had hungry mouths to feed back home if her husband was off fighting on some battlefield.

He sat back in his chair and smiled across the room at her. "No, thank you, ma'am. I believe I've had enough."

"How about some coffee and a piece o' pie to finish things off? I made apple this mornin'."

"Don't see how I could say no to that."

"Smart man," said one of the several older fellows seated together at the central table. "Rosalyn makes the best pies in town." The man shoved his chair back and stood. "The soldier's tab is on me, Rosalyn."

"You bet, Harold."

Jack turned his attention to the gentleman approaching his table. "I appreciate your generosity, mister, but you need not cover my meal."

"I insist," the man said as he limped closer. "It's the least I can do for someone riskin' life an' limb out there. Name's Harold Marlan." He extended his hand across the table.

Jack immediately stood to shake hands. "Jack Fuller. Nice to make your acquaintance."

"Same here. You fight in that battle over at Buffington Island last week?"

"Yes, sir, I did."

Without invitation, Mr. Marlan pulled out a high-back chair and sat down at Jack's table. Jack sat back down. Not that he minded the company; he just wasn't in much of a mood for conversing, as tired as he was…not to mention distracted by thoughts of tomorrow's errand.

"Haven't seen you around before. You on guard duty with the other soldiers in town?" Mr. Marlan asked.

"No, I'm here on other business. I'll be leaving sometime tomorrow."

"That so?"

Rosalyn delivered Jack's apple pie and cup of coffee. Jack nodded his thanks, doing the same when she carried over a pitcher and topped off his water mug.

"You stayin' at the Union camp tonight?" his new friend inquired.

"No, I'll be checking in at a local hotel. The thought of a bed with a real mattress truly appeals."

The man gave a low chuckle. "I'd offer you a room at my place, but the missus would have my head if I didn't give her at least a day to prepare for company. She likes to have everything just so."

Jack smiled. "It's no problem. You've already been more than kind and hospitable. I'm told I'll find lodging on North Street."

Mr. Marlan nodded. "There's a place called the Appalachian, built just a few years ago—before the war, in fact. It's nothin' fancy, mind you. There're also a couple o' boardinghouses."

"I'm sure I'll find something suitable. I'm not hard to please." Jack dug into his pie, finding it just as delicious as he'd imagined. Paired with his coffee, it worked like a charm to finish off his meal.

"What sort o' business you got in Ripley? Sure ain't yer normal stoppin'-off spot. Not much happens 'round here. Think the men who've been charged with keepin' the peace are gettin' awful bored. Ain't seen many Rebs in these parts since they arrived."

"I'm heading out to the farm of one Private Orville Stiles. Do you know him?"

"Orville Stiles." He scratched his balding head. "I know 'im, but not well. He an' his li'l Mexican beauty have a farm outside of town. Off Church Street, I believe. Church winds around a bit. You'll take it a mile, maybe two, an' then you'll turn right on a two-track road. Not sure it even has a name. There's a school there. You'll go past that, then turn left on another two-track trail. You should find the farm on that road. It's not a far patch. You got you a horse?"

"No, sir." He might have told him about the encounter he'd had with the ornery farmer, but he thought it best to keep that to himself.

The fellow's eyebrows shot up. "Then how'd you get here?"

"Um…on my own two legs."

Mr. Marlan grinned. "You're young. I s'pose long hikes don't bother you none."

"Not really, no."

"Why don't you go on over to the livery and rent yerself a horse?"

"I'll think on it. Thanks for the directions."

"The Stiles plot is small, maybe five or ten acres, if that. Not much of a farm. It sits in the foothills, so it's a pretty craggy terrain, not too suitable for farmin'. Orville inherited the plot from his father's brother, Ned Stiles, before he got hitched. Orville's always kept to himself. He does odd jobs outside o' farmin' to make do, but he sure don't fare well. Don't know how he's supported his family all these years. I hope he's sendin' money back to that pretty wife o' his. Hear-tell that's why he joined, so's he could make a bit o' extra money. Although from what I been told, the South don't pay their soldiers much a'tall. Around these parts, you'll find folks of both Confederate and Union persuasion. I'm Union, if y' hain't already guessed."

Jack smiled as he mulled over Harold Marlan's earlier words. How was the woman going to make do, now that her husband had passed? Well, it wasn't his problem to worry about. His job was to deliver the letter her husband had left her, then return to his unit.

"How much longer you in for?"

"I will have served three years come November. I can muster out at that time unless I'm of a mood to stay on."

The fellow eyed his uniform. "I see by them shoulder boards and those gold buttons on yer coat that you're a lieutenant. I'm guessin' you're a fine soldier."

Jack shrugged. "I do my job. I'm no better than the next fellow."

"An' you're a humble one at that." Mr. Marlan gave him a slow grin.

Jack smiled but said nothing.

"Well, if'n I'd been younger, and if'n it weren't fer this here bum leg, I would've joined the Union." He blew out the last puff of his cheroot, then threw down the stump of the cigar and ground it beneath the sole of his boot. Smoke wafted across the table and tickled Jack's nostrils. He never had been one for the habit and it seemed to him that ever since the government had started taxing tobacco sales to fund the war, he'd been in the minority.

"You say you got business out at the Stiles farm, eh? Hope Orville ain't in some sort o' trouble. Or, worse, dead. This state's already lost too many soldiers on both sides."

Jack's stomach knotted, but he tried not to show his discomfort. "I'm afraid it's that way wherever you go. I, for one, will be glad when it's over."

"Won't we all? It's a sorry war. I been readin' 'bout it every chance I get. 'Course, I ain't sure the newspaper's givin' us all the details."

"Probably for the best."

The bell over the door jangled and two Union soldiers entered, smoking stogies. Jack watched as they paused to scan the place for a table and then chose one at the front, next to the window. They must not have noticed Jack, or they surely would have saluted, since he outranked them. They pulled back two chairs, seated themselves, and took puffs from their cheroots, looking rather proud of themselves.

Rosalyn gave a little scowl before approaching their table. Evidently, this wasn't their first time in her restaurant. "What'cha want this time, soldiers?"

The larger one guffawed. "Somethin' you ain't willin' t' give us. At least, not yet. We'll wear y' down, Rosie, don't you worry."

They both gave a whoop of laughter, as if they considered themselves the world's best joke-tellers.

Rosalyn visibly stiffened and tipped her head back. "I'm talkin' 'bout the menu, fellas. You want yer usual? Beef gravy on bread an' a scoop o' potatoes?"

One of the soldiers reached out and ran a hand down her bare arm. She flinched and stepped out of his reach.

Jack clenched his teeth. If there was one thing he could not abide, it was Yankee soldiers abusing their status, particularly when it came to women.

Rosalyn planted her hands on her hips. "I repeat: what can I get y' from the menu?"

The larger soldier smiled pertly at her. "*I* repeat: what we want ain't on the menu."

More explosions of laughter.

"Hey, soldier, mind yer manners," said one of the old fellows who had dined with Mr. Marlan.

The soldier turned his head. "Oh, yeah? How 'bout you mind yer business, y' ol' redneck? We ain't talkin' to you. And only thing we wanna hear from you is words o' gratitude fer keepin' the peace in this podunk town."

Jack had heard enough. He pushed back in his chair with such force that the legs made a screeching sound loud enough to turn heads. Standing as straight as a post, he glared at the two soldiers who were just now seeing him for the first time. Their jaws dropped in an almost comical manner.

Rosalyn gave the sorry soldiers a satisfied expression and walked back to the kitchen, sending Jack a small smile as she passed him. He acknowledged her with a nod, then put his hat on his head and tipped the brim at Mr. Marlan. "Excuse me, Mr. Marlan." His gaze shifted to the soldiers. "Seems I have some business to attend to."

"Help yourself, Lieutenant."

Nearly every patron in the restaurant, including all the older men seated around the circular table, sat at attention and looked on with evident interest as Jack approached the two soldiers. They made no move to escape, only sat there, slack-jawed.

"Afternoon, gentlemen." Jack reached their table and planted his feet firmly on the floor. "Lieutenant Jack Fuller of the Forty-Fifth Ohio Infantry. What unit are you serving with?"

They scrambled to stand and salute him. "Company B, sir," they said in unison. "Of the One Hundred Forty-Second Regiment, New York Volunteers, sir."

"At ease. Names?"

"Pardon?"

"What are your names?"

"Oh! Clive Horton, sir, and this here is Mike Farmer."

Both men shifted their weight nervously. The one named Clive bore a red scar going down his left cheek.

"Who is your commanding officer?"

"Lieutenant Reginald Bond, sir," Horton answered. "He ordered us to stand guard inside the main city blocks. There's others keepin' watch on the outskirts o' town."

"That right? A commendable post—but it would be even more so if you followed proper protocol."

"Oh, but we do, sir," the one named Mike Farmer hastened to say.

"Not in a respectful manner."

Both men wrinkled their brows in a show of confusion.

"I overheard your inappropriate talk with Miss Rosalyn. I would suggest you never return to this establishment. I shall plan to visit your lieutenant on my way out of town tomorrow to issue the order. In fact, I would suggest you vacate the premises immediately."

"But…we ain't eaten yet," Mike whined.

Jack said nothing, just straightened his shoulders and glowered at the men.

"Y-yes, sir," Clive sputtered. "No need to visit our unit though. We promise not t' come here again."

"Is that a fact? Just the same, I think I'll drop by—for good measure. I'd like the chance to meet Lieutenant Bond."

The men merely stared at Jack until he added, "I thought I asked you to leave. Shall I make it an order?"

"Oh, no, sir, we're leaving. Come on, Clive." Mike saluted Jack again, then nudged his friend in the side. Clive followed suit, though not with equal enthusiasm.

Even though he wasn't obliged to do so, Jack returned the salute. The two men hefted their gunnysacks, glanced around the place once more, and made for the door. When they had gone, Jack moved to the window and watched them cross the street, their steps fast, their mouths in motion, no doubt cussing him out. He didn't care. He'd chased them off—for good, he hoped. Behind him, a small crowd of onlookers applauded. He turned around and put up his hands. "No need for thanks, folks. I hope you've seen the last of those two."

"They been nothin' but trouble ever since the Yanks done come t' town, sir," said Rosalyn. "I thank you for orderin' them out."

"You're mighty welcome." Jack made his way back to his table.

Harold Marlan stood as he approached. "That was downright admirable. I've half a mind to walk you to your hotel and pay for your housin' as well."

Jack laughed while gathering his gear. "Mr. Marlan, you've been too generous already. I'll be just fine. I'm going to head on over to North Street and get a nice bed for the night." As he made for the door, he tipped his hat and smiled at the other diners, all of whom smiled and nodded back at him in farewell.

7

I ain't never been so humiliated in all my life. I'd like to give that good-fer-nothin' Lieutenant So-and-so a piece o' my mind," Clive groused as he and Mike headed west on Main Street.

"Lieutenant Fuller, I believe he said," Mike inserted.

"Yeah, yeah. Fuller." Clive cursed under his breath. "Did y' catch the way he talked to us—like we was nobodies? Idiot. I'd like to give 'im a piece o' my mind."

"Yeah, you've said," answered Mike. "I'd've liked to've told 'im off, too, but we got to watch ar'selves. He's already sayin' he's gonna talk to Bond. You think he will?"

Clive shrugged. "Even if he does, we won't get much more 'n a slight reprimand."

"Maybe so," said Mike. "But the last thing we need is Lieutenant Bond diggin' into ar' business. If he finds out how we been robbin' folks blind, we'll be court-martialed, maybe even hanged."

Clive knew his friend was right, but that didn't quell his anger any.

"That fellow had no business usin' his rank against us. Still, he *is* our superior, an' I don't wanna rock the boat none. Right now, we got the ideal job, standin' guard in this stinkin' li'l town. Beats hand-to-hand combat. Things've been goin' pretty good for us, too, with all the extra cash we been gettin'."

Clive shook his head as he thought to himself. "We oughtta go back to Rosalyn's some night after closin' time. Teach that woman a lesson."

Mike frowned. "I ain't so sure that makes sense…'specially since that lieutenant just told us we cain't go back there."

"Since when do you obey every order, Farmer? You been runnin' burglaries right along with me, hain't ya'?" Clive sneered.

"Sure, sure. I'm just sayin', we gotta be smart."

Clive's boiling blood slowed to a low simmer. The men stopped beside a brick building and leaned against it, puffing their cigars in the glow of a nearby streetlamp. Swarms of bugs circled the light. "Speakin' o' burglaries, what if we paid another visit t' that little she-devil Cristina Stiles? We stopped by her farm a month ago 'r so. I reckon she's probably pretty unsuspectin' right about now."

Mike stood straighter. "You mean, tonight?"

"Why not? Think about it. It's a quiet night; nobody's expectin' any trouble. We're off duty now that Brooks and Moser relieved us of our posts, and the next few hours are ours to do with as we please." He eyed his partner with raised brows. "We ain't had supper yet. Let's go out to the Stiles farm an' order that Mexican she-devil t' rustle up some good eats. Afterward, we'll have ar' way with her."

Mike's brow crumpled into a grim frown. "That's plain dumb. She's got those little ones. What're we supposed to do with them?"

"I don't know. Lock 'em up somewhere? We'll figure it out as we go. Come on, it'll be fun."

Mike paused for only a moment, then threw down his cheroot. "If you ain't the craziest coot I ever did know."

"You're just as bad, y' slow-witted weasel."

"Careful. You hang out with me, you know. What's that make you?"

Clive dropped his own cheroot, ground it out with his boot heel, and tossed a grin at Mike. "Smarter."

"Hah. You keep tellin' yerself that."

"You ready?"

"O' course, I'm ready."

They laughed all the way to the livery and rode out to the farm. Good thing they hadn't been drinking, or Clive might not have been able to find his way back. They left their horses tied to a tree in the woods and sneaked toward the tiny cabin, their guns at the ready, just in case the lady came out shooting. So far, the place looked as lifeless as a morgue, but they kept their approach silent and slow. On the porch, Clive pressed his ear to the door, listening for any sounds coming from within. Hearing nothing, he pushed the door open and entered an apparently empty house, Mike on his tail.

"Maybe they're hidin' in the loft," Clive whispered over his shoulder. "Go check it out. I'll keep watch down here."

Mike stepped forward and began a slow climb up the ladder, one rung at a time, his rifle cocked and leveled. Once he'd peered around, he looked down and shook his head. "Ain't nobody up here. Y' think they're out in the barn?" He descended the ladder faster than his ascent.

Clive walked to a window and pulled back the curtain to survey the backyard. "Nope. It's as still as death out there, save for that milk cow chewin' 'er cud. Ain't any horses out there, either, and I don't see a wagon. I bet they went into town. Too bad we didn't see 'er. We could've given 'er a real scare just by walkin' past."

Mike laughed. "Yeah, we missed a great opportunity."

"Well, while we're here, might as well make ar'selves at home and fix a meal."

Mike grunted. "I ain't no cook."

"You ain't good for much, are y'?" Clive chortled. "Go out to the springhouse an' get me some cured pork, if you can find it. I'll make us some pork and beans. With this bread"—he snatched a fresh-baked loaf from the counter—"an' some butter or jam, we'll have us a fine meal. Best of all, there won't be no cleanin' up. We can watch that lil' hellcat do it whilst we got a gun pointin' at 'er. Won't that get 'er good?"

While Mike went in search of provisions from the springhouse, Clive ransacked the kitchen cupboards for a pot and some cooking utensils, his mouth watering as he anticipated the tasty meal. It was just a shame the Stiles woman wasn't there to prepare it for them.

After their supper, with stomachs fully satisfied, the men stretched out comfortably, Clive sprawled on the bed, Mike seated on a chair with his legs propped on a stool. "Where d' you think she could be?" Mike asked, taking a swig from the jug of whiskey he'd found on a kitchen shelf.

"Who knows?" Clive growled. "I was hopin' she'd come home whilst we were eatin'. Pass me some o' that bark juice."

Mike took another gulp before passing the bottle to Clive. "Y' don't think she's stayin' away 'cause she knows we're here?"

Clive spat. "No way she oughtta realize we're here. We been careful. Hid the horses, killed the fire after cookin'…." He returned the whiskey to Mike.

"Well, we can't hang out here forever," Mike said, helping himself to another swig. "We gotta report back before eleven."

"I know." Clive got to his feet, swaying slightly. He steadied himself on a bedpost. "Let's fill ar' bags with whatever loot we can find and then head back. It's gettin' awful dark." He lifted the whiskey bottle from the table, then scowled at Mike. "You done drank most of it." He swallowed the rest of it. "Get movin', you buzzard."

"Yeah, yeah, don't be so bossy."

While Mike emptied a wooden bowl of tomatoes, Clive set the empty bottle on the table and grabbed a warm blanket off the back of a chair just because he wanted to make sure the Stiles woman would notice it missing. "Here're some candy sticks," he said, snatching a jar from the cabinet and dumping the contents into his bag. "These'll make for a nice lil' snack."

Mike chuckled. "You're cruel, you know that?"

"My mother used to say the same thing."

"Yeah? Well, she was right."

"I liked stayin' overnight at Miss Clara's, Maw," said Elias the next morning as the family drove home in their wagon. "It was fun. I didn't expect we'd get to do that."

Cristina smiled. "Neither did I, an' you're right. It was fun."

"It was fun playin' hide the thimble an' checkers an' blindman's bluff."

"Sure was. We oughtta play more games, don't y' think?"

"Yes!" squealed Catherina. "Can we play hide 'n seek tonight?"

"That sounds good t' me," Cristina replied.

"And can we stay at Miss Clara's house again sometime?" Catherina asked.

"We'll see. Either way, you shouldn't be invitin' yourselves like you did last night. That's not usin' the best o' manners. First, you're askin' t' take home kittens, an' then you're askin' for pie, an' then—"

"I'm glad she asked if we could spend the night," Elias inserted, "'cause I don't know if Miss Clara would've thought t' invite us otherwise."

They all shared a laugh while Cristina steered the horses onto their farm. She reined them in and then set the brake.

"Mama, look! By the front door!" Catherina exclaimed. "Where'd those pretty flowers come from?"

Cristina glanced at the cluster of blossoms lying on her tiny porch. She immediately recognized the blooms as having come from her own garden. "I have no idea," she fibbed.

"I'll take the horses out back," Elias offered, evidently not at all curious about the flowers and their origins.

"I'll come, too," said Catherina.

Elias groaned. "You don't have t' follow me everywhere I go, y' know."

"I can if I want to. Isn't that right, Mama?"

Cristina barely heard their chitchat, her mind too preoccupied by the flowers. "That's fine," she muttered absently.

Elias immediately set to work unfastening the harnesses. "Well, if you're gonna follow me, might as well make yerself handy."

"What's that mean?"

"It means I'm gonna give you a job, and if you don't like it, don't follow me to the barn."

"What should I do?"

"Here. Hold these reins. Don't drop 'em."

"I won't. I'm good at this."

"Yeah, yeah."

Soon, Elias led the team of horses away, still mumbling his irritation, with his sister following close on his heels. Meanwhile, Cristina remained seated in the parked wagon, her eyes focused on the strange bouquet of flowers, her head rattled by the questions of who had put them there and why. At last, she mustered the presence of mind to climb down. She gave her yard a quick scan but saw nothing out of the ordinary. Then she reached up and snagged her rifle from beneath the wagon seat. Shouldering it, she cocked the barrel, then gingerly climbed the two steps to her front stoop and slowly bent down to retrieve the flowers. They had come from her garden, all right—globe thistles, peonies, and coneflowers, to name a few—a lovely bouquet, had she assembled it herself.

She tossed the flowers back down and cautiously opened the door, poking just her head inside to check if anyone was about. Once satisfied that the room was clear, she entered, and her nose caught a whiff of fried pork and cooked beans. What in the world? Dirty dishes, soiled pans, a rumpled bedspread, an empty whiskey bottle tipped on its side, and misplaced pieces of furniture all called her nerves to attention. And then she spotted it—the scrawled note on the table. She lowered her rifle and went to pick up the paper. Quick as light, her eyes traced the words.

Remember us? We come calling but you wasn't here. Too bad we missed you. We'll be back soon. Next time you can cook for us.

Incensed, she crumpled the note into a ball, marched to the fireplace, and quickly tossed the dread thing onto the still-hot cinders. She immediately regretted doing so, for what if she found herself in need of concrete evidence of the soldiers' wrongdoing? But it was too late. Just as she reached in to retrieve the paper, a few sparks set it ablaze.

She stood back and watched the note disappear, word by disgusting word. *Thank God we stayed at Clara's last night.* She frowned. Thank God? Where in tarnation had that thought come from? Surely, God, or whatever deity there might be, had nothing to do with her decision not to come home until that morning. Such a senseless notion, with her own wishful thinking to blame. She must clean up this mess—and forget about how she'd happened to stay at Clara's. First, though, the children.

She walked back outside and stepped down from the landing. Glancing around, she noticed, in addition to the tracks of her own horses and wagon wheels, a set of large footprints, clearly made by men wearing boots, leading to the house and also away, toward the woods. It irked her that she hadn't noticed the tracks before going inside. She simply had to learn to be more diligent, so as not to be caught off guard again. She searched for evidence of additional horse tracks but saw nothing. The soldiers must have either walked to her house or left their horses in the woods.

"How dare those fools!" she muttered to no one in particular.

"Whatcha doin', Maw?" asked Elias as he came around the corner of the house.

She couldn't very well keep the break-in a secret. "I'm afraid we've had…some intruders."

"Again? How d' you know?"

She nodded toward the house, and he ran past her to look inside.

"Them dang varmints!" he yelled, his voice trembling with a tone closer to fear than anger. He ran back outside. "D' you think it's the same men?"

"Who're y' talkin' about?" Catherina wanted to know.

"No one, honey."

"Well, do you?" Elias prodded.

"I…yes, I'm sure it's gotta be," Cristina said quietly, choosing not to bring up the handwritten note.

"Who're y' talkin' about?" Catherina repeated in a whine.

"Them mean, nasty, no-good Yanks!" Elias shouted, stepping back into the house again.

This time, Cristina followed him, helpless, not knowing how to calm him. "Elias, please try t' control yer outbursts 'round yer sister."

Elias bent down to right a chair, then pushed it under the table. His reddened face displayed a mix of fury and fright, and Cristina could almost see the war going on inside him, his ten-year-old self longing for manhood, yet the boy in him terrified at the mere thought of it.

He picked up a soiled dish from the table, then set it back down. His eyes scanned the room. "They think they own this place, Maw," he grumbled.

"They might think so, but they're sorely mistaken. An' I'll see to it they understand that fact the next time they set foot on my property."

Elias stared at her with his piercing brown eyes, so like his father's. "How you gonna do that?"

Cristina sighed. "I don't know. Guess I'm countin' on knowin' what t' do if an' when the time comes."

"Think you'll shoot 'em?"

She pressed her lips together and studied the floor. Finally, she said, "I'll do whatever it takes t' protect you and your sister."

Elias straightened his shoulders. "I'll do it, Maw. I'm the man o' this house now."

She abruptly raised her head and glared at her son. "Don't talk like that, Elias Stiles. You are not the man o' this house. The man o' this house is away, which means I'm the one in charge."

Catherina tugged at her sleeve. "Who you gonna shoot, Mama?"

"No one, dear. At least, I hope I don't have t' shoot anyone."

Catherina began to whimper.

Cristina knelt down to enfold her in her arms. "I'm sorry, honey. I don't want you worryin'. Let's clean up this mess and get on with our day, shall we?"

And so they did, for the most part. But a picture of those nasty Yanks shuffling through her belongings kept popping into her mind, and she could not shake it until she'd gone out to the barn, rifle in hand, to search the outbuildings and assure herself that the soldiers had indeed left her property. The question remained, though: when would they return? The note had said "soon." Would it happen while she and her children slept? Tonight? Or next week? Would she be able to protect her family? Would she be fast enough on the draw?

What if the men returned while her family was away again and, this time, waited in hiding for them in the springhouse or the attic? What if they stayed all night in the barn, only to catch her little family unawares when they went out to feed the animals and milk the cow? All morning, her mind did not stop racing. She thought up the most horrific scenarios while scrubbing down the house...while weeding the garden with the children...while kneading bread dough...while standing at the well to pump another pail of water....

"Maw! You can stop pumpin' anytime," said Elias. "The pail's over-flowin' and you're makin' a river."

"Oh!" She stopped, looked down at the pail, and gave a nervous laugh. "No wonder it was gettin' so heavy. Silly me."

"You were daydreamin', weren't you?" said Elias. "I know what that's like. Y' get your mind so full o' thoughts, y' don't know what to do with 'em all, so y' start weavin' stories—mostly bad ones."

She set the pail down and blinked at Elias. "Gracious, Elias. How would you know that?"

He gave a brief smile. "I don't know. Just smart, I s'pose. I kinda been doin' the same thing myself this mornin', ever since we found ar' house all a mess."

She nodded, struck by the impression that her son was growing taller before her very eyes. Still lost in thought, she picked up the pail and climbed the front steps.

"I don't think they'll come back today, Maw."

At the door, she turned. "No? Why d' you say that?"

"Well, think about it. First time they came was 'bout a month ago, ain't that right? I think they'll play it safe. Are you goin' to the sheriff today?"

"The sheriff? No. I doubt he'd do anything, bein' that it's an Army matter."

"Well, he could at least go out to the Army camp and talk to the one in charge."

Cristina was not about to inform her son of the soldiers' threat. "Let's talk about somethin' else, shall we?" She turned her gaze to Catherina, playing across the yard in the dirt with a wooden spoon and a couple of pans.

"Catherina, come inside now," she called. "Mama doesn't want you out here by yerself."

"Aww, do I have t' come in?"

"You do. Besides, it's almost time fer our noon meal, and I'll need yer help."

"You wanna try one o' my dirt pies?"

"Sure," Cristina said.

"Not a jugful!" Elias proclaimed.

Cristina gave him a warning glance. "Elias, can't you play along?"

He rolled his eyes. "I ain't eatin' dirt."

"You aren't, not 'you ain't.' And you'll pretend."

Elias heaved a big sigh and Cristina laughed.

For just a moment, she forgot all about the hideous Yanks who had broken into her home and robbed her of food and her favorite blanket, a patchwork quilt Orville's mother had stitched for him when he was a boy. Having that stolen had hurt deeper than a stab and made her miss Orville all the more.

"I guess I am hungry," Catherina confessed, throwing down her wooden spoon and jumping up.

"Me, too," Cristina put in, although she wasn't certain she could manage to eat with the lump in her throat. She turned and followed Elias into the house. "Elias, would you mind slicin' up some bread?"

Not a second later, the door slammed shut. There stood Catherina, breathing hard, her face red, her eyes wide. "Mama, th-there's a—a Union soldier comin' up the road!"

Cristina whirled, her skirts flaring. She grabbed her rifle off the wall, went to the window, and peered out. "You sure it was a soldier you saw?"

"Yes, I'm sure!"

"Just one?"

"Uh-huh."

She turned and faced her children. "All right. Both o' you go up in the attic, and don't come down till I tell you it's safe."

Catherina started whimpering.

"But, Maw," Elias protested. "I don't think you—"

"Just do as I say. Catherina, you go first. You've gotta be brave, both of you. Elias, take care o' yer sister. Now, go on up there." They scampered up the ladder without further argument.

Positioning the butt of the stock in the pocket of her shoulder, just above her armpit, Cristina opened the door with one hand, then used her foot to pull it the rest of the way open. She stepped out onto the porch, her cheek gently resting against the stock.

8

"ome out where I can see you, soldier!" the woman shouted. "Don't be foolin' with me neither. I'm not takin' any more o' yer monkeyshines. You hear me? I'm done with you, done with both o' you! Step out now!"

Peering out from behind the trunk of a huge sycamore tree, Jack did not know what to think. He'd decided against simply approaching the house without warning, not knowing what to expect, and now he was glad he had been cautious. The woman had a rifle aimed right at him. "Don't shoot, ma'am," he yelled. "I don't know what, um, 'monkeyshines' you're referring to. I'm here on an errand of a serious nature."

"Yeah, I just bet you are. Step out!"

He wasn't sure he dared to, not with a gun pointing straight at him. "You'll have to put down your rifle first," he called back.

"Not gonna happen. I'll lay you flat 'fore you get a chance to whistle one note to your scallywag friend."

"Well then, I don't know why I'd step out if you're planning to shoot me."

She didn't say anything to that, so he didn't move. He considered tossing his own rifle out on the ground in plain view, but that would render him totally helpless—not a chance he wanted to take, in case she turned out to be a madwoman. Harold Marlan had referred to Stiles's wife as a "Mexican beauty," but hadn't mentioned her being a crazy, gun-toting one. Jack could simply shout out his message—that her husband was dead—and then make a run for it, or he could stay and try to talk some sense into her before breaking the news. He decided to stay and try to reason with her.

"I've got something I need to give to you," he said.

"Forget it, soldier. I don't want anythin' from you."

Ever so slowly, he stuck his head out to get a tiny glimpse of her, and, just like that, a bullet sizzled by, blowing his hat right off him. He lurched back, shocked by the accuracy of her aim. "I mean no harm," he called out, a little rattled by the narrow miss. "I repeat, I have something I want to give you."

"And I repeat, I don't want anythin' from you—'cept to be left alone, once an' for all."

"Once I give it to you, I'll be out of your hair. You have my word."

"Uh-huh. You think I trust you, y' dirty, rotten Yank? Where's yer friend, by the way?"

"My friend?"

"Don't play dumb. Is he hidin' out? I'll take y' both down. I know what you've been doin', and I'll not have you snoopin' 'round my property anymore, you hear?"

"I hear you, ma'am, but…I believe you have me mixed up with someone else."

"Stop playin' games with me."

"No games. You are Mrs. Orville Stiles, correct?"

Again, she gave no response. The only sounds he heard were the mooing of a cow and, in the distance, the squawking of chickens. "Ma'am? Are you there?"

Still nothing.

He decided to chance it. Slowly. He wouldn't throw his rifle down but would hold it over his head. That ought to ease her mind. "I'm coming out!" he called by way of a warning.

But the second he emerged, he knew he should have thought twice. A thunderous shot bellowed through the air, and in the next second, an explosive shock to his body sent him airborne. He flew backward at a powerful speed and landed on his back with such a tremendous thud that, for at least a minute, he couldn't catch a single breath. He just lay there, unmoving, unfeeling, drifting in a sea of blackness and murky shadows that had no form or meaning. In the distance, he heard a voice he couldn't distinguish, and then another one, the spoken words making no sense to his mind. He hadn't enough wits about him to open his eyes. Soon a lifeless sensation came over him, as if he hung somewhere between heaven and earth, and he wondered for the briefest second if he hadn't died, and the voices belonged to angels who'd come to take him home.

"Is he dead, Maw?" came a faint voice.

"I told you not t' come out till I said to."

"But is he dead?"

"I—don't know."

A tiny whimper sounded. "You shot 'im, Mama. Is he a bad guy?"

"I thought so, but…I'm not sure. Now that I look at 'im…."

A strength of will came over him about the same time a stabbing pain in his side awakened him to the present. With everything in him, he worked to open his eyes so he could get a sense of his surroundings. If he were going to die, he had to at first get the message across to Mrs. Stiles that he had a letter for her.

A groan came out of him, almost of its own accord.

"Maw, he's still alive."

"So he is."

"P-please," he muttered. Slow, staggering breaths eked out of him, and he felt a cough well up in his chest. "There—there's a note for you in my bag. It's from—from your husband."

"What?" The woman quickly snatched his bag from under his head, and he groaned at the painful movement. Instinctively, he put a hand to the left side of his waist where it pained him the most, and he felt a wet, gooey substance seeping through the fabric of his pants. He lifted his hand for a look and instantly went queasy at the sight. He'd been in the war nearly three years and managed to dodge bullets from all sides—until now. And the person who'd shot him wasn't even a soldier but a woman dressed in plain clothes, her black hair flying in the breeze. What a rotten deal.

He closed his eyes again, too weak to sit up, but wishing he could assess his wound. Was he dying?

Time passed, and Jack seemed to go in and out of consciousness. He awoke with a start when he felt severe pressure to his side and heard someone barking orders. "Elias! Take one o' the horses and hurry over t' Miss Clara's. Tell 'er I shot somebody an' need help right away. She'll know what to do."

"But, Maw, he's the enemy."

"He is, but—he's not. Just go. Don't ask questions."

Jack heard the sound of rapid footfalls. His nostrils filled with dust as someone ran off.

"Catherina, there's a clean basin o' water on the table next to the potatoes I was gonna peel. Carry it out here, an' do yer best not t' spill it all over. Run to the house, but walk back here with the basin."

"Yes, Mama," came the wee, shaky voice.

The pressure on his wound increased, and Jack could tell that Mrs. Stiles was doing her best to stop the bleeding. He opened his eyes a crack, then managed to ask, "Did you read the letter?"

She kept her eyes on her task. "I did, but there's no time t' talk about that now."

"I'm sorry."

"Shush. No flappin' yer mouth."

He closed his eyes again, but not before he caught her wiping a tear from her cheek. She'd gathered enough evidence from the letter to realize that her husband had died. Dare he tell her who had killed him? Not now, he decided, or she'd surely finish him off. He swallowed hard and tried not to retch. Still, the pain was so sharp, he doubted he'd be able to hold back for long.

Just then, a horse galloped past. "Ride as quick as y' can, but be careful," she called over the rumble of hooves.

"Why'd you shoot me?"

"Here, bite down on this handkerchief." Ignoring his question, she stuffed the cloth in his mouth without warning, and he nearly gagged. "It ain't been used but once, t' wipe the sweat from my brow." She eased her pressure on his wound for a moment and took a look. "Doesn't look too bad, actually. Seems the bullet went through yer waist at the front an' came right out the back. At least Miss Clara won't have t' remove the bullet. I guess I'm not as good a shot as I thought."

He lifted one hand to his mouth and removed the handkerchief just long enough to say, "You blew my hat right off."

"Lucky shot."

He stuck the cloth back in his mouth and bit down hard. It felt as if she'd set his side on fire. He lifted his head as best he could but couldn't see any flames. His head dropped down again on its own.

"Here, let's get you propped up a bit." She stuffed his bag back beneath his head once more, almost like a pillow.

"Maybe it wasn't yer time t' die." She paused. "Unless you're of a mind that I finish the job."

He moaned as he shook his head back and forth.

She gave a little laugh, as if this were any time for humor. "I thought you were someone else."

He'd gathered as much.

"I'm comin', Mama," said the little girl.

Mrs. Stiles turned her head to the side. "Take yer time, honey. Best to arrive with a little bit o' water than none."

"I'm concentratin'," the girl said.

"Good. You keep it up."

When the girl set the basin on the ground, a splash of water washed over Jack's face, giving him a bit of relief from the blazing noonday sun. He continued biting on the cloth, finding that it did help to ease the pain.

"I'm gonna remove my apron from yer wound, mister, an' throw some clean water on there so I can get a better look at it. You just keep bitin' down on that handkerchief."

He said nothing, just squeezed his eyes shut and prepared to wince, or, worse, cry like a baby. It took everything in him to do neither, but his stomach steadily grew queasier, and he knew it was just a matter of time before he brought up the pancakes Rosalyn had made him that morning.

9

The soldier yowled like a banshee when Cristina, with Clara's assistance, helped him to his feet. "I can walk by myself," he said with a willful tone. He tried to take one step and faltered. Both women caught him before he went down.

"Clearly, you cain't," Clara said. "You've got a bad injury, an' you jes' threw up the contents o' yer stomach, so you're a mite weak. Now stop actin' like a mule and hold on t' us."

The soldier relented and tossed a heavy arm over Clara's shoulder, then Cristina's. Cristina nearly caved under his weight.

"Now, go real slow-like," Clara instructed him.

"I'm not about to run a race," the soldier said.

Elias and Catherina walked on the other side of Cristina, Elias holding the reins of both his horse and Clara's as the animals trailed behind, while Catherina carried the empty basin. "Y' oughtta've finished 'im off, Maw," Elias mumbled. "If he'd been a deer, you woulda got 'im right smack in the heart."

"Stop that talk, Son. This is no time for spewin' vile talk."

"But he's a good-fer-nothin' Yank."

"I'll give y' that," said Clara.

"Just never mind that now. I'm obliged to save the man's life if I can. If he dies, then I'll have t' live with the knowledge that I killed a man. Plus, I might go to jail."

"Jail? Who would take care o' me an' Catherina?" Elias asked.

"Good point. I guess you'll have t' do yer part."

"I guess. How 'bout I finish 'im off? They wouldn't throw *me* in jail."

"Stop with that nonsense talk," Cristina said.

"Yes, please do," the soldier muttered.

It took a great deal of maneuvering, but they managed to get the fellow into the house and across the room to the straw bed. He would take over Cristina's spot, at least for the time being, and she and Catherina would sleep on pallets next to the fireplace. Soon, she would have to tell the children that their father had died, but that wouldn't happen tonight. Not with this Yankee present. She wished to know the full story about Orville, but she knew she couldn't stomach it now. Her heart and soul longed to escape into the deep, wooded hills and scream to the heavens, but she would have to delay that response until a later time.

"Bring me some hot water. I'm gonna clean his wound best I can," Clara said, waking Cristina from her trancelike state.

"Yes, ma'am." She hurried over to the fireplace, reached for a couple of pieces of wood that were stacked to the side, and stoked up the fire. After pausing briefly to wipe her sweaty brow with the back of her hand, she set the black Dutch oven over the hot coals and then stood there staring down at the water, waiting for it to begin bubbling.

"Don't...you have...a doctor in town?" the soldier muttered between labored breaths.

"Pfff." Clara grunted. "He ain't worth his weight, soldier. His eyes is gettin' so bad, he cain't tell a lame cow from a shade tree; plus, he's ailin' 'imself, so more an' more folks're makin' do on their own. I hear-tell a younger doc's supposed to be comin' in t' take over his practice. Until then, we jus' keep hopin' there ain't no emergencies."

"Isn't this an emergency?"

"Well, we ain't gonna know that till I assess the wound, will we? Or until the buzzards start circlin' overhead. Now, turn on yer good side."

He turned over, but not without a loud moan. Cristina kept her gaze averted, thankful that Elias had found Clara at home, and that it wasn't her who had to minister to him. Her mind was torn. One part of her wished she'd been a better aim, and the other part harbored deep guilt for shooting a man who'd intended nothing more than to deliver the news of her husband's passing—and the letter Orville had written her. She'd read it only once, quickly, and longed for a few minutes to herself so she could pore over it in greater depth. Some of the phrases he'd written started coming back to her. *"I'm not fit to be your husband.... I love you and the children.... My mind is not working right.... I am having awful dreams.... Forgive me for leaving you...."*

In spite of her effort to hold back her emotions, a stray tear dropped from her eye. There was a deluge more where that one came from, but she refused to let them out.

"That water 'bout ready?" Clara asked.

Cristina swiped at the tear before turning her head. "Just startin' to boil."

Her children sat at the table, and while she couldn't see their faces, she knew they were gaping at the stranger sprawled on their mother's bed.

Really, she'd had no business shooting him, even if her intent had been to protect her household. He was an innocent man and had tried to correct her mistaken identification of him, but she'd been too frightened, and perhaps too stubborn, to listen to reason. She'd shot him without any consideration of the potential consequences. And now that she'd seen him up close, she realized he didn't even remotely resemble either of the two Yanks who'd attacked her.

What would happen to her when the Union Army discovered she'd shot one of its own? Would they throw her in jail for attempted murder? Or, worse, might they hang her? She had no family to speak of and, thus, no one to whom she could entrust her children. Clara was too old to be responsible for them.

The soldier writhed about, drawing Cristina's attention back to the present. She used a ladle to fill a wooden washbowl with steaming water. After grabbing a bar of lye soap and a clean cloth and towel from an overhead shelf, she quickly yet carefully carried it all to Clara. Somehow, the older woman had managed to remove the man's bloodied jacket and then pulled his blood-soaked shirt from his waistband, exposing the awful hole the bullet had made. *Her* bullet. The very thought made Cristina's stomach churn. She'd never shot anything but animals. Sometimes, even doing that bothered her, especially if the animal had made eye contact with her before she pulled the trigger. Had she known for sure this fellow had been one of her attackers, it wouldn't have bothered her nearly as much—or maybe not at all. She already knew *their* intentions.

"All right, mister. Lay real still, now," Clara instructed. "I'm gonna dab at the wound an' see if I can clean it up." She dipped the cloth into the bowl of steaming water, then lifted it out and let it cool some before wringing it out. When she applied it to the wound, the man let out a yowl that gave everyone but Clara a jolt. "Hm. Looks like a few o' yer guts is stickin' out. I'm gonna have t' push 'em back in." Then to Cristina, "You got any whiskey?"

Cristina blinked. "I'm afraid not. There was a bottle that belonged to Orville, but those...those fellows stole it."

"What fellows?" the soldier asked weakly.

"I'll tell you later."

The soldier lifted his head slightly and looked at Clara. "What'd you say you were going to do to me?"

Clara paid him no mind but steadied her gaze on Cristina. "What about some tonic? Did you happen to get some from that medicine man that stopped by a few weeks ago sellin' wares and whatnot?"

"Oh, yes. I did buy somethin' he said would help ease the pain if one o' my youngins took a fall or had a stomach ache. I also bought some long strips o' cotton fabric for usin' as bandages."

"Good, good. Fetch whatever you have."

Cristina did as her friend instructed. After shuffling around in her upper shelves next to the fireplace, she finally laid a hand on the bottle and then the bandage fabric. She took a few steps and delivered the items to Clara. "I thought you might've brought some o' yer own curin' oil."

"Didn't have time to think about it. I'll bring some when I come by tomorrow."

"Tomorrow? Aren't you gonna spend the night?"

"Naw. I gotta get home to my animals."

"But what if he…?"

"Dies? You should've thought about that 'fore you shot 'im, my chuckaboo. Matter of fact, you should've jus' finished 'im off."

"Hey," the soldier said, raising his head again.

Clara flicked her wrist at him. "Oh, never mind. Y' ain't gonna die. Not if I fix y' up right."

Clara held the bottle at arm's length and squinted as she seemed to study the contents listed on the label. "Humph. This stuff oughtta make you sleep straight through the night."

"What is it?" he asked.

"Here, open yer mouth."

"What is it?" he repeated.

"Oh, bother. It's called Dr. Sam's Medicinal Pain Cure. S'posed t' cure fevers, gut pain, head pain, an', well, I guess pretty much every pain known to man. Right now, maybe I should take a swig of it, seein' as you're bein' a pain, yerself." Clearly, the soldier did not see the humor in her last sentence. "All right, then, open yer mouth so I can pour this down yer gullet."

He wrinkled his brow at her, and Cristina couldn't help but notice the square set of his sun-bronzed jaw, the fine crinkle lines at the corners of his deep blue eyes, and the full lips that now seemed to have set in a firm line. "Y' might as well do what she says, Yank," Cristina told him. "Miss Clara's not one to give in when she makes up her mind about somethin'." His blue eyes drifted to Cristina, and she looked at him squarely. "Go on, now. Open up."

"Fine." He opened his mouth and allowed Clara to pour some tincture down his throat. He nearly choked on the substance, then yelped and clutched at his wound. Clara held the cloth tight to the area and waited till his coughing subsided. With her other hand, she tossed her long, white braid over her shoulder so that it fell down the middle of her back. "You done?" she asked, sounding about as uncaring as the restless wind.

The soldier swallowed. "I think so."

"Good. Now, don't move so's I can clean this out." She resumed her ministrations. This time, instead of watching her friend, Cristina focused on the soldier and even took a bit of pleasure in watching him squint and hearing him squeal. He succeeded in keeping his body still, but his face certainly did a number of contortions as he whipped his head from side to side. At last, he settled down some.

By now, Elias had edged up next to Clara to watch the "operation" in progress. "Looks ugly," he remarked. "Maw, you got 'im a good one. You shoulda shot a little closer to the middle, though."

"She ain't as good a shot as she thought," said Clara. "But now that he ain't dead, we got to do what we can to keep him alive."

Elias frowned. "Why?"

"'Cause it's the humane thing t' do, I guess."

"But he's a Yank."

"I know, and we hate Yanks, don't we, Elias." Clara turned to her patient. "What's yer name, anyway?"

He didn't answer, perhaps too pained to do so. Or maybe whatever had been in that elixir had numbed his speaking abilities.

Clara kept talking as she continued performing curative measures on his wound. Cristina had no desire to observe and, really, no wish to even assist. She felt a mounting resentment toward the man, even though he'd taken a great risk in coming here to deliver her late husband's letter. It certainly wasn't necessary for him to make the trip. He could have sent someone else. And why was it a Yank, rather than a Confederate officer, who'd come to break the news of Orville's death? Was his unit even missing him yet? Maybe Orville had withdrawn so much from the rest of his company that his superiors weren't yet aware of his absence. Cristina's heart ached something fierce at the prospect.

As early as tomorrow, she ought to load this fellow on the bed of her wagon and deliver him to the nearest Yankee cavalry. The one outside Ripley should do just fine, although it was there that those two wicked soldiers were staying, and she couldn't risk having them see her. Not only that, but what would the cavalry do to her? They had a right to arrest her and could easily throw her in jail. What then? Her stomach burned with anxiety.

She snuck a peek at Catherina. The poor girl trembled lightly, her eyes wide with unspoken fear. Cristina crouched beside her daughter and hugged her. The little mite had seen far too much in her five, almost six, short years. How would she and Elias react to the news of their daddy's passing? So far, Elias had not asked about the letter the soldier had delivered. Cristina could only hope he'd been too preoccupied to have noticed her reading it, for she was at a loss as to how to convey the dreadful truth.

⌒

"If that Lieutenant Fuller paid Bond a visit, you'd think we would'a heard about it by now," Clive mused quietly to Mike. The two were seated at the supper campfire gnawing on pieces of jerky. It was approaching six o'clock, but dusk had not yet fallen. They'd had a day off from regular duty and had spent their time helping a few other men to reinforce a bridge. When they'd returned to camp, around four, they'd fully expected a reprimand. Not that they were disappointed not to receive one.

"Well, maybe the fine lieutenant had a change o' heart. Either he decided it wasn't worth the trip over here, or he didn't leave town today as planned," answered Mike under his breath. There were only a few other soldiers sitting around the fire, but they seemed too engrossed in their own conversations to overhear.

"Wonder what he was doin' here, anyway. It ain't like Ripley's a major metropolis," Clive muttered.

"Who knows? Maybe he took the day off to visit a relative. It could've been anything."

"Yeah."

They fell silent for a moment when the other soldiers stood, stretched, and then nodded their good-nights. Once alone with Mike, Clive said, "We should start plannin' our next snatch."

Mike frowned. "I think we should give it a good rest for now, don't you?"

"I'm runnin' outta cash."

Mike shook his head. "You buy too much booze. Why, in just the last hour, you done guzzled down two bottles o' whiskey. You need to slow down, or you're gonna end up blurtin' out somethin' that'll give us away."

"I can hold my own."

"We'll see. Just don't be doin' or sayin' anything stupid," Mike warned.

Clive chuckled. "I'll do my best. All right, we'll give it a week."

"Good deal. Pass me another strip o' jerky."

Clive did so, and then glanced at the sky. "Looks like rain tonight."

"Feels like it, too. Air's hot an' clammy. 'Course, this fire don't help none."

They sat and stared at the dying flames while they finished their dried meat. In due time, they both stood. "See you in the mornin'," they told each other, almost in unison, before heading to their separate camps.

10

In the middle of the night, Jack awoke in pain. Disoriented, he scanned the room like a wild man, trying to figure out where he was and what had landed him in this strange house, not to mention this bed. It took him all of a minute to reorient himself to his surroundings and then to come to grips with what had transpired. He'd been shot by that Stiles woman and he had a strong feeling that either she or that boy of hers would soon finish him off. His head spun with pain, and he felt the beginnings of the hot and cold shakes overtaking him. He had a great urge to relieve himself, so he pushed away the lightweight blanket covering him, only to discover he was wearing a nightshirt of some sort over the bandage that other woman had wrapped around his waist. What was her name? *Miss Clara.* Yes, that was it—a rather testy old woman.

The house was dark, save for a low-burning lamp across the room that created eerie shadows. It was a tiny abode with a fireplace and a few rustic-looking pieces of furniture. In the glow cast by the embers in the fireplace, he thought he saw a couple of bodies asleep on the floor—Mrs. Stiles and her daughter, perhaps? It irked him that he'd taken over the bed, but, doggone it, she was the one who had shot him, so he shouldn't feel too guilty.

There was a door catty-corner to the fireplace and Jack thought it might lead out back to an outhouse. Even so, he decided to go out the front porch door, since it was closer, and walk around the side of the house. He let his eyes adjust before he used his right arm to heft himself up. He couldn't help the tiny groan that escaped his lips at the surge of burning pain on his left side. He longed to unwrap the bandage and get a look, but he supposed it was best to leave it be—at least for now. He pushed himself further up, and then, carefully and slowly, swiveled around until his bare feet found the rough planked floor. Somehow, he had to find a way to get out of here tomorrow. He no longer had a horse and he knew for certain he couldn't walk all the way back to camp. Maybe Mrs. Stiles would assist him in getting back to his unit. Surely, she would oblige him if he asked. But that was a long way to expect her to take him and then to drive all the way back home to Ripley. He would have to think on it.

Taking care not to make a sound, he stood, then promptly tumbled backward on his rear, hitting the mattress hard. The jarring of his wound caused his stomach to churn and his head to reel. Where was his stamina? Most days, he had the strength of an ox, but now he felt about as weak as a newborn lamb. Under his breath, he gave a low growl of frustration.

A moment later, he made another attempt to stand, this time steadying himself before taking his first step and then another. As he inched his way toward the door, he ran into a chair. He quickly grabbed hold of it before it toppled. He stood still for a few seconds to gather his wits. At last, he set out again, only to step on something hard—a tool of some sort, or perhaps a small toy. He kicked it aside and proceeded.

Just as he was about to reach for the door latch, a harsh whisper brought him up short. "What d' you think you're doin', soldier?"

He turned and saw, across the room, the silhouette of a woman with waist-long hair wearing what looked to be a long nightdress. Great. He had awakened Mrs. Stiles. He was not a self-conscious man, but he

wasn't used to having women gawk at him in his nightshirt, either—
what she could see of it, anyway. His brief marriage to Marilee had poi-
soned his desire for women, particularly pretty ones. Still, he wondered
how she felt, seeing him dressed in a shirt that had no doubt belonged
to her deceased husband. Miss Clara had probably been the one to
put it on him, though he had no recollection of anything after she'd
poured that awful, sour-tasting tincture down his throat. The last thing
he could remember was his coughing spell, and so, then and there, he
resolved not to allow another drop of that rotten stuff past his lips. He
needed to keep his mental faculties about him.

"I was going to find my way to the outhouse, if you don't mind."

"Oh. Well, you needn't do that. There's a cauldron beside yer bed. I
can empty it in the mornin'."

"Empty—no! I'll go outside, thank you."

"Then wait till I wake Elias. He can help you."

"No need. I'll be fine."

He swayed a bit, then reached for the wall with his right hand and
steadied himself.

"Yes, I can see that." She turned her head in the direction of the loft.
"Elias!" she called.

"I'm awake, I'm awake." The boy shuffled down the ladder. "Y' really
thought I could sleep through all this racket?" He reached the bottom
rung and stumbled across the room toward the door. "Come on, Yank,
I'll help ya'. It ain't—*isn't*—a short walk, though."

"I'll make do on my own."

"I said I'll take y'," the boy insisted in a cranky tone.

"I'm a grown man," Jack replied sternly.

"Oh, for pity's sake. Soldier, stop yer arguin'. Just take 'im, Elias."

Jack felt duly reprimanded.

Lord, get me out of here tomorrow. Please.

But when tomorrow came, Jack quickly realized he wouldn't be
going anywhere for a while. Sometime after he'd closed his eyes and
managed to get back to sleep, a raging fever hit him like a hot brick,
and by morning, he could barely lift his head, let alone walk outside

to relieve himself. With her own brand of ingenuity, Mrs. Stiles, with Elias's help, hung ropes from the cabin's rafters and draped some quilts over them for makeshift curtains. Jack now had some privacy…and the cauldron came in handy after all.

In a panic, Cristina again sent Elias to Clara's, telling him to insist that she come immediately. Elias arrived home ahead of Clara and took his horse out to the barn for his rubdown. When her friend arrived, Cristina met her out front. "He's real sick, Clara. I don't know what t' do."

"What's wrong with 'im?" Clara handed down a satchel to Cristina, then dismounted and led her horse to the hitching post, looping the reins around it several times.

"He's hotter 'n blazes." Cristina handed the bag back to Clara.

"Sounds like the putrids have set in."

"The putrids?"

"His wound 's gone green, no doubt. That's done caused the fever. I'll prob'ly need to take off that bandage and dig out the pus. Probably stinks to high heaven, too."

"I didn't notice that."

"Well, nonetheless, I'm pretty sure I know what we're dealin' with. If it gets any worse, gangrene'll set in, and then it's life or death."

"Oh, no. We can't let 'im die. He looks t' be a high-rankin' officer, from all those stripes an' whatnot on his uniform. What's the Army gonna do t' me when they find out…?"

"Now, now. Stop yer worryin', girl. Let's go inside before it starts rainin'. Air's thick enough to cut, and I'm sticky as glue. Need to wash my hands real good 'fore I look at the patient, too. I was shovelin' cow dung when Elias showed up."

They stepped inside and found Catherina asleep on the rug in the middle of the room. Not surprising, since no one had gotten a good night's rest. Cristina gently picked her up and carried her over to the pallet, which she'd moved further from the fireplace and the kitchen commotion. She smoothed the hair away from Catherina's rosy face, then stood and walked over to Clara, who had plunged her hands into the basin of water on the table and now scrubbed them with lye soap.

Clara gave Cristina a sideways glance. "How you doin', now that you've known of Orville's passin' for a full day?"

"I actually haven't taken much time t' think about it," Cristina admitted. "I know it's real, but it hasn't hit me full on, probably because it's been so long since I last saw 'im."

"It's true you've had to accustom yerself t' makin' do on yer own. You long been livin' the life of a widow, whether you want to admit it or not."

"I suppose you're right." Cristina reached for a towel and held it at the ready.

"A woman does what she's gotta do to survive when her man's not about. You've done well, Cristina, and don't you forget it. When my Melvin passed on, well…." She glanced up at the ceiling. "I'd say it took me till sundown to get myself back on track."

"Sundown? You mean, less than a day?"

Clara arched an eyebrow at Cristina. "I was a mite better off without 'im, y' know."

"Clara!"

"It's the truth, my young chum. He liked his moonshine an' it made 'im mean. Real mean. Broke my arm once." She stated the fact as if she were talking about the weather.

"No!" Cristina put a hand over her open mouth. "You never told me that."

"Well, now y' know. When he keeled over one afternoon from too much booze, I wasn't all that sad. I s'pose his heart gave out. I'll never know. Anyway, you can be real glad your Orville wasn't like my Melvin."

Cristina and Orville hadn't had the perfect marriage, either, especially in the beginning. But they'd grown to love each other in a comfortable sort of way and, of course, the children had brought them closer together.

"I still haven't told the children. They haven't yet questioned why this nameless soldier's here and, as far as I know, they're clueless about the letter he delivered."

"This letter…did Orville give you reason to believe that he—"

"I read between the lines, Clara. He made it very clear he didn't want t' go on. His death wasn't an accident, I'm certain of it. The way he wrote the letter, well, he knew it was the last one he'd be writin' me. That's what hurts, Clara. He didn't love us enough to…."

Clara laid a wet hand on Cristina's arm. "Now, now, don't start talkin' like that." She kept her voice at a whisper. "He wasn't of a clear mind, Cristina. You've gotta remember that. He wasn't right." Clara took the offered towel and dried her hands on it.

"I know."

A groan sounded from behind the curtain of quilts, and Clara glanced that way. "I'm comin', mister." Clara picked up her bag and gave it a pat. "I'm armed and ready. Let's go have a look at our patient, shall we?"

Over the next several days, the soldier tossed and turned, moaning and muttering, "What's that? Get off of me. Go! Get away from me!" He often batted at his blanket and at the air, and otherwise stared ahead with a glazed expression.

"Why's he keep talkin' weird like that?" Elias asked one day when he returned from tending to Clara's animals. He'd assumed that responsibility while Clara stayed at the Stiles home to ensure the soldier had round-the-clock care.

"His mind's gone soft," Clara said. "It's the fever. He's got no idea where he is and he's imaginin' all sorts o' things."

"Like what?" Elias asked.

Clara shrugged. "I'm not sure, my dear, but it's not uncommon for folks sufferin' high fevers to hallucinate." She turned her full attention to Elias. "How're my animals farin'?"

Elias shrugged. "Near as I can tell, they're happy as ducks in a pond. I been lettin' the cows out to pasture after I milk 'em, and the old horse follows 'em. The cats are eatin' up the mice and drinkin' the milk I squirt at them, the chickens been gobblin' their feed an' drinkin' their water, the pig's been diggin' in the mud but eatin' good, and yer goats an' donkey are fine as can be. They been gettin' real used to seein' me twice a day, and, truth told, they'll prob'ly be sad when I quit comin'. You think ol' Gus is doin' all right at yer neighbor's house?"

Clara laughed. "He's doin' just fine, I'm sure. Mr. Winston'll feed 'im real good. The ol' dog won't even want t' come home. Anyway, you're a fine farmer, boy. Someday you'll have yer own land and animals, and you'll be a great success."

Elias turned his attention to the soldier. "Why won't his fever stay down?" he asked. "Ain't, ur, haven't you been puttin' cold cloths on 'is forehead all the time? He seems t' come around some when the fever goes down, but then it shoots right back up again."

Clara gave a thoughtful glance at the restless patient. "I know. Go pump me another pail o' water, Elias, would you?"

"Okay, but I sure wish somebody would explain t' me why you're tryin' so hard to keep that Yank alive," he groused.

"Only reason yer maw shot 'im was 'cause she thought he was one of them two that broke into yer house," Clara explained. "We don't want yer maw goin t' jail over this, so we gotta do what we can t' keep the feller alive. Now go get the water please."

"I will, but why'd he come on ar' property in the first place?"

Cristina tsked. "Elias, just go fetch the water."

The boy snatched up the pail, turned abruptly, and stalked outside in a huff. Sometimes his moods changed faster than a bull's.

Clara shook her head. "Forget about that boy and his ways for now, Cristina. He's just a'growin'. Just get a couple o' more cloths for me. We'll work harder on this fever. Maybe we haven't done the best we could."

Still unconscious, the soldier suddenly tore off his blankets. His nightshirt was disheveled up to his knees, revealing a pair of hairy, muscular legs and feet as tall as a donkey's ears and as wide as a soup ladle. He yanked at his coffee-colored hair and brushed his whiskery jaw with the back of his hand, his movements jerky and uncontrolled. At first, Cristina did nothing but stare at him, her own nerves almost paralyzed.

"Cristina, go! Time's a'wastin'."

"Oh! Of course." She scurried to the sink past Catherina, who sat at the table with her cloth dolls. From the shelf overhead, she snatched two more folded cloths, then hurried back to the bed.

At the same time, Elias returned with a pail of water, which he set on the floor next to Clara. "I'm goin' out to the barn to clean the goats' pen an' to feed an' water 'em," he announced.

"Thank you, Elias. See to the other animals while you're at it, would you, please?"

"Sure, Mama. I'd rather do any manner o' work than stand here watchin' that Yank roll all over the place like some madman. That's all he been doin' for days now."

"Elias Eduardo, stop bein' so hateful."

"Why? He's a Yank. I thought you hated all Yanks. Paw's Confederate. Should you really be tendin' to someone he's fightin' against?"

"I don't hate this man. I don't even know him."

"He's Union. Ain't that enough?"

This time, he didn't bother to correct his use of the word "ain't" and she didn't bother to mention it. "Let's just work at bein' a little more civil if we can. I know it's hard for you, but make an effort, would you?"

"Paw wouldn't like it. Not one bit."

She froze for a moment and swallowed hard, staring at the bucket of water he'd set on the floor. Had Cristina really done this to Elias— had she taught him to hate? Her heart suddenly ached at the thought. "We'll...talk about this later. Keep an eye out for unwanted visitors. I can't be out there with you, so be careful."

"Should I take the gun?"

She paused to consider his question, sensing Clara's eyes on her.

"No," she finally answered. "Just be alert."

He did not respond, simply walked to the door and left the cabin.

Catherina looked up at the sound of the door closing. "Where'd Elias go?" She'd been so engrossed in her play, she must not have overheard the discussion—to Cristina's relief.

"He went out to the barn, honey."

"I'm goin' out there, too."

"No, stay in the house."

"But I wanna go outside."

Cristina thought for a moment. "All right, but run to catch up with Elias. I don't want you playin' outside alone. Stay close to your brother, but don't pester him. He's not in the best of spirits."

"I never pester him."

Cristina just smiled as Catherina carefully laid her dolls down on the table and raced out the door. "Elias! I'm comin'!" she sang out. Cristina could just imagine Elias rolling his eyes and muttering under his breath. Well, so be it. Perhaps his sister's presence would manage to cheer him.

Clara lifted the water pail and set it on the wooden stand next to the bed, then dipped a cloth into the water and gave it a good wringing-out. And then she held it out to Cristina.

Cristina merely stared. So far, she'd been content to sit back and let Clara handle the ministrations.

"C'mon, take it. You're gonna rub 'im down from the waist up and I'm gonna do 'is legs. We gotta treat this fever more diligent-like."

"But…how can I? His nightshirt—"

"Well, unbutton it."

"What?"

"Cristina, you've seen a man before."

"I know, but—this man's a stranger."

"And a Yank, I know."

"No, I wasn't gonna say that."

Clara stared hard at her. "Looky here, honey, do you think I like takin' care o' him any more 'n you? He isn't even mine t' tend, but you're my best friend so I gotta help you. Like I told Elias, fer yer sake, I want the feller t' live. Unbutton the top part o' his nightshirt an' apply that cold cloth to 'is face, neck, an' chest. While you get started, I'm gonna look in my bag t' see if I can find somethin' that might help. Not so sure I can get 'im t' swallow anything, but I'll try. Go on, now. Git on it."

It was the first time Clara had used a stern voice with Cristina. Still, she'd not so much as shaken the hand of another man since last seeing Orville, so the thought of tending to this unnamed soldier gave her a bit of a chill. But she swallowed her discomfort and set to work while Clara started sorting through her satchel. After some shuffling, she pulled out a bottle and held it at a distance to study the label. "This linctus might not help the fever, but it'll settle 'im down. Nothin' much t' be done about that 'cept to keep bathin' 'im. Rub the insides o' his wrists with the cold cloth, Cris. That's s'posed t' help cool the rest o' the body."

Methodically, Cristina did as her friend bid her, trying not to pay too much attention to the man's brawny arms, his broad shoulders, or his overall girth. She turned over a callused hand, palm up, and rubbed the wrist, then repeated the procedure on his other hand, reaching across him to lift the hot, heavy arm. She'd never been around such a large man, let alone touched one, and a wave of guilt washed over her for even noticing his appearance. She really had not yet grieved the loss of Orville, save for a few tears that she'd shed on her pillow the last several nights before drifting to sleep.

The soldier's teeth chattered as his mouth emitted strange, nonverbal sounds.

"What d' you think he's sayin?" Cristina asked.

Clara snorted. "Gibberish. Like I was tellin' Elias, a high fever can make a body do odd things. His head's not right."

"You think he's gonna…?" She hadn't wanted to ask the question.

Clara shrugged. "Cain't say."

Cristina's hands paused briefly, but she kept her eyes on the sick soldier. "I really don't wish 'im ill, Yank or not. It's my fault he's lyin' here." She paused a moment. "Clara, d' you think I've taught Elias to hate?"

"Now ain't the time for talkin'. Just tend to this soldier."

"All right."

Clara moved in beside Cristina, filled a measuring spoon to the brim from the bottle, and bent to lift the man's head so she could give him the linctus. It took some doing, but she somehow managed. The soldier's lips were already parted due to his teeth chattering, so Clara eased his mouth open further. "Here, soldier, I'm givin' you some medicine. All you have t' do is swallow it, y' hear?"

Of course, he didn't answer, didn't even acknowledge that he'd heard her, but he did open his mouth a bit more when the spoon touched his lips. After swallowing the liquid, he set to coughing, so Clara tried to get him to sit up, but he clearly did not intend to cooperate. At last, the coughing subsided on its own and Cristina released the breath she'd been holding.

They had worked for at least an hour to bring down his temperature when, at last, the fever subsided and the man fell into a peaceful slumber. "The worst is over fer now," Clara said. "That don't mean it won't come back. Fer now, he rests. I'm gonna have t' go home t'night. I appreciate Elias givin' my animals food an' water, but their stalls need muckin' an' I got eggs t' collect. You'll be fine. You know what t' do."

Cristina dreaded the thought of taking care of the man by herself, but she knew Clara had her own things to attend to. "What if he dies?" she asked quietly.

"Then we'll bury 'im. At least nobody'll be able to say we din't try t' help 'im."

"I don't want a dead man in my bed."

Clara gave a little chuckle. "Well, he's sleepin' soundly now. Let's try t' think good thoughts."

"Do you want some supper before you go?"

"No, I'll fix somethin' at home."

Cristina's next words were interrupted by the sound of the children's thundering footsteps. They burst through the front door.

"Mama, we had fun!" Catherina exclaimed. "Elias pushed me on the big swing. I din't even pester 'im."

"Is that right?"

Elias grinned. "Well, she pestered me a little bit, but that's okay."

Relief fluttered through Cristina as she realized Elias's bad mood had passed. "That was nice of you to push yer sister."

"She tried pushin' me, but I only went about a foot high. Then it started t' rain, so we came in."

"Oh, dear!" Cristina turned and patted Clara's arm. "Now I know you have to go. Thank you for comin' and all your help and thank you fer the encouragement."

Elias turned his attention to the makeshift curtains. "Is that soldier still talkin' to 'imself?"

"Not at the moment. Say good-bye to Miss Clara." After a round of parting hugs, Clara left and Cristina sucked in a deep breath. "All right, then, let's rustle up some supper, shall we?"

"What're we havin'?" Catherina wanted to know.

"How about Miss Clara's specialty—stick soup?"

Both children moaned but then giggled and Cristina found, for the first time in a while, that a smile came naturally. Her children had a way of kindling joy with hardly any effort.

11

ell, I think we can safely say Fuller changed his mind 'bout payin' Lieutenant Bond a visit," Clive mused as he and Mike patrolled the rain-soaked sidewalk up and down Main Street. They'd been reassigned to their posts in town, so he could only assume the officer they'd met at Rosalyn's a couple of weeks back had decided not to follow through on reporting their behavior to the lieutenant. Good. With any luck, they'd seen the last of him.

"Even so, we should prob'ly proceed with caution," Mike replied. "And I don't think we should return to Rosalyn's 'cause a bunch o' customers heard the lieutenant order us to stay away. No point in stirrin' up more trouble jus' fer some eats."

"Yeah, you're prob'ly right. That don't mean we can't have ar' fun with Rosalyn if we happen t' meet up with her some night in a dark alley."

Mike jerked his head up. "You're the devil 'imself! How you 'spect t' run into her in some alley?"

"Well, we might have t' do a teeny bit o' plannin'."

"What'd y' have in mind?"

Clive shrugged. "Don't know exactly. I guess one o' these nights, when Privates Brooks and Moser relieve us of our duties, instead of goin' straight back to the unit, we could hang around town an' then, when the restaurant closes, come up on 'er."

"What if she ain't the one who locks up the place?"

"She's the owner, ain't she? Well, I guess we won't know till we get there. Ain't no law against standin' in an alley, is there?"

Mike laughed. "Good point. We're pretty much the law around here anyway. Ripley's sheriff's an old codger and, frankly, I think he's mighty glad we're here to assume his responsibility o' keepin' the peace. When folks see our uniforms, they assume we're doin' our job protectin' the community. I ain't seen more 'n a couple o' men wearin' badges. This place seems peaceful; folks prob'ly ain't accustomed to seein' much crime, 'cept for the occasional drunk that's up for a fight. Still, we gotta be sneaky. We want folks t' keep trustin' us."

A commotion up the street had them turning their heads. "Well, speak of a drunken spat."

Someone had thrown a couple of fellows out of a saloon and into the road. "Go sleep it off, you jug-bitten bilkers," yelled the big fellow who'd tossed them on their backsides. The drunks cursed and spat as they clumsily tried to get to their feet.

With a quiet nod between them, Clive and Mike set off toward the squabble. Throwing their weight around was what they did best.

Before bedtime, Cristina told the children a ridiculous little story about a piglet and its mother that she'd made up on the spot. They had giggled at her storytelling and she'd warmed at their sweet presence. What would she ever do without them? With Orville gone, it left just the three of them and that realization somehow gave her an added dose of determination. They would make it, their little family of three, no matter how difficult. She would see to it. At the close of her silly story, she tucked Catherina into her pallet and kissed her on the cheek. The girl's eyelids already drooped with sleepiness.

On the other side of the quilted curtain, the soldier stirred with a groan. She feared she was in for a long night with him.

She patted Catherina's arm one last time, then quietly stood and followed Elias up the ladder to the loft to tuck him in as well. "You don't have t' keep tuckin' me in at night, Maw," Elias said over his shoulder. "I'm growin' up, y' know."

"Nonsense. I'll be tuckin' you in at least till you start growin' yer first whiskers."

"Maw, I'll be a man by then!"

"True enough and still home with me, I hope."

Elias's rustic little attic loft suited him fine, with two small windows at either end, a little wooden table that held some old toys and a few books that he read by lamplight, and a chest that contained his clothes—three pairs of trousers, three shirts, and a few pairs of socks and underclothes. Cristina marveled at the way the years scooted by with nary a care.

Elias lay down on his cot and Cristina sat down beside him before drawing his lightweight blanket up close to his chin. "I know it's hard for you, havin' that soldier in our house. Hopefully, he won't be here much longer."

"I'm sorry I went on so much about him in front o' Miss Clara. I guess that wasn't very nice of me."

"Well, you're forgiven. We all have outbursts from time t' time."

"Do you s'pose the soldier'll die in yer bed?"

"Good heavens, I hope not."

"Where is heaven, anyway?" he asked.

Her stomach lurched for no good reason...except that she didn't have an answer for him. "Why ever would you ask such a thing?"

He shrugged. "I dunno. You said 'Good heavens' and it made me think about it. Is heaven a real place?"

"Well, I don't know. I suppose it is."

"Who gets to go there?"

Again, her stomach pinched. "Well, I can't say I know fer sure."

"Ain't you curious?"

She *was* curious, but the question had no easy answer, at least to her manner of thinking. "I suppose."

"I wonder who knows."

"Maybe a preacher would know."

"But we don't know no preacher."

"True enough."

Neither of them said anything more for a long moment. Night had rendered his attic room dark, save for the lantern light coming up through the opening to the main house below.

Elias lay there and stared at the ceiling. "What d' you suppose Paw is doin' right now?"

Cristina's heart thumped an extra beat at that unexpected question, but she tried to remain calm and unaffected. One day soon, she would have to tell her children the truth about their father. But she wasn't ready to do that tonight.

"I…I couldn't tell you, honey." It was an honest answer.

"You get any mail from him lately?"

Another skipped heartbeat. "Um, a while ago. He said he was tired of the war. He's seen some terrible things."

"If I were at his side, I could make him feel better."

"But then you wouldn't be at *my* side and how would that make me feel? Besides, you do like to refer to yerself as the man o' the house."

He seemed to ponder her words for a bit. "I guess you're right. I'm where I'm s'posed t' be for now."

She tilted her head at him. "Sometimes you're a real wonder to me. You're growin' up before my eyes, and I'm not sure how I feel about that."

He gave a slanted grin, followed by a long yawn. "You always talk like that. Maw, I'm gonna grow up, whether you like it or not. Like Miss Clara said, I'll have my own land and farm someday. But don't worry, you'll still have Catherina."

"Yes, that's true."

Downstairs, the bedsprings squeaked, and the soldier moaned again.

"I s'pect he needs a drink of water an' maybe another cool cloth on his forehead," Elias said.

"I s'pect so." She leaned down and kissed her son on the forehead. "Dream nice dreams."

He turned over on his cot and closed his eyes. Cristina guessed he had fallen asleep before she reached the top rung of the attic stairs.

~

His body burned like the blistering sun and yet it shook with chills. It made no sense to Jack's baffled mind. He tried to lift himself up, even open his eyes, but no part of him wanted to oblige. So he lay there like a wilted weed, parched and miserable, even though the cool cloth stretched across his forehead, and the soothing touch of another cold cloth running up and down his arms and across his chest, did bring a measure of comfort. Earlier that day, he'd envisioned spiders and other critters crawling on the walls, dangling in front of him, and scuttling across his body, but thank the Lord, those hallucinations had passed. Now, if he could just find the strength to open at least one eye even a slit, or, at the very least, utter the word "water"—though he wasn't sure whether his churning stomach could handle as much as a drop, and he didn't want to retch all over himself.

The female voice he kept hearing seemed far off and hard to distinguish, though it was probably nearer than he thought. As much as he tried to straighten out his tangled mind, his surroundings remained wrought with perplexing noises. His name was Jack Fuller and he was a lieutenant in the Army. That much he knew, though he couldn't recall the name of the major who he was supposed to report to. Had he made it back to the base? Was it his mother's voice he heard? Was she planning his funeral?

"Try t' calm down, mister. You'll get better soon. Here, take a sip o' water." A hand held a cup to his mouth, and so, despite his queasy stomach, he took a few swallows. She must not be his mother or she wouldn't have called him "mister." The pain in his side had dissipated for now, but that was only because he couldn't seem to move anything but his head. Was he paralyzed? The sudden notion had him frantically moving a finger and then a toe. As he lay there in his dreamlike state, he released a tiny sigh of relief. *Jesus.* Just saying the name in his head helped to calm him.

"I'm gonna go lie down fer a while, soldier. You try t' sleep, now."

There came that voice again, oddly familiar, yet distinctly foreign. Where was he? Questions stormed his wracked brain, but he managed to ignore them enough to drift back into a restless sleep.

When he awakened, the curtain of quilts was open and the cabin was dark save for a tiny glow from the low-burning lamp across the room. He heard noises outside—the distant howl of a coyote, the nearby squawks of chickens, and the sound of something skittering past the side of the house that shared a wall with his bed. Probably a rabbit or some other varmint. He coughed, then groaned from the pain. That took care of the silence indoors. He found he'd regained a bit more consciousness now that the wretched fever had let up. He lay in a pool of sweat, his memory starting to come back in small bits. The woman named Mrs. Stiles had shot and wounded him. Ever since then, he'd been making a hospital of her one-room cabin, with her laying cold cloths on him and another woman named Miss Clara who poured insufferable doses of awful-tasting tincture down his throat. Was she trying to kill him?

He turned his head and noticed an empty chair beside the bed. A straw hat, which must have belonged to *her*, dangled from the chair arm. Had she been sitting there, keeping vigil? Just the notion of it made his body quiver—and not because of the fever. He'd noticed, during moments of coherence, that the man in town had been right to call Mrs. Stiles a Mexican beauty. Instinctively, Jack wanted to know about her—where she'd come from and how she'd landed in Ripley. Of course, his next thought was one of self-reproach. She might be very pretty, but she was also newly widowed. Besides, ever since his botched marriage, he'd told himself he didn't want or need the company of another complicated woman. What was wrong with his head that he should allow himself the briefest twinkling of attraction? Good grief, that fever really *had* affected him.

He shut off those thoughts and turned his attention to the wooden bowl on the small table nearby. A wet cloth lay draped over the edge. Though his temples banged with pain and his wound still hurt clear to the heavens, he let his eyes keep wandering to the animal hide stretched out on the wall next to his bed—a bear, perhaps—and then to the broom propped in the corner by the front door. His chest gave a peculiar rattle, producing a coughing spell. He winced with pain and tried to suppress the cough but couldn't. He pulled himself up with a great deal of effort, thinking that sitting would ease his discomfort. The motion caused the damp cloths that had been draped over him to fall at his side, so he picked them up and draped them over the edge of the basin with the other one. He straightened the damp nightshirt, then flung his legs around until his feet landed on the plank floor. He fumbled with the buttons of his nightshirt, but soon gave up on trying to close it all the way. With even greater effort, he stood in order to stretch his weak muscles, then wobbled a bit before regaining his balance. His head swirled and an awful wave of nausea came over him. He let loose another cough, which landed him right back down on the mattress. The coughing continued until he was sure he'd awakened everybody, including the farm animals. More sweat soaked his nightshirt, so he splashed himself with some water from the basin beside him. The cool liquid felt refreshing as it dripped down his body, but it also produced a fit of wracking chills.

The bandage wrapped tightly around his waist constricted his breathing and he wished to loosen it, but he had no idea how to go about doing so, with this nightshirt confining his movements. Still hacking, he managed to reach the quilt curtain and pull it closed. If he'd had the strength, he would've gone outside to relieve himself. He begrudgingly bent down and reached for the black cauldron Mrs. Stiles had provided. What a humiliating situation. Feeling at least somewhat relieved, he replaced the kettle's lid, then shakily removed his arms from the nightshirt sleeves and pushed his shirt down so he could work on the bandage, starting at the beginning, where Miss Clara had tied it off. Slowly, he loosened the knot, then proceeded to unwrap the cloth from his body, one layer at a time, going around and around, and gaining relief the more he loosened the fabric. His wheezing chest yielded another coughing spasm, but this one didn't last as long as the others. About the time it stopped, the door squeaked open. On instinct, he reached for his rifle, but, of course, Mrs. Stiles had put it somewhere.

"Soldier?" came the voice on the other side of the curtain.

He relaxed a bit. *Mrs. Stiles.* And all this time, he'd believed her to be sleeping soundly on the floor by the fireplace. She must have taken a walk to the outhouse. He envied her the luxury.

"What're you doin' up?" she asked. "How're y' feelin'?"

"Like I could outrun a wildfire."

"Ha! I find that hard to believe. Why'd you get outta bed?"

"I'm taking off this bandage."

"Don't you do that! Miss Clara'll have yer hide."

"It's too tight. I'll put it back on." He coughed again.

"I wonder why you're gettin' that cough. I could hear you clear out in the necessary. Is yer chest hurtin'?"

"Not really. More like tickling."

"Okay, I'll get you some elixir."

"Some what?"

"Some elixir I bought from a travelin' merchant."

"It's probably just flavored water."

"Well, whatever it is, we'll try it."

Her voice trailed off, as did her footsteps. He realized he enjoyed listening to her speak with that Southern drawl. In spite of his condition, he felt the corners of his mouth curl upward in a tiny grin. Refocusing on his task, he tried to examine his wound, but in the dimly lit room, it was difficult to discern how bad it looked. He told himself he'd be better off not knowing, then rewrapped the bandage around his waist and worked to tie it off. On the other side of the curtain were the sounds of feet shuffling and items being moved around.

"You don't happen to have another nightshirt I could borrow, do you?" he called out.

"Yes, I—I'll get that, too."

He didn't miss the slight falter in her reply and a flood of guilt washed through him. How ill-mannered of him to assume he could borrow her husband's clothing.

Several minutes later, she stuck her arm around the side of the curtain and dropped some clothing on the bed. "You'll find a clean nightshirt and a pair o' drawers in that pile. When you start feelin' better, you can put on the trousers and shirt. They're all new, never used. Orville bought 'em off a salesman 'fore he went to war, but they wound up bein' too big. You're a mite bigger than him, so I figure they'll fit you good an' proper. Also, when you're feelin' up to movin' to a chair, I'll change yer beddin'. I'm sure it's startin' t' smell."

"Thank you, and—I'm sorry for imposing. I'm also sorry about your husband."

She didn't say anything in response.

He wondered what questions she might have about the way her husband had died, or if she even wanted to know. He wouldn't offer any details unless she asked. "I appreciate all you've done for me. How long have I been here?"

"It's been a number o' days."

"I've lost all track of time."

"You been sleepin' a lot."

His bandaging complete, he shakily stood and stepped out of the soiled nightshirt, put on the clean one, and then sat back down, exhausted from the activity. "You could've taken me to the nearest Union division, you know. There's a camp outside Ripley."

"I don't trust the Union Army. They're like t' throw me in jail for what I done to y' and I don't know what would happen t' my children."

"They won't throw you in jail, ma'am. I'll see to that."

"You may say that now, but I can't take any chances. I'll nurse y' back t' health—with Miss Clara's help, that is—an' once you're strong enough, you can be on yer way. Here's the elixir I promised. A measurin' spoon, too." She stuck her hand around the curtain again. "Fill it to the brim an' swallow the stuff in one gulp."

"One gulp, huh?"

"Yes, one gulp. I've used it once and it's not somethin' you want t' take yer time swallowin'."

"I see." He reached for the medicine bottle and the spoon and when his hand brushed her palm, he felt calluses. This was a hardworking woman, someone who spent long hours in the sun tending her garden, milking the cow, hauling hay, maybe even chopping wood. On top of all her farm chores, she was raising two youngsters all on her own. His heart went out to her, as did a great deal of respect.

"Would y' like somethin' t' eat? You haven't been awake long enough to partake o' much nourishment. Miss Clara an' I been forcin' water an' chicken broth down yer throat, but that's about all."

"It's the middle of the night. I couldn't ask you to fix me anything right now. You need to go back to bed—if I haven't ruined your whole night's sleep, that is."

"I've been sorta restless anyway. Don't know as I'd be able t' get back t' sleep. If you want t' try eatin', I can fix y' somethin'."

"Well, since you put it that way...I don't have much of an appetite, but perhaps a piece of bread?"

"With butter and jam?"

"That would be nice."

"I'll get you a cup o' water, too."

He listened to her retreating footsteps as he poured the elixir into the measuring spoon and then brought the utensil to his mouth. Right away, the smell of the stuff about burned the insides of his nostrils. He held his breath and downed the fluid in a single gulp, then promptly gagged.

"I warned you, didn't I?"

His face scrunched at the horrible aftertaste and he sought for his breath. "I think a teaspoon of rust water and mud would have gone down easier."

She didn't respond, just made puttering noises across the room and he imagined her slicing a loaf of bread and then spreading a nice, thick piece with some jam. Next came the wonderful sound of trickling water. He looked forward to quenching his thirst. He also looked forward to when he wouldn't be as dependent on her for meeting his most basic needs, which made him think of the cauldron under his bed. He would not ask her to empty it. No, sir. He'd already made up his mind to carry it out to the privy when he got up the strength.

Soon, two hands reached around the curtain with a plate and a mug. "Here y' go, soldier. I hope it all stays down."

"I'm much obliged, ma'am." He took the offerings and set them on the nearby table. Then, after surveying himself to ensure he was adequately covered—his nightshirt concealed all but his legs from the knees down—he decided to open the curtain halfway so he could see her.

She let out a breathy gasp at the sight of him. He did the same, but probably for a different reason. "Lovely" was the only word that came to mind, even dressed in a shabby-looking, floor-length nightgown that allowed only her bare feet to peek out. Long hair the color of coal fell down the front of her, nearly reaching her waist. He'd had no idea it was that long. Of course, he'd not yet had the opportunity to study her at close range. Although the room depended on a low-burning lantern and the dying embers of a fire for light, it was enough to reveal her roundish face and dark, penetrating eyes. She pursed her lips, revealing dimples he hadn't noticed before.

"Wh-what are you doin'?"

"I just thought we might talk a minute or two, while I eat my bread…unless you'd rather try to get back to sleep. You're probably too exhausted to—I…"

"All right," she said, stopping him mid-sentence. She sat down on the chair next to the bed and then readjusted it to face him. "I guess that would be nice. If you're up to it, that is."

"Sure." He never thought he'd see the day when he actually longed for a woman's company again. Not after what Marilee had done to him.

12

In the dimly lit cabin, Cristina could make out the soldier's ashen face. He was weak and she hoped these few bites of bread would help him to start regaining his strength. "I'm sorry I shot you, mister. I feel awful guilty."

"You shouldn't. You were doing what you thought you had to do to protect your home. I didn't approach you in a safe or smart way, so I'll take the blame."

"That's mighty generous o' you t' say. Where d' you hail from?"

"Lebanon, Ohio," he answered between bites. "I'm the oldest of three boys. My name's Jack, by the way. Jack Fuller. Sorry I never had the chance to introduce myself."

"Well, you been sorta laid up. Tell me about yer family." She had no idea why she wanted to know anything about him, unless it was to admit that he intrigued her, never mind that her husband had just made a widow out of her.

"Well, it's just my mother and us kids now, as my father passed away five years ago. Mother gets along very well though. You remind me of her, in a way."

Something prickled inside her when he said that, but she dared not entertain the warm feeling. "From Ohio, you said? You farmers?"

"You guessed it. Corn's our main crop, but we also keep several acres of beans, carrots, lettuce, potatoes, and the like. We have dairy cows and beef cattle, too, so it's a busy place. Jesse, the youngest, is home overseeing things while my other brother, Joseph, and I are away. I joined up early; Joey joined after Lincoln put out a plea for seventy-five thousand volunteers. Jesse would've joined, too, but, with his being the baby of the family, our mother drew the line—and so did we."

"Any o' the brothers…um, married?" She'd been curious about the soldier's marital status, so now seemed as good a time as any to ask the question.

"No. Joey's a widower. His wife succumbed rather quickly to a cancerous disease. Left him with four youngsters."

"That's tragic."

He finished off his bread and sipped at his water. She waited to see if he would elaborate. "His kids have suffered a great deal and they've coped by becoming what you could call a handful. After Beth died, my brother came down with a malaise he couldn't shake, and he became a little neglectful of the children. My mother tried to help, but she took ill for a few months and couldn't deal with it. Then, with the war and Lincoln's plea for volunteers, my brother just sort of dropped everything and left. In truth, I think he was glad for an excuse to escape. I tried to talk him into staying home, but he refused to listen to reason. After he joined, he worked his way up the ranks in record speed—probably in an effort to block out everything else. He's captain over a good-sized company, but he can't manage his own household."

Cristina couldn't imagine deserting her children, although she could almost understand the man's desperation. Many were the times she'd experienced a sense of helplessness. "I'm sorry t' hear that. Who takes care o' his children?"

He gave a dry, almost cynical chuckle. "He's gone through three nannies, last I heard. It could be more by now."

"Are they really that hard t' handle?"

There came that low chortle again. "Like I said, they're a handful."

His eyes drooped from fatigue, but she wanted to keep him talking just a bit longer, just enough for her to broach the subject that had her the most curious. "I'm sure those kids have made you swear off marriage."

"I've sworn off marriage, all right, but not because of them. I was married once, just long enough to learn my lesson."

That was not the answer she'd expected. But then, she supposed she didn't know him well enough to predict his responses. "Really?"

He nodded. "I thought she was a fine, upstanding Christian woman. Then, one morning a few months after we got married, I woke up and found her gone. She left a note saying she was sorry but it wasn't going to work out. I was heartsick, of course, but then, a week or so later, my brothers told me they'd been suspicious of her since the day I brought her home. They did some sleuthing and discovered she had another man on the string."

"Why did she marry you?"

He gave a cold smile. "I guess she wanted what money I had. I found out too late that she'd pretty much drained my bank account."

"That's awful. You're divorced, then?"

"Not exactly."

Now he really had her curious. She decided to rephrase her question. "So you're separated but still married?"

"That's not it either. I make a pretty good riddle, don't I? Actually, when I went to the lawyer to seek divorce papers, with a bit of digging, he determined she'd been married before—twice, in fact—and she hadn't divorced the second husband, so technically, we were never legally married. The whole thing was a hoax. Of course, she'd duped her second husband, too. Last I heard, he had obtained a divorce and she's currently working to find a fourth husband. Or maybe a fifth, for all I know."

She felt genuine pity for him. "Did you ever get your money back?"

"No."

"Didn't you press charges?"

"Didn't want to bother. It was only money. Besides, it was my own fault for not doing my own sleuthing when I first laid eyes on her.

Looking back, I suppose I was too taken by her beauty to want to bother with the truth."

"Well, I'm sorry y' went through all that."

He took another swig of water.

"Would you care fer some more bread? Or anything else?"

"Thanks, no. The bread was quite good." He patted his stomach, then pushed his fingers through his tousled, dark brown hair. "Your turn."

"My turn?"

"Your turn to tell me about yourself—where you hail from and how you met Orville."

Her face went hot at the mere thought of discussing her own sorry existence with this soldier. "'Fraid my life's pretty boring. Besides, you need yer rest. You're awful weak still from that fever an' I know that wound still bothers you. I see you wincin' every now an' then."

He grinned. "I'll be fine, nurse. I shared a bit about myself, so it's only fair you do the same."

She liked his smile, but quickly scolded herself for taking note of it. Inhaling deeply for courage, she blurted out, "Well, how's this? I married Orville without hardly knowin' him."

His eyes came to life. "How did you meet?"

"He started workin' at the store my father owned in southern California Territory. Daddy hailed from Mexico and he learned pretty quick that he could profit from the gold rush by providin' a service to miners. So he opened up a laundry an' supply store. Orville had traveled to California Territory in hopes o' findin' gold an' when that didn't work out, he started lookin' fer work. Daddy hired him, never suspectin' he would soon whisk me off to Virginia."

"Seriously? How long did it take him to steal your heart?"

"I…I sorta stole his heart actually. I could tell right off he liked me an' when he started talkin' 'bout a house in Virginia he'd inherited from his uncle…" Cristina paused and swallowed hard. "It's not a very happy story, but if y' wanna hear it…."

"I do."

Cristina felt her cheeks flush. The only person she'd told about her past was Clara and she could not understand what compelled her to bare the details to this soldier. Clearing her throat, she began. "When I was young, my father—well, the man I thought was my father—would beat me often an' for no particular reason, other than he got in the mood fer it. I was fourteen when I found out my real father lived in Boston. That explained why José hated me so much." She gave a bitter laugh. "I'd always wondered why my skin was so much lighter than my parents'. I'm told that it was after I was born that my mama took to drinkin'. In most of my memories of her, she's lyin' on a mat on the floor, drunker 'n blazes. When José beat me, she was always too drunk to defend me. Besides, I always felt she resented me." She folded her hands in her lap and peered up at him. "I told you it wasn't a happy story."

His mouth sagged. "I can see why you wanted to leave home." His eyes showed genuine sympathy, even though she'd not been looking for it.

"I know it sounds awful, but truth is, I used Orville as my ticket outta there. I barely knew the man, but when he asked me to marry him, I didn't think twice. Lookin' back, that was prob'ly a dangerous decision, but I was desperate. I married him in secret, scrawled a note to my mama, and then we left California as husband an' wife. I became a full-fledged Virginian before the ink even dried on our marriage certificate."

"No regrets, then?" he asked.

"None. I wrote a letter to my mama a few months after we settled in Virginia to let 'er know where I was. Got no response. Then I found out about five years ago, by way of a letter from my mama's friend, that Mama had died. I think she drank herself to death."

"Oh, Cristina. I'm so sorry."

The tenderness with which he uttered her name filled her chest with such unexpected emotion that she had to bite hard on her lip to keep any tears from falling. "Thank you." A few silent moments passed before she drummed up the courage to speak again. "Orville was a kindhearted man I came to love over time. It was a...a comfortable arrangement. We didn't have a perfect marriage, but it was good. And yet, Orville...he had his insecurities. And the war, well, it made things worse for him. I wish he'd never gone, but he had a sense of loyalty that drove him. In the end, based on the letter you gave me and several others I received before that, I think he stopped thinkin' straight."

His eyes flickered a little. "There's no question war can do strange things to a man's way of thinking. He loved you though. He wanted to make sure you knew that."

"Did he say that?"

"Indeed he did."

"You spoke to him, then, before…before he died?"

"I knelt at his side, yes. He was very adamant that I deliver the letter to you."

"So, you came upon him after he'd been shot?"

"I—yes, you could say that."

"How long did he lie there before…before you found 'im?"

"I—I don't know if you really want the details."

She glanced away. "Y' might be right." She took a shaky breath. "I don't much like t' think about his final breaths. It hurts too much. He was a good man, my Orville."

"I'm glad that the risk you took, running off with him as you did, proved worthwhile. Glad he proved to be a decent and kind human being."

"Yes, he was that. It took us a long time to get to know each other. You can't force love, you know."

"No, you certainly can't. It doesn't work that way."

How had they gotten onto the topic of love? She'd said too much, pouring out such private thoughts to a man she barely knew. "Look how I've rambled on!" she blurted out. "I'm sorry, mister."

"No, don't apologize. Really. And, please, call me Jack."

"All right…Jack." The name felt strange on her lips. Suffering saints! What had gotten into her?

"Now, if I may ask you a question…?"

She sat up a little straighter. "O' course."

"That day you shot me…I seem to recall your saying something about thinking I was someone else. Just who did you think I was?"

"Oh." She blinked a few times, debating whether to tell him. Then she made up her mind to trust him and charged ahead. "Back in early June, two Union soldiers attacked me at home."

He jerked backward and the abrupt movement provoked a coughing spell in him—his first since taking the elixir. After a few seconds, he regained control and stared at her, his deep blue eyes aflame like twin suns. "Tell me exactly what happened."

"Well, I was standin' at the table, makin' bread, when they burst through the door like wild bears. First, they demanded money an' when I said I didn't have any, one of 'em threw me to the floor and started poundin' me with his fist while the other stood guard at the window. I tried t' fight back, but he pinned me down so I couldn't move. Why they thought I'd have money is beyond me. Didn't they get a good look at my run-down cabin before they barged inside?"

His brow creased with worry and also something like fury. "Did they do…anything else to you?"

"No, thank my lucky stars. My kids were hidin' in the barn, but still…. They did threaten t' come back, though, which is what I thought was happenin' when you showed up."

He shook his head and narrowed his eyes. "I'd like to get my hands on those 'soldiers.'"

She chuckled softly. "You look 'bout ready fer a brawl."

"I'm serious. You say they told you they'd be back?"

"Yes. An' they already have. They came back a couple o' weeks ago."

"What?"

"We weren't here though. The three of us spent the night at Clara's house, which we'd never done before. We were havin' so much fun, the children begged t' stay. Next mornin' when we came home, the house was a mess. Smelled like cheroot smoke, too. They'd eaten my food and left a note so I'd know who'd been there."

His brow furrowed. "I wonder if they're just a couple of deserters, or if they're stationed outside Ripley with that infantry camp. Did you happen to notice any distinguishing marks on either of them that might help you identify them?"

"Oh, I can identify 'em, all right. One of 'em has a scar on his face and the other…well, he's pretty plain-lookin', I guess, but I'd recognize 'im anywhere. Saw 'em both in town not so long ago, in fact."

"What?" He gawked at her.

"I walked right past one of 'em, but he was conversin' with somebody an' didn't appear t' notice me. I about froze when I saw him, but I managed t' scoot on past and slip inside a store with my youngins. We waited till he crossed the street before we left."

Jack rubbed his whiskered jaw and then gave his head a little shake. "I'm trying to think where I saw a man with a scar, but I can't recall it right now. Hm. But it makes sense now why you shot me that day. You assumed I was one of them."

"Yes and I'm sincerely sorry for that."

"I trust you reported those thugs to the local sheriff."

"No, they warned me not to."

"And you listened to them?"

"They said they'd hurt my children if I told and I believe 'em. They're that evil."

He tipped his face downward, keeping his eyes on her. "The sheriff needs to know."

"No! And you can't report 'em either. I've told Clara the same. Those men were not foolin' with me. They were serious."

"I'm a bit stuck right now and as weak as a lame cat, but you should really notify the sheriff."

"I don't want to talk about it anymore." She stood up, sorry now that she'd shared so many details with him. What had she been thinking? "You should probably get some rest now. You've been sittin' up a long time."

He tilted his head at her. "You know, I've been sitting here listening to your story and thinking how awful life has been for you, but I'm also struck at how you managed to escape California at just the right time and with just the right person. I think too about how you stayed at Miss

Clara's that night when you said you'd never done so before. No telling what might've happened if you'd been here when those scalawags came back. Sure seems like you've got the hand of God on you, protecting you time and again, and I'm wondering whether you've been aware of that, or whether the idea's entirely new to you. Now, I don't mean to pry, but I happen to know that God works in people's lives sometimes well before they even know Him. Do you have a personal knowledge of God?"

It wasn't a question she'd ever entertained and she had no idea how to respond, so she simply gave him a mute stare.

His eyes softened. "What about a basic knowledge of God, never mind personal? Do you have a Bible?"

She shook her head. "My mama did, but I was never allowed t' look at it. She called herself Catholic but didn't really practice 'er faith. I've heard bits an' pieces o' things, fragments of incomplete stories. That's all."

"Well, it's never too late to get to know Him. He's a good and loving God who sent His only Son Jesus to earth to live among people and to save them. Jesus was God, but He was also man in the flesh."

"I've heard that part. I heard He died on a cross 'cause some wicked people hated Him, but that's where I get lost."

The kindly smile on his face made her heart skip a beat and she inwardly scolded herself.

"How about I loan you my Bible so you can find out some things on your own? You could start by reading the book of John. It gives a summary of Jesus's purpose in coming to earth—and explains why He willingly sacrificed His life for the whole world."

She drew a quick breath and put a hand to her chest. "Oh, I couldn't take yer Bible. No, that's too personal a thing. I'd be afraid o' droppin' it, or tearin' a page, or dirtyin' it up."

There came that smile again! And there came another skipped heartbeat, but she couldn't tell whether that was a result of her silly attraction to him or because she was about to lay her hands on a Bible for the first time. Some kind of unnamed hunger stirred inside her, but it wasn't of a physical nature. No, this was a hunger she couldn't put her finger on. Perhaps it came from her loss of Orville and her resulting loneliness, or perhaps it came from a simple desire to discover, once and for all, if God truly existed.

"If you want to hand me my sack, I can dig out the Bible for you. And no need to worry about tearing or soiling any pages. Remember, that book has been on the battlefield."

With a pounding heart, she leaned down and picked up the heavy bag, then laid it on the floor next to his chair. He fished around inside for a moment and produced a worn-looking leather-bound tome, which he then placed in the hand she hadn't realized she'd held out.

She ran her palm over the pebbly leather and experienced an unexpected chill. Just what would she find in these pages? Would she find the truth, or become more confused than before? Unexpected moisture gathered in her eyes. Embarrassed, she wiped it away.

"It's all right to cry, Cristina. You don't have to be strong every hour of the day."

"But...." An unforeseen sob came out of her. "Since Orville left, I've had no choice." Now, actual tears rolled down her cheeks. Mortified, she used her sleeve to wipe them off her face. "I'm sorry, I...I don't know why I'm cryin'."

His large hand came to rest on her forearm and the gentle pressure only precipitated more tears. He patted her, then started rubbing little circles into her skin. "Don't apologize. You shouldn't try to hold back tears when it's the natural thing to let them fall."

"I—I don't know why he did it, why he didn't just come home to us. I d-don't get it," she said between sobs. "He just—gave up and let some dumb Yank shoot 'im. I'm—mad at 'im fer that and I'm mad at the Yank."

He kept his hand on her arm. "That's natural. You should be mad, but don't let your anger turn to bitterness. Remember, he wasn't thinking straight and the Yank who shot him probably felt threatened and simply acted on instinct. We soldiers are trained to shoot the enemy. That's war, Cristina."

She sniffed several times, then started to regain some composure. "He was a good father an' a faithful husband."

He cleared his throat. "You are not the only wife in this blasted war waiting at home for a man who's not coming back."

That sobered her. She sniffed again and wiped her entire face with her apron. Good glory, she was a blubbering mess! "Do you think the war'll end soon?"

"I can't say." He'd removed his hand from her arm. "Gettysburg may have turned the tables for the Rebs, but we'll have to wait and see."

"I know." She let out a shaky breath. "We should try t' get some sleep. You look awful pale."

"I'm not as strong as I'd like to be, but I predict I'll live."

"I should hope so. I would hate to think all my nursin' was for naught."

He gave a light laugh, which spawned another wave of coughs. She reached for his cup on the table and handed it to him. He sipped between spams, and soon the episode passed. He set the cup back down. "Well, I thank you for your company. It was…good to talk to you."

She stood. "It was and I thank you for puttin' up with my ridiculous cryin' spell. An' fer the Bible. I'll, um, look fer some time later today to start readin' it." She took two steps backward. "Well, good night, then. Let me know if…if you need anything."

"I'm sure I won't need a thing. I hope you can sleep."

"Yes. And you."

When it seemed they'd both run out of words, she walked to her pallet and lay down. She glanced across the room in his direction, but he had already drawn the curtain closed.

13

Jack had so hoped that, after staying up talking with Cristina and then drifting into a semi-restful sleep, he might have been getting better. But now he tossed from one side to the other, seeking a comfortable position. His wracking coughs were getting the better of him and his raging fever had returned with a vengeance. His chest hurt and catching a complete breath didn't come easy, for it always spurred more coughing.

Cristina and Miss Clara worked tirelessly to bring down his fever. He appreciated their efforts more than he could express, but he wondered if they were really helping. To make matters worse, his wound had reopened, so Miss Clara had had to remove the bandage and dig out more infected tissue. He overheard her musing aloud whether he might have contracted pneumonia, just like General Stonewall Jackson, and didn't everybody know what had happened to him! Then Elias chimed in, saying death would serve the soldier right for coming onto their land in spite of his mother's warnings. All their talk was anything but reassuring, so he felt almost relieved when his loud coughing precluded any further eavesdropping.

Lord, I need Thee, he prayed over and over throughout the day. *Please heal me, Lord. I need Your divine touch. Holy Spirit, come and heal my body.* He always ended his prayers with, *But above all, Thy will be done.* As the day went on, his strength waned to the point where he could scarcely pray and he gradually sank into a cough-wracked, raging-hot stupor. What was happening to him?

All day and then into the night, Cristina and Clara did what they could for Jack. During periods of rest, Cristina sat at his bedside and read from the book of John, just as he'd suggested she do. Clara kept saying she couldn't figure out Cristina's fascination with the book, but she finally stopped pestering her about it and, after midnight, fell asleep on Cristina's pallet. This time, Clara made arrangements with a neighbor to feed her animals in her absence so that she could alternate shifts with Cristina of sitting with their patient. Clara's presence—and her pool of knowledge from having read extensively from medical texts and treatises—was a great relief to Cristina. Her father had been a physician, which had stirred Clara's interest in medicine. Cristina had once asked Clara why she hadn't pursued medicine herself, to which she'd replied that Melvin wouldn't allow it.

Around three in the morning, Jack suffered a serious bout of coughing. Overtaken by spasms, the poor man gasped and choked and gasped some more. Cristina found herself holding her own breath, as if she were the one fighting for air. When he finally relaxed, Cristina touched his brow and found it to be scorching hot. She laid down the borrowed Bible and went to work on him with more cold cloths, bathing the full length of his arms, his chest, and his face, and even wetting down his hair, in the hopes of lowering the fever. In between cold compresses, she administered another teaspoon of elixir. He seemed barely to notice, swallowing the stuff without a fight. Every five minutes or so, she removed the cloths from his body, plunged them back into the cold water, wrung them out, and reapplied them. He muttered the name of Jesus off and on, but Cristina thought that if God were going to help him, one would think He would have stepped in by now. Clara still slept and Cristina didn't want to wake her. The poor woman hadn't slept at all the previous night because she had helped one of her cows give birth to her first calf and stayed in the barn for several hours afterward to make sure the mother did not desert her baby. Cristina put her head on the edge of the soldier's bed and drifted into partial slumber.

Sometime later, a touch on her shoulder had Cristina bolting upright. Clara stood over her. "Go lay yerself down, Cristina," she whispered. "I've had enough sleep."

Clara stretched and surveyed Jack. The man slept, but fitfully, his chest rising and falling as his body sought air.

"What time is it?" she quietly asked Clara.

"Nearly six. Sun's not up yet, but it will be soon. Sorry I slept so long. When them youngins wake, I'll feed 'em breakfast an' try to keep 'em quiet. After you've gotten a decent rest, I'll go home long enough t' feed my animals, check on Betty an' 'er calf an' do a few chores. Then I'll come back."

Cristina wiped her eyes, which stung from fatigue. "Are you sure you don't mind? Comin' back, that is?"

"Not a'tall." Clara glanced at Jack.

"He still sounds bad. His fever was ragin' all night an' he kept makin' noises. An' mutterin' the name o' Jesus."

"Pfff. Lotta good that's gonna do."

"I don't know, Clara…I been readin' from the Bible Jack loaned me an' I'm startin' t' wonder if there isn't some truth t' his religion. I've read the gospel o' John 'bout three times already, in between preparin' an' applyin' cold compresses an' then I went on t' read two other books by John's name, one and two. I don't know if all my readin' is gonna amount t' anything, but at least it's opened my eyes a bit. John talks about us bein' children o' God—he says God's our Father. I never had an earthly father, so it's a little hard for me t' grasp, but the idea of havin' a Father that actually loves me sort o' hits me in the heart."

Clara stared at her like she'd lost her mind. "Go lie down, girl. You look 'bout ready to topple."

With myriad questions still tossing around in her head, Cristina rose. "You're right. I'm tired." She walked to her pallet and lay down, glad her children still slept, and put aside her questions for the sake of slumber—at least for now.

After a few hours' rest, Cristina resumed her nursing duties while Clara went home to take care of her chores. When she returned to Cristina's, she offered to fix a meal and Cristina was happy to accept. As Clara stood at the fireplace boiling some eggs, she quietly expressed uncertainty as to whether the soldier would make it through the night. Cristina's heart sank at the thought. She didn't want him to die. Meanwhile, Elias said he didn't give a fig about "that Yank" and Catherina asked if she could have her bed back.

Cristina cringed at her own children's callousness. And then, for the first time in her life—and in earshot of her children and Clara—she prayed. "Lord, please let Jack Fuller live."

At that, the house grew silent, save for Jack's rattling chest and the crackling logs in the fireplace. The next words she spoke were almost as unexpected, even to herself: "I'm takin' the wagon into town, to that Methodist church on the corner."

Clara's head jerked up. "What for?"

"I'm gonna see if I can find the preacher."

"The preacher?" Elias asked.

"What's a preacher?" Catherina wanted to know.

Cristina decided now was not the time to explain. "I want t' see if he'll come an' pray fer Jack."

"Why're you callin' that soldier by 'is first name?" Elias demanded.

She ignored that question, too, and skimmed Clara's weathered face. "I'll be back within the hour. You all right if I leave the kids with you?"

"O' course, but you be careful. You never know who's out and about. Remember those Yanks who been causin' y' trouble."

"I'll take my rifle. Do you have yer pistol?"

Clara patted her side under her blouse. "Never leave my house without it."

"Good. Like I said, I won't be long." She smiled at Elias and Catherina, then gave Jack a hasty glance. Within minutes, she'd rounded up the horses, harnessed them to the wagon, and made for town. She had a strong feeling there wasn't time to waste.

⌣

"Well, if that don't beat all. Ya see 'er? That spitfire Mexican gal just drove past goin' faster than a jackrabbit runnin' from a prairie fire. What d' you s'pose she's up to?" Clive mused.

"Ain't got the slightest idea. You sure it was her? I ain't never run across 'er in town," Mike replied.

In another half hour, their replacements would relieve them of their post and then it would be on to the saloon for some food, booze, and a good poker game. "I never seen 'er in town neither, but that was her, fer sure. You think we oughtta cancel the poker game an' follow 'er?"

"What fer? I ain't in the mood tonight. I got my mind on that poker game 'cause I'm feelin' mighty lucky. You go follow 'er, if you want."

Clive watched the dust settle from the woman's spinning wagon wheels. Pure curiosity had him in its clutches, but Mike was right. It served no purpose to follow her. Not tonight anyway. "Guess you're right." He patted the pocket where he kept his coin purse stashed with currency. "I'm plannin' on doublin' what's in my purse tonight."

"Now you're talkin'."

⌣

A middle-aged woman of ample size, with graying hair and wearing a homespun dress, opened the parsonage door and greeted Cristina with a warm smile. "Well, good evening, miss. What can I do for you?"

Cristina didn't know whether to curtsy, thrust out her hand in greeting, or simply blurt out her name and her reason for paying a visit. She went for the third option. "Good evenin', ma'am. My name is Cristina Stiles. Might the preacher be about? It's rather urgent I speak to him."

"Yes, Reverend Wilcox is in. I'm his wife, Edith." She leaned closer. "This is my husband's study hour, right after supper. But if it's urgent, I shan't hesitate to fetch him right quick."

"I'm sorry—"

"No, not at all. Come in, come in."

Cristina stepped across the threshold and immediately thought that she'd never entered a warmer, more welcoming home.

The woman ushered her to the parlor, then turned and extended a hand. "Nice to meet you, Miss Stiles—or is it Missus?"

"Uh, Missus. That is, until recently. 'Fraid my late husband, Orville, was recently...killed. In the war."

"Oh, my. I am so very sorry to hear that. What a terrible loss for you. Do you have children, my dear?"

Cristina nodded. "A son who's ten and a daughter who's six. I've not yet found the right opportunity t' tell them the sad news, though."

"I see. Well, I'm sure that when the right time comes, the Lord will give you the proper words to say."

"I—yes, thank you."

The corners of Mrs. Wilcox's mouth curved upward with understanding. "I'll get my husband, dear. You take a seat and relax."

Cristina sat down on a large divan facing a fireplace, but she did not relax.

In less than two minutes, a balding, portly gentleman dressed in a white shirt and a pair of brown trousers held up by suspenders entered the room. He introduced himself and quickly sat in the chair next to the fireplace, his hands folded between his knees as he leaned forward a bit. His wife did not return to the parlor, no doubt because she sensed a need for privacy. Niceties out of the way, the reverend asked Cristina what he could do for her.

"Sir, there's a wounded Union soldier at my house that my friend Miss Clara Woodrum and I been tryin' t' nurse back t' health. This soldier is a man o' faith and I...well, I've been readin' the Bible a bit myself lately an' I thought it might be a help if you were t' ride out t' my house and offer up a prayer for 'im—if you can spare the time, that is."

"Well, of course, I can always spare the time to pray for someone, dear lady, but might I get a little background information first? How is it that you happen to have a wounded soldier in your home?"

"He was shot, sir."

"By Rebels? Why didn't his unit carry him back to his camp?"

"Not by Rebels, sir, and his unit is stationed a bit too far away."

His graying eyebrows slanted in a frown. "I don't understand."

She hesitated just slightly, then blurted out, "I shot 'im, sir, but it was, well, accidental, mostly. He came on my property and I thought he meant me harm. Instead, he came bearin' news o' my husband's death at the hand of a Union soldier."

"I see. Did you report the incident to the Army?"

"No! And I'm tryin' to avoid that if I can. I don't know what the Army'll do t' me and I've got two youngins who need me. I've got no one else. I'd rather the sheriff not find out about it, either, or he might turn me over. Please, Reverend, can I trust you not t' say anything?"

He cleared his throat and bit his lower lip. "When did all this occur?"

"The soldier's been at my place a few weeks, sir—I've lost track o' time—and we thought he was recoverin', but now Miss Clara believes he may've gotten pneumonia. I'm worried he might die from cough an' fever, an' then his blood—it'll be on my hands." She hung her head and wept quietly.

Over her sniffles, the reverend kept trying to reassure her. "Everything will work out…. It wasn't your fault; you acted in self-defense…. You've been through a great deal of hardship with the loss of your husband…." But his caring words only made her cry the harder, until Mrs. Wilcox returned to the parlor, sat down next to her, and slipped both arms around her. She pulled Cristina close and that embrace was her complete undoing. Every mixed-up emotion flowed out of her in a river of tears—her sorrow at losing Orville, her awful sense of guilt for having shot a man, her worries about the future, her perplexity over the existence of God, and her confused feelings about Jack—until every last drop of moisture in her eyes was spent. And the kindly Mrs.

Wilcox said nothing, just held her close and rocked her as she would a frightened child.

At some point, the reverend had slipped out of the room, but now he stood in the doorway. "I'm ready to go if you are. It's too bad the new town doctor isn't here yet. For now, there is no one nearby who can treat this soldier's ailment. One option, I suppose, would be to drive him up to Ravenswood and then cross over the Ohio and get him to a facility. Or we could put him on a wagon and take him to Charleston."

Cristina raised her head, knowing her face was red and puffy. She regained her composure as much as possible before saying, "I'm afraid he might be too sick to move, sir. Miss Clara isn't sure he'll survive the night."

⌒

Jack had always taken breathing for granted. Now he had to concentrate with all his might on every breath—the rise and fall of his chest, the brief durations of his inhales and exhales, the pain that had settled deep in his rattling lungs. Miss Clara checked on him regularly, sometimes lifting his head to give him a drink, other times removing a hot cloth from his forehead to dip it in cold water, wring it out, and put it back. He wanted to thank her but didn't have the strength.

Outside, he caught the sounds of horses' hooves and the squeak of wagon wheels in need of oiling. There were scuffling footsteps and quiet introductions and then Elias piped up, "We ain't never—er, *haven't* never—had a preacher in ar' house before."

"Well then, we might have to fix that, young man," spoke a male voice.

Jack did his best to clear his head of the cobwebs that seemed to have tangled there. A preacher had come? *O Lord, may it be so.* Had he come to pray with him for healing, or to help usher him into heaven? Either option suited Jack just fine; although, upon hearing Cristina's voice, he decided he would like to remain on earth a little longer, if the Lord willed it.

Someone pulled open the curtain and Jack opened one eye, blinking a couple of times to make out Cristina's face. She stood over him, silhouetted by the ebbing daylight. "Are you awake, Jack? The preacher from town has come t' pray fer you."

Jack's heart leaped. Oh, how he needed divine encouragement right now. *Thank You, Lord. You know just what I need before I even speak it.*

"Hello there, sir. I hope you don't mind my intrusion," the preacher said, moving in next to Cristina. Cristina stepped back a bit and was joined by Miss Clara and her children, the four of them making a semicircular line at his bedside. Their eyes were as round as pancakes, as if they half expected him to pass into glory and they didn't want to miss the show.

Jack managed to open both eyes a little wider.

"I'm Reverend Herb Wilcox from Ripley Methodist Church in town," the preacher said, placing one hand on Jack's bare shoulder where the sheet covering him had slipped. "I understand Mrs. Stiles accidentally shot you and now, on top of your bullet wound, you're suffering a bad cough and high fever. I'd like to read some Scriptures to you, if it wouldn't be too much bother, and then pray for you."

Jack gave a slow nod and then allowed his eyes to rove over his audience, including the preacher. He didn't want to die in front of them. *Lord, give me strength. I believe in the power of Thy holy name.*

As Reverend Wilcox seated himself on the chair next to the bed and began leafing through his Bible, Jack's body gave way to a dreadful torrent of coughs. The reverend kept his hand on Jack's shoulder as he waited for the coughing to subside. Once it did, he began reading, slowly and with confidence. "Psalm one-oh-three. *'Bless the LORD, O my soul: and all that is within me, bless his holy name. Bless the LORD, O my soul, and forget not all his benefits: who forgiveth all thine iniquities; who healeth all thy diseases; who redeemeth thy life from destruction; who crowneth thee with lovingkindness and tender mercies; who satisfieth thy mouth with good things; so that thy youth is renewed like the eagle's.'"*

From there, Reverend Wilcox moved to another passage of Scripture, then another, and another, all of them having to do with God's ability to heal and restore. The more he read, the easier Jack's breathing became and the greater the amounts of air that flowed through his lungs. It felt like a tender breeze blowing through him, cleansing as it moved upward from his feet through his body till it reached his head, then traveling back down again. The preacher read about God's amazing love, grace, and mercy for His beloved children and how He longed to heal His people from their diseases, both of body and of mind. Then he closed his Bible and talked some more about healing, saying that while faith played a part, it was what God *willed* that was always best. "God wants us whole, son, but more than that, He wants our whole heart." That statement stuck to Jack's heart like glue to paper. *God wants me whole, but He wants my whole heart more. Yes, Lord, I am Yours. All of me for all of You.*

Jack had never experienced anything like this, never known such remarkable peace and rest. It was in that very moment he knew that either the Holy Spirit had begun a healing work in his body, or He planned to usher him right through the pearly gates. Whatever the case, when the preacher set to praying, the Lord's very presence moved in and Jack could only pray the others sensed it, too.

14

Exactly one week after the preacher's visit, Cristina could barely believe the transformation Jack had undergone. Although he remained weak, his cough lingered, and his appetite had not fully returned, he had shown remarkable progress. His wound had closed up, and while he said it still pained him some, Clara could find no evidence of infection. She had a hard time accepting how quickly he had healed, but she wrote it off as pure coincidence rather than having anything to do with the reverend's having prayed and read aloud from the Bible.

In light of the soldier's dramatic improvement, Clara had stopped coming to Cristina's on a daily basis. It had been three days since her last visit. Jack had started getting out of bed more often, spending time seated in a chair while reading his Bible and walking on his own to the necessary. He'd even joined the family at the supper table the past two nights. Catherina had started warming to him, but Elias kept his distance, turning up his nose at Jack anytime he tried to initiate conversation. Cristina wished her son would be more polite, but then, she reminded herself that Jack wouldn't be around much longer, so what did it matter?

The realization that he would soon be leaving always hit her in a strange way. A part of her longed to get to know him on a deeper level and another part ran from the very thought. How could a woman possibly have feelings for another man so soon after losing her husband? Nothing about the notion sat right with her, so she repeatedly pushed her attraction aside. Still, they'd had so many lovely conversations at night when the children were asleep, most of them revolving around God and the limitless things He could do in people's lives once they came to trust Him as their Lord and Savior. Just weeks ago, that idea had been completely foreign to Cristina, but now she found herself wondering if she shouldn't give God a try.

"Is that soldier leavin' soon, Maw?" Elias asked one morning while he and Catherina helped Cristina tend the animals. Elias seemed to enjoy all of the livestock chores—except for mucking out the stalls and pens. He even liked to take care of the pigs Cristina butchered every fall. Catherina, on the other hand, had a greater interest in collecting eggs and gardening. She had a keen knowledge of plants for a six-year-old and rarely had to ask if something was a weed.

"I don't know," Cristina answered as she squeezed out the last bit of Rita's milk. The cow lowed in response and Cristina gave her an affectionate pat. "He's still pretty weak, but he's gainin' strength every day."

"I'm gettin' tired of 'im." Elias plunged a pitchfork into the hay in the goats' stall, beginning the mucking process while the goats grazed with the horses in their hilly pasture.

"I know you are, but we've gotta be patient and try a little kindness."

"I don't think Paw would be happy knowin' he's here."

His statement pierced her heart and she decided then and there that today would be the day she would reveal the secret she'd been harboring for far too long. She simply couldn't shield her children from the news of their father's passing any longer.

"Mama, after we're done in the barn, can we go play on the swing?" Catherina asked.

"Perhaps, honey. We'll see."

"Are you gonna make me a new dress soon?"

"I have the fabric, but I haven't had time."

"You said you was goin' to make me a new rag doll, too."

"I'll find time to do that, I promise."

"I'm plannin' on fishin' later," Elias announced.

"Not without me."

Elias groaned. "Maw. I don't need you at my side every minute."

Cristina's throat clogged with emotion. "As much as I'd like to, I can't forget about those wicked soldiers. We won't be entirely safe until that Union camp leaves Ripley." She stood up from the milking stool and picked up the pail by its rusty handle, making a mental note to buy a new milk pail next time she went to town. Thankfully, she'd not encountered the soldier with the facial scar since that day she'd had to duck into Miss Harriet's Hat Shop. With any luck, he and his pal had been reassigned. "Let's walk Rita down to the pasture now, all right? Then we'll take this milk to the springhouse to store till tomorrow, when I can make some cheese an' butter. And while we're down there, I want to talk to you both about somethin' very important."

"What is it?" Elias asked.

She remained silent as she unwrapped Rita's lead from the post. The dear old cow gave a gentle moo and followed the trio through the open barn door and out into the dazzling morning. A few chickens followed along, squawking as they strutted down the hill.

"Whatcha' need t' talk t' us about?" Elias asked again.

"Just…oh, I'll tell you once we get to the stream."

"Tell us now, while we're walkin'," he insisted.

Her son could be a determined, if not stubborn, young fellow, always demanding detailed explanations and impatient to a fault if he didn't get them. Most times, she managed to satisfy his questions with direct, brief answers. Unfortunately, the subject at hand was not a matter she could tackle in haste.

"In due time," she said.

"Is it a secret, Mama?" Catherina asked.

"No, it's just…somethin' I've been waitin' t' talk t' you about."

"Is it somethin' good?" Elias asked.

"Please, no more questions for now. Let's just take care of our chores first."

Elias let out an exaggerated sigh. "Here, I'll lead Rita the rest of the way and you and Cath can take the milk to the springhouse. I'll meet you down there."

"That's a good idea." They parted ways but all too soon reunited. Cristina directed her children to sit on a grassy patch near the springhouse on the banks of the cool, swift-flowing stream.

Her eyes grew moist in the corners even before she uttered her first word. Quietly, she sat there, trying to figure out exactly how to proceed. A raw sensation swirled around in her gut, a distraction that robbed her of the ability to think straight.

Elias drew his face into a scowl. "Somethin' ain't right. Maw, what is it?" He tilted his face downward and stared at the ground, then started plucking clumps of grass in fistfuls. Catherina, on the other hand, playfully picked a wildflower and handed it to Cristina, then pointed at a turtle sitting on a log. It was a lovely August morning, already warm, but with a gentle, cooling breeze.

"Um…." Cristina stretched out her legs and flattened her faded floral skirt across them. Her dirty, worn shoes peeked out from the hem of her skirt. Her children, meanwhile, were barefoot by preference, their callused heels as tough as leather. "I'm havin' a hard time knowin' how or where t' start."

Elias's head shot back up. "It's somethin' bad, ain't it."

"I…I'm afraid so."

Tears came to his eyes. "I don't wanna know. It's somethin' to do with Paw, ain't it? Is that why the soldier came? I been wonderin' that all along. Is Paw hurt? Is he in some hospital? How would a Union soldier know about Paw bein' in a hospital? Why didn't a Confederate come t' tell us?"

Cristina squeezed her eyes shut and raised her face skyward. She'd had no idea that Elias had put all these tangled thoughts together. How much torment had these questions caused him? Everything stood still. Even the birds ceased singing in that one long, heart-stopping moment. *Lord, if You're up there, I could use some help.*

Feeling Catherina nestle against her, Cristina opened her eyes, swallowed, and took a deep breath as she sought the right words. "He's not in a camp hospital."

"Where is 'e then?" Elias asked, his tone desperate.

"He...he...I'm so sorry t' have t' tell you this, but yer paw...he was shot on the battlefield...and killed."

Faster than a brush fire spreads, Elias jumped to his feet, grabbed his head with both hands, and began to scream as he raced around in a circle. "No, no, no!" he wailed, his shrieks of grief tearing at her soul. Catherina also started crying, though her tears seemed to be more from fright and confusion than from sorrow. For her, the notion that her daddy would not be coming home had not yet begun to settle in. Cristina quickly rose, bringing Catherina with her. The three of them embraced and, at first, Elias went willingly into her arms, hugging tight and sobbing into the curve of her shoulder, his tears drenching the fabric of her dress. But half a minute later he stepped back, his red, teary eyes disbelieving, as he gave his head a vehement shake. "It ain't true, Maw!" he blurted out. "It ain't!" His tears flowed like rivers.

"I'm so sorry, but it's true."

"No! I won't believe it!" Sniffing, he quieted a bit and asked, "Is it really true, Maw?"

She gave a slow nod and reached for him, but he took a giant step backward. "Why'd you wait so long t' tell us? Why didn't you let us know right off? We deserved to know!" His tone rose several pitches, quivering with every word.

Catherina couldn't stop her flow of tears, so Cristina bent and picked her up. The child wrapped her legs and arms around her, snuggling her damp face into Cristina's neck.

Cristina turned back to Elias. "I—I can't explain that exactly. I suppose I wanted to find the right time, but there just never was one. Things have just been so hard ever since—"

"It's him, that Union soldier, what's made everything so hard!"

"Yes, but I also needed to think on your paw's passin' on my own before I could tell you about it. Then just today, I reached the point where I knew I couldn't keep the awful news to myself anymore. Your father, he wrote a letter to me before he died. Apparently, he carried it in his pocket for some time, though I couldn't tell you fer how long. Jus' before he died, Jack Fuller found 'im on the battlefield and kneeled over 'im. Yer paw, he asked Jack t' deliver the letter."

"Where's the letter? I wanna see it," Elias said without a second's hesitation.

She had kept the letter tucked in her pocket, but she hadn't intended to show it to her children. How would they react?

Elias swiped at his face and eyed her squarely. "Read the letter to me—to *us*."

"Oh, I'm not sure—"

"I want to hear the letter, Maw. Where is it? In the house?"

"No, it's…it's in my pocket."

He lowered his face to the ground. "Read it. Please."

"Why don't you read it yourself? I'm not sure yer sister…she isn't ready t' hear this."

"Fine. Can we sit down?"

"O' course."

They walked to the nearest shade tree and planted themselves under it.

Once seated, Catherina in her lap, Cristina took out the letter that she'd already read a hundred times and unfolded it. Seeing the words once again made her want to refold it and tuck it away forever, but she knew Elias wouldn't have it.

"Lemme see it, Maw," he urged her.

"All right." She handed over the letter and a sense of dread filled every corner of her heart. As she watched his eyes scan the page, in her mind, she recited the sad message she had read over and over, still trying to understand it.

My dear Cristina,

First I want you to know that I love you and the childern. Please tell them for me. I did not tell them or you enuf, but I do love you all.

Second, I have bin away from you for two long years, so, shurly, you are getting used to my absence. At least I hope you are. I trust that you are making good on the farm all on your own. This war has been terrible. I've seen more death from gun battles and disease than anyone should ever have to witness. A large number of my friends have past into eternity.

I'm not fit to be your husband, Cristina, and so I fear I cannot stick around much longer. My mind is not working right an I am having awful dreams. I can't think strait or make much sense of anything. Them nightmares wake me up and then my heart pounds hard for hours afterwords. Everything in front of me seems filled with despair. Even if I waited till my time was up, I'd be such a mess when I got home, you would not know what to do with me.

I'm sorry. Forgive me for leaving you. And forgive me God. I just do not have it in me anymore. It feels like the Yanks are winning anyway.

Good-bye, my love.

Your husband,
Orville

After he finished reading the letter, Elias stared at the page for a moment, then folded it up again and handed it back to Cristina without meeting her eyes. Then he resumed pulling grass by the fistful. His breath came out uneven and his jaw was clenched tight. Cristina waited for him to speak. At last, he straightened his shoulders and held his head up, the tears on his cheeks starting to dry. "How'd he die?" The cool manner in which he asked the question almost startled her. "Was it a stray bullet? Cannon fire? Sickness?"

Cristina sighed. "I don't know."

He wagged his head at her. "What do you mean? Didn't you ask the soldier?"

"No. I...I'm not sure we need t' know."

"Well, I do."

Cristina frowned. "Elias Eduardo Stiles, you are only ten years old. I will decide when and if you need t' know the details. I don't want the memory of yer father's life bein' tainted by the manner in which he died."

"I ain't a baby!" Elias screeched, his anger showing in his blood-red face. Catherina sobbed quietly, still nestled in her mother's lap.

"I know that, Elias, but...well, all right. A soldier shot him and Jack was the first person t' come upon 'im. Jack said yer paw said he loved—"

Before she could finish, Elias leaped up and set off toward the road, walking fast.

Cristina scrambled to her feet, lifting Catherina with her. "Elias, stop! I want us t' talk some more." She took several hurried steps to catch up with him before she realized she wouldn't get very far holding her daughter, so she set her down.

Elias stopped and turned around. "I'm mad at Paw! That letter makes it sound like he didn't wanna live!"

She took a step forward and used one hand to shield her eyes from the sun, her heart beating at a fast clip. "I know. Why don't you come on back so we can talk about it?"

He gave her a good long stare. "I'm leavin' so don't bother comin' t' look fer me!" That said, he turned and sprinted toward the road.

Leaving? She repeated the word in her head before it dawned on her what he meant. "Elias Eduardo, don't be ridiculous! You come back here this minute. D' you hear me? Turn around!"

"I ain't gonna, Maw. Don't come after me," he yelled.

"What is this nonsense? Stop right now, Elias. Stop! Do you hear me?"

But the louder she called, the faster he ran, his bare feet carrying him up the steep, stony hillside until he disappeared altogether over the ridge.

15

Jack awoke to the sounds of yelling. The noises were too distant for him to identify their source. He was still weak but definitely on the mend and, in his heart, he knew he had no one but God Almighty to thank for that. He would swear till the day he died that God had healed his sick body when that preacher paid a call.

Jack pulled the curtain back. Seeing no one about, he slowly rose, determined to figure out the source of all the racket. "Stop right now! Do you hear me?" came a shrieking voice, which he finally recognized as Cristina's.

He pushed himself up, then stood, taking a moment to steady himself. Next, he secured his pants at the waist, fastened the buttons of his shirt, stepped into his boots, and then pulled the curtain open the rest of the way. He hadn't reached the point of being able to do anything quickly, but he'd certainly improved, thanks to Cristina's watchful care, not to mention her tasty meals.

Before he returned to his unit, he would have to make a new mattress for Cristina, since this one reeked from all of his sweat and was flattened out to boot. The question remained of when he would feel strong enough to leave. It wouldn't be tomorrow or the next day, but soon, he hoped. He figured he could at least start sleeping in the barn, perhaps as early as tonight. It stumped him that no one from his platoon had come looking for him. Surely, Major Marsh would have sent out a search party by now.

He glanced around the little one-room house. Everything had its place and despite how small the home was, Cristina kept it as clean as a new penny. His heart wrestled a bit at the thought of leaving. He'd accustomed himself to his surroundings, even grown fond of the kids, even though it was clear Elias couldn't stand him. As for Cristina, he hadn't the right to think of her as anyone but a friend who was recently widowed. Whenever feelings of attraction for her circled his heart, he gave himself a good scolding. Those kinds of thoughts weren't even proper.

Another loud cry, more like a scream, split the air. A sense of urgency to see whether someone was injured quickly overtook his sensibilities. He walked to the door, opened it, and looked outside. Seeing nothing, he stepped out into a splash of sunlight. He had to use one arm to block his eyes from the rays as he tried to make out his surroundings. Once he got his bearings, he walked to the side of the house to survey the back-yard, grateful for the mild breeze.

Right away, he spotted Cristina and Catherina down by the stream. He'd bathed in those waters a couple of nights ago after everyone else had retired and found it most refreshing. He focused his attention on Cristina. She took the little girl's hand and started walking quickly toward the edge of the property, dragging the crying child with her as she passed the garden and followed the pasture fence. "Elias, come back here!" she yelled.

Jack glanced up the road, his eyes following it to the place where it veered to the side, the path hidden by trees and thick brush. He failed to see Elias.

"Come back!" she hollered again.

With her back to him, she did not notice his approach. "Cristina?"

She whirled around and put a hand to her brow. "Jack. I thought you were takin' a nap."

He passed over her remark. "Do you need some help?"

The little girl ducked shyly behind her mother, but not before Jack noticed her puffy red cheeks and eyes. Why had she been crying?

"I—no, but thank you."

He stepped closer, unsure if he had any right to ask, but also feeling somewhat responsible for all the commotion. "Is there anything I can do? I see Elias has taken off on you."

She sucked in a breath and straightened. "I finally told the kids 'bout their father's passin'. It came as a real shock to Elias."

"I'm certain it did. Do you want me to try to fetch him?"

"He doesn't want anything to do with you. He sure as the sun and moon won't come back if *you* call his name."

Jack gave a low chuckle. "I know he doesn't like me. Can't say I blame him any, seeing as I've completely disrupted your household."

"Well, it was my fault fer shootin' you."

"You've said that enough times."

She pushed some hairs out of her face and gave a shy smile, revealing her dimples. "As a trained soldier, you should've known better than to approach a home unarmed."

"Duly noted."

She fumbled with her apron and stared out at the road. "I wish he'd come back."

"I know you're worried, but you shouldn't be."

"He said he was runnin' away an'—an' not t' come lookin' for 'im."

"Most boys run away. More than once. I surely did."

"You did?" She tossed him a curious glance. "What reason did y' give yer mother fer runnin' away? Did you go back home on yer own?"

"I returned on my own, yes, because I was hungry and I couldn't even tell you the reason I ran off. I'm sure it had something to do with my brothers. Because I was the oldest, I was always told to set a good example. I imagine I grew weary of my duty." He laughed to himself at the recollection.

Although it was a cooler day than some, the sun still burnt through his shirt. He glanced skyward. "Your little house is pretty comfortable, considering the hot weather."

"It's not half bad, especially with the windows open."

"Did Orville's uncle build the place?"

"Yes, some forty or more years ago."

He wanted to keep her talking in an effort to ease her worries. "You never told me about Orville's parents. Are they still living?"

"No. They both took ill and died 'round the same time, back in fifty-five or fifty-six. I never met them. Orville was an only child."

"That's unfortunate."

She looked out at the vacant road again. "Elias is gonna be hungry soon."

"Which will prompt him to come home."

"He'll be gettin' awful thirsty, too."

"All the more reason for him to turn around. He likely needs time to let the news about his father settle in. There's a lot of emotions stirring inside him right now."

She transferred her eyes from the road to him. Even from about five feet away, he noticed the moisture collecting in them. The natural thing would've been to move closer and offer a comforting touch, but he didn't dare. "Things will get better."

She dabbed at her eyes, then straightened her back. Little Catherina had picked up a stick and now drew shapes in the dirt. "How can you be sure?"

"Because that's the way life goes. Hard times come upon us and we somehow muddle through them. It helps a great deal, though, if we can learn to lean on God for strength."

"I read somethin' along those lines in the Bible."

Hope flickered in his chest. "Is that so?"

She nodded. "It's interestin'—all I've read—but it can also be hard to understand."

"It's normal not to grasp everything immediately. Don't be afraid to reread confusing passages as many times as you need, or to ask for help.

I'm happy to tell you what I know and I'm sure Reverend Wilcox would gladly explain anything if you simply asked him to."

"Do you remember much about that night the preacher came? You were burnin' with fever."

His mind went back to that night. "Why don't we go sit in the shade and wait for Elias to come back?" He pointed to a spot under one of the giant oaks in her backyard. "Shall I bring you some water?"

"No, I'm fine."

They moseyed over to a tree and situated themselves beneath it, Catherina leaning against her mother's side. A few feet away from them, Jack sat with his back pressed into the tree trunk. "As for that night the preacher came"—he pulled a few blades of grass from the ground and studied them—"I remember it well. The Lord was in that room."

Cristina drew a deep breath. "You started gettin' better right afterward. Clara says it's all on account o' coincidence. She says yer body just turned the corner on its own."

"I'd agree with that, except for the fact that I felt something happening to me as the preacher read from the Scriptures and prayed. There was a warmth running through my body."

"That was the fever."

He chuckled. "I can see why you would think that. What I mean to say is, I felt an odd, prickly warmth running up and down my body. That's never happened to me before. In that moment, I clearly remember saying to myself, *God is healing me*. Until you experience something similar, it's difficult to understand. You know, believing in God takes faith on your part. You're never going to have all the answers, so if answers are what you're looking for, you'll be searching a long time."

She clenched her jaw and he could see the struggle inside her. He wouldn't press her.

"I suppose," was all she said.

Catherina squirmed and wrinkled her nose. "I gotta use the outhouse."

"Okay, honey. Go ahead. I'll watch you from here."

The child jumped up and darted off, her two braids flying behind her and her knee-high skirt flaring.

"She doesn't understand about her daddy," Cristina said. "She'd just turned four when he left. Elias, though, his mem'ries are strong. He looked forward to Orville's return, prob'ly more than he ever expressed. Before he ran off, he said he was angry—angry at his paw fer wantin' to die and angry at the Yank who shot him."

Jack dreaded the moment she would learn the truth—if it ever came. He said nothing, just pulled up a few blades of grass and stared blankly at them.

"I wish he'd come walkin' back down that road," she said after a few moments.

"Don't worry so. He'll be back before you know it. He just needs time. I bet you anything he's holed up under a tree beside the road, thinking about how hungry and thirsty he is. He'll return any minute now."

But morning turned to noontime and noontime to afternoon. And Elias did not return.

16

Despite her mounting anxiety, Cristina managed to rock a restless, weepy Catherina to sleep after a late lunch of soup and biscuits. She laid the child on her pallet and covered her with a thin blanket. Catherina rarely napped anymore, but today had been especially emotional, so it was no surprise when the poor girl fell into a deep slumber. At that point, Cristina and Jack went back outside to watch for signs of Elias.

"I can't take it much longer," Cristina fretted. "I know you said t' give him time t' cool down, but I'm gonna have t' go up that road and drag him back down by his ear if he doesn't come back in the next half hour."

"Does he have any secret hiding places?"

She thought hard. "None that I know about. There's the fishin' hole, but that's no secret. He just spends time down there fishin' and swimmin'. O' course, he didn't take any fishin' gear with 'im, so I'm certain he's not down there. He knows I don't like him goin' off by himself since the onset of the war, either, 'specially since we've been havin' problems with those two Yanks." She expelled a loud sigh. "Now I'm startin' to worry he's fallen out of a tree or somethin'. What kind o' mother am I? I let him go off on his own and didn't even chase him. He could be…I don't know, lyin' unconscious in the dirt." Her fears escalated until Jack shushed her with a mere touch to her arm.

"Don't jump to conclusions."

"I'm not. I'm thinkin' 'bout the possibilities."

"Take some deep breaths instead."

"Don't tell me how to behave!" she shot back.

His mouth formed the beginnings of a smile that did not come to fruition—a good thing, too, or she might have slapped him. "All right," he said after a long sigh. "You've called his name with no success, so either he's gone further than your voice can reach or he hears you but would rather ignore your calls. You're dealing with a brokenhearted boy, remember, so it may take more time."

"You said it might take a while five hours ago! I want him home *now!*"

Jack scuffed the toe of his boot in the ground, then removed his hat and ran his fingers through his hair. Putting the hat back in place, he looked up and surveyed the vast terrain stretching before them. "I'll go out there and bring him back."

"But we already discussed that. He won't come if you call his name. Besides, you're still weak."

"I'll be fine and he'll come out of hiding if he's desperate enough. You go back in the house and wait for your girl to wake up."

She didn't argue further. She wanted her son home and she needed this soldier's hunting and training instincts to help accomplish that. "I'll run down to the springhouse and get the milk pail. I can churn some butter while you're lookin' for him. Keep my mind busy."

"Good idea."

"You should ride rather than walk. Take Starlight, the black-and-white Pinto. He's very docile, but he's also a good, fast runner when it's needed. You'll find the saddle and whatnot on some shelves by the door. Ropes 're hangin' from a long nail."

"I'm sure I'll find what I need. It might be good for you to pump some cold water and put it in a jar. I could also use some cloths in case he's hurt and I need to clean him up. You might put something together for him to eat, too. He'll be hungry and thirsty both."

"Yes, I'll do all that." She hurried down the hill to the springhouse while Jack set off for the pasture. At last, she had a job to do, something that gave her purpose and a sense of productivity.

In a matter of minutes, she made it back to the house. Jack had secured Starlight and taken him to the barn for saddling. Once in the house, she set the pail down, then moved about procuring items for Jack to take on his search for Elias: a jar of water, a hunk of cheese, a small loaf of bread, and a big oatmeal cookie. Of course, she also removed his rifle from the rack next to the door, along with a knife. She had no idea if he'd need either one, but there was no sense in taking chances. Her heart soared with fresh hope. *Please come home to me, Elias. Lord, please help Jack find him.* The realization that she'd just prayed gave her pause. She still had no idea whether praying really helped, but at least she'd had the sense to whisper it in her head. *Faith,* Jack had said. *This process of finding God takes faith.* She mulled that over for a little while.

In due time, Jack brought Starlight to a stop in front of the house. Cristina rushed outside and handed him the items she'd prepared. He carefully tucked each article in a secure spot in the saddlebags, then gave a little wink. "Try not to worry, Cristina. I'll bring him back," he said with a comforting tone.

"I'm trustin' you t' do just that."

"How about you place your trust in God rather than in me?"

"I did pray a prayer a few minutes ago."

His eyebrows arched. "That's good."

"But I don't think God heard me because I said it in my head."

"He's God, Cristina. He can read your every thought."

"Oh." She stepped back and squinted up at him. "Well, I guess I'll see you when you get back."

"Yes, you will." He touched the brim of his hat and then rode away, Starlight kicking up dust as he trotted off.

Back in the house, Cristina checked on Catherina, still sleeping, then went out to the lean-to to prepare the ingredients and supplies she would need for churning butter. Once everything was ready, she picked up her wooden paddle and started praying and plunging, praying and plunging. And hoping with all her heart that God would take notice.

⟝⟞

Jack followed the winding road up the hill past the place where a small cornfield met its end, keeping his ears and eyes on full alert. When he reached the crest, he reined the horse to a stop and listened closely as he scanned his surroundings.

"Dear Father in heaven," he prayed aloud, "please lend me wisdom and guidance as I search for Elias. You know exactly where he is, Father, for nothing is hidden from You. In fact, You are looking down on him in this moment and perchance even whispering words of comfort into his spirit. He is grieving the loss of his father and I can only imagine what kind of sorrow he's feeling. Please help him know how to deal with his pain, even as he is out there. Lead me, Lord; guide me with Your hand of mercy and the light of Your love. I'm trusting You because You are a God of grace."

Years of training had honed his tracking skills. So far, nothing stood out as peculiar, so he nudged Starlight forward, down a gulley and up another small hill. West Virginia's mountain roads curved and slanted and dipped so severely, it was a wonder a horse could navigate them. But horses were sturdy critters meant for travel, so Jack pushed the animal onward, both of them with ears keen to the sounds around them. Every so often, Jack would whisper, "Did you hear that, boy?" and Starlight would halt and his ears would swivel. It seemed to Jack that they were working as a team. A rabbit darted across their path, but the horse must have seen enough of those not to react. Jack leaned forward and patted the Pinto's neck reassuringly. "Where is that boy, Starlight?" Again, he reined the horse to a stop. All around them, a host of singing crickets, choirs of tree frogs, and any number of finches, cardinals, chickadees, and warblers chattered back and forth.

"Elias!" he called into the warm breeze. The horse didn't budge, just inclined his ears. "It's me, Jack Fuller. I'm trying to find you because your mama is very worried! If you're hiding, why don't you consider coming out?" He waited for some response as he and Starlight continued their slow trek up hills and down again, up another hill and then around a bend, and then, alas, into another gulley. Would the boy have journeyed this far? The opposite direction would have led him into town and Jack didn't think the boy wished to encounter anyone in particular, not after just learning about his father's passing. No, Jack's instincts told him the boy wanted to escape.

As they went along, the image of Cristina Stiles flashed across Jack's mind. She was so pretty, no question there, but he had to remind himself she had a wounded heart. It would be a long time before she desired another man. No, for now, he would simply pray for her—pray that her longing for God would grow and that, in time, she would find the courage to believe He loved her and had a special plan and purpose for her life.

He reined in Starlight again. "Elias!" he called out. Up ahead, he saw a clearing in the woods where he could look out over the rolling hills, but no movement caught his eye. He pivoted in all directions in the saddle, the worn leather squeaking beneath his weight, and looked to both sides of the dirt track. Spying a few broken branches on a bush to his right, he made the decision to dismount. He slid off the horse's back, then walked to the area to inspect it. A few twigs had been gnawed, indicating an animal had done a bit of munching, perhaps a deer. Overhead, a hawk spread its wings and flew off. Some twigs cracked and fell behind him— some squirrels bickering back and forth? He blew out a sigh, straightened, and then turned on his heels to take one last look. Nothing. He mounted up again and the horse trotted on, Jack's senses so keen that even his own breathing echoed in his head.

A few minutes later, a sound in the distance brought all his nerves to attention. He nudged the horse toward the noise, which amounted to a low, whining cry, almost like that of a wounded puppy. What could it be? "Elias?" he called. There came the sound, but Jack couldn't determine from where, or even what it might be. "Elias?"

"Help," came the faint call.

He urged the horse on another twenty feet or so, then stopped him and jumped down to the ground. Pain shot through his side at his careless maneuver, but he ignored it. A couple of raspy coughs rattled out of him, too, but he wouldn't let those slow him down. Nothing mattered now but finding the boy. He looped the horse's reins around a low-hanging tree limb, then grabbed his knife and gun and the other supplies Cristina had bundled into a cloth sack.

"Elias, where are you? Can you call out?"

"Here," came the wobbly response.

"I'm coming. Stay right where you are."

"Help," the boy cried faintly.

"I'm coming. Your mama will be so glad to see you." Jack pushed his way through thick branches, some of which slapped him hard in the face. He trudged on, ignoring the pain.

Up ahead, he saw a patch of blue. Elias's shirt? At last, the boy came into view. He lay sprawled on the ground. "A snake bit me," he sobbed.

"A snake?" Jack tried not to show his alarm. The boy had already rolled up his left pant leg to reveal the unmistakable snake bite. Jack went down on his knees and loosened the twine around the opening of the cloth bag. He reached for the jar of water, unscrewed the lid, and lifted the boy's head so he could drink. Elias took his fill, then plopped back down.

Jack studied the bite. It had swelled to at least an inch in circumference and was as red as a beet. "Did you get a good look at the snake?"

"It was—tan—I think—or more like brown. With dark triangles on it."

"Triangles?"

"More like slanted bands. Where's my maw?"

He ignored the boy's question and thought about the snake's description. A northern copperhead, perhaps, but likely not a rattler, to his great relief. Still, a copperhead could be deadly if it dispensed the right amount of venom. "How long ago did it bite you?"

"Am I gonna die? Where's my maw?"

Jack moved closer. "How long ago did the snake bite you?"

Elias chewed his lip. "Fifteen minutes maybe." He swiped at the few remaining tears on his cheeks. "At first, I took off runnin', but then I remembered my paw tellin' me that you shouldn't run after a snakebite 'cause that just makes the poison move faster. So I lay down and hoped my maw would come find me. Is there a bunch o' poison in my body, Yank?"

"There's probably some, but your paw was exactly right when he told you not to run. You're also amazingly calm, which is a good thing."

"Well, I've had t' learn t' be brave. Why'd you come lookin' fer me an' not my maw?"

Obviously, Jack hadn't won any points by being the one to find him. "Well, first off, your sister's sleeping and, second, I'm better trained at looking for people. Your mama's worried sick though. She wanted to come, but I'm not sure she'd have found you. By the way, didn't you hear her hollering for you to come back after you ran off?"

"'Course, I heard 'er, but I wasn't in no mood then. My paw died y' know."

Jack's throat tightened. "I know, Elias, and I'm mighty sorry about that."

The boy winced and reached out to grab his left leg. "It's burnin' worse than a curse, Yank."

"That's why we're going to get you back to your house. Do you think you can walk to the horse if we go slow?"

"Sure. Are you gonna ride behind me?"

"We'd get there faster if I did."

Elias frowned and lifted his lip in a snide way. "All right. If you have to, I guess."

Clearly, Jack would not be making a friend in Elias anytime soon—not today, at least. "Before we go, I'm going to take this cloth and tie it around your leg to try to keep any venom that might be in there from moving any higher on your leg. It may or may not be too late for that."

The boy's eyes shot open. "Y' mean, the poison's gonna travel through my whole body if you're too late—even to my brain? I might be dead by tomorrow mornin'?"

"At the rate you're talking, I think you'll survive. Like I said, it's a good thing you laid down and waited for help. Must be you had enough faith that someone would come along sooner or later."

"I had faith that my maw would find me—not you."

Jack couldn't help the chuckle that came out of him as he worked to tie the cloth around the boy's upper leg, just above the kneecap. "Well, I'm mighty sorry to disappoint you." He finished tying off the cloth, not so tight as to cut off the blood flow, but at least to slow it down some.

"Ain't y' gonna suck out the venom?"

Jack shook his head. "That doesn't work, plain and simple."

"What does work, then?" Elias asked while Jack helped him to a standing position.

"Put your left hand on my shoulder and try to lean on me. We'll go on up to Starlight that way. You don't want to put too much weight on that leg. What works? Hmm. That's a tough question. Time, I suppose." Jack halted briefly and reached inside the sack. "Here. Your maw packed you a little something to eat." The boy eagerly devoured the cheese and bread as they slowly meandered through thick brush and lush green overgrowth.

Jack stopped and reached into the bag. "Have some more water, Elias. And here's a cookie your maw packed, too." A half-smile came to Jack's lips as he watched Elias bite into the cookie and they continued on their way. "Yes, good ol' time should heal that ol' snakebite. Of course, we first need to see if you'll even survive the night."

"Huh?" Elias jerked his head up and Jack could feel the boy's steady brown eyes studying his expression. Jack kept his gaze pointing straight ahead, his face as serious as an old owl, although he wanted to laugh. He did not foresee the boy taking a turn for the worse—not if he'd gone this long without suffering any dire consequences. Most likely, he'd only have a sore leg for the next few days.

"It—hurts—like fire," Elias sputtered as they walked.

Jack paused. "You need me to carry you?"

Elias set his mouth in a firm, stubborn line and huffed. "You kiddin'? Ever since my maw shot you, you've been as weak as a lily-livered lizard."

That did it. He scooped the boy up and over his shoulder, letting him bellow at the top of his lungs. Of course, the maneuver proved a foolish choice for Jack, who had not yet regained even a fraction of his former strength. Nevertheless, he went on trudging through the woods, pretending he had the strength of a bear. All the way, the boy cater-wauled and screamed at the top of his lungs for Jack to put him down.

"Hush your mouth," Jack chided him, "or somebody'll hear you and think you're dying."

"I might be. Y' said so yerself."

"Did I? Well, maybe I ought to put you down, go on back to your house, and tell your maw I couldn't find you."

"You wouldn't!"

"Try me."

After that, the boy shut his mouth until they finally reached the horse, where Jack at last placed Elias on the ground. "There. Was that worth all your yowling?"

A sheepish expression crept across the boy's face, but he clearly wasn't about to apologize—or even thank Jack for his trouble. Jack might have laughed if it weren't for the renewed pain tugging at his insides. "Better mount on the wrong side, boy, or your left leg's gonna be in a heap o' hurt. You want some help?"

The boy tried to mount unassisted, but he couldn't do it. "Ow!" he yelped.

"Feeling a little off, are we?"

"I guess."

"Here. Let me give you a boost." Jack cupped his hands together down below Starlight's right stirrup. With his chin still set in a stub-born fashion, Elias put his right foot in Jack's hands and gingerly swung his left leg over while Jack hoisted him up. Once the boy was situated, Jack climbed up behind him, reached around for the reins he'd looped over a branch, and then clicked at the horse and nudged him with his heels. With that, off they went. Although Elias clearly hadn't wanted to, he ended up resting his tired frame against Jack's chest. While the snake probably hadn't issued a full dose of venom, its bite had been enough to weaken the lad.

Halfway home, Jack broke the silence between them. "Your maw's going to be mighty glad to see you."

"She's gonna be mighty mad at me, too."

"Oh, I think she'll be too relieved to be mad at you, but I do hope you'll promise her you won't go running off like that again. You being the man of the house and all...well, she needs you around."

"I know. I'm not sure why I ran off in the first place."

"You were hurt and angry and sad and didn't know what else to do, I suppose. I'd probably have done the same thing at your age. You've got a lot of weight on your shoulders, Elias. You acted on impulse, that's all. Did you have some time to think?"

"A little, I guess, but I don't wanna talk about it."

"I can respect that."

They rode the rest of the way home in silence.

17

Cristina could not stop fidgeting. Back and forth she went from one window to the next, watching the road for any sign of Jack's return with Elias, and then going outside to pace in hopes she'd catch them coming down the hill. She'd accomplished little in the way of housework, save for making a small bowl of cream and then churning butter, which she'd shaped into a cube, set on a plate, and covered with a piece of cheesecloth to keep the flies away.

No matter that she tried not to allow it, her mind continuously spun terrible scenarios: Elias had been so overcome with heat that he'd fainted in the field and lacked the strength to get up and keep going. Or, worse, he had tripped over something, broken a bone, and could no longer walk. Unless some kindhearted person came upon him, he would starve to death. The possibility also existed that he'd gotten so lost in the woods or in a farmer's field that he'd turned himself around and now traveled in endless circles. The very worst, of course, was the possibility that he knew exactly where he was, but had chosen to run away for good, never to return. He had found someone willing to give him a ride and off he'd gone to the next town…and the next…and the next. He might even find himself taken slave to some horrid farmhand who'd decided to work him to the bone with nary a break. He would suffer from lack of water and nourishment until he collapsed and withered away to die in a remote area, frightened and alone. Oh, but her imagination did have a way of running off with her, taking her into deep, dark places that she never wished to visit!

Back in the house, she checked again on Catherina, who'd been asleep for far too long. Cristina knew she ought to wake her daughter, but she didn't have a bit of positive news to share and she wasn't in the mood for more of her tears. No, she would let her awaken on her own.

She walked around her little house, circling the table situated in the center. It was a rustic cabin, at best, but it had served her little family just fine all these years. Orville had wanted to build them something bigger and better someday; a mountaintop cabin had been his dream, even though Cristina had said their existing cabin suited her fine. Looking back, Cristina realized he'd never been content, always wishing to be smarter, more talented, stronger, and wealthier—and moping that he made a lousy provider, no matter how often she tried to assure him otherwise. It made her wonder how long he'd suffered on the battlefield, fretting that he couldn't send home enough money, haunted by the sights he'd seen, his mind constantly telling him what a failure he'd been. Her heart broke for him, causing yet another slew of tears to gush out the corners of her eyes and down her cheeks.

She thought about Jack out there hunting for her son and repeated the prayer she'd sent up in silence earlier that day. A part of her wanted to know God better, but another part of her fought against the idea. Why should God—if He existed—pay her any mind? She had nothing to offer Him in return. She walked to the window once more and stared out, then lifted her apron and gave her face a good swipe. Thirsty, she went to the counter to grab a tin mug, then headed outside to the pump for a drink of cool water. She had barely closed the door behind her when she spotted Starlight rounding the bend at the top of the hill, bearing Elias and Jack. It didn't matter how hot the temperature or how great her thirst; she threw down the mug and broke into a run.

"Elias!" she shouted. "You found 'im! Where was 'e? Elias, you scared me. Why—" She stopped mid-sentence when it became clear something wasn't right. "Elias, what's wrong?"

"I'm—sorry, Maw," he muttered as Jack reined Starlight to a halt.

"Never mind that now. Here, let me help y' down. Why's yer pant leg rolled up? What's happened?" She seemed unable to control her incessant flow of questions.

Jack rose up in the stirrups, shifted his weight to his left foot, and then swung his right leg around behind him and dismounted. Then he reached up and helped Elias get down. When the boy's feet hit the ground, Cristina snagged hold of him and drew him close. He leaned heavily against her. Most of the color had gone from his face.

"I'm afraid he's suffered a snakebite," Jack explained. "I found him in the woods. Thank God he made some noise so I could locate him."

Cristina sucked in a deep gasp, knowing full well West Virginia had its share of venomous snakes, especially in the forests and creek beds. She forced herself to calm, not wanting to make matters worse by overreacting, and gave Jack a penetrating look. "I hope you know how grateful I am."

He nodded. "Take him inside and put him on the bed. I'll be in as soon as I wipe down Starlight and give him a drink. Your son should be fine."

"So long as I don't die," Elias added with an exaggerated moan.

"It wasn't a rattler, was it?" Cristina asked, throwing a fast glance at Jack.

He took Starlight's reins. "From the description Elias gave me, I'd guess it was a northern copperhead."

"It hurts bad," said Elias.

"Best get him in the house and situated on the bed. The sooner he gets off his feet, the better."

Cristina nodded quickly. "Thank you again, Jack."

He tipped his chin at her and smiled before turning to lead Starlight around the side of the house and to the barn.

Cristina started for the house. "Come on, Elias. Let's get you inside."

"Do—I—have to lay in the same bed as that Yank?"

"Don't be silly. He might well have saved yer life."

"He's still a Yank."

"Yes, well…we're gonna forget about that fer now."

The boy said nothing more on the subject, just limped along beside her. Once in the house, she made him sit on the bed so she could give him a top-to-bottom inspection. Upon checking his feet, she turned up her nose. "Blessed saints, Elias, you need a good bath. These feet 're as black as coal."

He plopped backward and heaved a loud breath. She took the opportunity to study the unsightly snakebite, red and swollen around the edges. Had the venom spread far in his body? He closed his eyes and gave a little moan. "It hurts awful bad, Maw."

"I'll get you a looser pair o' pants an' a clean shirt t' wear. You'll be more comfortable." He didn't answer, just reached down and wiggled out of his raggedy trousers.

Cristina scurried up the ladder to the loft and rifled through his chest of clothes. After finding what she needed, she scooted back down. Catherina started to rouse when Cristina tiptoed past her. The girl turned over on her pallet and opened her eyes for a moment before lazily shutting them again.

Soon, Jack came in, his face and body betraying his exhaustion. "I can't thank you enough fer findin' 'im," she said. "I know it must've been hard, summonin' the energy to go out an' search."

He approached the bedside. "Elias did well to alert me to his whereabouts. Though I think he was a mite upset that I was the one to come to his rescue." He chuckled.

Cristina frowned at her son. "Elias, you should be grateful Jack found you when he did. You might've laid out there all night. How would that've been?"

The boy answered by way of a mere shrug.

"Did you thank 'im yet?"

"Thanks," Elias muttered.

Jack grinned. "You're welcome. Glad I found you."

"What should we do for this snakebite?" Cristina asked, trying not to sound anxious. "Tell me an' I'll do it."

"Well, for starters, I suggest you make a poultice of herbs. Do you have a good supply?"

"I do. I can boil up the concoction I've used for bee stings. He's...he's gonna be all right, isn't he?" She couldn't keep her voice from shaking as she forced out the words.

"The soldier said I might die tonight." Elias's voice sounded exceedingly weak.

Jack's sandy eyebrows lifted a fraction as an expression of amusement flashed across his face. "I think you've twisted my words around." Then to Cristina, he said, "If the bite had been truly serious, he would be far sicker by now. Most poisonous snakes don't wish to waste their venom on something they don't plan to eat. My guess is the critter administered just enough to scare off the boy...and cause him plenty of pain. Now for that poultice."

"Yes, right away." While Cristina stood over the fire, boiling a small amount of water in a kettle and dropping in a blend of herbs and aromatics that she kept stored on a shelf in the lean-to—dried yarrow leaves, aloe, and clay to absorb the venom from the wound—she kept glancing over her shoulder at Elias. He thrashed around a bit, but Jack whispered something to him that seemed to settle him down. She wished she'd been able to discern his words. Was Elias starting to warm to the soldier? As Cristina stirred the mixture, she thought about the prayer she'd offered up. Had the Lord answered it in leading Jack to Elias, or would Jack have found him regardless? Had God intervened, or had Elias's rescue been a matter of mere coincidence? Elias was home and that fact should have sufficed, but she still had an itch to know.

"So, y' think it was a copperhead that bit 'im?" she asked, giving a half turn while she continued stirring.

"That's my best guess based on Elias's description. At the very least, I'm satisfied it wasn't a rattler."

"I was tryin' to get past it, but there was too much thick brush," Elias said, his voice quiet. "I think I stepped on its tail."

Cristina cringed at the thought. How she feared the slippery, slithery critters, no matter that she lived deep in a region where they thrived, or that she was prone to encountering the nonvenomous varieties frequently in the garden.

"I'm guessing you riled him up just by sharing the woods with him, but he wouldn't have bitten you had he not felt threatened," Jack said. "And if it was a rattler, you would have heard it."

"Ouch!" Elias reached up and clutched his left leg with both hands, then winced. "It feels like somebody just sliced me with a knife."

"It will probably bother you for a couple of days," Jack told him.

"Have you ever gotten a snakebite?" Elias asked him.

"Thankfully, I've managed to avoid it."

"Then how come you know so much about them?"

"I read a lot. When you're in the army, there's a great deal you have to know."

"Hm." Elias quieted a moment. "I guess my paw didn't know enough t' stay alive."

"Your paw knew plenty, believe me. War is a terrible thing."

Cristina listened on as she stirred her healing concoction. It warmed her to hear them talking. She removed the kettle from the fire just as Catherina rose from the pallet and wiped her eyes. The girl brightened when she spotted her brother lying on the bed. "Elias!" She walked toward him.

"Yes, yer brother's home," Cristina said, "but he's feelin' a bit sick, so you should try not t' bother 'im."

"Why's he sick? Did he eat somethin' bad?"

"No, he didn't eat anything bad."

"Well, then—"

"A big ol' snake bit me, Catherina. It was about as long as this room."

"Elias, don't exaggerate," Cristina admonished, knowing full well Catherina swallowed everything her brother told her.

Her daughter's eyes grew big and round. "A real snake bited you?" She edged closer, half hiding behind Jack. "Where?"

"On my leg."

Catherina peeked around the man for a better look, then made a squealing sound. "I'm never goin' outside again!" She turned and dashed over to Cristina.

Cristina smiled as she poured the boiled herbs onto a cloth she'd moistened, then spread them out flat with the rounded edge of a spoon.

"Don't worry, honey," said Jack. "You'll not be seeing a snake anytime soon."

"How d' you know that?" Elias argued. "I didn't think I'd be seein' one either and then, snap! A big ol' copperhead gets me right in the leg. It hurts like fire, too, Catherina. You don't never wanna see a snake like what I saw today."

"All right, that's enough," Cristina said. She added the clay, then folded the thin cloth over the herbs, refolding the corners over that to form a triangular shape.

"I didn't think I'd see one either," Elias repeated, "but look what happened to me."

Cristina carried the poultice across the room. "Here you go, Jack. And, Elias, if you could try to be a little less descriptive around yer sister, I'd appreciate it."

Jack took the poultice and gave her a small glance. "Are you feeling better now that he's home?"

"Very much."

"God answered your prayer, didn't He?"

She considered his words. "I…suppose."

"Don't forget to thank Him."

"I won't."

Jack turned and placed the poultice on Elias's snakebite. The boy yelped when the cloth came in contact with his skin, but Jack's straightforward manner seemed to calm him. In fact, Cristina noted his very presence had a way of soothing all three of them.

18

Soon as Brooks an' Moser relieve us of our duties, we'll find us a private spot somewheres to change outta these uniforms. You got your plain clothes in yer duffle bag?" Clive asked as he and Mike concluded their patrol of the town's perimeter in front of Lou's Livery on West North Street.

Mike groaned. "I got 'em. You've only asked me that five times already."

"Well, I'm just makin' sure. Can't run the risk o' bein' identified with the Army t'night."

"Just what are y' plannin' on doin' with that Rosalyn woman?" Mike asked.

"Well, what do y' think, blockhead? We ain't had any fun with a woman in a long time. Use yer imagination."

Mike frowned. "What if she reports us?"

"She ain't gonna talk. We'll threaten her like we did that Mexican spitfire. She'll keep 'er mouth shut, all right. Don't worry none."

Clive reached into his rear pocket for his pouch of tobacco, took out a wad, and stuffed it in the side of his mouth as he leaned back against the post of a streetlight.

"Where we gonna hide out till she closes up the restaurant?" Mike wanted to know.

"I'm thinkin' in the alley across the street. It's gettin' near dark now. By the time she walks out, it'll be black as tar."

Just then he spotted Tom Moser and George Brooks strolling up the sidewalk in their direction. "'Bout time you slowpokes got here," Clive grumbled.

Tom rolled his eyes. "Anything to report?"

The two exchanged glances before shaking their heads. "Things been pretty calm all day," Mike said.

"In other words, we're in for a boring night," George quipped.

Mike chuckled. "With a little luck."

"I'd rather have a little action," Tom put in. "Maybe the saloon'll get rowdy."

Clive snickered. "You could always go in there and pick an argument just to get things started."

Tom gave a slight frown. "I'd rather bring order than chaos to a situation."

"Well, in the end, that's all any of us wants," Clive amended. "Peace an' order an' all that."

George nodded. "That's what we're here for, after all. Though I did overhear some talk that our time in Ripley might soon be comin' to an end."

"What's that?" asked Mike.

Clive scowled. "Where'd you hear that?"

George shifted his weight. "Round the fire at suppertime, one fella mentioned hearin' it straight from Lieutenant Bond."

"That so?" said Clive. "Who's gonna replace us?"

"Word has it the town doesn't think we're needed any longer," Tom supplied. "Most o' the conflict ended at Buffington Island. Not much chance o' the Rebs comin' back, considerin' the loss they suffered. I think it's a pretty good chance we'll be marchin' on to the next battleground, wherever that may be."

Clive did not like the sound of that. So far, this had been the easiest stint he'd had since joining up two years ago. He didn't like the idea of having to face any more Rebs.

He gave Mike a hearty slap on the shoulder. "Well, let's be on our way back to camp, shall we? I plan on crawlin' into my bedroll early tonight. If I play my cards right, I won't even talk to a single soul." He yawned. "I'm plain whipped from all that sunshine today."

Mike nodded, playing along. "I'm ready to head back to camp myself. You fellas do your best to maintain control around here," he said with a chuckle.

George dipped his head, his mouth forming a straight line. "Will do. Maybe we'll head over to the sheriff's office and see if he's made any recent arrests."

Clive laughed. "The local sheriff ain't much good for anything. Far as I know, he spends most o' his time sittin' in the station playin' cards with his two deputies. I ain't hardly ever run into him on the streets."

With that, Clive and Mike moseyed down the sidewalk. Once they were out of earshot of the other men, Clive spat his wad of tobacco on the wooden sidewalk. "Can you believe we might get our walkin' orders soon?"

"Don't worry. Wherever we go, it's bound to have wealthier folks to rob."

"I ain't talkin' 'bout that. I plain don't want to go out on the field again."

"You scared?"

"I ain't scared," he lied. "Just bored with this idiotic war."

"Well, I can't blame you there, but there's nothin' we can do about that."

"We could always defect."

Mike's head jerked in Clive's direction. "You mean go missin'?"

Clive felt a slow grin emerge. "Maybe."

"You dumb stinkweed. You wanna go to jail? Or, worse, get hanged?"

"They'd have to find me first." Clive laughed a little, though he wasn't exactly kidding. "Come on, let's get movin'. Soon's we know the coast's clear, we'll find a deserted alley where we can change. This is gonna be a fine night, I can feel it."

Mike shook his head as they walked along. "You're a bad egg, you know that?"

"An' just what d' you think *you* are?"

"A bad half-dozen, I s'pose."

Clive laughed until tears formed in his eyes. Mike could make him laugh, he'd give him that.

After changing into the plain clothes they'd bought secondhand just days ago, the men dawdled around on side streets, peering in store and office windows and biding their time until sunset, when they started making their way over to Rosalyn's. They kept their eyes out for the useless sheriff and, of course, Moser and Brooks, but Clive wasn't worried. On their trek, they stayed as concealed as possible but didn't run across a single pedestrian, save for a couple of passed-out drunks they had to step over to reach the alley across the street from Rosalyn's Restaurant. The sounds of loud fiddle music and an off-key piano rang out from the saloon as they neared their destination. At last, huddled in the shadows, they had a good view of the eatery. A couple of fellows appeared to be cleaning the place up, one sweeping and the other wiping tables.

"Do you see her?" Clive asked.

Mike shook his head. "Just that cook and that older-lookin' fella with a broom."

Clive squinted, trying to see better. "Where could she be?"

"No idea."

"Well, she must be in the back outta sight. We'll just wait."

They stood there another ten minutes or so, impatience churning. "Clearly, the restaurant's closed now," Mike observed. "They dimmed the lights five minutes ago."

Clive nodded. "Let's walk over there an' see what we can find out."

"What an' show ourselves?"

"They won't recognize us outta uniform. Keep yer head down."

They moseyed across the road, stepped up to the building, and peered through the front window. Clive gave a light tap on the glass with his knuckles.

"Sorry, fellas, but we're closed," said a man with a broom. "Come back tomorrow."

"Can't we just get a cup of coffee?" Clive asked.

"Sorry, coffee's gone. We're closed."

Clive cleared his throat. "You got anything to tide us over till mornin'? We just arrived in town."

"What're you doin'?" Mike hissed through his teeth.

The fellow with the broom started toward the front door. Meanwhile, the other man—perhaps one of the cooks—lifted his apron over his head and hung it on a nail at the rear of the restaurant, seeming not to care about their inquiries for sustenance.

"Just stick with me," Clive muttered. "Change of plans."

"A change— What're you talkin' 'bout?"

The broom-wielding man came to the door. "I told you we're closed."

"How 'bout just a few pieces o' bread?" Clive asked. "We been travelin' all day."

"Where're your horses?" the man asked.

"Got stolen this very mornin'. We're sleepin' outside o' town tonight and then headin' up to Ravenswood tomorrow. We both got sawmill jobs waitin' fer us up there."

The man crinkled his brow and hesitated, then started to fiddle with the lock on the door. "Well, Rosalyn wouldn't be happy 'bout this, but she ain't here, so I suppose—"

As soon as the door opened a crack, Clive pushed it the rest of the way, knocking the old man back against a table. The man quickly righted himself, at which point Clive stepped forward and pressed the barrel of his gun to his chest. "Open the money drawer."

"The money drawer?"

"You heard me, you ol' coot. Give us all yer cash."

The man stood there, dazed as a drunk.

"Now!"

He finally moved, limping over to the counter where the cashbox sat. He fumbled with the latch until Clive gave him a good jab with his gun. Once he'd opened the lid, Clive pushed the fellow out of the way and snatched all the paper money from inside, stuffing it in his pocket. "You did real good," he sneered. Then he stepped back, motioning for Mike that it was time to make a run for it.

Just then, he heard a loud click and looked up. There stood the other man who'd been wearing an apron, now holding a rifle aimed at them. "Put down that money!" he ordered.

Everything that happened next was a blur. Two guns fired—first Mike's and then the other fellow's, but only one man went down. *Mike.* With no time to check on his friend, Clive made a beeline for the back door, shooting as he went. Down went the fellow with the rifle. Clive couldn't believe his luck at having escaped unscathed. He ran up the dark and deserted street until he came upon a lone horse tied to a hitching post. After tearing the reins off the post, he mounted the beast and rode away, as fast as a windstorm, his heart pumping fast, no destination in mind except to escape. He patted his pocket and blew out a breath of relief when he felt the wad of money still tucked there. Leaving Mike behind caused him a brief stab of regret, but he himself was alive and that was all that mattered for the moment.

19

*J*ack sat at the table and watched as Cristina moved around the little cabin like a restless hornet. She'd done everything there was to do for her son and now that he slept soundly and she'd put Catherina down on her pallet for the night just ten minutes ago, she couldn't seem to stop hurrying about. She'd already swept the wood floor and wiped the same counter for the fourth time, so now she started dusting every other space, even beneath lamps, books, and tintypes.

Jack's own body ached from fatigue, but something kept him from walking out to the barn, where he'd decided to spend tonight and any remaining nights until he mustered the energy to hike the return trip to his unit. He set down his glass of sweet tea and shook his head. "Do you ever just sit and relax?"

Cristina jumped at the sound of his voice.

He chuckled. "I didn't mean to startle you. Did you forget I was sitting here?"

She gave a nervous laugh. "I suppose this whole fiasco with Elias runnin' off has got my nerves in a tangle." She walked to the counter and dropped her rag into the round washbowl on top, then wiped her hands on a towel, untied her apron, and hung the garment on a hook next to the fireplace. She gave a tiny sniff, straightened herself, and ambled over to the table, where she pulled out a chair and sat down across from him. She sighed as she folded her hands atop the table.

"It's been a trying day for you," Jack commented. "You started by telling your kids about the death of their father, which led to Elias's running off and then your fretting for hours till his return, only to find he'd suffered a snakebite. That's a lot for one day."

Cristina nodded. "I hope he doesn't take a turn for the worse—like you did."

He smiled. "He'll be all right, Cristina. I'm sure of it. Look at him. He's sleeping comfortably."

She pivoted her body a bit to glance at her son, then switched her gaze to Catherina, asleep on the floor. "They both are." She turned around to face him once more. "Did I thank you fer all you did today?"

"Several times."

"Well, I can't help it. You might well've saved 'is life."

"Since the snakebite wasn't fatal, he probably would've picked himself up after a while and walked back home."

"Maybe so, but you kept 'im from havin' t' do that and I'm mighty grateful."

"I didn't want any ill to befall him any more than you did. I thank the Lord He answered our prayers and led me straight to him."

She gave a slow, thoughtful nod, but didn't prod him with questions. Instead, she rose and walked with purpose to a cabinet against the wall, pulled open a drawer, and retrieved what looked like the letter Orville had sent with Jack.

Jack held his breath as she carefully unfolded the paper and then lifted her dark eyes to him. "Would you mind if I read it to you?"

"Not at all, but only if you're sure you want to."

"I'm sure."

As she read, a bit of moisture gathered in his eyes. *Lord, but she is a lovely woman*, he thought—and with that silent admission, he admitted to himself his growing feelings for her, feelings he hadn't dared examine until this very moment. How could it be that in so short a time, she'd put such trust in him and he'd begun falling in love with her?

She finished reading the letter with nary a sign of emotion, refolded it, and laid it on the table. "I've already cried rivers," she said, meeting his gaze again. "The tears come an' go."

"I'm sure they do. I shed more than a few tears when Marilee left me, though we hadn't been married nearly long enough to acquire many memories and she left me for entirely different reasons. Looking back, my crying was probably due more to sheer embarrassment than true sorrow. My family all saw it coming; I was the oblivious one." He chuckled quietly.

She didn't share his mirth. "It must've been real hard fer you t' have loved 'er an' then lost 'er so quickly."

He sobered. "You're right about that." He slid his finger around the rim of his cup and elected to change the subject. "Your children are mighty blessed to have you as their mother."

She raised her chin at him and swept her hair to one side of her forehead, giving him a better view of her entrancing eyes. "I've had t' learn t' make do. I grew independent of Orville long ago. As much as I loved havin' 'im around the house, I knew what I had t' do to keep us all alive. Before you came, I was sewin' pillowcases, towels, an' mattress covers an' knittin' blankets, mittens, hats, what have you, t' sell at the dry goods store on Sycamore Street. I also sell eggs in town. Ha'n't had much time fer any o' that lately, though."

He shifted in his seat, took another long drink of tea, and then set the empty cup back on the table. "I'm to blame for that. I'll make it up to you somehow."

"You'll do no such thing. I'm just glad t' see you recoverin'. You must be anxious t' get back t' yer Army camp."

It was the first time in a long while she'd mentioned anything about his leaving. "You must be anxious to get me out of your hair, huh? I've certainly caused a lot of upheaval. I'm a little perplexed that no one's come to fetch me back."

"Maybe they don't know where t' find you."

"No, I told Major Marsh of my plans to come to Ripley. He could've sent someone."

"Well, maybe he assumes you were delayed. I'm sure he trusts you t' return."

"I suppose. At any rate, I should be well enough to start my journey back in a few days."

Her expression flickered with an unreadable emotion. Would she miss him as much as he would miss her and her children? He wanted more time to see if anything could come of their newfound friendship. They'd started out on the fiercest, rockiest ground, but over a period of weeks, they'd started enjoying each other's company and she'd started trusting him, with proof in the letter from Orville that she'd shared with him. There was much more to her, greater depth and intensity, and he wanted to know it. He wanted to know it all. As many times as he'd told himself that another woman would never find a place in his heart, he hadn't truly meant it. Not since meeting Cristina Stiles.

"I will admit yer bein' here has made me a bit less fearful o' those awful Yanks who burst through my door back in June."

"You haven't seen any sign of them since that night they came into your house while you were gone, have you?"

"No, but maybe they know you're here an' they're stayin' away on account o' that."

He wanted to reassure her. "You're very brave, Cristina. You're plenty smart, too. They caught you off guard once, but I doubt they'll manage to do it twice."

In one fluid move, she rose once again from the table and walked to the cabinet, this time withdrawing a glass. She picked up a nearby pitcher and poured herself some water. Turning around, she leaned against the cabinet and said to him, "Don't assume such things about me. I do what I have to fer my family, but I'm no hero and I don't consider myself overly brave either."

Across the room, Elias let out a tiny moan, and Cristina started in his direction. But she paused when a snuffling snore and the rustling sound of the boy turning over in bed indicated he was all right. Jack studied Cristina. She had a raw, tender side to her that he admired, but right now, she looked plain tuckered. These had been trying days for her, what with seeing to his care on top of managing her household and completing her daily farm chores. It was very possible that she had not actually sat down and just relaxed for a long time. Perhaps she never had. A sudden notion came to him and he voiced it immediately. "How would you like me to make you a sandwich and some coffee?"

Her mouth gaped as wide as a church door after Easter services. "What?"

"You haven't eaten more than a few morsels of food today. I've been paying attention. How do you expect to continue at this pace without adequate nourishment?"

"I've never had a man wait on me before."

"No? Not even Orville?"

"Certainly not. It wouldn't've been proper. I never saw my mama's husband ever lift a finger for her either."

"Well, forgive me for saying so, but that sounds a little lopsided. I grew up watching my father treat my mother to much-needed periods of rest." He grinned to himself at the memory. "My father doted more on Mother than he did on any of us boys. I don't think I mentioned this before, but my mother gave birth to a baby girl who died before her first birthday. I was nine at the time; my brothers were seven and five. It was a hard thing for all of us, but Mother suffered the most. Sarah was sweet but so very small and weak, even from the start. After her death, I believe my father wanted to do everything he could for Mother to make her life more bearable. She is a woman of great faith who looks to God daily for strength and courage, but even the greatest faith can't wash away sorrow. Father did all he could to ease her pain and Mother often said, 'If it weren't for the Lord above and your daddy's sweet love, I'd be lyin' in my own grave.' Witnessing Mother's faith—and Father's, too, for that matter—made me desire to follow God and never stray." He stood up then and ambled over to the cabinet where Cristina stood. He opened the cupboard door and took out a mug. "Would you like some coffee?"

She wrinkled her brow at him. "I'm sorry, but I'm still confounded by this whole idea." She glanced down at her cup. "Um, this water, here, is quite enough, thank you."

"Well, all right, then, if you're sure. Now, about that sandwich."

"I couldn't allow you t'—"

He gently but purposefully laid a hand on her thin shoulder. She flinched at his touch, so he lightened his grip even more as he lowered his head to look into her eyes. "How about I go see what you've got in the springhouse while you go sit down and enjoy the quiet?"

"But…but you yerself must be exhausted. I can hardly—"

"Stop worrying about everyone else for a change and try to relax."

She looked powerless to move.

He chuckled and dropped his hand, then went to the door. With his hand on the knob, he said without turning, "When I come back, you'd better be sitting down."

"Yes, sir," came her soft reply.

He stepped down the rocky bank leading to the springhouse, then crossed a narrow footbridge, opened the squeaky door, and stepped inside. He shivered slightly in the cold, damp air, but the sensation was almost a relief on such a warm and muggy evening. He searched the shelves, reading handwritten labels on jars and scanning the contents of various containers and platters before he settled on some cured beef wrapped in brown paper, a bottle of milk, some cheese, and a jar of pickles. He swathed the beef and cheese in a piece of cheesecloth he found folded on a shelf, then picked up that package, along with the milk and pickles, and walked back out, clumsily closing the door behind him. He could only pray this plan to "dote on" Cristina didn't backfire.

What was that idiot lieutenant Jack Fuller doing here? Clive poked his head carefully around the side of the big feed barrel he'd jumped behind and gritted his teeth. It was him, all right. Who could forget that towering physique—or that self-possessed expression of authority he wore on his face? Even now, Clive bristled at the sight of him, anger whooshing through his blood as he recalled what dupes the man had made of Mike and him. They'd been toying with Rosalyn, merely teasing. Innocent fun. But the killjoy lieutenant hadn't seen it that way. No, he'd thought it his duty to call them out on their behavior—as if it were any of his business.

Clive watched through the barn window, still trying to catch his breath as he sized up the situation. He'd had to run most of the way to the farm after the stupid horse he'd nabbed after fleeing the restaurant had gone lame and he'd had to desert it on the side of the road. It was a struggle to quiet his breathing with his heart thundering against his ribs. Did the Fuller fellow have a romantic involvement with Mrs. Stiles? Had he deserted the Union and was he now seeking refuge with her? Doubtful. Otherwise, he wouldn't have gone out of his way to exert his authority at the restaurant. Still, what was he doing here? Whatever the case, he'd made a fine predicament for Clive, who'd considered this particular farm the perfect place to lie low until he could make it to that run-down barn where he and Mike had hidden their loot.

With Mike gone, he had to make some fast decisions. He thought about Mike, but only in a fleeting manner. The last time he'd seen his friend, the man had looked awfully…well, dead. Clive knew he should feel a stronger sense of regret, but the realization that he was the sole possessor of the money and items they'd stolen together somehow soothed his sorrow. He grinned to himself. It was all his now—the stuff they had stashed together, as well as the items Clive had secreted away without Mike's knowledge. Of course, he would have to wait till things settled down before retrieving the loot and leaving Ripley for good.

As the lieutenant disappeared inside the Stiles home, Clive gave an inward growl. He'd counted on finding that gal at home alone, not with a male visitor—and not just any male visitor but Jack Fuller, of all people. No matter. He would simply alter his plans yet again. This might actually prove to be the perfect time to get back at the self-righteous lieutenant.

20

Cristina gave a little start when Jack reentered the house. She sat up straighter in her chair and watched as he closed the door behind himself. My, but he's tall! she thought yet again. And such broad shoulders.... She'd grown accustomed to looking after him while he lay prone in bed; now that he was up and moving about, his commanding presence almost rattled her.

He gave her a slanted grin. "I think I found enough items in the springhouse for a simple meal."

"You really don't have t' do this," she said, even as her stomach growled.

He walked past her into the kitchen and set to work as if he hadn't heard her, as if waiting on her were second nature to him. His movements fascinated her, for never before had she witnessed a man toiling in a kitchen.

He found a knife and cut several pieces of bread. Next, he snatched a fresh tomato from the wooden bowl on the table and started slicing it. While he worked, he hummed in a soft, melodious way and she couldn't help but smile to herself.

Several minutes later, Jack brought her a plate on which he'd arranged a sandwich, a hunk of cheese, and two pickles. He set it on the table, placing a cup of milk next to it.

"You're too kind." She stared at the plate for all of 30 seconds. "I don't know what to say besides thank you. It looks delicious."

"You're very welcome. And now, if you don't mind, I'd like to say a quick prayer of thanks. After that, I'll make myself a sandwich and then I'll join you. How would that be?"

"Uh, good. I mean, all right. Thank you."

He bowed his head and began praying before she'd even closed her eyes. "Our Father in heaven, we thank You for answering our prayers regarding Elias. Thank You that he's safe and sound and that his snake-bite was not more serious. Please help this family as they cope with the loss of their husband and father. And Lord, we thank You for this food and we ask that You would use it to nourish our bodies. In Your name we pray, amen."

Hearing the prayer, brief though it was, filled Cristina with a wondrous sense of peace and awe. As soon as Jack returned to the kitchen area, she dove into her sandwich, savoring its taste more than perhaps any she'd had before because she hadn't had to lift a finger to make it.

By the time Jack joined her at the table, her sandwich was long gone. "That tasted amazin'. Best sandwich I ever ate."

Jack chuckled. "I doubt that, but I'm glad you enjoyed it. My mother made sure to teach my brothers and me the basics of cooking. And when you're in the Army, you learn pretty quick how to make yourself a meal—that or settle for the Army's rations, which are hardly enough to sustain a child, let alone a grown man."

"D' you hear much from yer brothers while on the field?"

He chewed and swallowed, then took a quick sip of water. "My brothers aren't much for letter writing, but my mother and I correspond regularly. She keeps me abreast of all the family news."

"Won't she be wonderin' why she hasn't heard from you lately?"

"She might, but she probably isn't overly concerned. She knows I get busy and that it's sometimes impossible to write. I suppose I'll find a bundle of letters from her waiting when I return to my unit. I'll write to her then."

"You gonna tell 'er you got shot by a crazy woman?"

He laughed. "Not till I get out. My brothers will find out in time and then I'll never hear the end of it. They'll probably take the story to Lebanon's local newspaper. I can almost see the headline now: 'Union Army lieutenant receives near fatal gunshot wound from West Virginia woman who wanted him off her property. Army now seeks aforementioned female for enlistment for her sharpshooting skills!'"

Cristina let out a great spurt of laughter, glad she'd swallowed her bite of food ahead of time. Goodness, she would wake her children if she wasn't careful. "That would be the day—my joinin' the Union Army! If anything, I'd fight fer the Confederates, like Orville did."

His expression turned inquisitive. "Why are you so devoted to the Confederate cause? Don't you want to see the preservation of these United States? And doesn't the institution of slavery strike you as immoral? I know folks argue to the contrary, but to me, the idea that a man can own a fellow human being like a piece of property is downright wrong."

A wave of unsettling emotions swept through her. "I…I guess from all o' Orville's rants. I heard 'em so often, I guess I started forgettin' t' think fer myself."

Jack looked uncomfortable for a moment before he smiled and glanced around. "Well, shall we wash and dry these dishes now?"

His offer came as a pleasant surprise. Not once could she recall Orville ever washing a single dish. Normally, by this time of the evening, Cristina would be in bed and probably asleep. But tonight was different. Jack was up and about, regaining his strength and looking much healthier…and she found herself wanting to prolong the evening. "You cooked, so I'll clean, but in the mornin'. Maybe fer now, we could just…sit awhile and talk some more?" She could scarcely believe her own boldness.

"I would like that very much." He glanced at the door. "It's a pleasant evening out. We could sit on the porch bench."

"That sounds…lovely." After checking on the children to ensure they were still sound asleep, she followed Jack outside, closing the door softly behind her. When he sat down next to her, his left knee grazed her leg ever so slightly and the contact sent her heart and mind into a regular frenzy. She enjoyed his company, but she wasn't sure she ought to be sitting so close to him. At the same time, she didn't wish to move. Did he have the same quivery feelings?

"Elias seems to be resting well," he said.

"Yes, I'm so glad of it. I'm—surprised he managed to sleep through all yer cookin' an' our talkin'."

"He wore himself out with such a long day of running, crying, and trying to outsmart a snake. Thank the Lord, all is well. He'll be sore for a while, but that's to be expected."

His mention of the Lord brought up more questions and Cristina felt this was as good a time as ever to ask them. "You know, just before you came here, I found myself thinkin' about God fer no apparent reason, wonderin' whether He was real. D' you think it was an answer to prayer that you came along?"

"God does work in some pretty amazing ways. Do I think He wanted you to shoot me? That's a question I can't answer, but I wouldn't be sitting here if you hadn't done that, would I? And you wouldn't have had a Bible to read. Don't think for a minute that you're not on God's mind every minute of every day."

She frowned. "But how could that be, when there's a whole world o' people out there? Can He think about all o' them at once?"

"You bet He can—and He does. In the book of Matthew in the Bible, Jesus says that not even one sparrow falls to the ground without the Father knowing about it and that even the very hairs of our head are numbered. What have we to fear, since we know we're more valuable to God than the sparrows?'"

"How is it you've got so much o' the Bible memorized?"

He shifted a bit and his arm brushed against hers. "I don't really. I've just read parts of it enough times to know where to find them. I will say, though, that the more you read the Bible, the more verses you'll come across that you'll want to memorize so you can recite them to yourself whenever you have need of whatever it is they speak of, such as strength or courage. How is your faith these days? Is it growing, do you think?"

"I don't know exactly. I think it's still on the small side."

"Jesus also says, in multiple places in the Bible, that even faith the size of a mustard seed is enough for Him to do mighty works in a life."

"My faith's prob'ly smaller than that," Cristina said quietly.

"It doesn't matter how great or small your faith is, Cristina. God looks at the heart and He understands our weaknesses. This very afternoon, I prayed and asked God to lead me to Elias. I prayed. I believed. God answered."

She crumpled her brow. "Maybe yer findin' 'im was just a coincidence."

"I'm not going to argue that point, but coincidence or not, Elias is home and since I prayed for his return, I'm choosing to believe it was by God's divine intervention that I came across him in the woods."

She sighed. "If only faith came as easy t' me as it does t' you."

"Faith is a gift God freely gives to those who ask."

She jerked her head up. "He *gives* us faith?"

"Of course. Think of it like this. If you believe in something strongly enough, then you have faith in it. Take this bench we're sitting on, for example. You trust it's going to hold us, right?"

"O' course. It's been a sturdy thing fer years an' years."

"Don't you realize that by sitting on the bench, you are placing your faith in it? You're trusting it to remain strong, steady, and sturdy. It lends comfort when you're weary. It holds you when you've grown tired of standing."

She carefully pondered his every word. "I guess so, yes."

"Well then, if you can have faith that this bench will support your weight, then surely you can have that same faith to rest your soul in Jesus Christ. He will hold you, give you rest, comfort you, and keep you safe and secure. Like this trusty bench, God is reliable. He's strong, steady, consistent, and truthful. He'll never leave you or cause you to fall; He'll never push you away and He won't grow weary of you. You can trust Him because He's stood the test of time—just like this old bench has."

Cristina liked Jack's illustration. She liked his gentle manner of speaking. She liked listening to him. He didn't judge her or look down on her. As if he'd read her mind, he smiled, and the lantern light coming through the window flickered on his face, making his expression quite irresistible. That's when it struck her afresh just how much she would miss him when he left. So silly, she knew, but she'd grown accustomed to him and the mere thought of his leaving made her sad. His presence gave her an added sense of security, even though she'd always prided herself on self-sufficiency.

"Thank you fer sharin' all that. I think…I think I'll really miss our talks once you're gone."

He quirked his eyebrows at her. "So you don't hate me as much as you first did?"

She couldn't help the nervous giggle that came out of her. "I don't hate you t'all now. And I was just marvelin' at how used t' yer presence I've grown."

"Well, it just so happens I've grown used to yours as well."

Her nerves jumped, but she managed to return his smile. "Have you, now?" she asked, her voice cracking.

"What would you think if—" He paused and let his gaze roam over her face.

She waited, her heart belting out a loud rhythm in her ears. "If…what?"

"What would you think if I kissed you?" he blurted out.

"Oh, I—" Should she allow it? Was it proper? She was recently widowed. While her head pounded hard with these questions, her soul soared and her heart filled with unexpected emotion. She dared raise her face to him and with that tiny glance, she read a new tenderness in his expression. "I…I guess…that would be all right."

Without giving her a chance to change her mind, he leaned forward and kissed her. She inhaled sharply at his touch. He kissed her cautiously, at first, but soon showed an eagerness she hadn't seen coming. A lurch of pleasure danced within her as he unknowingly transported her back in time to when she was a silly, breathless girl of eighteen. But, mercy, Orville had never kissed her like this! His lips explored, sending her into new spirals of excitement, into a world of invisible warmth and security, of contentment and dizzying emotion.

His arms came around her then and drew her close, one hand caressing the small of her back. A delicate thread of hope formed in her heart. Could it really be that, on the heels of losing Orville, she might be falling in love with another man? It seemed impossible and yet, there it was—that desire inside her, that yearning for love and tenderness and companionship.

But what was she thinking? She had nothing to offer in return. What man in his right mind would—? She failed to finish her thought because he tugged her closer to him and her arms encircled him almost of their own volition, clinging to him as tightly as a bowstring. To think that only moments ago, they'd been merely talking and now, they'd locked themselves in so warm an embrace, she couldn't imagine ever wanting to be free.

They both came up for a second's breath but then just as quickly claimed each other's lips again. Shivers raced up and down Cristina's spine, in spite of August's heat, and for the next few moments, all they did was revel in each other's presence. He kissed the pulsing hollow of her neck; she kissed his whiskered cheek as it brushed past her. He dropped gentle kisses across her forehead; she dipped her head to kiss his throat.

When the series of dreamy, shiver-inducing, soul-reaching kisses finally met their end, he peered deep into her eyes. Breathless and shaken, both sat there on the bench, in awe of what had just happened. Neither spoke a word. In the silence, questions started racing through Cristina's head. Did he have regrets? Should she be ashamed? What was he thinking? Good gracious, what was *she* thinking? She couldn't read his eyes and she doubted he could read hers. A few more pounding seconds of silence passed, until she could take it no more. She jumped up from the bench and walked to the edge of the tiny wooden porch. The dark sky was lit by countless stars and a half moon. The only sounds for miles around were the gentle rustling of trees in the evening breeze and the distant call of an owl. She stared out at the road where, only hours before, her heart had soared as she watched Starlight crest the road carrying two riders. How could so much have transpired in so short a span—her heart going from stressed to thankful to rapturous and then to fretful? *Lord, help me,* she prayed in her head. Odd how her tiny prayers had started coming with greater frequency.

Jack also got to his feet and stood behind her, his breath falling on the back of her neck and on the part between her two braids. "I don't know what you're thinking," he whispered, breaking the silence.

A sudden shyness came over her. She folded her arms across her chest and kept her spine straight, thankful that he did not touch her again—at least for now.

"I want you to know I…I have strong feelings for you," he tacked on.

She put one hand across her mouth to keep from gasping but kept her shoulders taut and her back straight, afraid to speak, lest her words come out a mumbling, jumbling mess. She didn't even know what to say because her mind had fallen into a tangled heap. He was a Yankee, through and through—a lieutenant in the Union Army, for goodness' sake—a man of strong faith who trusted God in all matters, who was calm and confident, well-spoken and educated. She, on the other hand, had little to show for her life—a runaway half-breed with no family, a pitiable widow with two children and nothing more than a sixth-grade education. She didn't consider herself ignorant, by any means, but she certainly didn't measure up to the likes of Lieutenant Jack Fuller.

"What are you thinking?" he asked.

At last, she found her voice. "I…I don't know." She kept her gaze fixed on the road. "I'm only just widowed. I shouldn't be kissin' you so soon after. It feels almost like I'm bein' unfaithful to Orville."

"I understand your feelings, Cristina. But your late husband is not here to judge you and God isn't judging you either. I kissed you because I care for you and I believe you care for me. Was it too soon after your husband's passing? Perhaps. But that doesn't necessarily make it wrong. It just means we have feelings for each other and you don't have to feel guilty about them. It's all right that we care for each other." He gently placed his hands on her shoulders and turned her around to face him. She'd kept her eyes looking downward, so he lifted her chin with his forefinger. "Are you all right? I didn't mean to make you feel uncomfortable."

She studied him intently. He was far too fine a man for her. She took a deep breath and blurted out, "I can't see much point in gettin' involved with each other. We aren't cut from the same cloth. Besides, you'll be leavin' soon. By the looks o' you, you could prob'ly set out as soon as tomorrow."

He arched his eyebrows. "I admit I'm doing much better and you're right; I could leave tomorrow, especially if you wanted me gone. Do you?"

She merely shrugged. No, she didn't want him gone, but she wouldn't dare admit it.

"Or I could stay another day or two and fix some things around your place."

That idea caught her attention. "Such as...?"

"Well, I noticed a loose hinge on your front door, and these steps could use some reinforcing. I noticed a few places in your pasture fence that could use some replacement boards, some broken wires in the goat pen...things of that nature."

Cristina raised her chin. "I'm capable o' fixin' most o' that stuff. I just haven't had time."

"I understand. But I would very much like to repay you at least a little for your kindness to me. I also intend to replace your mattress."

Her head shot up at that statement. A new mattress would be purely delightful. "Really?"

"It's the least I can do."

"Thank you." She cleared her throat. "I...I think it's best we don't... kiss anymore."

His lips quivered with a tiny smile. "I'll do my best to mind my manners. I also intend to sleep in the barn for the remainder of my time here, starting tonight. I've taken up space in your little house long enough."

"You don't mind sleepin' in a smelly barn?"

"Before the war, farming was my life, Cristina. That smell is second nature to me."

She tilted her head and gave him a sidelong glance. "I enjoyed talkin' t' you tonight. And all the other nights."

"So did I."

She appreciated that he didn't try to wrap her in another embrace. She needed her wits about her.

"It was our talks that awakened my feelings for you," he added.

She eyed him carefully and pursed her lips, unsure how to proceed. "I'm glad you're feelin' better," she finally said.

He smiled. "I've got you and the Lord to thank for that."

"More the Lord than me."

He lowered his head a trifle closer to hers. "Are you starting to believe that?"

"Yes." Now *that* felt good to admit. "But I'm still not all the way there."

He shook his head. "I wouldn't want you making any kind of decision until you were a hundred percent sure of yourself. Just remember, though, faith is the key."

She gave a slow nod. "I know." Then she studied her bare feet for a moment before wiggling her toes and saying, "I think I'll go in now. I need to check on Elias and then give these feet a thorough scrubbing before bed."

Jack stepped back. "I'll just gather my things and head out to the barn. I think I'll take my bath down at the stream."

They both tiptoed inside, where Jack collected his items before they quietly bid each other good night.

Once Jack had closed the door behind him, Cristina heaved a quivery sigh and looked at the ceiling. "Lord," she whispered, "can You hear me? My heart is all a jumble. How am I supposed t' feel about Jack Fuller? Is it too early fer me t' care for him? Shoot, I'm probably not even supposed to notice another man yet." She continued staring upward, waiting for a sign, though she knew not what to expect. Would God answer in an audible voice? And if not, then just how *did* a person know when God was speaking? Was it possible to hear His voice and recognize it as distinct from one's own conscience? Was there even a difference?

Exhaling loudly, Cristina moved to the bureau and retrieved her shabby nightgown, along with the tattered outer garment she would drape around herself for walking out to the necessary later on. Her thoughts were so scrambled that all she could think to do to unravel them was to finish readying herself for bed and then open Jack's Bible to begin rereading those passages that had stood out to her earlier. If she could muster the faith to believe, perhaps God would speak His truth into her spirit.

21

Clive woke and stretched his aching body. He'd spent the night in a natural cave honed into a rocky ridge a mile or two upstream from that puny Stiles farm. With his Union jacket his only covering, he'd gotten chilly overnight and he was determined to search that day for a clothesline from which he could snatch a pair of men's pants and a couple of shirts. Maybe he would even find a clean blanket. His growling stomach told him it was time to rustle up some breakfast. He'd raided the Stiles springhouse the previous night, using a lantern he'd nabbed from her, so at least he had a light source and enough food to last him a few days. If it hadn't been for that vile Jack Fuller, he could have slept on a warm bed of hay. Granted, barns stank to the heavens, but this war had hardened Clive to a lot of things—the stench of death, for one—so the smell of a barn was nothing.

Getting to his feet, he looked around, glad for the solitude. His only companions were some flitting birds and yapping squirrels. On the other side of the stream was a field of dried-up corn and, beyond that, a low mountain range. West Virginia had its share of hills, gullies, rivers, and streams, and in his two years in the Army, he'd probably traversed and forded just about every one of them. "I'm done with that nonsense," he muttered to himself. "The Army's seen the last o' me. Once they've called off their search, I'll skedaddle outta here and head to wherever I want. Maybe Florida, or…who knows? I may end up in Texas." He shrugged. "Wherever I go, I'll see to it no one ever hunts me down."

He bent over and began picking up an assortment of sticks and dead branches so he could start a fire and cook the eggs he'd raided from that pretty hellcat's henhouse. He continued along the bank of the stream until he'd collected an adequate amount of kindling. Just as he was about to head back to the cave, something further upstream caught his eye. He spied a young, dark-skinned boy wading in the water. Clive ducked behind a bush, not wishing to be seen until he knew the nature of the boy's mission. The boy spread his hands over the surface of the water as he slowly maneuvered his way around in a methodical fashion. Fascinated, Clive watched until, suddenly, the boy plunged his hands into the water and pulled out a fish. The kid caught a fish barehanded! Not some measly little guppy, either, but a sizeable fish, which he held out and admired. Clive waited a few minutes to make sure the boy was alone, then watched for a chance to reveal himself. If he played his cards right, he'd be adding fish to his breakfast menu.

The boy climbed out of the water and carried the fish upstream and around a bend, so Clive laid down his kindling, jumped up, and followed at a distance, taking care to stay hidden. About five minutes later, the boy stopped at a small campsite where sticks and branches arranged like a small tepee waited to be ignited. He sat down on a rock, laid the fish out on a piece of cloth, took out a knife, and chopped off its head. Clearly, he was accustomed to living on his own.

Clive stepped out from his hiding place and slowly approached. "Hello there, boy!"

Fast as light, the boy jumped up and had a rifle aimed at Clive.

Why wasn't this kid in the Army? Clive raised his arms over his head. "Steady, boy. I ain't got no gun on me." Foolish of him to have forgotten it. He'd always depended on Mike to remind him.

The boy's eyes went as round as mountain apples as he kept the gun trained on Clive, saying not a word. Clive had to think fast.

"I saw you catch that fish. Mighty clever o' you. I see you're about t' make yerself some breakfast. I got me some eggs and bacon back at my camp if you want t' share."

The boy shifted his weight, his threadbare clothes hanging on his scrawny body. A spark of interest shone in his eyes, though he kept his rifle aimed.

"Where's yer family?" Clive asked, trying to earn the kid's trust.

The boy shrugged. "Got none."

"No? Well then, you an' me got that in common. Where you from?"

"No place."

"Ah. Somethin' else we share. I lost both my parents before the age o' fourteen. I been roamin' the wilds ever since." He wasn't about to disclose his association with the Army, on the chance the boy had gotten word of a wanted soldier in connection with a robbery and shooting at Rosalyn's. "Can I lower my arms? They're goin' numb on me."

The boy gave a simple nod but kept that rifle at the ready. Smart kid.

"How 'bout it? Should I go back fer my grub? I bet between the two of us, we could make a mighty fine feast."

The boy licked his lips.

"I don't mean no harm," Clive went on. "In fact, I got a proposal fer you that could earn you some money, if you're up fer hearin' about it."

Another spark set off in the boy's eyes. He gave a small nod, which Clive took as a yes. He turned on his heel. "I'll be back right quick." Without looking back, he made for his campsite.

When he reached the cave, he grabbed his rucksack and rifled through it, looking for his tattered notebook and a pencil. After locating both, he hurriedly scrawled a message on the top sheet, then tore it off, folded it, and stuck it in his back pocket. He grinned to himself. What a perfect plan. Now if he could just pull it off. He felt for his coin purse, relieved to find it still in the front pocket of his pants. He unbuttoned the pocket and withdrew the purse, then opened it and dug around until his fingers clutched hold of one of the liberty-seated half-dollar coins he'd taken from the old man's house. He held it up to the light and smiled. Then, closing his fist around it, he picked up the potato sack that held the food he'd lifted, threw the sack over his shoulder, and headed back to the boy's campsite.

In his absence, the boy had started his fire and had even put a pan on top of a rusted piece of metal to begin heating it. By all accounts, he seemed to be an expert at independent living. He couldn't be much older than twelve or thirteen, about the same age as Clive when he'd set out on his own. The boy looked up when he returned and raised his rifle, though not as high this time. He'd started trusting Clive, just as he'd hoped he would. "Looks like you got things under control. Here's some more grub." He set down the sack and was glad to see the boy lay his rifle on the ground beside him. "The eggs should still be intact, I wrapped them real careful-like in cloth."

The boy's gaze darted to the bag. "Open it, then," he ordered. Bossy little thug. Clive would've put him in his place if he hadn't been about to present him with a proposal.

Later, the boy started to relax while fixing the eggs and bacon along with the fish he'd scaled, gutted, and cleaned. He had skills Clive could only dream about. "Where'd you learn t' cook like that, boy?"

"I worked in the massuh's kitchen."

"Oh, yeah? Where was that?"

"South Carolina."

"You run away?"

The boy shook his head. "Walked out right after the war started. Things was in a mess in the big house. Nobody seen me go and I di'n't tell nobody I was a goin' neithuh. I never looks back. Not once."

"You got no family, eh?"

"I got sold down in Georgia when I was real young. Never knowed my mammy. Somehow, I ends up in South Carolina with the massuh's family. But they's history now."

Clive could've sworn he detected a bit of a smile on the boy's face. "You happy, then?"

"I likes not answerin' t' nobody. I gets by."

"How d' you make do with no money?"

"I makes a few cents here an' there by workin' fer folks, but mostly I lives off the land an' I'm good at it."

"I can see that."

For a moment, neither talked; they just stared at the sparks and flames beneath the pan of food. "You in the Army?" the boy asked.

"Me? Naw," Clive rushed to answer. "I ain't got no interest. How come you didn't join? There'd be a place fer you in the Union."

"I ain't got no interest neithuh. I'd have t' talk t' folks an' I like my life like it is, peaceful an' private."

Clive took that statement as a hint that the boy would be glad when Clive got out of his hair. Within minutes, the boy produced a couple of tin plates and two forks from his holey rucksack. He scooped their breakfast onto the plates, then handed one over to Clive. "Thanks, boy. You got a name?"

The boy shook his head.

"No name? Really?"

"Not that I know of. The massuh called me Raisin."

"Raisin, eh? That what you go by, then?"

"I don't much care what folks calls me, long as they don't botha me. I never stays in one place for longer 'n a day or so."

"You don't get tired o' wanderin'?"

"Do you?" the boy shot back, his round eyes probing. He had an edge to him that put Clive in mind of a mule. If he didn't feel like giving an inch, he'd make you wait till you were on your last legs and about to keel over.

"No, I like my life jus' fine," he lied.

They both scraped their plates clean around the same time. "I'll take these down to the stream an' wash 'em," Raisin offered.

Clive handed over his plate, then watched as the boy picked up the frying pan and carried all the dishes down to the water's edge. While the boy washed and rinsed, Clive mentally reviewed his plan. When the boy returned, he stuffed the dishes and pan back inside his rucksack, then threw some dirt on his fire. He did everything in rote fashion, as if he'd done it a hundred times before—which he probably had.

"That was a fine breakfast, kid. Thanks fer indulgin' me."

Rather than reply, he merely gave a fast nod of the head. He didn't sit, his way of dismissing Clive to return to his own campsite. Clive knew he had to act fast. He brought out the liberty-seated half dollar from his pocket and held it up for the boy to see. "How'd you like t' earn more than a cent or two?"

The boy's eyes widened, unable to conceal his obvious curiosity. "Where'd you get that?"

"I got money, boy. Plenty of it."

"I thought you was a wanderer."

"That don't mean I can't have money on me. Anyway, back to my question." He retrieved the note and handed it over to the boy.

The boy took the paper, unfolded it, and stared at the words. "I can't read."

"'Course you can't. You don't have to read the message. You just have t' deliver it to the right person. When you get back, I'll give you this half dollar. How's that?"

The boy's round eyes suddenly narrowed. "Who'm I s'posed t' deliver it to?"

"I'll give you all the details in a minute. You interested?"

"How do I know you'll be here when I get back?"

"Well, you gotta trust me."

"I ain't dumb, white man." He eyed Clive's hand. "I see you gots a gold ring there. You give me that as a promise t' pay. If you ain't here when I get back, I keeps the ring."

"You're a tough young bird, ain't y'?" Clive wiggled the ring off his finger. He'd won it in a round of poker back in '61 while stationed in southern Pennsylvania. The fellow had been madder than a hornet when he'd thrown it on the table, saying it was some kind of heirloom. Clive had put it on his finger right there under the guy's nose and laughed all the way back to his unit.

"You'd best return, boy. I want that ring back."

"Give me the details," Raisin said, bending to stuff the ring in the front pocket of his rucksack.

"All right, all right. Listen up."

22

Jack worked all that next day and into the evening mending fences, repairing porch steps, and fixing broken hinges. He secured the lock on Cristina's front door and filled in every little hole in her walls to ensure no drafts would penetrate them when colder weather set in. He also replaced the stuffing in her mattress, filling it with a mixture of straw and several bags of feathers she'd been saving for several months. When he carried the freshly stuffed mattress into the house and laid it out on the bed, he thought Cristina would fall over with outright joy. What he wouldn't have given in that moment to bottle up her expression to look at later! And, oh, what he wouldn't have given to wrap his arms around her slender frame and kiss her silly once more. Of course, that wasn't to be, as she'd made it clear she didn't think any further kissing would be appropriate. He could only hope she would soon have a change of heart.

Elias had rested on Cristina's pallet for a good share of the day but, by early afternoon, said he felt much better. With his mother's permission and Jack's approval, he followed Jack around, limping as he went, but watching with a great deal of interest. Bit by bit, Jack got him to say a few words; by suppertime, Elias had warmed to Jack by a few more degrees. Jack smiled to himself at the notion that he might be winning him over, if only by tiny increments.

If only Jack could sleep on the new mattress. His first night in the barn had been even more restless than expected. For one thing, the barn didn't offer much in the way of comfort, with all its extra sounds and smells. On top of that, he'd had trouble keeping his thoughts about Cristina under control, not to mention his growing attraction to her. He spent hour after hour wondering what to do about them and also praying for guidance and wisdom. He knew he couldn't linger at the little farm much longer than a couple of days and yet there was a large part of him that couldn't bear to leave. He'd regained most of his strength, his cough was nearly gone, and the gunshot wound had healed almost completely, so he'd run out of excuses for staying. But he knew he was falling in love with Cristina and it seemed that leaving her would be the hardest thing he'd ever had to do. And yet, two things bothered him. First, he had to find a way to tell her that he'd been the one to shoot Orville. He could not go on deceiving her into believing he'd just come upon her husband on the battlefield. Second, he had reservations about falling in love with a woman who did not share his faith in Christ. He was familiar with the passage in 2 Corinthians 6 that warned of the danger of "yoking" oneself with an unbeliever. How could a man and a woman be joined together in marriage, connected as they faced the trials and triumphs of life, if they did not share an equal measure of faith in, and love for, God? He couldn't press her into making a decision to follow Christ just because he wanted to share his life with her. No, that sort of decision had to come from a personal conviction only God could plant in her heart.

After supper, everyone helped to clear the table. Elias limped to the little counter next to the sink, where he set down his dishes. Jack made the boy sit down so he could unwind the cloth bandage and check the bite. It pleased him to see that no infection had set in. In fact, the only indication that he'd suffered a bite were the fang marks and the reddish area surrounding the bite. "It's looking good for a snake bite that's only a day old. I have a good feeling that snake didn't wish to waste any of his precious venom on you."

"I pro'ly wouldn't have tasted very good either, bein' as I was all dirty with sweat."

Jack tossed back his head and laughed. "You might be right about that." Satisfied, he rewrapped the bandage.

"Which reminds me, Elias, you and Catherina need baths tonight," said Cristina.

"Aww, do we have to?" asked Elias.

"Do we got to, Mama?" Catherina piped in.

"Yes, but since it's a warm night, I'll take you down to the stream t' bathe."

"Hooray!" Elias cheered. "That's better than an old sponge bath any day."

"Can Jack come, too?" Catherina asked.

Jack caught Cristina's eye and winked at her. "I'd be happy to tag along if your mother doesn't mind. I could use a dip in the stream, myself."

"It's fine by me," Cristina answered.

"Are you gonna take a bath, too, Mama?" Catherina wanted to know.

"No, Catherina. I will wash up after you've gone to bed."

They all worked together to tidy up the kitchen area and while they moved about, Jack noted a peaceful atmosphere among them. Elias and Catherina teased each other, while he and Cristina shared secretive smiles, as if they had the ability to read each other's thoughts. Had she, too, been pondering those marvelous, tender kisses of the night before? Had she replayed them in her mind as he had done all day? He mentally berated himself for so quickly setting aside the belief that he had no business forming a relationship with her until she gave her life fully over to God. *Lord, forgive me my many weaknesses, particularly this newfound love for Cristina forming in my heart.*

Just as Cristina washed the final dish and Jack dried it, approaching horse's hooves alerted them to a visitor. "Somebody's comin', Mama!" Elias ran to the window. "It's that preacher who paid a call last week."

"Reverend Wilcox?" She hurried to the window herself to peer out, then went to the door and opened it wide. "Reverend! Welcome. You didn't bring yer lovely wife?" Jack moved to the door then and stood behind the little family, towering over Cristina's head.

"No, I'm sorry she couldn't come," he answered with a cheery smile. He removed his hat and set it on the buggy seat next to him. "She did, however, send her best wishes along with some fresh cornbread, apple butter, and a platter of sugar cookies." The children both squealed with delight. "I hope I'm not disturbing your supper. It is rather late, I'm afraid."

"No, no, not at all, Reverend. Come on inside," Cristina said. "We just finished cleanin' up."

The preacher grinned down at them, then turned and picked up a large basket covered with a yellow gingham cloth. Without being asked, Elias went outside to assist the preacher with the basket and take the reins from him. "Thank you, young man. I can see your mother has raised you well."

After climbing down from his rig, the stocky gentleman walked up the freshly repaired front steps and entered through the open door, Elias following soon after. Spotting Jack first, the preacher gazed up with assessing eyes. "My, I'd say you're looking much healthier than the first time we met. Are you feeling better?"

"Much better, Reverend. In fact, I've regained my strength and a good share of my energy, thanks in large part to those healing words you so eloquently prayed over me."

"Well, I can't take any credit for that. I merely acted as God's agent. He did the healing work. But it's humbling to know He saw fit to work through me."

His eyes traveled from Jack to Cristina and back again. It occurred to Jack that the man might be trying to gauge what sort of feelings had developed between them. With arched brows, he asked, "Now that you're on the mend, are you planning to head back to your regiment?"

Jack put on a matter-of-fact air, not wanting to reveal any feelings of dread at having to leave. "I am, actually. Probably in a couple of days. In repayment for the care I received from Mrs. Stiles, I've been making a number of repairs around her property. It's the least I can do." Then, for good measure, he tacked on, "I've also moved out to the barn."

The reverend nodded. "I assumed as much."

"The soldier made Mama a new bed mattress!" Catherina announced. "She's gonna sleep on it tonight."

"Is that so? Well, I'm sure she appreciated that. Are you going to miss Mr. Fuller when he leaves?"

"Yes 'cause our papa died and when Mr. Fuller goes, we won't have no man around here anymore." To Jack's knowledge, it was the first time Catherina had mentioned her father's passing. Cristina had said she doubted her six-year-old fully grasped that her father wouldn't be coming home. Perchance the girl comprehended more than either of them knew.

Catherina lifted her face to Jack. "I wish you wasn't goin'."

His heart melted a little. "My division needs me, Catherina, but I will definitely miss you." He took a step closer and touched her petite nose.

The preacher gave a low chuckle. "Well, it appears you've made quite an impression around here, Mr. Fuller."

"Please, call me Jack. If I've made an impression, I hope it's a positive one. I know I probably wouldn't have survived had it not been for the watchful care of Cristina and Miss Clara—and, of course, the Lord's divine intervention. I thank you again for coming out when you did, Reverend."

"Well, you have Cristina here to thank for that. She's the one who came knocking on the parsonage door."

"Yes and I'm glad she did. I experienced divine healing and no one will persuade me otherwise."

Cristina hurried across the room and retrieved a wooden rocker, positioning it near the preacher. "Sorry for my manners, Reverend. I should've offered you a chair earlier."

"No need, really," he said, even as he sat, the chair creaking under his weight. "I hadn't planned to stay more than a couple of minutes. I merely wanted to check on the patient, deliver the baked goods Mrs. Wilcox made, and, well, invite you and your children to Sunday services this week."

"Oh! Well, thank you very much. I'll think about that."

"What're 'Sunday services'?" Elias asked.

"Well now, that's a fine question," the preacher said. As he talked, everyone found a place to sit, Cristina and Jack on the long bench, and Elias and Catherina on the braided rug in front of the minister. He explained that Sunday school started at 10 a.m. and the church service at 11, that Sunday school was for all ages where one could learn Bible lessons and listen to stories, and that the church service started out with singing and then a message from the preacher. "I think you'll truly enjoy it," he said by way of a conclusion.

"I wanna go, Mama," said Elias.

"Me, too," said Catherina. "Does they have any little girls my age?"

The preacher leaned forward and patted her head. "We do, indeed. There's little Susannah Garner and young Johanna Bixby and a few others. I'm sure you'd all be fast friends."

Catherina clapped her hands. "I wanna go to Sunday school, I wanna go to Sunday school," she said in a singsong fashion. She whipped her head around, making her long braids fly. "Can we go, Mama? Can we?"

"We'll have t'—" The clomping sound of a horse's hooves had Cristina stopping mid-sentence. She rose and hurried to the window. "Why, it's Clara. She doesn't usually stop by this time o' day." She threw wide the door.

"I've got some news," Jack heard Clara say.

"Well, come on in then."

Clara rushed in rather breathlessly and looked around, her gaze pausing on the preacher. "Didn't mean to interrupt yer visit. I could come back."

"No, no, I only stopped by for a minute," Reverend Wilcox said. "You go ahead." He started to stand.

"Please stay, Reverend," Cristina said. "No need for you to hurry off." The preacher lowered himself again. "What is it you wanted t' tell us, Clara?"

Clara looked at the children. "Elias, would y' mind takin' Catherina out to the swing and givin' her a few pushes?"

Elias frowned. "Why?"

"Because she asked you to, young man," said Cristina.

The boy sobered and took his sister's hand and the two walked outside. Jack shifted his position on the bench as an uneasy sensation came over him. What did Clara have to share that would have prompted her to ask the children to leave?

"I believe I know what you're about to tell them," Reverend Wilcox said to Clara. "I had half a mind to mention it myself, but for the children."

Clara nodded at him. "I figured you'd know since you live in town."

Cristina shot Jack a worried glance.

Jack nodded silently, then switched his gaze to Clara. "What's going on?"

"There was a robbery and a shootin' at Rosalyn's Restaurant," Clara blurted out.

Cristina covered a gasp with her hand.

"Appears to have been two Army fellas what did the crime, but the Army's stayin' real quiet on the matter. They're doin' their own investigation. Jeb Walters, who works at Rosalyn's, said two fellas came into the restaurant an' demanded all the money in the cashbox."

"Were they wearing Army uniforms?" Jack asked.

"They weren't, but I'm gettin' t' that. Jeb thought one o' the fellas looked familiar once he got a closer look. Turns out it was one of them Army men who's supposed to be guardin' the town. And I got a good feelin' I know just who he's referrin' to."

"Is that so?" the reverend asked. "You'd best report it to the law if you have an idea."

"Pardon, Reverend, but I'll get to that in due time. Anyway, just as Jeb opened the box to get the money, another man—one o' the restaurant cooks, I believe, named Lyle Richards—came in from the back o' the restaurant and opened fire. He shot down one o' the robbers, but the other man got away—after shootin' Lyle dead."

"That's just awful," Cristina exclaimed.

"Cristina." Clara spoke in a low voice, eyeing her with an intensity Jack had never seen before.

What, exactly, was happening here? Jack's head spun with a myriad of questions. "So are you saying you think Union soldiers disguised themselves as ordinary citizens to commit this crime?"

"Me an' everyone else, Mr. Fuller! That's the rumor floatin' around town anyway."

"And you think you know their identities?"

"'Course I do! I gotta assume Cristina told you 'bout the two Union soldiers who attacked her a couple o' months ago. One had a scar goin' down his face. I've spotted that fella on more than one occasion an' Cristina has, too."

"Wait a minute," the reverend interrupted. "You say you were attacked, Cristina? I trust you reported the incident."

Cristina hung her head. "I didn't. I…I couldn't. Everyone stop talkin' about this, please." She covered her face with her hands and began to cry.

Jack couldn't help but reach an arm around Cristina's shoulders and give her a comforting squeeze. She didn't fight him; if anything, she seemed to welcome his nearness.

"Cristina, we can't stop talkin' about it," Clara persisted. "Those men're the same ones who robbed Rosalyn's restaurant and now Lyle Richards is dead. It's high time we reported those crooks. They're from that unit camped outside Ripley, Mr. Fuller, and the Army's sayin' they're missin' a man. 'Course, the Army don't give us no details, only tells us to be on the lookout—and not to open our doors fer no one. Everyone's assumin' the other man's dead, since Jeb said he wasn't movin', but the Army don't say. All they tell the public is that one's in Army custody. I doubt even Sheriff Barton knows the full truth. It's downright frustratin'."

The mention of a facial scar burned a hole of familiarity in Jack's mind. He sat there thinking on it until it suddenly dawned on him. He'd met the man and his cohort the day before he'd come out to Cristina's place. The two men—privates Clive Horton and Mike Farmer—had been stirring up a problem for Rosalyn and now it seemed they had broken their promise to never return to her restaurant.

Just then, the children came back inside, Catherina tearfully reporting she'd fallen and scraped her knee. Cristina quickly wiped her own tear-stained face, then hurried to her daughter's aid. At the same time, the reverend announced his leave-taking and Clara said that she, too, needed to be on her way. They all wished each other a good, safe evening, and within five minutes, the little house had returned to normal. Well, as normal as one could possibly hope it to be, considering the new information that had been shared.

Jack thought about his next move. Tomorrow, he would pay a visit to the local squadron leader and report what little he could offer. Perhaps he would also learn the fate of the soldier who'd been shot. At the same time, he would inform the Army of the attack on Cristina by privates Horton and Farmer, along with news of the break-in while she'd been away—whether she approved or not. She could not continue withholding information because of a threat those thugs had made against her children. He would see to it that the Army granted her protection.

And if he had his way, the assignment to protect her would go to him.

23

Once their guests had gone, Cristina instructed the children to put on their swimming clothes. She gathered towels and some soap powder and the four of them walked down to the stream. She intended to bathe Catherina right away, but instead, she and Jack sat on the bank and watched the children swim around in the shallow water. It was cold, as always, but on hot nights such as this, the children found it refreshing. "What are you thinking?" Jack asked, as they sat there in silence, eyes on the children.

Rather than look at him straight on, she tipped her face to the setting sun. "I don't even know what to feel or think. On the one hand, I'm feelin' guilty fer not reportin' those awful men. Perhaps the Army would've dealt with 'em in one way or another and then there'd've been no robbery. Lyle Richards wouldn't be dead." That last statement gave her pause. She sniffed, then swiped at the moisture collecting in the corners of her eyes. "But I couldn't be sure the Army would believe me if I came forward. I had no idea how much influence those fellas would have over their commandin' officer. For all I knew, they would convince 'im I was lyin'. On the other hand, those men beat me so mercilessly, they had me convinced that if I went to the law, they'd kill my children."

A tear escaped one eye and she quickly wiped it away. "Now one of 'em is runnin' free, Jack—and I fear fer anyone who crosses paths with 'im." She pulled her knees up to her chest and hugged her legs through the dog-eared fabric of her plain-woven skirt.

Jack cleared his throat. "If you're feeling responsible in any way, you need to let that go, Cristina. Those men are responsible for their own actions. You cannot blame yourself for what happened at Rosalyn's. It's tragic that one of Rosalyn's employees died, but it had nothing to do with you. You were right to put your children first and to do what you thought would keep them safe. I will tell you this, though: I intend to visit that Army camp tomorrow. I hope you won't mind if I borrow your horse. I want to leave at first light."

Her head jerked up. "Why are you goin' there?"

"To tell them everything I know: how those fellows, the scar-faced Clive and his friend, Mike, beat you and later broke into your house while you were away. Army officials need to know these men were up to no good long before the incident at Rosalyn's."

Cristina gawked at him. "How d' you know their names?"

"I ran into them the day before I came here. I was finishing supper at Rosalyn's when they came in and started causing a disturbance. I ordered them not to return to the restaurant and also announced my plan to pay their lieutenant a visit the next day. And I intended to do just that on my way back to my unit, until I got...waylaid. The whole incident escaped my mind—until tonight."

"Are you gonna tell 'em I shot you?"

"Well, not unless it comes up."

"What if they throw me in jail?"

He inclined his head at her and smiled. "They are not going to put you in jail. You acted in self-defense."

"Still...my children could be in jeopardy."

"Your children will be fine."

As if on cue, they turned their attention to Elias and Catherina, who giggled and squealed as they engaged in a splashing match. If Elias's snakebite still bothered him, he didn't show it. Cristina had bandaged it again in order to protect the wound as much as possible while he swam, but she intended to remove the cloth and lather up the wound for a good cleaning before he got out of the water.

She lowered her legs and stretched them out in front of her, studying the toes of her tattered shoes. An unexpected sigh snuck out of her lungs.

"I hope you know that I'll do everything I possibly can to keep you and your children safe," Jack said. Leaning closer, he whispered, "I mean it, Cristina. Do you have any idea how much I care about you? I didn't expect to feel so strongly toward you in so short a time, but I can't deny that I do."

Her pulse skittered at his whispered words and her lips burned with the memory of their kisses from the night before. She had to say it. "I…I care about you, too." There. Relief washed over her. But in its wake came another wave of shame and guilt over allowing herself a romantic attraction so soon after learning of her husband's passing. Some would call it altogether improper. She dared not look at him, keeping her eyes trained on her children.

He reached one arm around her shoulders and tugged her closer. It was hard to formulate a coherent thought with him so near. "I'm glad to hear you say that," he murmured close to her ear. "I wondered if you were feeling the same."

"But…I don't know."

"What don't you know?"

"It seems too soon."

"I understand your reservations, but I hope that if you're feeling something for me, you won't run away from it but will rather hand it over to God and let Him work it out according to His perfect plan."

"But I haven't yet learned t' trust Him like you. How d' you…how d' you let Him 'work somethin' out'? An' how can you know His plan?"

He gave a gentle chuckle. "It's really not that hard to do. It's a matter of surrendering your heart and life to Jesus Christ, God's Son. It's admitting that you're a sinner who needs saving. It's repenting of any wrongful deeds or thoughts you may have had and asking for God's forgiveness.

It's turning away from your old ways and saying, 'Here I am, God. Make me a new creation so that I can live the life You always intended me to live. Help me to live according to Your plan, not mine.'"

She finally dared to look into his shining blue eyes and gave him the tiniest smile. "I thought you said it was easy. That sounds like a lot."

He grinned back. "Now you're toying with me." He tapped the tip of her nose and gave her shoulder gentle squeeze with his other hand.

Noticing Elias glance up at them, Cristina quickly inched away from Jack. "Best not let the children see us sittin' so close. 'Specially Elias. He might grow suspicious."

Jack dropped his arm. "I understand your uneasiness, but how long will you hide the way you're feeling?"

Cristina sighed. "He just found out about his daddy an'—"

"I know that. I'm not trying to diminish his sorrow, believe me. I know the grieving and healing process will take him some time. But even today, I noticed him starting to warm a bit to me. As for Catherina, well, I don't think it will take much time at all to win her over."

"Yes, just in time fer you t' say good-bye." She straightened her spine, folded her arms, and focused her full attention on her children romping in the water.

He inhaled a loud breath. "Ah, is that it? You think once I go, you won't see me again?"

"It *is* wartime."

"Indeed, it is. And none of us but God knows the future. I could very well die on the field, Cristina, although I will continue trusting God to keep me safe until I'm due to muster out, in a few short months."

She poked her finger through a small hole in the side of her skirt and mindlessly made it bigger. "What of it?"

"What of it? I would like to come back here when I'm discharged— if I'm welcome. Would I be?"

Dare she hope that something might truly come of their relationship? More likely, he would return to the field and forget all about her.

When she didn't respond, he leaned in a bit closer. "I'm going to ask something of you though."

Ah, so there *was* a condition. She might have known. She raised her head and regarded him with somber curiosity.

"Would you promise to keep reading your Bible?"

"*My* Bible? I figured you'd take it with you when you left."

"No." He touched her chin and gently lifted it, causing a shiver to scamper down her spine. "Consider it my gift to you, all right? And I ask only that you keep reading it, and that you'll do so with an open heart and mind. That's all."

She nodded.

"Good. And would you take Reverend Wilcox up on his invitation to church?"

She nodded again, this time a little faster—and with a newfound hope welling up in her chest. "Maybe I could even interest Clara in joinin' us."

A wide smile broke on his face. "Now wouldn't that be something!"

She giggled. "A miracle, that's what it would be."

His expression sobered a bit. "Miracles *do* happen."

"What're you two talkin' 'bout?" Elias asked, standing still in the water to stare at them.

"Us? Oh, nothin' in particular," Cristina replied. "You done swimmin'?"

"Not yet. Aren't you gonna get in?"

She shook her head. "That water's too cold fer me. I'll wash up with warm water later on."

Elias looked at Jack with a sly smile. "What about you, Jack? You comin' in—or are you too scared?"

Cristina glanced at Jack in time to see his eyebrows shoot up in surprise. With staid calmness, he slowly rose to his feet. "Was that a challenge, young man?" He moved toward the water, his steps slow and measured, and Elias's eyes went round with gleeful surprise.

Catherina let out a frightful squeal at the sight of Jack's approach. She scrambled out of the water and ran to Cristina, who laughed as she enfolded her daughter in a towel and sat her in her lap. Elias gave Jack a wild splash, hitting him square in the face. Jack recoiled with a little yelp. "This is war!" he declared, quickly bending to remove his shoes and socks before venturing into the water, long pants and all. Elias kept splashing Jack, backing up as he did so. Jack reciprocated with bigger splashes, advancing on the boy until they both cut loose a series of roars and hoots and more raucous splashes. Before long, they were shoving each other playfully while belting out riotous spurts of laughter. Cristina could hardly believe her eyes as she watched their horseplay. This was something new for Elias. It had been two years since he'd had the chance to play with his father…not that Orville had done much playing when he was home. He'd been too busy trying to make a living and really wasn't the playful sort to begin with. Reading stories to the children at night had been his way of spending time with them. Although he lacked a formal education, he had always been a proficient reader and delighted in introducing Elias, especially, to such titles as *Moby-Dick* and *Twice-Told Tales*. Cristina was grateful he had tried to be a good father.

Jack and Elias wrestled for a few more minutes until Cristina brought out the bar of lye soap and instructed her son to start washing himself.

"Aw, Maw," he protested, "I'm clean enough."

Jack gave the boy a gentle shove. "Better do as your mama says."

Without further argument, Elias came up on shore and took the soap from Cristina, then returned to the water.

"Here," Jack said to him, "let me take off that bandage so you can give that snakebite a good cleaning." Elias stuck out his leg and allowed Jack to untie and then unwrap the fabric bandage.

Cristina held her breath while Jack surveyed the wound.

He nodded to himself, then turned to her. "It's healing nicely," he called out.

She exhaled in relief. "That's good t' know."

Elias proceeded to wash his face, arms, and legs, then handed the soap to Jack, who scrubbed his own face and arms. "I could use a good shave, but I'll do that in the morning," he announced to no one in particular.

Cristina stood to her feet. "Come on, Cath, let's go get you clean, as well."

They walked down to the water's edge and Jack passed the soap to Cristina. Their hands touched in the exchange, during which they also exchanged glances and tiny smiles. Feeling suddenly shy, Cristina turned her full attention to her daughter. Taking off her own shoes, she slowly dipped a toe in the water. "Aah!" she screeched. "This water's colder than a dead man's nose. How can you possibly swim in this?"

Jack laughed. "I believed you to be much more daring, Mrs. Stiles."

She ventured one step forward, then retreated abruptly, shivering.

"It ain't—isn't—cold when you get used to it, Maw," Elias insisted.

"Oh, no?" She sneaked a glance at Jack and found him wearing a roguish grin.

"Perhaps she needs a little splash…what do you think, Elias?" Jack said.

"Yes!"

Cristina put on her sternest face as she pointed her index finger from Elias to Jack and then back again. "Don't you dare!"

Jack reached down and lobbed a little sprinkle at her.

"Hey!" she squeaked, jumping back.

Then Elias splashed her harder.

"Stop that right now!" she ordered, except her tone apparently didn't convey how serious she was, for the two kept up their splashing until the fabric of her dress was thoroughly soaked, chilling her to the bone. She might have escaped to the bank, but a little taste for revenge started stirring in her gut. "All right, you two, that's it. Y' best step back, Catherina, if y' don't wanna get wetter."

"No, I want to!" the girl squealed with a giggle. Soon, a full-out water war was under way and Cristina somehow found herself right in the middle. It was the most fun she'd had in…well, she couldn't remember the last time she'd given herself the freedom to play with such abandon. Elias was right: after staying in the water for a while, one did grow accustomed to the frigid temperature.

When everyone had finally tired of the water battle, Elias and Jack collapsed, breathless, on the riverbank, while Cristina finished scrubbing Catherina with the soap. Both children wanted to know if they could repeat the game the next day.

"Sorry, pal," said Jack, "but I'll be heading back to my unit either tomorrow or the next day. Got a bit of business in town to see to first though." At that comment, his eyes drifted to Cristina, no doubt to gauge her reaction. She tried to remain aloof, not wanting to be overcome with emotion.

24

*P*eeking out from behind a tree deep in the woods, Clive watched as Lieutenant Fuller and the Stiles family made their way from the stream to the house. *Look at them*, Clive thought, *all cheery and cozy.* Lieutenant Fuller sure didn't look like he was ailing at all. Surely, the Army would come for him soon. And once the problem of Lieutenant Fuller went away, Clive would revisit the dark-skinned kid, seal the deal with him, and then move in on the little Stiles family.

He glanced down at his left hand. Perhaps as early as tomorrow, he'd be wearing his ring again. He cautiously peered around the tree trunk once more and watched the foursome disappear inside the house. Satisfied it was safe to move, Clive headed back to his cave. He would return at first light in hopes of witnessing his plan starting to come to fruition.

⌒

Jack stepped onto the porch to sit in the warm breeze and gaze at the night sky while giving Cristina some private time to talk to her children, read them a story, and otherwise complete the bedtime routine. She had agreed to join him outside when the children were tucked in and now he thought about what it was he intended to tell her that evening. *God, may my words come out right and may she take them to heart and not be offended. Above all else, I want Your will to be accomplished in my life—and in hers. Please work in her spirit and draw her unto Yourself.*

Jack gazed up at a black sky peppered with glowing stars and a crescent moon—and pondered his long hike back to camp. He didn't want to leave Cristina and her children, but he knew his time had come. He would first visit the local Union camp's superior to offer the details he knew about Clive Horton and Mike Farmer, then return to Cristina's and finish any odd jobs that needed doing around the farm. If all went according to schedule, he would start his trek back the day after tomorrow. The only thing that might delay his departure would be a heavy thunderstorm. Barring a weather event such as that, his time here had nearly reached its end.

Heaviness came over him at the thought of saying good-bye. And yet, he told himself, it wouldn't be forever. Lord willing, he would return once he mustered out, perhaps even sooner, if he could talk Major Marsh into granting him orders to return to Ripley to help with the search for the despicable man who'd beaten Cristina, broken into her house a few weeks later, and, more recently, murdered a man during a robbery at Rosalyn's.

Several minutes later, the front door creaked open and Cristina stepped out onto the porch. He made a mental note to oil the door hinges before setting off.

He hadn't noticed until now that she'd changed out of her wet clothes and donned a different dress. "What a lovely night," she said, looking up at the sky.

"Lovely, indeed," he replied, his eyes fixed on her. "Shall we take a little walk?"

"Oh, I wouldn't want to go far."

"Of course not. Maybe just up the road a piece and back."

"Yes, that sounds nice."

He extended a hand to her and once she'd clasped it, they descended the porch steps and strolled slowly down the driveway toward the road.

She interlaced her fingers with his and glanced up at him. "The kids sure enjoyed themselves t'night. I haven't heard them laugh that hard in I don't know how long. Thank you fer playin' with 'em."

"The pleasure was mine. They gave me so much joy, especially in light of the fact that I have to leave you soon. I don't want to go, you know."

She gave him a brief upward glance. "I—I don't—want you t' leave."

At the edge of the road, they stopped walking and faced each other. He couldn't help himself; he leaned down and kissed her on the forehead.

Her breath caught.

He leaned back and looked into her eyes. "You've unlocked my heart, you know,"

In the moonlight, she gave a hint of a smile. "I have?"

"After my brief marriage to Marilee, I made a promise to myself to never fall for another woman. I'd managed to keep that promise, too—until I met you."

He detected another hitch in her breath. "Is that so?"

He reached down and gently lifted her chin with his index finger. "I don't think you know how much you mean to me."

"I…I'm beginnin' to think I might."

"Do you need some reassurance?"

She released a shaky breath. "I still think it might be too early."

"And you might well be right, but I can't deny my growing feelings and I don't think you can either. I admire you for the way you care for your children. I admire your strength and courage and perseverance in the midst of very difficult circumstances. I admire how hard you work to keep this little farm afloat, the chores you do on a daily basis without so much as a single complaint. I admire your spirit and the sacrifices you make for your children. If it came down to it, I know you'd lay down your life for them."

She put two fingers to his mouth to shush him. "Y' give me too much credit."

"Not at all," he murmured. He reached up and took her hand, opening it with the palm facing upward. Then he brought it to his mouth and kissed each callus. Next, he lowered her hand, tracing each callus with his index finger.

He felt a trembling in her hand before she withdrew it and tilted her face at him. "Well, I admire you, as well."

"Is that so?"

"Indeed, it is. I admire you fer yer strong faith an' fer the way you've been so patient with me as I try t' figure out who God is. I admire you fer yer courage an' fer yer desire t' serve not only God but yer country and fer yer principles an' convictions. I admire you fer the way you've worked t' win over my children, especially fer helpin' Elias t' open up."

"Well, that's been easy. I think your children are wonderful and I have developed a deep fondness for both of them."

She opened her mouth to say more, but he stopped her efforts with a kiss—slow and gentle at first, but one that soon turned breathless, especially when she stood on tiptoe and wrapped her arms around his neck. *Lord, I am drowning in my love for her*, he prayed, slipping his own arms around her small frame, clinging, kissing, whispering, trembling, and, at last, relaxing in the oneness he felt with her. He had but to murmur the words "I love you" and everything would be complete, but he couldn't quite bring himself to do that yet. Certain requirements had to be met before he dared express his deepest emotions—a declaration of her faith in Jesus being foremost, as well as his revealing the secret he'd held for far too long. Still, that did not keep him from kissing her, as his emotions swirled and skidded.

Several blissful moments passed until he reluctantly set her back from him, took her hand in his once again, and led her up the road to resume their walk, serenaded by the song of crickets, the hoots of owls, the distant warble of a whip-poor-will, and the gentle rustling of trees. It was a peaceful night and yet his heart wrestled within him. How would he ever say good-bye to Cristina?

In the middle of the road, he drew a stop and dropped her hand. His pulse pounded in his ears as he tried to arrange in his head the words that had to be said. "I...I have something to tell you. I don't know if this is the right time or place. Then again, I don't know if there ever will be a right time."

Worry lines etched her expression as she tilted her head to look at him. "What is it?"

"It's...it's about Orville."

She sucked in a loud breath. "What about 'im?"

"There's no easy way to say it."

She kept her gaze fixed just over his shoulder, her expression impassive. "I s'pose you should just say it, then—if it's somethin' y' feel y' must say."

He wondered then if perhaps she already sensed what he was about to tell her. Maybe she didn't want to know the truth. He waged a silent argument with himself over whether he should speak of it at all. If it turned out that she would rather not know the truth, could he keep it to himself for all time? Then again, could he live with himself, knowing he harbored such a secret? Somewhere deep in the dense woods, a mourning dove gave up its sad cry, giving voice to Jack's current emotional state.

"You once said you don't like to think about your husband's final breaths because it hurts too much."

"I prob'ly said somethin' like that."

"Do you recall the details I relayed to you about his...passing?"

Her eyebrows rose in inquiry. She scratched her temple, then shifted her gaze to the ground. "I...well, from what I recall, you said you came upon him just as he was breathin' his last—after he'd been shot, that is, and you bent over him t' hear his final words. He told you he had a letter in his pocket intended fer his wife. He asked that you deliver it since there was no one else t' ask." She raised her head. "How am I doin'?"

He didn't dare touch her for fear of her reaction to his next words. "Actually, I never said that I came upon him after he'd been shot. I...I think you sort of put those words in my mouth and I failed to correct you."

She frowned. "What do you mean?"

He took a deep breath. "I mean...I am the one who shot him, Cristina. He stepped into my line of fire. I shot him and watched him go down."

"What?" The single word came out as a whisper. An inexplicable look of withdrawal, even betrayal, washed across her beautiful face.

"I'm sorry, Cristina. I should have told you right from the beginning, but I was afraid you'd finish me off. After that first encounter, I just couldn't find the right time to tell you."

She backed away from him, her dark eyes glittering with anger—or even hatred? He couldn't quite tell the difference, especially with the moon and stars overhead as their only light.

"I'm sorry," he said again. "Say something, would you?"

"What is there t' say? You deceived me."

"I didn't deceive you. I meant to tell you all along, I just—"

"You could've told me earlier, before I...before I...."

"Before you what? Fell in love with me?"

"No! I don't love you—an' I never will." She abruptly spun on her heel and started walking briskly back toward the house.

"Cristina! Cristina, listen to me, please." He hurried after her, quickly overtaking her with his long strides.

She stopped and faced him but wouldn't meet his eyes. "There's nothin' more t' say. You killed my husband. I can't look at you knowin' that. It changes everything."

"It doesn't have to, Cristina. We can work through this."

"Maybe you can, but I can't." She hurried off again and didn't slow her pace until she came within steps of her front porch, where she stopped again and turned. In the moonlight, her face showed obvious anger and a hint of loathing; mostly, though, he read pain, twisted and smoldering. Tears pooled in the corners of her eyes. "I think we should say good-bye right here an' now."

"What? But...I was going to finish a few projects for you tomorrow."

She gave her head a violent shake. "There isn't another thing I need or want from you."

"I can't leave without at least saying good-bye to your children."

"I'll have some breakfast ready fer you in the mornin'. You can say yer good-byes then."

"Cristina, don't do this. Please. Orville wanted to die. You said yourself you understood as much from his letter. He had his rifle aimed right at me and then he turned it aside at the last second, just before I thought it was either shoot him or die. Why does it matter so much that he stepped into my fire rather than another soldier's?"

"It does, that's all. I can't continue somethin' with you, knowin' it was you who ended my husband's life. I just…I just couldn't. And that's all there is to it."

He reached out and touched her bare arm just above her wrist.

She recoiled. "Don't. Good night, Jack. There's nothin' more t' say."

"You're wrong, Cristina. There is a lot more to say. Please, won't you reconsider and hear me out? We've known all along that I would have to leave, but I don't want my departure to be filled with bitterness and ill feelings."

She pivoted on her heel and climbed the steps. Putting her hand to the door latch, she turned slightly, only far enough to show the side of her face. "It is unfortunate that things had t' end like this, but it's fer the best."

"It's not for—"

"Good night, Jack." She disappeared into the house, locking the door with a loud click.

25

Cristina abruptly sat up from a fitful sleep and stared across the dark cabin. Something had awakened her, though she knew not what—unless it was just her aching heart. Despite her new mattress and her exhausted body, she simply couldn't get Jack off her mind. She slowly lay back down and stared at the ceiling. Before drifting off, she'd tossed one way and turned another, mulling over recent events—everything from the fun the four of them had had in the water to all that Jack had so selflessly accomplished for her on the farm to the kisses they'd shared after the children went to bed...and then to the fateful admission he'd made concerning Orville.

She hated the way they'd left things. It was foolish, perhaps even childish, of her to react in so harsh a manner. Even though it sickened her to think that he had been the one to shoot Orville, if she were completely honest with herself, she would have to admit her own suspicions along those lines, even though she'd never dwelled on them. Could she ever love Jack without always remembering what he had done to her first husband? Would she ever be able to put that awful truth behind her and move forward? She lay there pondering these questions and also thinking about some of the Bible passages she'd read of late—lessons about love and forgiveness.

She finally determined that, yes, with God's help, she could move forward. Need she share with her children that Jack had been the one to kill their father? Certainly not right now, if ever. What possible good could come from their knowing? She understood now why Jack had told her though: he didn't want the secret hanging over his head. He knew that if he didn't get it out in the open sooner than later, the knowledge could easily haunt him for years, maybe even forever. He'd *had* to tell her and that made sense to her, now that she thought about it. She made up her mind that when he came in for breakfast, she would settle matters with him and tell him that he need not rush off on her account. In fact, the very notion of sneaking a few more delightful kisses before he departed excited her.

Just as the day was dawning, there came an unfamiliar noise from outside—footsteps? Horses' hooves? Stray animals intent on getting at her chickens? She reached for the rifle lying next to her and quietly slid out of bed, being careful not to tread on the trundle bed where Catherina slept. With her bare feet firmly planted on the floor, she glanced overhead in the direction of the loft, where Elias slept, and hoped he would stay that way. Crouching low, she crept to the front window and silently pulled back the curtain to peer out. She saw nothing but heard the distinct neigh of a horse. Had Jack decided to saddle up Starlight to visit the Army camp outside Ripley, with plans of returning him before hiking back to his unit?

Another neigh sounded, different from the first, giving the impression that there was more than one horse. Cristina tiptoed to the side window next, peering out with care and feeling grateful to Jack for repairing the locks on both the front and back doors the previous day. Her heart pumped a little harder, but she ordered herself not to panic. After all, Jack was just out back in the barn. Any imminent danger would have a hard time catching him by surprise, considering his keen instincts and his training.

She raised her head just a tad for another look outside. Still, nothing seemed amiss. Had Starlight or Thunder escaped the fence? She supposed it was possible Jack had failed to secure one section in his repair work yesterday. Leaving that window, she crept to the third and final window, to the left of the fireplace and beside the back door. No sooner had she lifted one corner of the curtain than she saw movement out by the barn. In the light of the rising sun, she made out several men on horseback, perhaps four or five, all facing the barn. One soldier occupied the driver's seat of a large open wagon. What in tarnation did they have in mind? Her pulse leaped with alarm, but she tightened her hold on her weapon, then quietly unlocked her door and opened it, wincing at the slight squeak the hinges made. No one appeared to have noticed, so she stepped out into the chill of the morning air, realizing then that she wore nothing but her long, tattered nightgown. How she wished she'd thought to don her robe. *Lord, give me courage and boldness,* came her silent prayer. *Keep my children safe. Guide me. Give me wisdom.* She could only hope God regarded her plea.

"Jack Fuller!" shouted one of the men. "We know you're in there. This is the United States Army. We demand that you come out unarmed, with your hands up."

Cristina's heart drummed hard as she stepped down from the wooden landing to the cool earth, then raised her rifle, resting its butt in the small of her shoulder. "What d' you think you're doin' on my property?" Her voice echoed in the still air, startling the horses into an uneasy prance.

One of the men looked over his shoulder. "Go back inside, ma'am!" he shouted. "We mean you no harm. We're here for one reason only and that's to apprehend Jack Fuller, who deserted his unit. Word has it he's hiding out here in your barn."

"I'm not hiding out." Jack emerged from the barn, hands on his head. "I'm Lieutenant Jack Fuller of the Forty-Fifth Ohio Infantry."

All the men on horseback had their rifles trained on him.

"Jack!" Cristina called, her own rifle aimed and cocked as she moved toward the barn. "What's happenin'?"

"Cristina, put the gun down," he instructed her. "These men are here to take me back to my unit."

"No, we're here to arrest you," another man said. "You do know desertion is punishable by death, don't you?"

"He didn't desert!" Cristina shouted. "I shot 'im and he had to stay here till he healed. He was gettin' ready to hike back to 'is unit t'day or t'morrow."

One soldier turned his horse around and approached her. "You shot him, did you? Maybe we ought to haul you off, too." He gave a hearty laugh, making Cristina's insides churn. "Don't matter. We heard otherwise. Got notice from the unit stationed right here in Ripley of a deserter in their midst, hidin' here in yer barn." He pushed his cap back and scanned her from top to bottom. "If I had you lookin' out for me, I might consider desertin' myself." Another cackle came out of him.

She aimed her rifle higher, with the fellow's chest in her sights. "You're on private property, soldier. I shot one man already and it wouldn't bother me one bit t' do it again." It was a giant fib, but she hoped it would work.

"Cristina, put down your weapon," Jack called out. "And you leave her alone, soldier, or I'll have you court-martialed."

The man on horseback laughed, keeping his gaze on Cristina. "Now, that's funny, ain't it? He'll have *me* court-martialed?" He looked over his shoulder at Jack. "You're the one bein' court-martialed, mister." He turned his horse then and left Cristina standing there, her mouth agape. "We ain't got time to mess with yer pretty little lady anyway. We came here fer one purpose only and that was t' retrieve you, Lieutenant Fuller. 'Course after today, you'll be stripped o' yer rank. You know that, right?"

"Didn't you hear what I said?" Cristina cried. "I shot 'im. He's been laid up for weeks."

"We'll leave that to the courts to decide."

"Jack, tell 'em!" she pleaded, marching across the yard with abandon. "Show 'em yer wound."

"We ain't interested in seein' no wound," the soldier insisted. "We were ordered t' deliver this no-good deserter to the authorities and that's just what we intend t' do. Now, you get yerself back inside the house and mind yer business."

She ignored his directive and stood there staring at the proceedings as two of the men dismounted and violently drew Jack's arms around behind him, fastening them securely at the wrists. Next, they shackled his ankles as if he were some kind of murderous criminal. Tears streamed down Cristina's cheeks as they gave Jack a hard shove toward the back of the hay wagon. Somehow, despite his bound ankles, he managed, with help, to climb to the back of the wagon, a gun barrel poked at his head the whole time. One of the soldiers gave him another push, nearly knocking him over, but Jack maintained his balance and slid to one side of the wagon, leaning back against the metal rail. "Listen, Cristina," he called. "Send a wire to my brother Captain Joseph Fuller of the Ohio Twenty-Seventh Infantry. Tell him I've been taken prisoner. He'll know what to do."

She bit her lip and gave a silent nod, powerless to do anything else. At last, she lowered her rifle, knowing it did no good when faced with five armed soldiers. They didn't want her; they wanted Jack, and nothing would deter them from their mission—no words, no weapon, and no tantrum on her part.

"Maw? What's goin' on?" Elias shouted from the back door.

"Get back inside," Cristina and Jack yelled in unison.

Instead of retreating, Elias raced to his mother's side and gawked at her, at Jack, and then at all the soldiers on horseback. "What d' you dumb Yanks think you're doin'?" he wailed without a hint of fear in his tone. "Where you takin' 'im? You got no business. He didn't do nothin' t' you."

"Shut up, kid, and do what you was told," growled one of the soldiers. "Get back inside."

Cristina put an arm around Elias and drew him to her side. He fought to loose himself, but she held tight. "Elias, shh. Don't say anything more," she murmured in his ear. "It'll only make matters worse."

"They can't do this," he whined, still trying to wrangle out of her grip.

"They can and they will," Jack answered calmly. "You stay strong, Elias, and do what your mother says. Take good care of Catherina and set a fine example for her." He turned pleading eyes on Cristina, "Keep reading your Bible and ask God to guide you. He will. He'll never fail you or forsake you. He loves you." She thought she saw him mouth the words, *And so do I.* She put her hand to her heart.

"Is the prisoner secured?" asked the fellow holding the reins.

"Yes, sir!" someone answered. "He'll be hangin' 'fore nightfall."

Cristina gasped. "No!" she yowled. "Jack!"

The soldiers paid her no mind, just turned their horses and headed toward the road, their backs straight, their gazes determined.

"Jack!" Cristina wailed as she and Elias ran alongside the wagon. Jack tried to say something, but one of the soldiers stuck his rifle butt to his mouth and stopped him.

When they reached the road, the driver turned the team toward town and with a loud "Giddy-up," the two horses set off at a gallop. Elias and Cristina stood and watched, despairing, until the wagon was out of sight.

Clive's grin filled his whole face as he watched the Army haul away that no-good lieutenant. He was especially cheered by the prediction that Fuller would be hanged before nightfall. Maybe the group of them would handle the deed themselves before ever reaching the lieutenant's unit. It wasn't unheard of for vigilantes to take matters into their own hands, especially when they went to battle day and night, risking life and limb, only to come across a coward who had deserted. While he doubted Fuller was that type of man, Clive congratulated himself for having gotten him off the farm belonging to that little Mexican she-devil. *My, what a spitfire she was, aiming her rifle at them!* He'd best wait a few days before he moved in on her, so he could catch her when she'd calmed down and was unawares. Clive needed was his stash, but he couldn't get to it unless he brought her with him. She would serve as his shield just in case someone recognized him from the restaurant robbery.

Stewing with impatience yet satisfied that his plan to get rid of Fuller had worked, Clive headed back to his hiding spot, where he could pay Raisin and get back his ring. He would spend the rest of the day in his cave with a bottle of whiskey for company.

26

ack had heard the soldiers arrive that morning and his immediate thought had been that they belonged to his own unit and had finally determined his location. He'd even breathed a sigh of relief that he wouldn't have to walk back. Now, not even an hour later, Jack's head spun with all manner of questions as he jounced along in the wagon, whose driver seemed bent on hitting every pothole he could find on their journey north. Who had reported his whereabouts to the Army and why? It had to have been someone from town, but he knew hardly a soul in Ripley. There was Clara, yet he doubted she would have uttered a word about his presence. She cared too much for Cristina to take that kind of risk—unless she'd suspected he meant trouble. But Jack had never sensed she was wary of him. No, it couldn't have been Clara. Then, there was the man he'd met in the restaurant the day before he went to visit Cristina—Harold something—but how could Harold have known that Jack had been shot and was laid up at Cristina's house? The only other people who knew of his presence were the Reverend Wilcox and his wife and he just couldn't believe either of them would declare him a defector.

On top of his mental anguish as he sorted through this list, his physical discomfort became excruciating. His back, neck, and arms ached because of his awkward way of sitting against the wagon rail, with his wrists and ankles still shackled. Even his wound, which had healed almost completely, now felt tender to the touch; if he happened to shift a certain way, pain shot through his side. Granted, he'd been feeling sore prior to getting picked up, probably due to all the work he'd done the previous day around Cristina's property.

He tried shifting his position, to no avail. Those soldiers had him tied up tight as a drum head. No way would he be breaking loose. All he could do was pray that as soon as he arrived at camp—or wherever it was they intended to take him—he would manage to contact Major Marsh and get this whole matter settled and behind him. Surely, the major would see to it things returned to normal in short order. Either he would reassign Jack to his prior company so he could resume his former duties, or he would relieve him of that duty and grant him permission to return to Ripley. Whatever the case, Jack reached a point of relinquishing everything into the Lord's hands, knowing God had his best interests in mind.

During the journey, the group stopped once by a stream for a drink of water and a snack, neither of which was offered to Jack. His throat was parched, but he was not about to complain, thinking it better to remain quiet than to create a stir. He didn't know these men, to what regiment they belonged, or under what jurisdiction they had picked him up. So he sat in silence, praying God would give him strength to endure whatever lay ahead—and that he would be spared execution.

It was several uncomfortable hours later that they stopped at a place entirely unfamiliar to Jack and the men dismounted. One of them approached the wagon. "All right, soldier. Come on down. The major's on his way."

Jack tried to conceal his sigh of relief. When Major Marsh showed up, he would order someone to untie Jack immediately. He struggled to bring himself to his feet with his hands still bound behind him. His knees had gone numb, so he wobbled as he tried to walk. Thankfully, the soldier was considerate enough to take him by the arm and help him down to the ground. The others from the group paid him no mind;

some of them started rolling cigarettes or stretching. A few soldiers from the camp wandered over to the wagon to have a look at Jack, but no one spoke a word of greeting. Jack recognized no one.

"Where exactly are we?" he asked the soldier who'd helped him.

"Meigs County, Ohio. You don't recognize it, do y'?"

"No, I don't recognize it—or see anyone from my unit."

"That's 'cause yer company moved on, mister," said one of the other soldiers who'd wandered over.

"My company moved on? Where? And why wasn't I delivered to them? I'm a lieutenant. I have my own squadron."

"Not no more, you don't," said another. "You're headed fer prison camp, last I heard."

"What?" Jack's head hammered in much the same way as it had when he lay suffering with fever due to his gunshot wound. "Where is Major Marsh? I need to speak with him."

One of the soldiers who'd participated in Jack's transport gave a hearty chuckle. "Don't think you'll be seein' him anytime soon."

Jack winced from his headache, which had mostly settled in his temples. What he wouldn't give to get these shackles off his ankles and wrists. "Why do you say that?"

"You'll find out soon enough."

"Can someone tell me where my regiment went?" He waited, but received only blank stares. "Anybody?"

"Heard they moved up north," someone finally offered. "But I couldn't tell y' where exactly. That's privileged information since you defected."

"You ain't got no rights anyway, mister." This from the one who'd first come upon him that morning in the barn and hauled him off to the wagon.

"Once again, I am not a deserter," Jack maintained.

One of the soldiers removed his hat and scratched his greasy head. He stuck his hat back on, then looked Jack in the eye. "Well, you'll have t' tell that t' someone other than Major Marsh, I'm afraid. Yer regiment moved on, without yer major."

Jack shook his head. "Without my…? What exactly are you saying?"

"Your Major Marsh keeled over of a heart attack several weeks back. Talk was, he died the very day you defected."

"What?" Jack bellowed. His thoughts went fuzzy on him as he tried to piece together this new information. "Dead? Are you sure? I mean, he seemed absolutely fine when I last saw him." He did seem to recall, however, suggesting to the major that he start thinking about retiring. The man had looked particularly old that day, even a bit haggard. Jack swallowed down a burning lump that threatened to choke him. "He was going to talk to Captain Timmer about assuming responsibility for my company until I returned. I'd planned to be gone only a couple of days."

The soldier chuckled. "Think yer plan fell through, mister. Last I heard, no one knew where you'd gone. Anyway, we got the message that you'd defected—came in a letter, with precise details of where t' look— so the major sent a group of us t' bring you in."

"Who sent the letter?"

"No idea. You'll have t' ask Major Freeland."

"Major Freeland?"

"He should be here any minute. You can save yer breath on us. We ain't yer judge an' jury. We're just the ones who brought y' back and it's been a mighty fine day fer us, if I do say so—sunny, pleasant, no fightin' amongst us. Shoot, we didn't even get a struggle outta you. We'll be sure to pass that tidbit along to the major if y' think it'll help yer case." The soldier slapped the shoulder of the fellow next to him. "Or maybe not." Then the entire group burst into raucous laughter.

The only one who didn't laugh, besides Jack, was the young man who'd helped him down from the wagon and now stood next to him, a firm grip on his arm—as if Jack planned to escape with shackles on.

"Let's go, fellas," the pettifogger said soberly. "Major'll be here soon. Don't know what's keepin' 'im. The rest o' you fellas, head back t' yer stations. Show's over." Then, to the man holding Jack's arm, he said, "Private, you stay with the prisoner."

"Yes, Lieutenant Yost, sir." He saluted his superior, as the foursome moved off toward the center of camp, along with any bystanders.

The private showed Jack to a shade tree with a simple nod of his head and a gentle tug on Jack's arm.

"So, that's Lieutenant Yost, is it?" Jack asked.

"Yes, sir."

Jack shook his head. "Is it really true about Major Marsh? He's really dead?"

"Yes, sir, he is."

"That's too bad. No wonder they assumed I'd deserted. The major probably didn't have a chance to inform Captain Timmer about my planned absence. I did tell one fellow I was heading out. He fixed me some eggs the morning I set off for Ripley, but I don't think I told him where I was going or why. I wonder if he told anyone that he'd seen me that morning."

"I wouldn't know, sir."

Jack looked at the young man and smiled. "Of course, you wouldn't. I'm more or less talking to myself, I suppose. What's your name, by the way?"

"Grayson Novak, sir. They call me Gray."

"Grayson Novak. Sounds like a good, solid name. Where do you hail from, Private?"

"Perrysburg, Ohio, sir."

"You can call me Jack—that is, if you have a mind to."

"Oh, no, I couldn't do that, you bein' a lieutenant an' all."

"Well, I thank you for the show of respect, but I'm just an ordinary fellow. Seems I'm a little less than ordinary right now, though, since folks believe I defected. I didn't though, in case you're wondering. I went to deliver a message to a woman whose husband, a Confederate soldier, had died on the battlefield. When I showed up at this woman's home, she felt threatened and shot me in the side. Then she took me in to tend to my injury, which, thank God, wasn't that serious. But I developed an infection and then a chronic cough, which laid me up for some time. I intended on starting the return trek to camp this very morning."

Private Novak stiffened, seeming uncomfortable. "It's probably not proper fer you t' be tellin' me all this. They just told me to wait here with you till the major arrived."

"Please don't let it concern you. I fully understand and wouldn't want to get you into trouble. Just so you know, it probably wasn't proper of your lieutenant to leave you with me either. What you're doing now, guarding a prisoner, is not a job for a private."

Private Novak took a quick, suspicious up-and-down glance at Jack.

"No need to worry though," Jack assured him. "I'm not going to try any funny business. I just thought I'd inform you of the proper protocol and let you know your lieutenant didn't follow it today."

The young man gave a sober nod. "They always give me the grunt jobs. Not that you're a grunt job, sir," he quickly added.

Jack laughed in spite of the uncommon heat and his utter discomfort. He needed these shackles off so he could move about, but he wouldn't put that burden on the young private. "You hail from Perrysburg, huh? I'm familiar with the area, being from Ohio myself. You seem like a decent, upstanding young man."

"Thank you, sir. I do my best t' serve my country well."

Their conversation ceased at the sounds of gunfire, the start of an afternoon drill. Jack thought about Cristina and the argument they'd had the previous night. How he wished he could have had one more chance this morning to talk to her about his feelings. He wanted to tell her that he deeply regretted having been the one to shoot Orville, that he'd taken no pleasure whatsoever in shooting him, and that Orville had been the first Rebel he'd shot—at least face-to-face. The image still haunted him and he wanted Cristina to know that. The first chance he got, whether he was in a prison somewhere or had been released to his unit, he would write her a letter and try to explain himself.

Finally, a stout man with a full dark beard and dark hair graying at the temples approached the pair.

Private Novak straightened, clicked his boots together, and, with his free hand, saluted the man. "Major Freeland, sir."

Major Freeland acknowledged the private with a dismissive nod. "At ease, Novak. So this is our prisoner, is it?" His eyes scanned Jack from his boots to his hat. "You don't look none the worse for the wear.

Glad the information we received didn't lead our boys on some pointless chase. How long ago did you defect?"

"Sir, I'm Lieutenant Jack Fuller from the Ohio Forty-Fifth Infantry. I did not desert. I left my infantry on or about July twentieth or twenty-first. I'm sorry I don't recall the exact date. I had to deliver a letter to a Confederate soldier's widow at the urgent request of the dying soldier. The woman shot me when I came on her property, thinking I meant her harm. She'd been attacked some five weeks prior by some renegade Federals, so her trust level was exceedingly low. She shot me in the side. If you'd untie my wrists, I could show you the wound."

The major appeared only mildly interested in Jack's explanation. He nodded to Private Novak, who immediately went to work untying the securely knotted rope. It took some time, but Jack finally moved his aching arms in front of his body and wiggled his fingers to get the blood flowing again. Then he lifted his shirt and turned his body so that the healing wound was visible to the men.

"Humph," the major grunted.

"I developed an infection and then a bad cough that may have been the start of pneumonia. The town of Ripley didn't have a doctor available—not an able-bodied one, anyway."

Major Freeland frowned. "So what you're saying, then, is that no one really knew you were hiding out there."

"I was not hiding out, sir. I was laid up. And Major Marsh gave me leave to deliver the letter."

"And who was it that nursed you back to health?"

"The widow...um, Mrs. Stiles." He read suspicion in the major's eyes. "And an older lady who came almost every day to oversee my care. She was the one primarily responsible for treating my wound and subsequent illness."

The major nodded, not so much in agreement as with wariness. "I see. And is this...this Mrs. Stiles, the recent widow—is she a sight for sore eyes?"

"Pardon me, sir?"

The major tilted his pudgy face at him, a curious twinkle in his eye. "You know what I'm getting at, Fuller. Did you develop an affection for her?"

Red-hot ire rose in Jack's chest. "What does that have to do with anything? I didn't even know this woman before her dying husband implored me to deliver a letter to her, one he'd written some time before he died."

"Hm, is that so? Let me see that wound again."

Annoyed, Jack lifted his shirt once more.

"How do I know that's not self-inflicted?"

Jack bit back every curse word he'd ever thought—as well as a few he'd even been guilty of uttering a time or two—and inwardly prayed for divine strength. "Sir, the bullet went in the front and out the back. Thank the Lord it didn't hit any of my organs. Even so, I was in pretty bad shape. They say some of my guts were sticking out."

"Hmm. Whatever happened, I can't just take your word for it," the major said. "Novak, take him to the prison tent and stand guard outside with your rifle cocked. I'll send several other men to stand guard with you." Then, to a stunned Jack, he said, "In the tent you'll find a pitcher o' fresh water, a cot to lie on, and some hardtack and a few other items for your nourishment." The major turned to leave.

"Wait!" Jack protested, stopping him. "You're actually putting me in jail?"

The major gave him a grin that held not even an ounce of mercy. "We don't take kindly to deserters. You oughtta know that. Whether you hang by sundown tomorrow is yet to be determined. Or maybe you'll simply be shot instead."

Jack could barely believe his ears. "You know what President Lincoln would say! He is highly opposed to the killing of deserters."

"Ah, so you're admitting you *did* desert."

"I'm admitting no such thing!" Clearly, Jack couldn't possibly stay one step ahead of the major. The man had already made up his mind about him.

"Bind him again, Novak."

"His hands, sir?" the private asked, a slight wobble in his tone.

"No, his hair. Of course, his hands."

"Just how am I supposed to feed myself, Major? Or take care of… certain necessities?" Jack had needed to relieve himself for some time now.

The major huffed. "Tie his hands in front of him. Keep his feet shackled as they are, a good eighteen inches apart." The major stood there watching as Novak retied Jack's hands. "Now see that those feet are still shackled securely." Again, he stood watching while the private followed orders. "Good, good. Now take him to the prison tent. I'll get some other fellows over there shortly." At that, he turned again and set off toward the center of camp, soon slipping out of view behind a tent.

Shocked by what had just transpired, Jack could do little but move along with the private to the prison tent. Jaw-dropping disbelief raced like wildfire through Jack's mind. How had he fallen into such a predicament in so short a time? He'd only told the truth and where had it gotten him? In jail, of all places. He said nothing as he trudged through dirt and brush on his way to the so-called prison tent. "I'm sorry, sir. This don't seem right," whispered the private. "Just so you know, I do believe you."

"Thank you, Private. That's something anyway. I don't want to get you into trouble though, so I wouldn't go talking to any of your comrades about my situation. I don't want any of them accusing you of taking sides with me. It could mean big trouble for you. You understand what I'm saying?"

"Yes, sir. Call me Gray if you like."

Jack managed a tiny laugh. "All right. But you call me Jack."

"Oh, no, sir. I couldn't, sir."

Jack grinned at the boy as they walked. Gray couldn't be more than seventeen or eighteen.

With his head, Gray motioned to the right. "This way, sir. The green army tent straight ahead."

Jack chuckled wryly. "Can't very well miss the big letters 'J-A-I-L,' now, can we?"

Private Novak led him inside the crude structure. Jack turned to Gray. "I'll be a model prisoner, Gray. No worries there. With God's help, this trial will work out for the good."

"You believe in God, then?"

"Indeed, I do. How about yourself?"

"Oh, yes, sir. I gave my heart to Jesus when I was knee high."

"Well now, that makes us Christian brothers, doesn't it?" Jack smiled as he surveyed the interior of the tent.

The private cleared his throat. "Uh, in case y' have need o' relievin' yerself, sir, there's a pot with a lid over in that corner," he said with a nod.

Jack smiled again. "I appreciate that. You must've read my mind. Oh, and I wonder if you could do me a favor, Private—that is, as long as it won't get you into trouble. Once the other soldiers arrive for guard duty, would you mind getting me a fountain pen and some paper so I can mail a couple of letters?"

"I don't see why y' shouldn't have that right, sir. I'll do my best to get those to you and I'll even take care o' the postage."

"Thank you, Private. You're a fine soldier. And if I might ask one more thing...?"

"Yes, sir. What might that be, sir?"

"Could you try to find me a Bible? I gave mine to someone else."

Gray brightened. "I have one I can give you. Fact is, I carry three Bibles with me at all times, sir, for just such occasions. When I give one away, I find another somewheres else."

"Really? Well, now I think even more highly of you than I did a few minutes ago. I thank you kindly."

Once the young man stepped outside, Jack quickly used the chamber pot. Then he dove straight for the water pitcher and rather than pick it up and pour some into the tin cup provided, he brought the spout straight to his mouth and gulped down almost half the contents. Next, he took a few nibbles of hardtack and chomped on a hard piece of dry meat. That got him to missing Cristina's fine meals and a wave of regret came over him. "Help me, Lord. I'm in a bit of a predicament, here." He set the pitcher down, shuffled over to the narrow cot, and laid himself down. In less than a minute, he fell asleep.

27

Cristina tried to stay busy, tried to keep the children occupied, tried to keep her mind on the present, but everything felt wrong. Catherina was cranky because she found out upon waking that Jack had left with nary a good-bye and Elias was livid because the Yanks had hauled him off for no reason.

"Actually, they think they had reason, Elias," Cristina explained. "They believe he deserted, so it was their duty t' treat 'im as a prisoner."

"What's 'deserted' mean?"

"It means they think he ran away from the army."

"But he didn't. He just came here bringin' that letter that Paw wrote y'."

"What letter?" Catherina interrupted between hiccupping sighs.

"You an' I both know he didn't desert, but apparently someone contacted the Army and gave 'em his name an' exact location, so they're treatin' 'im as someone who left active duty without permission."

"What's 'permission'?" Catherina asked.

"But you explained everything t' those men," said Elias.

"But that doesn't mean they believed me." Cristina's head pounded from all the stress and anxiety she felt.

"Where d' you think they took 'im?"

"I have no idea, honey, but I'm sure when his brother receives the wire we sent first thing this mornin' from the telegraph office, he'll get right t' work determinin' Jack's whereabouts."

"I hope his brother is as smart as Jack," Elias said, tearing off a piece of bread from the loaf Cristina had been preparing to slice and popping it in his mouth.

She picked up a knife and a large potato and started peeling it, not even knowing what she would do with it. All morning and again after the noon meal, it'd been question after question from her children and Cristina had no real answers for any of them. Now she had to figure out what to make for supper and she barely had the gumption for preparing it. That's why she didn't even reprimand Elias for ripping another piece of bread from the middle of the loaf. Earlier, she'd gone out to the springhouse for some dried meat and found several things missing. At least, she was pretty certain they were missing, unless she'd used them in a meal she couldn't recall. She finally chalked the whole thing up to Jack's having made her a fine little supper and Clara's having gone out there to retrieve some things when she'd been helping with meals and such while Jack had been so ill.

"I didn't think I'd ever like 'im," Elias said while noisily chewing the bread.

Cristina smiled. "And have you now decided you do?" In that moment, she chose to fry up some chopped potatoes, onions, and eggs, and serve them with hot biscuits and ham gravy. That should make for a suitable meal. All she needed to do was stoke the stove and take down the fry pan.

"He's not so bad after all. It's gonna feel strange without 'im here."

"Yes, well, we'll have to accustom ourselves to it, won't we? We've known all along that the day would come when he'd be leavin'. Matter o' fact, he was prepared t' leave today or t'morrow—before those Union soldiers came an' hauled 'im off."

"D' you think we'll ever see 'im again?" Elias asked, tearing off yet another piece of bread.

This time, Cristina did give his wrist a light slap. "No more. You'll spoil yer appetite." Then she huffed out a sigh. "I don't know if we'll see 'im again, Elias." In her heart, she desperately hoped so. In fact, early that morning, she'd shed tears in the outhouse, the only place she knew of where she could escape the children for a moment.

What a horrid good-bye it had been between her and Jack, especially after last night. Even now, just thinking about it made her eyes water. She quickly picked up an onion and started peeling it, so as to have an excuse if her tears started falling.

Outside, a horse's neigh and the squeak of wagon wheels alerted them to someone's arrival. Elias ran to the window and pulled back the curtain. "It's two ladies with flowery hats. The man that's drivin' 'em looks like the owner of the livery."

"What?" Cristina dropped her knife, hastened to neaten her mussed hair, and took a swipe at her perspiring face with the hem of her apron, which she then untied and draped over the back of a chair. My, but she must be a terrible sight for visitors.

"The livery man's helpin' the ladies down," Elias announced.

"Oh, my stars. How do I look, Elias?"

He turned from the window and gave her a hurried glance, then shrugged. "I don't know. Like my maw, I guess."

At all the excitement, Catherina leaped up from the floor where she'd been playing on the braided rug with two cloth dolls. "We don't never get company 'sides Miss Clara!"

"Both o' you, be on yer best behavior!" Cristina blurted out, just as a light knock sounded on the door.

"Should I open it?" Elias asked.

"No!" Cristina cleared her throat. "I'll do it. Step aside." Once the children had done as told, she placed her hand on the door latch.

"Open it, Mama!" cried Catherina.

"I will. Just—hush. Please." Her heart thudded with trepidation. Who could possibly be calling? She straightened her shoulders, put on the best smile she could muster, and, with forced calm, opened the door. Two middle-aged women—one rather short and plump, with rosy cheeks, the other, tall, slender, and refined-looking—greeted her with friendly smiles and slight curtseys. Never had anyone curtseyed to Cristina. She didn't know whether to return the gesture or simply speak a word of greeting.

She went for the latter. "Good afternoon. May I...help you?"

The two women glanced at each other, and the taller one nodded at the shorter, who looked back at Cristina with another smile. "Begging your pardon, ma'am. I'm Sarah Parsons and this is Alberta Burley. We attend Ripley Methodist Church and were recently informed of the loss of your beloved husband in the war. We've come to offer our condolences and to give you a little something, if you don't mind."

Mrs. Burley turned to the driver, who stood next to the buggy. "Mr. Garvey, would you mind bringing the covered dishes from the back compartment?"

With a nod, the gentleman retrieved two large covered dishes and carried them to the door.

Cristina could do little but stare at their offering.

"What's under that towel?" Catherina asked, peeking out from behind Cristina.

"Baked chicken and some cooked greens," said Mrs. Parsons.

"Guess you don't gotta cook supper after all, Maw," Elias said.

Cristina could hardly believe her eyes or ears. "But...I never expected...."

"Of course you didn't, dear," Mrs. Burley said with a tender tone. "But it would be quite negligent of us not to pay you a call. We have a few more items we'd like to offer you on behalf of our congregation—if you don't mind, that is. But first, would it be all right if Mr. Garvey stepped inside and laid these dishes on your table?"

"Oh! Yes, o' course. Here, let me clear a place. Please, come in. Excuse the mess an' my terribly cramped house. I'm afraid I'm not very well set up fer guests. Not that you're not welcome," she added hastily.

"That's very sweet of you, dear," said Mrs. Burley, as she and Mrs. Parsons stepped over the threshold after Mr. Garvey and glanced around.

"Why, this is a fine-looking cabin," Mrs. Parsons commented. "Did your husband build it?"

"No, he—his uncle passed it on t' him."

"Really? What was his uncle's name?" Mrs. Burley asked.

"Ned Stiles. Orville would sometimes mention Uncle Ned, though I don't think he knew him well. My husband grew up in Charleston and on his uncle's passin', the cabin went to him, some dozen or so years ago."

Mrs. Burley smiled broadly. "My living stars, I remember Ned Stiles. He was quite a bit older than me. An only child, if I remember right. His family pretty much kept to themselves. I've lived in Ripley all my life and have seen my share of families come and go from these parts. I'm sorry that I—*we*—never made an effort to call on you until now. I'm afraid we neglected our Christian duty. The reverend's sermons have been quite convicting of late. He's been challenging us to make a better effort to get to know folks about town and to be more mindful about extending a helping hand when the need calls for it. Which reminds me…Mr. Garvey, would you mind bringing in those other items?"

"Not at all, Mrs. Burley." Mr. Garvey turned and disappeared out the open door.

"Excuse my manners—please, won't you, um, have a seat?" Cristina rushed to remove her apron from the chair where she'd left it, then took to rumpling it into a ball in her hands. "I'm afraid I don't have a bountiful supply o' chairs fer visitin'. There is that rockin' chair over there, if you've a mind to sit in it."

Mrs. Parsons smiled. "Don't worry, dear. We have no intention of staying. Besides, you have supper waiting on you and we wouldn't want it getting cold before you have a chance to taste it."

"It does smell awful good," Cristina said.

Mr. Garvey returned, bearing two large baskets heaped with items.

"What on earth?" Cristina gasped.

"Mama, I see a doll's head peekin' outta there," squealed Catherina.

Elias's eyes were two big circles as he surveyed the baskets. They brimmed with building blocks, books, wooden puzzles, and other children's items. Cristina could only stand there with her mouth agape.

"I—I don't understand." Her hand went from her chest to her mouth and she knew she must look as white as a ghost, no matter that the sun had burned her cheeks yesterday when she'd forgotten to wear her hat in the garden.

Mr. Garvey set the baskets on the floor and grinned at Elias and Catherina. "This is for you youngins. You two go right ahead an' see what's inside." Then he turned to the ladies. "While they're doin' that, I'll go out an' get that other basket if y' want me to, Mrs. Burley."

Mrs. Burley nodded. "Please do that, Mr. Garvey. Thank you."

The children dug into the baskets with a frenzy, making oohing sounds and laughing with great joy.

Cristina finally found her voice. "I don't even know how to thank you ladies. You've gone far an' above what I ever imagined possible. Goodness, I didn't expect a visit, but now that you're here, I must say, I'm honored."

Mrs. Parsons beamed. "It's our pleasure. The reverend told us about the injured man staying out in your barn. Is he in need of anything?"

"Oh! No, he—he left early this morning."

"Ah, I see." Mrs. Burley nodded. "Well, I'm glad you were able to help him."

"It was the preacher's prayer fer healin' that made all the difference."

"He did mention that he'd come out to pray for him. Praise the Lord for His divine work."

Cristina hoped Elias wouldn't chime in about the soldiers who had come to take Jack away, but she needn't have worried, the way he and Catherina were diving into their baskets of goodies. She looked over and saw him studying a hand-carved wooden horse and wagon, complete with harness straps and reins.

"I never had a doll like this one!" Catherina exclaimed, holding up the china-faced figure for Cristina to see.

"Y' must be very careful with it, Catherina. That's a very special dolly and you'll want t' cherish it always."

Catherina brought the doll close to her chest, hugging and rocking it. "It's my best doll in the world, Mama. I like my other ones, too, 'cause you made them, but I like this one better."

Cristina laughed at her daughter's excitement. "I don't blame you, honey. Yer other ones are all made o' rags."

"Sometimes, those are the best kind," Mrs. Burley said.

"Look at 'er, Mama," said Catherina. "Ain't—isn't—she the prettiest thing you ever saw?"

"Absolutely, honey. The finest." The fabric alone on this particular doll had to have cost a fortune and Cristina couldn't help but wonder at the women's generosity. "Thank you again," Cristina told the pair, who were still standing, despite her invitation to take a seat.

Mr. Garvey reentered with another basket brimming with items. He set it on the floor in front of Cristina with a bit of a thud.

"What…is this?" Cristina asked.

"This, my dear, is for you," said Mrs. Parsons.

Seconds went by before Cristina remembered to breathe. She put her hand over her mouth to cover the gasp. This got Elias and Catherina's attention. They left their own baskets of goodies and gave hers their full attention. "Mama, you gots some presents, too. What's in there?" Catherina asked.

"Oh, my goodness. I—I don't know what to say."

Mrs. Parsons smiled. "You need not say anything, dear. Just have yourself a look. I hope these items will serve you well in your sweet little house. We tried to find things that every housekeeper should have on hand. I think you'll find a new lamp, a blanket, some wash towels, some bright new fabrics for stitching, and a few bars of Pears Soap."

Cristina's head shot up. "Pears Soap? But…that's so extravagant! I don't know how I can accept all these wonderful gifts."

Mrs. Burley patted her arm. "It's our pleasure to give them to you, my dear. Why, you've lived out here for years and I don't think we ever met before. And that's a pity."

"Well, I do pretty much stick to myself. My kids an' me, that is."

The women exchanged a quick glance. Mrs. Parsons cleared her throat. "We'd be much obliged if you'd accept one more thing."

"One more thing? Oh, but I—"

"Yes, one more thing," Mrs. Burley insisted. "We'd be obliged if you'd accept our invitation to church tomorrow morning."

"Let's go!" Elias exclaimed.

Cristina gave her children a hasty glance and then, without further thought, nodded with a smile. "We'd like that very much. Thank you fer the invitation."

Both ladies clapped their hands daintily, as if they'd just won a large cash prize. Cristina laughed at their enthusiasm, then sobered. "I've never been t' church, y' know. Orville wasn't much for it an' I wasn't raised t' go to church, so...."

Mrs. Parsons shook her head. "No need for explanations, dear. You just show up at ten o'clock and we will be there at the door to usher you inside. Sunday school comes first, followed by the church service at eleven. Your children will adore Sunday school. Your boy, especially, will enjoy seeing some of his school friends, I'm sure."

"I don't goes to school yet, but I will soon, won't I, Mama?" Catherina said.

Cristina rested her hand on her daughter's shoulder. "Yes, dear, in a few short weeks, you'll be goin' t' school fer the very first time."

"But I don't know no kids yet," she said, drawing close to Cristina's skirts.

Mrs. Burley leaned down slightly and patted Catherina gently on the head. "After tomorrow, you will have some new friends. How will that be?"

Catherina brightened and bobbed her head up and down.

Mrs. Parsons cleared her throat. "Well, we should be on our way. I see Mr. Garvey has already retreated to the wagon. It has been a pleasure meeting you, Mrs. Stiles."

"Likewise," said Cristina. "Please, call me Cristina. I don't know how t' thank you fer...everything. I can't remember the last time anyone showered us with gifts. I think perhaps it's—"

"Never!" said Elias. "We haven't never had anyone give us nothin'."

Cristina cringed at his speech but quickly reminded herself that her own was nothing to brag about. She walked the ladies to the door. "Thank you, again. I'm much obliged fer your kindness. And thank you again fer the invitation t' church. We look forward to comin'."

Both ladies beamed.

Cristina turned to her children to remind them of their manners, but they beat her to it.

"Thank you for the presents," said Elias without any prompting.

"Yes, thank you," echoed Catherina.

The ladies nodded, the pretty feathers in their hats swaying.

"Oh!" Cristina touched her head. "I don't own a nice hat. What do I wear t' church?"

"Not to worry, my dear," Mrs. Parsons assured her. "Some of the local farmers come into church smelling like hogs, but do we turn them away? Of course not. You just dress yourselves any old way you choose and you'll fit in just fine."

Cristina couldn't help the relieved giggle that came out of her. "Well then, we'll see you in the mornin'." She waved good-bye to Mr. Garvey, who returned the gesture before helping the ladies into the wagon, their fine skirts flaring as they stepped onboard.

Good gravy! Cristina didn't own a single fancy petticoat. The nicest dress she had was her red and white gingham. That would have to do. Perhaps she would put her hair up, if she could find that fancy comb she'd brought from California. The more she thought about it, the more excited she became. As for her children, Elias had one pair of good trousers that were getting a bit too short. She could take the hem out of those tonight. And, last she looked, he had one clean shirt. That should do. Catherina would be fine; she'd look pretty in anything. Cristina gave Elias a thorough looking over. "Oh, my gracious, Elias Eduardo, you're in desperate need of a haircut. Why didn't I notice that earlier?"

He looked up and frowned. "Is this what goin' t' church is like? Dressin' up an' tryin' t' look like somethin' we ain't—*aren't?*"

"No, it's about showin' some respect and takin' a bit o' pride in our appearance. I'll get the scissors. Go sit at the table."

"But I'm hungry," Catherina whined. "I thought we was gonna eat what them ladies brought."

Cristina tsked. "I'm sorry—you're right, of course. We'll eat first. Then we'll cut yer hair, Elias. Looks like we've got a busy night ahead of us!"

"I wish Jack was here so's he could go t' church, too," Elias mused.

A lump of sudden sadness lodged in Cristina's chest at the unexpected reminder. "I wish the same thing, Elias."

"Maybe he'll come back someday."

She eyed her son. "Would y' really want 'im to?"

He looked off toward the front window for a few moments. Then he gave a slow nod. "I ended up likin' 'im. He did save my life, after all."

"That's quite a claim," Cristina remarked. "Your snakebite wasn't poisonous, remember?"

"Yeah, but that's when I started thinkin' he wasn't so bad."

She smiled and ruffled his hair. She dared not admit to her children her own feelings for Jack. She'd only just started admitting them to herself.

⌒

Clive watched from the barn window as the visitors drove away. He was of a mind to sneak up to the house and peer in the window just to see what was in those baskets that'd been carried in, but if that pretty lil' hellcat was still on edge.... Naw, he shouldn't risk it. But he *would* get a good night's sleep in the hayloft now that Fuller was gone. With any luck, that bootlickin' lieutenant would be hanging from a tree before dawn. Clive hoped so anyway. The Army didn't look kindly on deserters. Which meant that if Clive wanted to save his own hide, he had to make plans for escaping this Podunk town—and soon. Maybe he would head for Texas, like he'd told Raisin. He could pretend to be a Confederate. The Union would never find him. But first and foremost, he had to get to his hidden stash. That's where that lil' Mexican gal entered the picture. She would obey him, too, if she valued those two little rapscallions of hers.

28

The morning dragged on with no news from Major Freeland. Jack had at least eaten some breakfast, if one could call it that—some hardtack, a soft apple, two stale pieces of bread, and a mug of murky, tepid coffee. He'd gobbled it all down after listening to his stomach growl off and on through the night. After mostly unsuccessful attempts to sleep, he'd fallen into a peaceful slumber toward dawn as, one by one, he'd handed over each heartrending worry to God. How was he going to get out of this "jail"? Would Major Freeland dare hang him? Had Cristina managed to send a telegraph to his brother? Did Ripley even have a telegraph office? What had gone through her mind, and Elias's, as they watched the Union soldiers haul him off in shackles like some common criminal? All these questions had bombarded him until he at last determined that worrying would get him nowhere. God had all the answers, he knew, so he'd relinquished each concern into His capable hands and then slept until an unfamiliar soldier woke him. "Here's some grub," he said gruffly before walking out.

Around his tent stood at least a dozen men, all holding rifles at their sides. What did they think him capable of doing? He had no weapon and he hadn't even tried to untie his shackles, never mind that he could probably do it with little effort if he set his mind to it. He'd be dead in less than a second if he tried to escape. So far, he hadn't heard one word of pity for his plight and he hadn't seen Private Novak since last night, when the young man had given him a Bible and exactly four pieces of paper, along with a fountain pen. The private had sheepishly explained that Major Freeland, thinking he'd detected a hint of empathy from him for the prisoner, had assigned him to dig trenches on the morrow. "I guess I can't come by after t'night," he'd whispered out of earshot of two soldiers nearby who were exchanging lighthearted banter and paying no attention to the private.

"That's fine, Gray," Jack had whispered in return. "You take care of yourself and obey your commander. Thanks again for the writing supplies. I'll figure out another way to mail any letters I might write."

Gray had shrugged. "Sorry."

"No, enough of that."

"Hey!" one of the other soldiers had yelled. "What're you doin' talkin' to the prisoner anyway? You want me t' report you to the major?"

"No, I wasn't— I—"

"He brought me a Bible at my request." Jack had held up the leather-bound book. "That's all."

"Oh. Well, get on yer way, Private. This prisoner ain't yer concern."

"Yes, sir. I'm goin', sir." He'd given Jack one final glance, nodded, and then turned and headed away from the tent. As Jack watched him go, he'd prayed a silent prayer of thanks for his delivery of a copy of the Good Book.

His noon meal was delivered by the same soldier who brought his breakfast, presented in the same gruff manner. "Eat up, mister, and here's some water from the creek." The man set the pitcher down with a plop so that some of the water splashed out and he carelessly lowered a plate of food beside it. The meal looked to be some kind of cooked meat. Squirrel, maybe? Jack decided he didn't want to know. Besides, he was too hungry to care. Along with the meat was a small boiled potato and a fair-sized portion of bread. The first thing he did was gulp down some water and then he went for the bread.

Outside, some sort of commotion had caused a stir, so that half the men assigned to watch his tent left their posts. Now would've been a good time to escape, but he didn't think he could have gotten very far, being as he hadn't even begun to loosen his shackles. Besides, his stomach seemed to be saying, "Eat or starve, take your pick." He ate, glad that, for a change, he didn't have to concern himself about the goings-on in the center of camp. They weren't his worry—unless, of course, the soldiers were casting lots for his clothing. That would be reason for concern.

He finished his bread, then rose to his feet and shuffled over to the opening of the tent. "What's goin' on out there?" he called.

"No idea, mister," one of his guards responded. "An' I ain't s'posed t' be talkin' t' you."

"I'm not trying to get you into trouble. I was just curious, that's all."

The guard said nothing more but simply stared straight ahead, so Jack gave a half-shrug and then made his way back to the little table next to his cot where his dinner plate lay, a potato and most of the meat remaining. He sat down, picked up his fork, and prepared to stab the potato when a loud voice gave him pause.

"Major, I demand you tell me where he is!" The familiar male voice had Jack back on his feet. Joseph? Could it be? Had Cristina succeeded in sending off a telegram? Jack returned to the tent opening. "Joey!" he shouted.

"Hey, shut up!" the guard barked, lifting his rifle and preparing to aim it.

"I hear my brother, Captain Joseph Fuller of the Ohio Twenty-Seventh Infantry."

"I don't give a spoonful o' spit if it's the president himself. I told you to keep quiet."

"Joey!" Jack yelled, his hands wrapped around the tent post as he looked through the narrow opening in the tent flap.

Just as the soldier raised his rifle again, Joseph came into view and shouted, "Put down that gun, soldier, or I'll blow off your head!"

The soldier turned at his voice.

"Calm down, Captain," said the major, following on Joseph's heels, almost running to keep up with him. "Both of you, put your rifles down. Sergeant Varner, we need to confer with the prisoner."

"There'll be no conferring, Major," Joseph maintained. "I demand you remove those shackles at once."

Jack stared at his strapping, six-plus-foot brother. He might have to kiss the ground Joseph walked on if his brother managed to arrange his liberation.

"Wait just a minute, Captain," sputtered Major Freeland. "You don't outrank me."

"No, but General George H. Thomas, second in command of the Army of the Cumberland, surely does. And this order clearly states you must release the prisoner into my custody." Major Freeland's brow crinkled like parchment as Joseph reached into his side pocket and retrieved a piece of paper resembling a telegram. The major snatched the paper out of Joseph's hand and began to scan it, rubbing his chin all the while, with a stubborn frown on his bearded face. At last, he passed the paper back, then looked at the soldier standing closest to Jack and gave a loud huff. "Remove the shackles, Sergeant, so we can release the prisoner to Captain Fuller."

The sergeant jerked his head back. "Sir?"

"Do as I say!"

The soldier did not move. "He's not a deserter, after all?"

"Don't ask questions, Sergeant! Just release the prisoner."

"Yes, sir." The sergeant snapped to attention and untied the rope that bound Jack's wrists, then got to work on the shackles around his ankles. Jack refrained from speaking to Joseph for the time being, but he had a number of questions for him. How he had found him—and so quickly? The last he'd heard, his brother was stationed in northern Pennsylvania. How had he gotten here so fast?

As soon as he was unfettered, Jack picked up the Bible from Gray and glanced once more around the place. He didn't have a single other possession, as he'd left Cristina's barn with nothing but the clothes he wore. He left the paper and fountain pen, in the hopes that Private Novak would learn what had happened and retrieve them later.

"Come on, Jack. Let's get out of here."

Jack turned and walked out, thankful for his freedom. What he needed now was a good shower. Did Joey have any sort of plan in mind?

⌒

The church service was the most interesting gathering Cristina had ever attended and she could hardly wait for her next opportunity to visit. First, there was Sunday school, where 20 to 30 other women gathered in a side room for a Bible lesson. One of the church ladies, Mrs. Silvers, stood at the front of the room and talked about two sisters named Mary and Martha, friends of Jesus, who had raised their brother Lazarus from the dead. Cristina remembered having read the account in Jack's Bible, but the Sunday school instructor had a way of bringing the story to life. More than once, Cristina caught herself leaning forward in her chair, not wanting to miss a single word of the teaching. At times, Mrs. Silvers posed a question to the ladies to inspire discussion. Cristina listened with rapt attention to everyone's input and even found herself wishing she had something to contribute.

After Sunday school, the roomful of ladies walked to the sanctuary, where Cristina met up with Elias and Catherina, who had been ushered into the large room by their own teachers. Catherina could hardly contain her enthusiasm over what she'd learned in class and she wished to explain it all that very minute. Elias nudged her in the side and whispered, "You'll have t' tell Maw about it on the wagon ride home. We're goin' t' church now."

"I thought we already did church," his sister said, somewhat loudly.

"No, that was Sunday school."

"Oh." She frowned then. "But I'm gettin' hungry."

"Catherina, shh." Cristina held a finger to her lips. A couple of ladies nearby giggled in response, then introduced themselves and welcomed the little family. Cristina hardly knew how to handle all the friendliness.

"Mrs. Stiles, what an honor to see you this morning," the reverend greeted her next in his deep, pleasant voice.

"Reverend Wilcox, thank you. It's our pleasure t' be here. We got a wonderful visit from Mrs. Burley and Mrs. Parsons last night and they invited us. Then, this mornin', they were kind enough t' meet us at the church door."

"They bringed us presents last night," Catherina announced.

"Ever so many nice things," Cristina affirmed. "I never could've expected such extravagance. They told us it all came from the congregation. I don't know how t' thank everyone. It was just such a—a blessin'."

"There's no need to thank us, Mrs. Stiles," said the reverend with a smile. "I'm certain everyone knows how grateful you are. I hope you don't mind that I spread the word a bit about your recent loss. I was hopeful that folks would reach out to you." A look of concern crossed his face then. "What's this I hear about Lieutenant Fuller? Mrs. Parsons told me just before Sunday school that he left yesterday morning. I didn't realize he was—"

"Some Yanks came an' took him," Elias spouted.

The reverend's forehead crinkled even more. "Is that so?"

Cristina nodded. "Somebody reported that he'd deserted, which, o' course, he hadn't. The Army got word o' his whereabouts and hauled 'im away, even though I tried to explain that he'd been shot and was recoverin'. They seemed not to want t' hear anything I had to say, just tol' me they were followin' orders by bringin' him in. One of them even hinted he might hang by sundown." Unexpected tears welled in her eyes. "I pray that wasn't the case, Reverend."

Compassion washed across his clean-shaven face. "I pray the same, but I have to believe they'd do a thorough investigation before carrying out something so drastic as a hanging. After all, both sides are desperate for able-bodied soldiers. I'm certain the Army will investigate Lieutenant Fuller's case and find him quite innocent. Surely his superiors will back up his story and, for that matter, verify his intention, which was simply to deliver a letter to you from your late husband."

Cristina sighed. "I hope you're right."

"Speaking of your husband's passing, how have you been holding up?"

"I take it a day at a time, Reverend."

"The Lord will help you through this, my dear, though it will take time."

She nodded. "I'm tryin' t' trust Him."

His smile conveyed a great deal of warmth. "Drop by the parsonage anytime and either Edith or I will be happy to discuss with you any questions you might have regarding spiritual matters."

"I appreciate that, sir."

The reverend moved on then, greeting other parishioners on his way to the front of the sanctuary. Meanwhile, the organist played with gusto, causing the instrument's pipes to bellow a cheerful-sounding melody. Cristina and her children found seats. Soon, Sarah Parsons and her husband joined them at the end of the pew. Cristina and Mrs. Parsons exchanged smiles.

Cristina thought how happy Jack would be to know she'd brought her children to church. Then she started worrying that he might never find out. Had her telegram reached his brother? More importantly, had it reached him in time? *Please, Lord, protect Jack.*

The music stopped as a man walked across the platform and stood at the podium. "Let us rise for the morning hymn," he said in a loud, enthusiastic voice. "Please open your hymnals to number thirty-one, "Come Thou Fount of Every Blessing.""

All around them, folks stood, so Cristina and her children did as well. Soon, the organist struck the right keys and made the instrument boom with delightful tones. Cristina listened in rapt wonder until she felt a gentle nudge from Mrs. Parsons. Glancing down, she saw the hymn book the kind woman held out to her. Mrs. Parsons pointed at the page and nodded for Cristina to take the book. They exchanged smiles before Mrs. Parsons returned to her husband's side and shared another book with him. Cristina fumbled with the notes of the song but soon began to catch on to the spirited tune. She tried her best to sing with the congregation, each word and every note putting a warm spot in the center of her chest. Gazing down at her children, she found Catherina yawning and Elias busy staring at his surroundings, too caught up in that to want to share the book with her.

After the song ended, the worship leader announced another hymn, this one titled "Marching to Zion," and Cristina thought she'd never heard a more joyful tune.

Later, the reverend delivered an engrossing sermon about a man named Saul, a Roman citizen who hated Christians and made it his mission to persecute them. One day, he was struck down by God Himself and lost his sight. He did not regain his ability to see until three days later, after a visit from a follower of Jesus named Ananias, who told Saul that God had great plans for his life. Soon, Saul gave his life fully over to Jesus and, from that day forward, preached the message of God's love to everyone he met.

Cristina almost wished for a divine encounter such as Saul's—not that she wished to go blind, but she wished for God to speak to her in an audible voice. Then there'd be no doubt she could fully trust and obey.

At the close of the service, Reverend Wilcox announced a potluck church picnic to follow. Neither Mrs. Burley nor Mrs. Parsons had informed her in advance of the event, so Cristina ushered her children down the aisle in preparation for leaving, but Mrs. Parsons stopped them at the end of the pew. "We didn't tell you yesterday about the picnic, Cristina, because we didn't want you feeling obligated to bring anything. I brought extra food to cover your family, including dishes and tableware. Please, won't you consider staying?"

"Oh, I—that is so nice of you, Mrs. Parsons, but…." However, she could think of no reason not to attend, other than the fact that she had nothing to contribute.

"You must stay," urged Mrs. Parsons. "The picnic is the perfect opportunity to get to know some of the other ladies while the children play."

"Can we stay, Maw?" asked Elias.

"Can we, please?" Catherina pleaded.

"Well, I…I suppose."

"Hooray!" The children shouted joyfully as they jumped up and down. Soon, a couple of boys Elias recognized from school invited him outside. When Cristina gave him a nod of approval, he dashed off. Then, a young mother with a daughter who looked to be about Catherina's age introduced herself as Charlotte Garner and offered Cristina her condolences, saying she'd heard about Orville's passing from another parishioner.

More and more women approached Cristina, many of whom she'd seen in town over the years but had never formally met. Her mind tried to take in each face and name, but the task proved overwhelming. Still, Cristina deeply appreciated their kindness. Even Miss Harriet from the hat shop was there, naturally wearing a splendid headpiece with blue lace and white feathers. In her musical voice, she told Cristina how delighted she was to see her again.

Once everyone moved outside, Cristina made a plate of food for herself and Catherina from the bountiful spread of potluck dishes, then sat down at a long table in the shade of a large oak next to Charlotte Garner and her husband, John. Wedged in between them was their little girl Susannah, and then Catherina. Across the table sat Sarah and George Parsons, as well as Alberta and George Burley. Several others passed by, some even stopping to offer a kind word of welcome to Cristina. The sunshine and mild temperatures put everyone in high spirits. Every so often, Catherina and Susannah would speak in tiny spurts, both shy and perhaps a bit nervous.

Cristina glanced across the churchyard and spotted Elias eating with several of his school friends, one of whom, she'd learned, was Susannah's older brother, Luke. What a wonder that Charlotte and her husband would have two children so close in age to Cristina's. After today, Elias would surely insist they never miss another Sunday service.

"Mrs. Stiles, how lovely to see you again."

Cristina turned at the voice and the gentle touch to her shoulder. It was the reverend's wife, Edith.

She quickly chewed and swallowed. "Thank you, Mrs. Wilcox. It's lovely t' see you again, as well. I enjoyed yer husband's sermon this mornin'."

"I'm happy to hear it. He also earned my approval with that one."

Mr. Parsons laughed. "Oh, come on, Edith, admit it—you wrote it for him."

The older woman chuckled. "No, but I did correct some minor errors in spelling and the like as I read through it. He prepares and delivers a fine sermon, but I don't know how he reads his own handwriting." She returned her attention to Cristina. "I do hope you'll come again."

"Oh, I will. I'm certain of it."

Edith soon moved on to greet other parishioners, she and her husband working opposite ends of the churchyard, apparently attempting to speak with everyone present. In due time, Catherina and Susannah asked to be excused and, with much enthusiasm, ran off holding hands, their little skirts flaring and their braids flying. The conversation at the table turned to the recent shooting and robbery at Rosalyn's Restaurant.

"Wouldn't surprise me none if the soldier gets away with it," groused a man at the far end of the table. "War always interferes with the course o' justice. Folks commit crimes an' there ain't enough men left in town t' uphold the law."

"I wonder if he skipped town that very night or whether he's still lurking around these parts," Mr. Garner said quietly.

"I'm inclined to think he's long gone," mused another fellow. "What would make him stick around town, knowin' the Army an' everyone else is lookin' for him?"

Cristina shuddered. She knew better than anyone how unsafe the town was if that awful Union soldier still lurked in their midst.

⌒

Clive felt his mouth water just watching his fish fry in a pan over the hot flames. He'd walked down to Raisin's campsite, bringing him a freshly caught fish to share for supper. He would give him the coin when the time seemed right. For now, he watched the kid prepare their meal, supplementing the fish with some wild greens, onions, carrots, and a couple of potatoes he must've found in somebody's garden.

Clive cleared his throat. "When you went to the Army settlement outside o' Ripley, what'd they ask you, exactly, 'bout that note I gave you?"

The boy flipped the fish over with a long fork. "They wanted t' know who gave it to me an' I said I di'n't know 'is name. Told 'em I cou'n't read, so I di'n't even know what it said."

Clive nodded slowly. "You done good, kid. You done real good."

Raisin lifted his hand, admiring the ring on his thumb. "It fits me good, y' know?"

Clive laughed. "It fits me better." He reached into his pocket and withdrew the coin.

"Which is worth more?" the kid asked.

"This coin." Clive held it flat on his palm so that it glistened in the sun.

"Liar," Raisin said, without a single blink of the eye. The kid had an uncanny way of making Clive feel uneasy, but Clive wasn't about to let him know that.

"That supper's smellin' awful fine."

"Ain't it?"

"You are a young man of few words, aren't you?"

Raisin shrugged. "I don't say much t' folks I cain't trust. Which means I ain't much fer talkin' t' nobody." He picked up a plate and scooped a portion of food onto it, then passed it over to Clive, who stood from the rock where he'd been sitting in order to accept it.

"Thanks."

"Welcome," Raisin mumbled. He served himself a portion on a plate, which he set on a log beside him. Then, still standing, he stretched out his arm and again studied the ring. "Still think it fits me right nice."

Clive harrumphed. "You ain't thinkin' o' double-crossin' me, are y'? I can draw my gun on you and run off with the ring an' the coin both. You know that, right?"

The next thing Clive knew, the kid had a pistol trained on him. Clive hadn't even had a chance to take his next breath. With a cunning grin, Raisin said, "I could blow you clear 'cross the Ohio. You know that, right?" The whites of his deep brown eyes flashed like strikes of lightning.

For the first time in a long while, fear hovered over Clive like a vulture. He gave a hearty laugh to cover it. "You're quick, boy. I was just joshin'. Here's yer coin." He extended his open hand without hesitation.

The boy eyed it with particular care. "Because we made a deal, I honor it. After t'day, though, I don't wanna see you again. Ever. That clear?"

"Clear as the sky above."

With no facial expression, the boy wiggled the ring off his thumb and they made the exchange.

They ate without speaking. The only sounds were the babbling of the stream, the scraping of forks against plates, and an occasional chirp overhead—though, oddly enough, even the birds seemed a bit leery about singing. When Clive had finished, he stood, nodded at the boy, and then followed the stream back toward his cave, where he planned to spend the night. The previous evening in the Stiles barn had been a nightmare, what with the hay and the stench of animals making his eyes water. He'd slept fitfully and left before dawn. So much for sleeping in the comfort of a roofed structure.

Prickles moved up and down his spine as he walked, half expecting to hear a gun being cocked, but when he rounded the bend and dared to glance back, he let out a loud breath of relief. No sign of Raisin. Fancy fearing a boy who couldn't be older than thirteen!

29

Jack spent a day with Joseph before leaving to reunite with his unit. He was grateful for a chance to catch up on the war as well as on life. They were having lunch at a restaurant near the stagecoach stop about 50 miles south of Columbus when Jack told his younger brother of his plans to return to Ripley as soon as possible. Joseph rolled his eyes. "Don't tell me you fell for the widow whose husband you shot."

Jack hesitated, then sheepishly conceded, "You might say that."

Joseph let out a long moan. "You're crazy, man. I thought you were done with women."

Jack chuckled. "I thought I was, too, but...she's different."

"She is, eh? Does she have money?"

"Money? No, why do you ask?"

"Jack, listen to yourself. Marilee didn't have money, either, remember? When she found out you did, she poured on the charm and like a hungry mouse, you ran right into her trap."

Jack didn't give a second's thought to Joseph's words. "Cristina has no interest in even seeing if I have money. I told her about our farm and I suppose she considers me successful. But if you think she's after my money, you're dead wrong. As for her pouring on any charm, she took special care not to show me an ounce. In truth, for the first several days I spent at her place, she wanted nothing to do with me. Sure, she helped her older friend to nurse me back to health, but she did so only out of a sense of obligation. After all, I was the one who delivered that letter from her husband."

Joseph gave three slow nods of his head, then crinkled his brow at Jack. "How in tarnation have you managed to dodge so many bullets in this blasted war but failed to miss the one a Rebel woman fired at you? You do know you're not going to hear the end of this, don't you? I can hear Jesse now. He'll tease you into Indiana."

Jack smiled as he thought about his other brother. "I know that, but you'll all stop laughing once you meet her. You'll see immediately why I fell so hard."

"Really? Is she pretty?"

"Prettier than a rose in June."

Joseph laughed. "You're getting all poetic, brother, which tells me you're already a lost cause."

Jack chuckled. "Not quite. I haven't yet expressed my love to her. I'm taking things slow because, truth is, she doesn't have a personal faith in Christ."

"Well, I can see why you'd be cautious, you being so spiritual and all." Joseph winked.

Jack sobered, not wanting his brother to misunderstand. "I may be a Christian, but I still sin as much as the next man. I make mistakes on a regular basis and am always having to repent and seek God's forgiveness. The good news is, He freely forgives out of the abundance of His unfailing love and grace. You should give God a chance to prove Himself in your life."

Joseph groaned. "Now you sound like Ma. 'Joey, I wish you'd go to church.' 'Joey, have you been reading your Bible?' 'Joey, you need to start praying more. What if you get shot on the battlefield? Are you going to heaven?'"

"Well, that's Ma." Jack shook his head, thinking about his mother's passion for evangelizing Joseph. "She's right, only perhaps a bit overzealous at times."

"No kidding. I know she means well. I'm just not like you and Jesse. I can't get past the fact that God gave Beth a tumor that took her life. I got four kids, Jack. What kind of loving God does something like that, takes a mother away from her four kids?"

"This isn't a perfect world, Joey. Bad things happen—to everyone, Christians included. It's how you handle tragedy when it hits that makes the difference. Do you turn to a loving God for help, or do you run the other direction?"

"I guess I ran the other direction. And I'm making it fine."

"Are you? Last I heard, you've gone through three or four nannies."

Joey gave a half-hearted smile. "Make that five."

"Five? In the last two years? Why so many?"

"Nobody can handle my four rascals."

"You see? Right there, that's something God could help you with if you gave Him half a chance."

"You think He could find me the perfect nanny?"

"It's about learning to trust Him, Joey, and that's all I'll say. I'm not going to be like Ma. You know everything you need to know about the gospel without my preaching at you."

Joseph laid his fork down and wiped his mouth with his cloth napkin. "Just so you know, I did send a telegram to that Cristina woman the day I rescued you."

Jack had jerked his head up and stared across the table. "You did? Why didn't you tell me?"

"I forgot, I guess. I didn't know you were so head-over-heels for her. I walked over to the telegraph office while you were sleeping in the hotel room."

"What did your message say?"

"Basically, that you were safe. I also thanked her for letting me know about the situation. That was it."

"She probably wonders why I wasn't the one who sent the message."

"Well, sit down and write to her, if you want."

"I plan to do just that, as soon as I get a few minutes."

Joseph checked his pocket watch. "We'd better get you to the stage-coach station. You're in for quite a jaunt to Knoxville. Didn't the ticket-ing clerk say you'd have five stops?"

Jack nodded. "It won't be a pleasant ride, I'm sure, but I'll make the best of it. At least I'm not sitting in that prison tent."

Joseph picked up the restaurant tab—good thing, since Jack hadn't a cent to his name. All his possessions, right down to his Army uniform, were back in Cristina's barn. His brother's generosity had bought him a new set of clothes and also his stagecoach voucher.

They walked to the station, taking steps that were slower than usual in order to prolong their time together. When they arrived at the platform, they faced each other. Joseph gave Jack a hearty shake of the shoulders. "You take care now, brother, and don't let any more bullets find you."

"I'll do my best. I've got two more months of duty before I muster out. I'm still hoping to finish out my time in Ripley."

Joseph sighed. "How in the world are you going to talk Major Jones into sanctioning that when you have an assigned company? You're an Army lieutenant, Jack. Have you forgotten your responsibility?"

"Not at all. I don't see why the army can't send me there to assist in the search and seizure of Private Clive Horton. I have a vested interest in finding him, since he and his deceased partner attacked Cristina in the privacy of her home."

"I understand that, but I don't see how you're going to convince Jones. It's not your regiment, not your unit. What do you plan to do? Switch over when you have only two more months of active duty in the Forty-Fifth? It's a bad idea. With what company did you say this Horton fellow is associated?"

"The Hundred Forty-Second Regiment, New York Volunteers."

"How in the heck do you think you can transfer from an Ohio com-pany to a New York one?"

"It doesn't matter what state you're from. A person can enlist from anywhere."

"You're not thinking of dropping out and reenlisting…?"

"No, nothing like that. I'm just going to put in a request and see where it takes me. It's in God's hands."

"Uh-huh. Well, be sure to send me a wire and tell me where God's hands dropped you."

Jack chuckled. "I'll do that. Thanks again for everything."

"Oh! That reminds me." Joseph reached into his pocket and withdrew his leather purse. Opening it, he retrieved some money. "Take this. It'll help you get by until you get paid again."

Jack didn't argue. "I owe you." He dropped the coins into his vest pocket, then fastened the button. They stared at each other for a long moment, then quickly embraced before backing up and bidding each other one last good-bye.

Several hours later, Jack stared out the window as the stagecoach bumped along toward Knoxville, Tennessee, where Jack was to meet with Major General Samuel Jones, commander of the department at East Tennessee, and receive orders to reconnect with his cavalry brigade and, hopefully, rejoin his unit. At one point, Union soldiers had stopped the driver and informed him that he would do best to avoid the Cumberland Gap, being as Confederate defenders occupied much of that area. So, the driver had decided to flank them some 40 miles to the north.

Much had changed since he'd left camp in mid-July. A few weeks after the Battle of Buffington Island in Meigs County, the Forty-Fifth Ohio Infantry had begun their advance toward Knoxville under the direction of Ambrose Burnside, head of the Ninth Corps of the Ohio. With the help of several other regiments, the Union managed to chase out all Confederate influence and take over Knoxville. Jack wondered how long he'd be in Tennessee. Probably at least long enough to ensure the Confederates stayed at bay.

Now the sole passenger of the coach, Jack felt his heart thumping hard as he anticipated his arrival in Knoxville. How would he be received? In what sort of mood would he find Major Jones? Did he even stand the slimmest chance of being sent back to Ripley? He glanced heavenward and whispered, "Have thine own way, Lord. Not my will but thine be done."

30

It had been two weeks since the incident at Rosalyn's and Clive was rather proud of himself for evading the authorities, even if he was desperate for a decent meal. As much as he'd wanted to hide out in the Stiles house with that gal and her ragamuffins, that would be darn near impossible since that "Miss Clara" seemed to come around almost every day. If he wanted to get out of Ripley, he had to play his cards right. He really had no interest in shooting anybody else. Creating any further disturbances about town would only diminish his chances of escape.

Yesterday, he'd been helping himself to some apples from an over-grown orchard when two fellas on horseback had met at a crossroad and stopped to converse. Clive had darted behind some apple crates and remained hidden while he eavesdropped on them. His ears had perked up when their talk had turned to Army activity. "I heard the Army moved on from Ripley," said one of the men. "Ain't seen nobody standin' guard about town no more. They must've figured that rogue soldier got away."

"That's the talk I heard, too. Good riddance to all of 'em, if y' ask me. Heard-tell there were a number of break-ins about town while they were here. Seems they had some renegades in their midst."

They touched on a few other topics before bidding each other good-bye and going their own way. Grinning to himself, Clive stood up and bit into a juicy apple. Now *that* was good news. His unit had moved on, which could mean only one thing: they had given up looking for him.

Still, he had to be cautious. Sneaky as a fox, he crept along till he reached the Stiles farm. He hid behind the trunk of the sprawling oak tree in the backyard and watched as an unfamiliar woman wearing fancy clothes settled the Stiles children in the rear seat of her wagon with two other youngsters. Once she'd gotten them situated, she lowered herself into the driver's seat and took the reins. She gave a little wave at the door of the house, then shouted, "I'll bring them home by suppertime. How does that sound?"

"That sounds jes' fine, Mrs. Garner," the Stiles woman replied.

"Please. If we're gonna be friends, you'd best call me Charlotte. Better yet, call me Char. All my friends do."

"All right, then, Char. An' you must call me Cristina. You kids be good at the Garners' house, y' hear?"

"We will, Mama!" shouted the Stiles girl. "Me an' Susannah's gonna have so much fun playin'."

Clive couldn't have dreamed up a more perfect scenario. With those two snot-nosed scamps out of the house, there'd be no need to tie them up as he'd originally planned. All he had to do was barge in on that lil' gal—just the way he and Mike had done before—hold his gun to her head and tell her what would happen to her and her family, and maybe even that Charlotte Garner and her kids, if she didn't cooperate. He'd have to move fast, so he could get out of this rotten town and move south once and for all. Too bad he wouldn't have time for a little manly fun with that ripe lil' Mexican cherry. He would have to find himself a cute Texas gal once he reached his destination.

He watched as the Garner woman reined her two-horse team in a half-circle and set off toward the road. He wouldn't move in on that Mrs. Stiles just yet. No, he would stand here for a few minutes and get his plan in place. And a fine plan it would be, too. By late afternoon, if everything went as scheduled, he would be riding out of town on her horse, having left her alone along some deserted road. Her job was simple. All she had to do was be his human shield…or his bartering tool…or maybe both. She'd come in mighty handy.

⌒

Ten minutes after her children's departure, Cristina already missed them, although she appreciated Charlotte Garner's kind gesture in inviting them over for the day. Goodness, this is how it would feel once they both started school. She dabbed at a bit of dampness in the corners of her eyes, just thinking about having to loosen her rein on Catherina. Was the child even ready for book learning? The fact that school ran for only a few months each year eased Cristina's mind.

She took a deep breath and looked around, assessing her tidy little house. Lately, she'd been keeping her mind busy with one chore after another—doing laundry, scrubbing floors, washing windows, performing various tasks around the barn—anything and everything that kept her from thinking about Jack and what might have become of him. She had received a telegram from his brother a few weeks ago, letting her know that Jack was safe and thanking her for notifying him. But there had been no word from Jack himself. She'd considered writing to him, but decided that would be inappropriately bold. If he wrote to her, she would respond.

But had he put her out of his mind because of the argument they'd had the night before the Army took him away? Maybe he'd thought it best to break all ties with her. She hoped with all her might that wasn't the case. She missed him—even more than she missed Orville—and it was time she admitted to herself that she'd fallen in love with him, no matter that she was newly widowed.

It was far from proper on her part, she knew. Gracious, she hadn't even dressed in the traditional black mourning attire of a widow. She should have driven straight into town soon after learning of Orville's passing and bought some black fabric to make a dress, but she hadn't even considered doing so. First, she considered black to be morbid; second, she'd started mourning Orville's absence some two years ago, when he'd set off to join the Army. Something had told her even then that he might not return. Looking back, she supposed she saw signs of malcontent well before he left. Many nights, he had moped about the house, complaining about a lack of sufficient money and wishing things were different so he could build a bigger house and barn, raise better cattle, and own more land. Despite her repeated insistence that their little farm suited them fine and that they had their whole lives ahead of them for pursuing their dreams, he'd never ceased grumbling about his so-called failures. Anything she said to try to ease his mind only made it worse.

Now that she had time to think about it, she wondered if he'd seen the Army as a means of escape. Had the responsibilities of home so weighed him down that joining the Army seemed his only recourse? A far-fetched idea, perhaps, but when a person lost the ability to reason, he sometimes did strange things.

Cristina gave her head a little shake and absently crossed the room to the trunk that held most of her sewing supplies. She opened it and began shuffling through the contents in search of the fabrics that had been in the basket of items brought by Mrs. Burley and Mrs. Parsons. Today, she would start stitching Catherina a new dress for school and perhaps even make a new shirt for Elias. With some of the money she'd set aside from selling eggs over the past year, she could buy each of them a new pair of shoes.

She moved about, gathering scissors, measuring tape, needle, thread, and a few other items, all of which she arranged on the table. She was retrieving the fabric she'd selected when she heard a knock at the door. No doubt it was Mrs. Garner, wanting to tell her something she had forgotten to mention, although Cristina hadn't heard the wagon coming back up the drive. Without thinking to investigate first, she set down the fabric and opened the door.

Her heart stopped. It was *him*—the cruel, felonious Union rat who'd beaten her in June—holding a gun. Rumor had it he'd murdered Lyle Richards, the restaurant cook. She'd thought him long gone.

"What do you want?" Her rifle hung just to her left, but she knew she would never manage to grab it quickly enough. Her mind pulsed with all manner of thoughts. *Do not panic*, she told herself. *Lord, please hear my prayer and help me.*

A sly grin spread across his filthy, whiskered face. "Did y' miss me?"

She would not favor him with a reply. Instead, she straightened to her full height, stood her ground, and refused to step back. Her heart pumped faster than a horse's trot, but she wouldn't let him know it. She concentrated on each measured breath. "I asked you a question. What do you want?"

"You'll find out soon enough." He pointed the tip of his revolver at her forehead. "In the meantime, no funny business, y' hear? It's convenient that Mrs. Garner took yer children for the day. Now I don't have to worry 'bout tyin' 'em up whilst you and I do some business."

"I'm not doin' any business with you, Clive Horton. Yes, I know yer name. I also know you t' be a murderer."

In response, he put the icy muzzle of the gun against her forehead, but she didn't budge. She would not show her fear. *Lord, help me. Give me strength.*

"Oh, you'll do business with me, girlie. And what d' y' mean, I'm a murderer? Last I heard, everyone's innocent till proven guilty."

"I believe there's sufficient proof, Mr. Horton, since the sole survivor at the restaurant recognized you. Not only that, the Army's lookin' fer you. You should've skipped town when you had the chance."

He tossed back his head and gave a growly laugh. "My unit left town, missy. And don't worry; I've got the perfect plan and you t' help me carry it out."

"I'll do no such thing, you—you lawless animal!"

He laughed again and rammed the muzzle hard into her forehead, no doubt making an indentation in her skin. She winced with pain. "All…r-right."

He gave an evil grin. "That's more like it. Now then, if you don't wanna get hurt, I suggest you follow my instructions, the first o' which is t' saddle up yer best ridin' horse—the one that can carry us both an' still make good time."

She blinked at him, frozen in place.

"If you don't start movin', I'll just shoot you dead right here and find somebody else ta help me. And won't it be somethin' for yer lil' scamps t' find ya dead?"

That's the last thing Cristina wanted—and she didn't want to put anyone else in danger either, so she decided to go along with his orders, at least for now. She would saddle Thunder, since the Appaloosa was bigger and stronger than Starlight.

He waved her onward and they moved onto the porch, where Cristina whistled to summon Thunder. When he approached, she led him to the barn and started preparing him for a ride, fully aware of Clive's gun directed at her the entire time.

"You missin' yer beau?" he sneered while she started on the saddle.

For a second, her hands stopped moving. "What d' you mean by that?"

"You know exactly what I mean. The good lieutenant—you missin' 'im?"

"How did you know he—"

A sinister-sounding chuckle came out of him. "You don't give me much credit, missy. I knew he was here. I been keepin' my eye on things."

"Spyin' on my family y' mean?"

He shrugged. "Call it what you want. Anyway, I was able to help out the Army once I realized yer beau was hidin' here. Don't think they'll let him off lightly fer desertin'."

She feigned nonchalance and resumed saddling Thunder, slipping the girth strap under his belly, then moving around to the other side to tighten and secure the buckle. "He didn't desert," she said, trying to keep all emotion out of her voice. "He was convalescin' from an injury. I shot 'im, thinkin' he was *you*, when he came to deliver a letter from my now-deceased husband."

"You sayin you were gonna shoot me?" His voice rose a couple of notches in pitch. "Now you've hurt my feelings." With the gun still aimed at her, he pressed his other hand to his heart. She gave him only half a glance. "I s'pose I oughtta thank the good lieutenant fer takin' a bullet fer me. Too bad he's probably already dead."

"Too bad indeed," she replied, pretending not to care one way or the other. "There. I'm finished."

"Good. Climb on up and I'll get behind you."

Cristina frowned. "Can't I put on some ridin' pants?"

"No time for worryin' 'bout that now. You think I ain't never seen a gal's legs before? Get on up there."

The last thing she wanted was to ride with him breathing down the back of her neck, but she put one foot in a stirrup and climbed up, then spread the fabric of her dress over her legs as much as she could, thankful that she'd at least chosen one with an extra-full skirt that day. Once she had gotten herself situated, Clive promptly climbed up behind her, then fumbled around in his pocket. A moment later, he handed her a kerchief.

"What's this for?" she asked.

"It's called a blindfold."

"I'm not puttin' that on."

He yanked it back. "Oh, but you are. I guess I'll just have to put it on for y' since yer stubborn as an ol' mule." He grabbed one of her wrists and squeezed until she was sure the blood had stopped flowing to her fingers.

"Ouch!" she yelped.

"Stop fightin' me, you little wench. Now, gimme yer other hand."

"What? No!"

He yanked her other hand behind her back and the next thing she knew, he was wrapping her wrists with what felt like coarse twine.

"Ouch! That's too tight. Why're you doin' this?"

"Shut up. You complain too much." He finished tying her wrists. "Now then, I'm gonna tie this kerchief over your eyes. I swear, if you fight me, I'll pop you a good one in the side o' yer face. Y' hear me?"

She gave a slow nod and settled down. At the moment, she was more angry than scared. How she longed to hurt him, maybe throw her head back to strike him in the chin. But where would that get her? He had a gun, after all. She sat still while he secured the kerchief over her eyes so that when she looked down, all she saw was a tiny slice of the saddle. "There, now. Comfortable?" He laughed. "Here, feel this?" He poked the gun barrel to the back of her head. "That's just a little reminder to you not t' make a sound. Not that we're gonna see anybody on our route."

"Where're you takin' me?"

"No questions either." He kicked Thunder into motion and they set off, his flabby arms brushing against her sides as he held the reins with his left hand and his revolver with the right. Her tied hands were plastered against his big gut. "Yer only job is t' do as I say—that is, if you wanna see yer kids again. You mess up and I'll find yer kids and that Garner family and do away with every last one of 'em. You got that?"

"Yes," she replied soberly. And began to pray.

⌒

On September 7, Jack moved his unit at a faster-than-usual pace toward the Cumberland Gap, their war-torn boots making loud, rhythmic thumps as each man tramped along the uneven path. Their assignment was to force a surrender from Confederate General John W. Frazer, who had repeatedly refused similar demands because he seemed to think he had sufficient manpower to defend the Gap. As they marched along with no time to spare, Jack prayed for success. Burnside had an iron-jawed will about him that set everyone's nerves on edge. If Frazer didn't surrender upon their arrival, things could turn violent. Jack wanted to avoid bloodshed if possible, even though he wouldn't shirk his military duty to protect the Union at all costs.

Jack had not managed to talk Major Jones into transferring him back to Ripley. Ever since the sudden demise of Major Marsh, things had been in a state of turmoil; even Major Jones wasn't altogether sure of his current responsibilities, having been uprooted from the One Hundred Twenty-Fifth Ohio Infantry to stand in for Marsh until a permanent replacement could be found. In the transition, some of Jack's company had departed—Jack knew not where—and important records had been misplaced.

Jack felt that he bore at least some responsibility for all the chaos, so he didn't press the matter with Jones. Best to wait till things cooled down—if they ever did—before he made another request for a transfer. Worst case, he would finish his two remaining months of active duty away from Ripley—and he would buy a one-way train ticket there the moment he was out. He wanted nothing more than to be with Cristina around the clock and he knew this with even greater clarity since leaving West Virginia. However, he also knew he couldn't rush God's plan. If God willed it, He would work out the circumstances and bring it to pass. Jack's only duty was to trust in the Lord's bigger plan.

He'd written exactly four letters to Cristina, but seeing as no mail wagon had visited the camp since his arrival in Knoxville, he'd been unsuccessful at sending them. He wondered what thoughts might be running through her head and whether she even cared that he'd been forced to leave in such a hurry. For all he knew, his departure had come as a great relief, especially considering how angry she'd been when he'd told her he'd been the one to shoot Orville. Would that knowledge end up erecting a wall between them that neither one would ever be able to tear down? Then again, she *had* sent the telegram to Joseph; wouldn't she have ignored his request if she hadn't cared what happened to him? The picture of her bewildered face on that morning lingered in his mind, her long hair undone and falling down her back, Elias joining her as they ran alongside the wagon until the driver reached the road. Jack had been helpless to do anything, shackled as he was, so he'd simply sat there watching them until they slipped from view, his heart a mass of untold emotion.

He gave his head several quick shakes as he marched along, trying to rid his mind of such distracting thoughts so he could concentrate on his duties. *Lord, please protect Cristina and draw her to Yourself. Help her to find You in the turmoil. And help me, Lord, to keep my focus where it needs to be—on You first, and then on my responsibilities to the Forty-Fifth Ohio Infantry.*

"How much longer do you think, Lieutenant?" asked Private Lewis Arden, who'd sidled up next to him on the trail.

Jack was glad for the interruption. "We'll stop sometime tonight for a brief rest before mobilizing again. We'll likely arrive shortly after that. You can bet we'll be exhausted, but our energy reserves will kick in when needed. We've a job to do and Burnside will make sure we accomplish it."

"Yes, sir! But I sure could use a horse about now."

Jack chuckled. His lack of exercise during his recovery had left him winded on the march. "I'm of the same opinion, Private. But together, we'll get there."

"Yes, sir. Onward and upward."

31

Cristina felt her braid come loose as Clive pushed Thunder along at a canter. Her hair was probably slapping the filthy man in the face. May it be so! "Where are we?" she asked over her shoulder.

"Didn't I tell you t' keep quiet?" he yelled in her ear. "I'll tell you what t' do when the time comes. Fer now, just keep yer yapper shut."

She pursed her lips, wishing she could give him a good shove off the horse. She dared not aggravate him too much, since she had no weapon, while he held a revolver as well as the reins. Besides, with her hands tied behind her and a blindfold over her eyes, she was completely helpless. She could tell by Thunder's occasional uneven hoofbeats that Clive had taken a less traveled road rather than a main thoroughfare. Apparently, in the time Clive had spent in the area with his Army unit, he'd familiarized himself with the territory. He kept demanding that the Appaloosa run faster and it wasn't long before Cristina could feel his lather soaking her skirts.

"You'd better slow down or my horse'll come up lame on you," she hollered, breaking the tense quiet between them.

To her great surprise and relief, he heeded her advice. If only she could determine where they were. They'd been on the road for probably a good twenty minutes now and Clive had yet to make mention of his intentions.

After a few more minutes, Clive drew Thunder to a halt. Upon stopping, the horse blew out a loud puff and snorted, then shifted his body. The blindfold made it difficult for Cristina to maintain her balance, but by some miracle, she managed to stay put. She wanted to ask why they'd stopped but kept the question to herself.

"All right, lil' lady, listen up. I'm gonna remove the blindfold an' untie yer hands, but don't you go tryin' nothin'."

He loosened the knot behind her head until the blindfold fell away. She blinked several times in the sunlight before her vision cleared and she could study their surroundings. They were on the crest of a hill overlooking a valley where there stood a ramshackle barn that appeared to be deserted, for tall weeds grew around it.

He worked to free her hands. Once he'd finished, she flexed her fingers and then rubbed her sore, red wrists. "What're we doin' here?" she asked.

"I'm gonna retrieve the stash me an' Mike stowed away."

"You mean, the money an' possessions y' got by robbin' from innocent people?"

He snorted. "Nobody's innocent."

"Well, I won't have anything t' do with it."

"Sure y'are—in a roundabout way, that is."

She didn't want to know what he meant by that, so she didn't ask for a clarification, figuring she'd find out soon enough.

"All right now. We're headin' fer that barn down there." He nodded. "Don't see nobody about, so this oughtta be a snap."

"Are you takin' me back t' my house when this is all over?"

He sneered. "You can find yer own way home. By the time you reach civilization an' report me to the law, I'll be long gone."

"I don't see why y' needed me in the first place."

"Wasn't sure what I'd be up against. Figured I'd use you as a bargainin' tool, if need be. Yer life in exchange fer my freedom. With you along, ain't nobody gonna shoot at me."

"How reassurin'," she muttered.

He nudged Thunder in the sides to start their journey down the knoll toward the barn, his gun barrel poking Cristina's ribs all the while. As they drew closer, an unnerving, eerie sensation came over Cristina, as if something bad were about to happen. *Lord, please give me courage an' strength an' help me t' make it back home t' my children.*

Clive directed Thunder to the other side of the barn, then reined him to a stop. "All right. Nice an' easy now, hop on down."

"How am I supposed t' get down with you blockin' me?" she asked him. "You get down first, then I'll follow."

"You think I'm stupid or somethin'?"

"I promise not t' ride off. It's awkward wearin' a dress in the saddle. You have to get down first so I can swing my leg over."

He huffed. "Oh, all right, but I'm warnin' you. Don't do anything foolish."

She knew she could probably attempt an escape once his feet hit the ground, but what would be her chances of surviving that success when he had a gun? He slid off Thunder's back and she immediately stood in the stirrups, swung her right leg up and around behind her, and dismounted.

He was right there to grab her by the arm and yank her to his side. Rather than balk at his rough handling, she chose to cooperate. She moved along without resisting as he led her into the musty barn. Several boards had rotted away and fallen off the sides, leaving gaping holes to the outside, and parts of the roof were open to the sky. "Over here, under these floorboards," he said, his voice husky with excitement as he pulled her along with him. "See the black notch in that board right there?"

Her eyes followed where he pointed and she nodded. "What about it?"

"Bend down an' lift that board. You'll see a brown cloth bag. Grab it."

She dutifully went down on her knees and gave the board a hard tug. At first, it felt too heavy to lift. But with some wiggling, wrangling, and tugging, she finally managed. She peered down into the darkness under the floorboard.

"Pick it up."

"Pick what up? There's nothin' here."

"What're you talkin' about? 'Course there is." He gave her a shove so that she landed flat on her backside. He inspected the space for himself, his gun still held at the ready. "What...? Where'd it go?" Then he jumped up, grabbed her by the arm, and yanked her across the barn with him. "Here." He stopped at another place in the floor. "Right there. Pick up that board."

"Which board?"

"Right there, stupid!" He pointed at a board that clearly wasn't nailed in place.

She crouched down and picked up the loose board, then peeked into the dark hole beneath it. "I don't see anything."

"What? Put your hand down there an' feel around."

She did as told, wincing as her fingers grazed spiderwebs and untold other debris. "There's nothing here. Are you sure you put something here?"

"O' course, I'm sure. I'm not some numbskull."

"You sure about that?" said a gruff male voice from behind them.

Cristina whirled around, and Clive turned, too, albeit more slowly. There stood Ripley's own sheriff, his chest puffed out as if he'd just won a trophy, along with two men sporting Pinkerton badges and holding rifles aimed at her and Clive. Cristina didn't know if she should be relieved or fearful. She immediately shot her hands up in the air. "I'm not with him! He forced me t' come along."

"Shut up!" Clive spat, suddenly yanking her by the arm, hauling her in front of him, and poking his gun into her back.

"Let the woman go, Horton. It's you we want," said one of the detectives.

"Yeah? Well, you ain't gettin' me. You're gonna have t' go through her t' get t' me."

"I don't think so," said the other detective. "What d' you got planned? Without your stolen money, you got nothin'. And you won't get far, even if we do let you go. 'Fraid you're surrounded."

Another armed Pinkerton agent stepped into view, as if to convince Clive the man wasn't lying. "Let the woman go, Horton."

"Can't do that. I aim t' leave this state and if I have to take her with me, I will."

"Don't be an idiot, Clive." The gravelly voice made Clive turn full around, bringing Cristina with him, his gun still rammed into her.

Clive let out a trembly gasp. "Mike? I thought you were—"

"Dead? Nope." Mike Farmer, with his hands cuffed in front of him, stood planted between a man dressed in Union blue and yet another Pinkerton detective. "I had a surface wound. Healed pretty quick, too. Disappointed?"

"No, 'course not, but—"

"I see you tried t' cheat me outta some of our earnin's. You planned that all along, didn't you?" Mike said. "See, I followed you one night when you snuck away from camp. I saw you transfer a big wad o' cash over to that other spot. I waited t' see if you would mention that to me. Y' never did."

"Y-you're wrong." Cristina felt Clive's body start to shake as he switched his weight from one leg to the other. He pulled Cristina even closer against him, his thick left arm hugging her tightly, making breathing difficult. "I was gonna tell you, honest, once—"

"Never mind, Horton," said the Union soldier. Cristina could only surmise he was Clive's commanding officer. Perhaps he'd stayed behind while the rest of his unit had moved on. "None of it matters anyway because it's over and it turns out you're the real idiot here. See, Private Farmer came clean with the law, so while he's going to spend *some* time behind bars for his wrongdoings, he will see the light of day again. You, on the other hand…you'll be a jailbird till your dying day. And probably hanged. You killed a man, Horton. At least Private Farmer doesn't have murder on his hands."

Clive's jagged breaths tickled the back of Cristina's neck. "Where's our stuff, Mike?" he demanded, completely ignoring the officer's remarks.

"Returned t' their rightful owners—everything 'cept the money we already spent."

"You dirty, double-dealin'—"

"*I'm* not the dirty double-dealer. That would be *you*."

"You—you told them…everything?" Clive sputtered. "That makes you the worst kind o' snitch."

"Both of you, shut your traps," said one of the detectives. "We knew you'd be comin' here one o' these days, Horton. We've been takin' turns campin' out in this beautiful meadow, just waitin' for you. Almost sorry to leave it, actually, but the game's over. It's time you dropped your weapon."

Clive remained still and silent; Cristina thought he might surrender. But then he dashed for the door, dragging Cristina with him and holding her so close, she could feel his every thumping heartbeat. He moved the gun muzzle to the side of her head and poked her so hard, she let out an involuntary yelp from the pain.

"I swear I'll shoot 'er if you try t' stop me!" he yelled.

Fear blurred Cristina's vision, and all she could do was pray silently, *Lord, be with me. Lord, keep me calm. Lord, get me through this alive.*

∼

Clive swallowed bile but kept his wits about him. He had to make a run for it, somehow, some way. He turned his head from side to side, searching in all directions, while keeping his arm firmly planted across Cristina's middle and his gun jabbing her in the skull, his finger on the trigger. "Everybody jus' make way," he demanded. "If this lady goes down, it'll be because you didn't cooperate."

"Just take it easy, Horton," said one of the Pinkertons.

"Put yer guns down, every last one o' you!" Clive shouted, his eyes darting from one man to the next. "Now!"

One by one, the men laid down their weapons. He couldn't help grinning at the feeling of empowerment that came over him. "That's good. Now…move outta the barn where I can see you." No one moved. "I said move!" he screamed. This time, they obeyed him like senseless hogs going to the slaughterhouse.

He waited till they were all outside and then he moved Cristina in front of him, still holding her tightly. "Call yer horse."

Thunder had been grazing in a nearby patch of grass. Cristina whistled and the horse lifted his head and approached them. "Climb on up," Clive instructed her.

"No." She shook her head.

"Get up on yer dumb horse, woman."

She shook her head once more.

Clive's ire was mounting fast. "Get up there, or I'll shoot you!"

That Stiles woman had the nerve to look over her shoulder at him and…and smile?! "Shoot me, Clive? Really? And destroy yer single chance at gettin' outta this alive?"

Anger boiled up inside him from head to toe. Who did she think she was? He was the one in control here, not her. Yet she calmly stood there, cocky and calm, while her horse pawed the ground as if to show his impatience.

Clive turned at a clicking sound behind him. A Pinkerton stood just a few feet away, with his revolver only inches from Clive's head. He must've had a weapon stashed in his belt. "Drop it, Horton," he barked. "You're done."

Before he had a chance to think through his next move, the woman wriggled violently in his arms, knocking him off balance. Within seconds, the men were on him, forcing him to the ground, snatching his gun, and tying his hands behind his back. He wailed as much from humiliation as from pain.

With the side of his face pressed to the hard ground and somebody's knee planted in the middle of his back, he laid eyes on Mike Farmer. His former friend wore a cold, smug grin.

32

Jack pulled out his watch when they started marching again after two hours' rest. Five o'clock. He dared not voice how weary he was because everyone else felt the same. Still, he would be glad when they reached the Cumberland Gap, surely before breakfast.

"I heard you got shot by some woman, Lieutenant. How'd that happen?" A private from his infantry, Robert Hauzer, had come up alongside him.

"I'm afraid you heard right," Jack replied, almost thankful for the distraction of conversation...although he would have preferred a different topic. "She mistook me for another Union soldier who'd caused problems for her. She shot me before realizing I meant her no harm."

"I guess you must be all healed up by now, huh?"

"I'm doing fine, thank you. The woman who shot me actually nursed my wound."

"That's pretty ironic—her shootin' you and then turnin' around and givin' you medical care."

"I think she felt somewhat obligated to help, particularly when she found out my reason for coming on her property was to deliver a letter to her from her deceased husband."

"The one you shot, you mean."

"How did you know about that?"

"News travels fast."

Jack grunted. "Indeed. What sort of rumors passed about my disappearance?"

"Oh, some thought you were dead, some wondered if you'd been snatched by some Rebs on the trail, and a few even considered the possibility o' desertion, though anyone who knew you well knew that just wasn't possible. You're about the most loyal soldier I ever met. Regardless o' the rumors, there were plenty concerned when you came up missin'. We didn't want you to come to any harm."

"I appreciate that."

"It was just a crazy, sad coincidence, Marsh dyin' o' heart failure before he ever had the first chance to tell anybody where you was goin'."

"Yes, I was deeply sorry to hear about Major Marsh's passing."

Their conversation stalled and soon, someone called Hauzer's name, so the private fell out of line to see what was wanted. Jack marched on, talking to other soldiers along the way, until he had a few minutes to himself again. In the solitude of his thoughts, his mind went to wondering about Cristina, as it did several times a day. How was she doing? Did she ever think of him? He so wished for a chance to mail her the letters he'd written. Did she think he'd forgotten all about her? He prayed not.

⌒

"Did y' miss us t'day, Mama?" Catherina asked as Cristina tucked her blanket up under her chin.

"I sure did, honey. More than you'll ever know."

Cristina thanked the Lord she made it back home before her children returned from visiting the Garners' farm. Both of them had talked almost continuously about all the exciting things they'd done that day— everything from wading in the pond, catching turtles, and climbing trees to eating Mrs. Garner's ice cream, playing with the barn cats, and watching Mr. Garner break in a horse.

"He fell off three times, Maw, but he kept jumpin' back on till he had that horse all calmed down," Elias explained now as he sat on the edge of Catherina's trundle bed. "I never saw nothin' like it. I wanna break in horses when I grow up."

"Y' do, do you? Well, we'll have t' see about that. I wouldn't want you hurtin' yerself."

"Someday I'll be too big fer you t' worry about."

Cristina shook her head. "Never."

"Not even when I'm a man and have my own farm?"

"Not even then." Cristina reached over to tousle his thick, light brown hair.

"I'm livin' here forever," Catherina announced.

Cristina smiled. "That would make me very happy."

"I bet you got bored today when we was gone," the girl mused.

Cristina burst out laughing. She couldn't help it.

"What's so funny, Maw?" Elias asked.

Cristina forced herself to sober. "Nothin'. Nothin' at all. I was just thinkin' 'bout today and how I'm glad it's over."

"Because y' missed us so much?" Catherina asked.

"Yes, exactly." She doubted she would ever divulge the full details of the day's events to either of them. But the news of Clive Horton's capture would soon be all over town, so she would have to explain it to some degree. Besides, she wanted them to know that they need never fear a repeat attack by Clive and his cohort. That knowledge alone gave Cristina untold peace and great relief.

"Mrs. Garner said there's church t'morrow. Are we goin'?" Catherina asked.

"We sure are. I wouldn't wanna miss it."

"Me, neither," said Elias.

Cristina stood and stretched. "Guess that means we should all get some sleep so we'll be bright-eyed in the mornin'."

"Can we start sayin' bedtime prayers?" Elias asked.

The question took her by surprise. She'd been doing a lot of praying lately, but never aloud. "I think that's a fine idea. Would you like t' lead us in prayer tonight, Elias?"

"Me? No, you do it. Our Sunday school teacher told us t' remind our parents t' say a bedtime prayer every night. She said it helps t' keep the bad dreams away."

A silly kind of shyness came over her at the thought of praying in front of her children. "Well, all right, then, but…can't say my prayer'll be very good."

"It's okay, Mama," said Catherina, reaching for Cristina's hand. "I think God'll still like it."

Overcome with gratitude for the sweetness of her children, Cristina closed her eyes, took a big breath for courage, and began: "Dear God, we thank You fer this bright an' sunny day. We thank you fer keepin' us, um, safe. An' fer listenin' to our prayers. May we all have a good night's sleep." She paused, trying to think if there was anything else she should say.

"Pray for Jack," Elias piped up.

Her heart took a little tumble at the mention of Jack's name. "Yes, please keep Jack safe—wherever he may be right now. And give us a good night's sleep."

"You already said that," Catherina said quietly.

"Shh!" Elias whispered. "God doesn't mind."

Cristina couldn't help but giggle. She'd fumbled through her first spoken prayer, but she had finished it, with her children's help. She hoped God had a sense of humor. "Amen," she finally said. What would Jack think about her praying with her children tonight—and praying for him, no less? An amazing sense of sweetness filled her spirit. She had prayed—out loud—and God had heard her. She just knew it.

"Can we do that ev'ry night?" Catherina asked.

Cristina clapped her hands. "Every night from now on."

Later, Cristina lay awake in bed, listening to Catherina's soft breathing on the trundle bed beside her, and reflected further on the day. She first recalled the moment Clive had burst into her house that morning and begun making demands of her. Then her mind traveled to many of the details that followed, from her blindfolded ride on a bumpy trail, to her fruitless search for his stolen goods, to the moment when the first Pinkerton detective showed up. Then she remembered the moment she'd defied Clive's demand that she climb back in the saddle, despite his threat to use his gun on her. The very notion now made her tremble. Where could that extra dose of courage have come from, if not from God Himself? She knew that He had heard her prayer for courage and strength and had granted those things when she needed them most. And she hadn't done a single thing to earn His love and watchful care.

She thought about how, after the men had hauled Clive away on a wagon they'd had stashed in the woods, Clive's commanding officer—an older gentleman by the name of Lieutenant Reginald Bond—had accompanied her home and the unexpectedly pivotal conversation they'd had during that slow, side-by-side ride on horseback. When Lieutenant Bond had complimented her on her show of bravery, she'd explained that she credited God with having answered her prayer for courage. He'd then commended her faith and asked to know when she had come to acknowledge God as her Lord and Savior. She hadn't known quite what to say. While she was nearly certain she'd sensed God's presence that day, she still wasn't sure if she was ready to call Him "Lord," or if she could count on him as her Savior. Surprisingly, she'd felt comfortable telling him as much and she'd admitted her difficulty in believing that God could love her and save her, seeing as she had nothing of value to offer Him.

At this, Lieutenant Bond had given a gentle laugh that had made her feel warm and accepted rather than embarrassed. "Of course, you have nothing of value to offer Him," he'd said. "None of us does. That's the reason we call it the 'grace of God'—it's a gift based not on our worthiness but wholly on Christ's sacrifice on the cross. No one—not even the most pious or most talented—could ever earn salvation. Christ died for our sins in order to bring each of us to God. Again, it wasn't anything *we* did, but what *He* did on our behalf. All we need to do is believe it and look to Him alone for salvation."

In that moment, things had started making a bit more sense to her—almost like a fog beginning to lift on a damp and dewy morning.

Now, hours later, Cristina turned over in bed and closed her eyes. "God," she whispered, "I…I wanna thank You fer this day." Just like that, her eyes filled with tears. "Thank You fer sendin' yer Son Jesus t' die fer sinners like me. Thank You that there's nothin' special I have t' do t' earn the gift of salvation, except t' trust an' believe You. That's what the lieutenant said anyway. Would You forgive me o' my sins, Jesus, and help me t' live fer You?" She could barely get the next words out because of the sudden emotion that clogged her throat. At last, she managed, "Would You be my Lord an' Savior?" She lay there in the stillness, wiping her damp eyes with her bedsheet.

Was that all there was to it? Was she a Christian now? The lieutenant had said all she had to do was trust and believe. "I believe," she whispered. Her heart swelled with unspeakable peace, even as her damp eyes started to grow heavy and her thoughts slowed down. A half smile found its way to her mouth as she pressed her palms together and tucked them under her cheek. *I'm a Christian. I have t' tell Clara.*

She awoke the next morning to gray skies, but the dreary weather did nothing to dampen her jubilant spirit. She tore the covers off and climbed carefully out of bed so as not to wake her dozing daughter. For as long as her children chose to sleep, she decided that, once she was dressed and ready, she would sit at the kitchen table and read her Bible—the Bible Jack had given her. Oh, if only she could tell him the news of her salvation. Perhaps she would go ahead and write the first letter. Yes, that is what she would do this afternoon and she would mail it from the post office while the children were at school tomorrow.

33

*J*ack's unit arrived tired and hungry at the gateway to the Cumberland Gap a few minutes short of seven o'clock the next morning. Word had it they'd marched sixty miles in fifty-two hours. "Exhausted" didn't begin to describe the way they felt. Even so, Jack heard nary a complaint. He did hear that, upon their arrival, Major General Ambrose Burnside sent a message to inform Confederate General John Frazer that his brigade was closing in on his position. Unless he surrendered immediately, they would surely overthrow him. And now, Burnside's men waited.

Many men took advantage of the break to lie down in the dewy grass and rest, heads propped upon their knapsacks. Jack, meanwhile, decided to walk ahead and try to locate Colonel Gilbert.

He found the officer sitting on a folding chair, talking with a few soldiers. As Jack approached the group, Colonel Gilbert glanced up at him. Jack clicked his heels and saluted.

"At ease, Fuller," the man told him. "How did your men fare?"

"They're tired but no worse for the wear."

Gilbert nodded. "That's good. We're hoping to receive our orders shortly. How did the rest of the contingent look as you made your way to the front?"

"They appear to be in good shape, sir. We're prepared to carry out our orders, whatever they may be."

"I'll send someone back to inform you as soon as I hear."

"Excellent." Jack started to turn.

"Oh, Fuller?"

Jack stopped and pivoted on his heel. "Yes, sir?"

"Well done. That's all."

"Thank you, sir." In some ways, it was good to be back in the field—to have a purpose, and, if nothing else, to make time pass. November couldn't get here soon enough.

The day wore on with no new information. By early afternoon, men had started taking up card games, reading, writing letters, smoking hand-rolled cigarettes, and snacking on whatever rations they'd packed. Jack leaned against a tree and closed his eyes. Within minutes, the rattle of wagon wheels roused him to attention. He opened his eyes and peered at the approaching wagon. When he read "U.S. MAIL" on its side, Jack leaped to his feet.

"Sorry I ain't got no mail for any o' you fellas," the driver shouted out the window. "I'm just passin' through, makin' my way to Maryville with a few stops in between. I'm willin' t' take whatever letters you might have ready for mailin' though. Is that anybody?"

Jack yanked open his rucksack and grabbed the four letters he'd penned to Cristina, his heart thumping wildly at the prospect of her finally hearing from him, never mind that they were short little missives that all said pretty much the same thing. He'd not been able to get her face out of his mind since that final morning when she'd watched the Army haul him away. He prayed that she was safe and that she and the children were thriving—physically, emotionally, and spiritually.

He approached the wagon with several men equally anxious to hand off their correspondence. They dropped their missives one by one into the canvas bag the driver held open. "I prob'ly won't reach Maryville till early tomorrow," the fellow said. "That's where these'll get sorted an' sent off."

A few cheers rang out. "Thanks, mister," said one soldier. "We ain't had mail fer days."

"That so? Could be your mail carrier's havin' trouble locatin' your unit. What're you all doin' hangin' out here?"

"Waitin' on orders," another soldier put in. "We're about t' chase some stubborn Rebs outta the Gap."

"Well, good luck t' you, and God be with you." With that, the mail carrier clicked at his two-horse team and set off.

A few minutes before three that afternoon, a messenger on horseback rode down the line, announcing that Brigadier General Frazer had surrendered his garrison. The sound of cheering filled the air and even Jack let out a whoop. Anytime the Rebs forfeited their weapons without the need for bloodshed was reason for celebration.

Then Jack sobered and sighed. The day wasn't over, by any means. They had weapons to confiscate and Rebs to haul off to wagons that would deliver them to prison camps. Still, the worst was over, and they could all rest a little easier.

⌒

Cristina sat at the table, her letter to Jack before her, and stared out the side window. Elias and Catherina had gone out to the barn to tend to the goats, cow, and horses, and now that those chores were finished, they were playing on the swing. Cristina couldn't see them but could hear their happy voices. It did her heart good knowing they could play freely with no threat of another attack from Clive Horton.

Her eyes trailed back to her letter. She decided to reread it, knowing she still had time to make additions before mailing it tomorrow.

September 10, 1863

Dear Jack,

I hope this letter finds you well. I am sorry for the way we had to part ways, but I'm glad your brother sent a telegram to let me know you were safe, at least for the time being. I hope you were able to convince the Army that you did not desert. Perhaps you know this by now, but it was Clive Horton who turned you in with those false allegations. He told me himself.

You may wonder how I came to talk to him at all. I do not wish to worry you. While the children were at a friend's house for the day, he took me captive, but it was not long until he was apprehended by his own lieutenant, the local sheriff, and some Pinkerton detectives. It is a great relief to me that both Clive Horton and Mike Farmer (who didn't die from that gunshot wound at Roslyn's, after all) are now behind bars.

I wanted to tell you that I am finally a genuine Christian. I've prayed and asked God to forgive my sins. I understand now that God sacrificed His one and only Son as payment for my sins. I thought I wasn't good enough, but it was actually Clive Horton's commanding officer who explained to me in a way I could understand that salvation is a free gift no one can ever earn. (How I came to talk to him is another story. I guess God had a hand in it.) I've been going to church and reading my Bible, and last night Elias and Catherina told me they wanted me to start saying bedtime prayers every night.

Clara has been visiting us off and on. I don't know what she will say when I tell her of my newfound faith. I hope I can convince her to come to church with us.

I hope you don't mind that I wrote you without first hearing from you. It seems overly bold, but I could not help it. Elias told me the other day that he misses you. That's something, coming from a boy who once hated Yanks. The children start school tomorrow. Catherina hardly seems old enough. I will miss them both during the day.

I pray that you dodge every bullet that comes your way. Better yet, I pray you don't have to dodge any bullets at all.

Best regards to you,
Cristina

She reread the letter several times and thought about her closing, wondering if she should have signed it differently. Would he think it too formal? Or not formal enough? She'd written with extra attention to proper spelling and grammar, pondering every word and reading the sentences in her head before actually putting them to paper. The result was far from perfect, but she'd done the best she could. Satisfied, she folded the note, then affixed a seal. Addressing it was the real problem because Jack had never given her a mailing address. She knew his infantry number, but that was all. She decided to call on a new tool in her arsenal: prayer. "Lord, if You want this letter t' reach Jack, please see to it that it falls in the hands o' the right sorter. Amen." It felt good to pray aloud and even better to know God heard her. Now it was up to Him to answer in the way He thought best.

The next morning at breakfast, Elias ate faster than a baby bird, full of nervous energy and excitement. Catherina, on the other hand, hardly touched her food. "I don't wanna go t' school," she said while slowly chewing. "My tummy hurts."

"Would you feel better if I took you on the first day?" Cristina asked.

Catherina nodded timidly.

"You don't need t' take us," Elias protested. He turned to his sister. "Catherina, I'll be right there."

"You aren't the same as Mama."

"I'll take you in the wagon," Cristina said.

Elias folded his arms across his chest. "I'm not ridin' in the wagon. Someone might see me."

"Oh, Elias, that's silly. Other mothers'll be there."

"No, they won't."

"Yes, they will."

In the end, Elias relented and agreed to be driven. And Cristina was hardly the only mother who showed up. Catherina clung close to her side, hanging on to her skirts. She perked up when she spotted Susannah Garner. Elias had already scooted off to be with his friends and hadn't even said good-bye. Cristina bent close to Catherina. "Will you be all right walkin' home with yer brother today, or should I come back with the wagon?"

"Come back," Catherina muttered.

"Mrs. Stiles, so nice to see you. And this must be Catherina." The schoolteacher—a pleasant-mannered middle-aged man named Mr. Harding—bent over and shook Catherina's hand.

Cristina was relieved to see her ofttimes-timid daughter give her new teacher a tiny smile.

Soon it was time for the students to head inside. Cristina gave Catherina a quick hug, then smiled as Charlotte Garner approached with Susanna. The little girls held hands as they climbed the stairs and disappeared into the building.

"It's not easy sendin' our youngest ones off to school, is it?" Charlotte mused.

Cristina shook her head. "It's not, but I'm not cryin' so I guess I'm takin' it a lot better than I thought I would."

"Well, good morning, ladies." Reverend Wilcox climbed down from his horse and looped the reins around the post outside the schoolhouse. "Mr. Harding asked me to come this morning to offer a prayer for the students."

"That's a lovely gesture, Reverend," said Charlotte. "Cristina and I have just left our youngest children at school for the first time and we're tryin' to decide whether to be happy or sad about it."

He chuckled. "There is something to be said for having more time to yourselves. I say, enjoy it while you have the chance." He turned his attention to Cristina. "Pardon me for changing the subject, but I understand you had a part in the seizure of Clive Horton?"

"That murderer who's been on the run?" Charlotte asked with a gasp. "Cristina!"

Cristina gave a rueful little smile. "Oh, dear, reverend. The news is out then?"

He nodded. "I heard about it just now at the livery. I'm sure there'll be an article in today's newspaper. At any rate, it's good those characters are both in jail. I was surprised to learn that the other fellow hadn't died in the shooting. I guess the Army wanted to keep it quiet until they caught Mr. Horton."

The three of them conversed a bit more before the reverend said good-bye and went into the schoolhouse. Charlotte wanted details about the capture of Clive Horton, so Cristina relayed them as best she could. Tonight, she would have to sit her children down and tell them what had happened. Best to do it before they heard a myriad of other versions of the story. She only hoped she would not be stopped by every person who happened upon her in town that day. Besides mailing her letter to Jack, she needed to stop at the mercantile to buy more thread for her next sewing project—a dress for Catherina and a shirt for Elias. She'd sent her children to school in clothes that were rather tattered, but as she'd surveyed the other students as they arrived, she'd realized Elias and Catherina wouldn't stand out. Most of the other children were also shoeless.

After she and Charlotte parted ways, she set off for town. To her great relief, she met up with only a few folks who'd heard about her part in Clive Horton's capture—a couple of customers at the post office and the cashier at the mercantile—and none of them pressed her for details.

She'd wanted to tell both the reverend and Charlotte about the prayer she had prayed, but the timing didn't seem quite right. Besides, she rather relished the idea of sharing that precious knowledge with Jack alone—God already knew, of course—for the time being. Something about telling Jack first seemed very special. She did, however, intend to tell Clara about the power of prayer the next time she saw her, which could be today or next week. One never knew when that spirited woman might come knocking.

34

Jack sat on the ground in the shade of a maple tree and read Cristina's letter for at least the fifth time. He pored over every word, reading and rereading the paragraph that described how she'd turned her life over to Christ. His heart rejoiced at the news, especially knowing she'd made the decision all on her own. Furthermore, it erased any reservations he might have had about asking her to be his wife.

Her brief account of her abduction by Clive Horton both intrigued and frightened him. He whispered a prayer of thanks to the Lord for protecting her and also for seeing to it that neither Clive nor Mike would ever bother her again. He smiled to learn that Elias missed him, but he wished Cristina might have said she did, too. He tried to read between the lines for any sign or hint that she hoped to see him again, or that she'd forgiven him for shooting her husband, but he found no such message. The sole regret she expressed was regarding the manner in which they'd had to part. Perhaps she meant she wished they'd had a chance to talk about their argument the previous night, so she could tell him she wasn't still angry. He at least knew she didn't wish him dead, so there was that.

Jack held the paper to his nose to see if he could find a trace of her scent. Silly, but he supposed that's what happened when a man grew desperate. He wondered if she'd received any of the four letters he'd mailed. If so, had she been as happy to get them as he was to get hers? When the mail wagon had rolled into camp earlier that day, he hadn't expected to hear his name called; even then, he'd assumed it was a letter from his mother. His heart had done a giant flip at the sight of the return address: "Cristina Stiles, Ripley, West Virginia." He'd nearly torn into the letter right there in front of everybody. Thankfully, he'd managed to exercise patience and move to a private spot.

He checked his pocket watch. Three o'clock. He had time to write back to her and even send the letter from the post office today, since mail delivery had resumed a normal schedule. He drew out some stationery and his fountain pen. Using his Bible as a hard surface, he began to write.

September 18, 1863

Dear Cristina,

I can't tell you how happy I was to hear from you today. Thank you for writing. I've written you exactly four letters, but we had a delay in mail going in and out of Knoxville, where I was stationed for a time, so I was unable to post them until a week or so ago. Let me just go ahead and tell you I'm missing you more than you know. I miss Elias and Catherina, too, and I often wonder how they are faring in school, especially Catherina.

I am managing to dodge every bullet for now. After securing a surrender at Cumberland Gap, the 45th Ohio Infantry has moved on to Sweetwater, Tennessee, some 40 miles south of Knoxville, where General Burnside has ordered us to occupy the town and maintain control of the railroad. There has been a series of engagements with Confederate forces, but the Union has dominated the Sweetwater Valley ever since capturing Knoxville. The tide can change quickly, so I'm in constant communication with my commanding officers, but

I'm grateful for the calm right now. I don't mean to bore you with details of war, but I wanted you to know where I am at the writing of this letter. I am unspeakably happy to know that you have given your heart and soul to Jesus. That has been my continual prayer for you, Cristina.

Jack paused in his writing, wishing he could tell her right then that he loved her. He didn't know how she might receive such news, however, and he also knew that such a declaration was best made in person. He also longed to tell her that he planned to return to Ripley upon being discharged from the Army, but that news, too, had to wait. In her letter, she'd given no indication she wished to see him again. He pondered his next words for a moment before picking up his pen once more.

Continue reading your Bible daily because that is how God will speak to you and how you will grow in your faith. God uses His holy Word to plant messages of love into your heart. I'm honored that I was able to give you my Bible. By the way, I came across a Union soldier who had an extra one he gave to me. See how God provides?

I am anxious to hear more details about this abduction you mentioned. I'm relieved that those two monsters are behind bars, but the thought that Clive Horton came onto your land yet again makes my blood boil.

Thank you for going to the telegraph office the morning I left Ripley. My brother was able to travel to where I was and arrange my freedom. We spent some time together before returning to our respective duties, but I guess I already told you that in one of my earlier letters.

I pray every day for you. Please tell Elias and Catherina that I think about them often and wish I could see them again. Take care of yourself.

Until next time…
Jack

He spent at least five minutes trying to decide how to conclude his letter. Seeing that she'd kept her closing simple, he did the same.

If only things between them didn't have to be so complicated.

With more excitement than Cristina could contain, she read all four of Jack's letters in the order in which he'd written them. The children had gone to bed an hour ago, so now, by lamplight, she reread them yet again while sipping coffee and nibbling on a piece of bread smothered with apple butter.

August 17, 1863

Dear Cristina,

Thank you for sending the telegram to Joseph. The Union soldiers that came to your farm that morning were from Clive Horton's company. They put me in a prison tent, and their captain was determined to doubt every word I said when I explained how I'd been recovering from a gunshot wound. He even accused me of having shot myself just so I would have an excuse to stay at your farm. I think he would've hanged me within 24 hours if my brother hadn't shown up. Joseph brought with him a telegram from Brigadier General George H. Thomas demanding my release. To this day, I don't know how my brother managed that one, but I'm glad he did.

I am being summoned by the major. Thank you again. I think of you often.

Jack

Cristina folded that letter and reread the next one.

August 20, 1863

Dear Cristina,

I was not able to mail the letter I wrote you a couple of days ago. The citizens of Knoxville, where I am currently stationed, are apparently receiving their mail just fine, but no mail wagon has visited our camp. Soldiers are in an uproar about it, but I keep telling them things will get ironed out soon enough.

The days have been uncommonly hot. I have been missing the stream that runs along your property.

It's time for me to help fry up some fish one of the fellows caught today. We'll be feasting tonight!

I hope you, Elias, and Catherina are doing well.

I can't stop thinking about you. I wish I'd been able to give you a proper good-bye.

Jack

A smile tickled the corners of her mouth. He couldn't stop thinking about her! She read that line again and again. And what had he meant by saying he wished they'd had a *proper* good-bye? Had he left with as many regrets as she'd had as she watched him ride away in the back of that wagon?

She moved on to letter three once more.

August 24, 1863

Dear Cristina,

Still no one coming to our regiment to pick up or deliver mail. We've determined it's not the U.S. Postal service that is failing us but a lack of mail carriers. The local citizens are receiving mail, but some Union camps aren't being serviced due to unrest ever since the Union started occupying the city. At any rate, I will continue writing letters, with plans to send them as a bundle when things open up.

In Knoxville, the tension is high. You'll find brother pitted against brother, father against son, and even husband against wife. Many longtime residents have fled town because of it.

Have you heard any news of a sighting—or, better yet, a seizure—of Clive Horton? I pray daily for your safety and for the protection of your children.

I'm sorry this letter is so short. We may be getting orders soon to move on toward the Cumberland Gap.

I sit here picturing you with your long dark braids falling over both shoulders. I never did tell you how pretty I think you are.

Jack

Cristina grinned and even felt herself blush at the way he'd ended this particular letter. He'd found her attractive? And thought about her braids? What else might he have observed about her? She gave her head a quick little shake, then folded the letter and set it on top of the others before proceeding to reread the fourth and final one.

August 30, 1863

Dear Cristina,

Still no mail wagon. This problem will soon come to an end, I'm sure of it. At some point, you will receive all my letters at once. I think that, for now, I shall cease writing until I've sent these four off to you. I don't have much else to tell you at this point, anyway, except that it is quite certain we will soon mobilize to the Cumberland Gap.

To date, most of my responsibilities here have consisted of helping to build fortifications around the city. It is the Union's hope to erect some 20 forts to keep the Confederates at bay. It isn't out of the question that the Rebels might try to reclaim the city of Knoxville. They won't succeed, I can guarantee you that.

I apologize for boring you with news from the front; it's just that there isn't much else new to share.

I keep picturing you working around your farm, tidying up your home, and cooking those wonderful meals of yours, and I wonder how you do it while also managing two very active youngsters. You are a wonder, Mrs. Stiles.

I think of you often and wish I could catch one more glimpse of your pretty smile.

Yours,
Jack

"Yours," he'd written. Cristina wondered how to interpret it, or whether it was a word that even needed interpreting. Good heavens, she'd probably read far too much into his every word. She needed to try to take them more at face value, as he'd intended them. Then again, he had mentioned her hair and her "pretty smile" and had called her a "wonder." Did he see something in her that she herself did not?

Tomorrow, when she penned her reply, she would tell him that nothing he'd written had bored her. She was interested in everything he was doing. Most of all, she wanted to know if he intended to visit her upon his exit from the army. He'd said he would muster out in November, but when, exactly, would that happen? She wished to ask him without coming across as overly bold. Such a dilemma. She was in love with a man but hadn't the courage to tell him, even on paper. Would she ever have that chance? Should she write that she forgave him for shooting Orville, or was that something better left unsaid until a future reunion—if that day ever came? He'd certainly not brought it up yet. Then again, the four letters she'd just received had been rather ordinary. Oh, dear. Would she be able to sleep tonight with her mind such a flurry of thoughts?

But she needn't have worried. Within several minutes of putting her head to the pillow, she drifted into sweet slumber—and dreamt that she'd floated out to sea in a large rowboat. At first, she'd been frightened, until she turned around and discovered Jack behind her. He had a puppy in his arms and was saying, "Let's go back to shore now so we can give this dog to Elias."

35

October 12, 1863

Dear Jack,

I have now received nine letters from you, which I continually reread to myself and also to Elias and Catherina, who enjoy them as much as I do. I am trying to keep up with you by writing every day. Please stop apologizing for telling me news of the war. I rarely have a chance to read the local newspaper, so I don't usually know what's happening, other than what you've told me and what I've heard about town. I saved the article about the capture of Clive Horton. You would probably find it interesting.

The children have now been attending school for a month and have been enjoying it. Catherina is already starting to read. I knew she was smart, but I didn't know just how smart until recently. Elias has fun being with his friends on a regular basis. They are both such chatterboxes when they get home.

Elias talks about you almost every day. He was asking me just yesterday when you would be mustering out of the army. He wanted to know if he will ever see you again. Of course, I did not know what to tell him.

The farm has been keeping me busy, but it has also been a good source of income lately. I sell eggs to the local grocer three times a week and I'm preparing to take the hog to Mr. Trigstead to slaughter, though Elias begs me not to. He and Catherina will soon return from school, so I had better start on supper.

I think about you often, too.

Cristina

October 12, 1863

Dear Cristina,

You have me very excited about mail call every day. We've been busy in Sweetwater, where I'm currently stationed. The Confederates are getting fidgety; it is clear they plan to attempt another siege on Knoxville. They'll be sorry, though, as Union troops have fortified the perimeter.

I relish news of life in Ripley. I'm glad to hear you're attending church faithfully and making friends.

Sorry this is so short. I need to settle a scuffle among some of the men and the mail wagon is on its way.

Yours,
Jack

October 16, 1863

Dear Jack,

   The children just arrived home from school wearing even bigger smiles than usual. They are excited because their teacher is taking the class on a nature excursion tomorrow. They are to pick up any interesting things they find along the way, take them back to their classroom, and write about their findings. Catherina will get help with her project from one of the older children. It's very nice the way the bigger children help the younger ones. She is learning quite a lot in a very short time.

   Elias and Catherina have just asked me to tell you they say hello and that they miss you. My boy has changed his stance on the war and now sides with the Yankees and I think you played no small part in that. The schoolteacher is also a Yankee, through and through, and I know Elias looks up to him. Many of the locals are still undecided about where they stand. My views are swaying the other direction, as well, but Clara remains a staunch Confederate. She is also quite mystified about my newfound Christian faith. While she doesn't discount the faith altogether, she claims that the Ripley Methodist church, and Reverend Wilcox, in particular, have given me a "cockeyed" view of life. I just smile and tell her they had very little to do with it. I had an emptiness in my life long before I met the reverend—and even before I met you—which, I learned later, was there because I didn't know Jesus as Lord and Savior. If you hadn't come along when you did, I might never have gotten a Bible or heard the gospel message that God loves me.

   The children are complaining about their growling stomachs, so I must sign off for now.

                                             Cristina

October 20, 1863

Dear Cristina,

You are doing a fine job keeping up with my writing. I feel I'm the one who must work hard to keep up with you. I'm sorry I haven't been able to find as much time as I would like to write to you, but the major has us busy almost around the clock.

The good news is, I will muster out in less than two weeks. Cristina, I must be honest: I miss you and the children, and I want to see you again, but I do not know if you want to see me. I would like to return to Ripley for another visit—and stay longer this time, if you would like me to. Of course, I would find a room in town. I know we have matters to discuss, and a dispute that neither of us has mentioned still hangs between us. I've been waiting to see if you would bring it up, but in case this is my last letter, I want you to know how very sorry I am that I shot your beloved husband. I don't know if you will ever be able to put that behind you. Please know that I won't come back to Ripley if you don't want me to. Should you feel that my return would be too difficult, then I shall make my way to my family's farm.

Tensions in the area continue to increase. I'm afraid there will be another Confederate siege on Knoxville, but, God willing, I will be mustered out by then.

I am yours,
Jack

October 22, 1863

Dear Jack,

I'm sorry I missed a few days of writing you. I came down with a fever and a terribly upset stomach. Clara spent a couple of nights here to see to my care and get the children off to school. I'm feeling much better now, but I'm sad to say that both Elias and Catherina have fallen ill. Elias has been spending most of his time lying on the floor by the fire because he's afraid he won't make it down the ladder from his bed in the loft in time to get outside. I do think he is turning the corner faster than Catherina.

I suppose you will soon muster out. Since you have not told me of your plans, let me just say I wish you the best of everything.

God be with you.
Cristina

After rereading the missive, Cristina quickly folded it, addressed it, and affixed a three-cent stamp. She then handed it to Clara, who'd offered to mail it today when she went into town.

"Thank you fer stoppin' by, Clara," Cristina said. "As usual, you've been more than generous with yer time and you have yer own animals t' tend."

"Well, I had to make sure you was still recoverin'," Clara replied. "You got yerself darned sick. I'm just glad I could help."

"I hope you don't get sick yerself. The kids said a few o' their class-mates were missin' last week. Prob'ly caught the same thing."

Clara shook her head. "Don't go worryin' 'about me. I cain't even remember the last time I felt under the weather. I think it must be those couple swigs o' whiskey I take every night at suppertime what keeps me healthier than a May flower."

Cristina laughed. "Oh, Clara, you make me laugh!"

"I hope we don't have t' miss church on Sunday," Catherina mused sleepily from where she lay on her trundle.

"You ever gonna come with us t' church, Miss Clara?" asked Elias, who'd stretched out on Cristina's bed with a book he'd borrowed from Mr. Harding. "I think you'd like it."

"We'll see."

"We'll see" was a lot better than "Never," which was the answer Cristina had always gotten when she invited Clara to church. Perhaps she ought to rely on Elias to do the inviting from now on.

"I'm glad t' hear you'd consider it, Clara."

"Yeah, we'll see. Well, I must be goin'. I gotta mail yer letter now an' pick up a few supplies. You sure you don't need anything?"

"No, we should be set, but thank you."

Clara glanced down at the letter. "What d' you hear from the lieutenant these days?"

"He writes often. He'll be discharged soon, but he hasn't said what his next plans are."

Clara leaned closer and arched her gray eyebrows. "I know what you're hopin' he'll do," she said quietly.

Cristina gave a dismissive wave of her hand. "Oh, stop it. I suppose if he wants t' see us again, he'll make a point t' visit."

"Have y' told him y' want t' see 'im again?"

Cristina cast her eyes downward. "That'd be awful forward o' me."

"He might be lookin' for a sign. Appeared to me he was startin' t' have eyes for y'. You might want t' rethink—"

"What're you talkin' about?" asked Elias, lowering his book to his chest.

"Nothin'. Miss Clara was just leavin'." Cristina jumped to her feet and opened the door. "Thanks again fer everything."

Clara grinned, revealing her crooked top teeth. "I'll see ya' soon, my bricky buddy."

Catherina took a long nap and awoke close to bedtime. The poor thing was still weak, but her fever had broken and she asked for something to eat.

"How 'bout some tea an' a huckleberry biscuit?" Cristina suggested.

"Okay," Catherina said in a wee voice.

"Can I have some, too?" Elias asked.

"Sure."

Cristina set the pot of water on the grill to heat it for their tea. The fire seemed a bit smoky, so she used the tongs to move the logs around a bit. After their snack, they all went outside to use the necessary, Cristina carrying Catherina. Once back in the house, they washed their hands and faces, then climbed into bed. Cristina offered to sleep on the floor so that Elias could have her bed, but he said he preferred the pallet next to Catherina's trundle. He still didn't feel quite up to climbing the ladder to his attic bed, which was fine by Cristina. When her children were sick, she liked to have them close by in case they needed her.

They said a bedtime prayer and then Cristina read a couple of Bible verses aloud. Elias asked if he could read by lamplight a bit before going to sleep and Cristina allowed it, but it wasn't long before she heard him breathing heavily. She reached over and snuffed out the lamp on the small bedside table. Within a matter of minutes, she, too, drifted into a deep slumber.

The next thing Cristina knew, distant noises echoed off the walls, sounds she couldn't identify, followed by hollow-sounding screams that seemed to come from miles away. Where was she—and why couldn't she take a deep breath? Blackness lingered over and around her, closing in like the worst kind of storm, hovering, choking…smothering. *Breathe,* she told herself. *Breathe.* But there seemed nothing *to* breathe. Her head felt light—light as air itself—apart from her, floating far, far away. And the heat…oh, how it singed and burned, like flaming fingers reaching out to grab her by the throat. Reality drifted away as darkness slowly swallowed her up.

Suddenly she felt a firm grip on both ankles as she was pulled, moved, by someone else's strength. She could not have helped for anything. Not a muscle in her could assist. Something, *someone,* screamed "Maw!" but even that was not enough to awaken her fully. Another distant, reverberating scream pounded at her closed-up mind, like a persistent knock at a door she could not reach to open. She tried to wade through the deep, thick cobwebs tangling her senses, but it was no use. There was no hope for it. If she had eyes, she couldn't open them; if she had ears, she couldn't discern what she heard; if she had a mouth, she couldn't utter a sound; if she had hands or feet, they refused to cooperate. She was useless…immobile…next to death.

36

Shortly after breakfast, Jack was summoned to Major General Samuel Jones's tent. "Word is the Confederates are on the move," the major told Jack. "You're due to muster out in five days, Lieutenant. I suggest you go now before you get caught up in a siege that'll keep you entangled for who knows how much longer. I've arranged for Captain Jack Timmer to take over your company. I'll issue your honorable discharge exit papers and you can report to Lieutenant Conklin to have him stamp them. He has also prepared your final treasury note in appreciation for your service. And I must say, Lieutenant, while I haven't known you all that long, it's been a pleasure serving with you." Jones saluted first—a gesture of honor, considering he outranked Jack.

Jack quickly returned the salute, expressed his appreciation, and confirmed that he would muster out according to schedule. After some further conversation, Jack left the major's tent in somewhat of a daze. He could barely contain his brimming gratitude, yet he had to be careful not to show it in front of the men who were facing an imminent skirmish with the Rebs. The first thing he intended to do was secure Lieutenant Conklin's stamp on his papers. Then he would send word to his brother Joseph of his early discharge—well, a few days early—and then wire his mother, for she would certainly want to know.

Mother and Jesse would expect him to board the next train out of Sweetwater and head for Lebanon, but he had other plans. He hadn't heard a word from Cristina regarding how she felt about his proposed return to Ripley, but then, she probably hadn't yet received his latest letter, in which he'd expressed his desire to see her again. Her most recent letter had shared more of the same general news and a very vague, noncommittal closing and signature. Jack decided the only way to know for sure how she felt, and whether he stood any chance of ever winning her heart, was to confront her in person.

If he stuck to his plan—taking a reasonable amount of time to bid farewell to the members of his unit and the friends he'd made along the way, packing up what few possessions he had, and cashing his treasury note at the bank—Jack saw no reason why he couldn't be on the train to Charleston, West Virginia, sometime this afternoon. He wouldn't arrive till tomorrow, considering all the stops along the way and then the necessity of taking a stagecoach to Ripley. But he would be moving in the right direction and that was all that mattered to him at this point. *Cristina, I am coming to Ripley, whether you like it or not.*

As expected, he arrived in Ripley the next day at one in the afternoon. Having eaten an early lunch in Charleston while waiting for the stagecoach, he now had no other stops to make except at Lou's Livery on West North Street, a short walk from the depot, where he planned to rent a horse. He decided he'd walked enough over the past three years and didn't have time to waste in getting to Cristina's house. In fact, he could hardly wait to lay eyes on Cristina. What would be her initial reaction at the sight of him? Shock? Delight? Confusion? Her emotions might run the gamut, but he hoped one of them wouldn't be anger. Whatever the case, he resolved to be prepared.

He reached the livery and headed inside, nodding to the two men he passed who were seated on a bench out front, talking quietly.

On his entrance, a livery worker approached him. "How can I help y'?'

"I'd like to rent a horse."

"Fer how long?"

"I'm not sure exactly. Let's say a couple of days. Can I extend my rental time if I need to?"

"Sure. I'll need you t' sign this sheet here an' tell me when you'll be back. If y' don't return the horse within twenty-four hours o' when y' say you'll bring it back, there's an automatic warrant out fer yer arrest."

Jack grinned as he signed the paper. "No worries there, mister. I don't plan to leave town on your horse." He might have told him his destination, but he didn't wish to raise any questions about why he'd be visiting the widow, not that this fellow necessarily knew who she was.

"I've got a few out in the stable if y' want t' come out an' take yer pick."

"That's not necessary," Jack replied. "If you'll just saddle up your best horse, I'll take that one."

"All right, then. It'll run y' fifty cents a day."

The price was steep but worth it. Besides, Jack had the money. "That's not a problem."

The fellow nodded, then gave him a quick scan before turning around and heading for the door at the back of the livery. In the meantime, Jack fished a dollar bill out of his coin purse, unfolded it, and laid it on the dirty counter. Just then, he overheard some of the men's conversation outside.

"Yeah, y' just wonder what'll happen next in Ripley," one of them said. "Overnight, it seems we went from peace an' quiet t' tragedy an' misfortune."

"Ain't that the truth," said the other.

"You goin' to the funeral?"

"Nah. You?"

"The wife says I should, but I hate funerals."

"Know what y' mean."

The men kept up their dialogue, but Jack had trouble discerning what either of them was saying.

Within a quarter of an hour, he'd finished his business with the stable worker, mounted the rented horse named Darby, and headed in the direction of Cristina's small farm, his heart pounding inside his chest.

The sun shone in the azure sky, but the temperature had dropped considerably since summer—a welcome relief, in his opinion. He wore a long-sleeved cotton shirt he'd bought in Sweetwater, along with his trousers, boots, and broad-brimmed hat. He'd also gotten a shave and a haircut, then paid a visit to the local bathhouse. He secretly hoped all his sprucing up would pay off, but only time would tell. The closer he drew to Cristina's road, the more jittery and jumpy his nerves became, the quick clip of Darby's hooves matching his pulse.

He turned the corner and saw the barn in the distance, but something looked wrong. He nudged Darby's sides to bring him to a gallop and when they rounded the bend in the road, Jack pulled back on the reins, brought Darby to a stop, and stared straight ahead. *What in the world?* His mouth gaped and his eyes went wide as he sat there looking at piles of ashes, half a fireplace, and a mound of debris and broken glass where Cristina's little house had once stood. His gaze darted in all directions. There hung the tree swing, moving faintly with the breeze. The tree from which it hung bore evidence of fire damage, some of its charred branches having fallen to the ground. He clicked at Darby and raced out to the barn but knew without needing to look that it stood empty, with nary an animal in sight, not even in the pasture. What had happened? He recalled hearing the men outside the livery talking about a funeral. Dread as dark as midnight seeped into his soul, but he quickly told himself not to panic. Surely, they'd escaped in time, but…. *Oh, Lord, it can't be. No, God. Please, no!* He reined Darby around and kicked him to speed toward town, praying all the while.

The first place he stopped was the Methodist church, thinking he might find the preacher at the parsonage. Many wagons were parked in the churchyard and there were horses tied to every nearby post, yet it wasn't Sunday. Jack turned just as two boys wearing farm clothes walked past. "Hey, do you boys happen to know what's going on in there?" he asked, nodding toward the church building.

"Funeral, I think," said one boy.

"A funeral?" Dread arose once more.

"Yeah, but I don't know who died."

"Me neither," said the other boy. "My ma didn't tell me."

Jack's heart took a terrible tumble. "Thanks." He started to turn Darby around, then glanced over his shoulder. "Why aren't you boys in school?"

"It's closed t'day so's our teacher could go to the funeral."

Jack nodded and thanked them, then gave Darby a gentle kick in the sides, urging him into a gallop up Main Street toward Rosalyn's Restaurant. Upon reaching the establishment, he jumped down and looped the reins over a post, then hurried through the door, the bell overhead giving a loud jingle.

"Can I help you, sir?" asked a middle-aged woman standing behind the counter.

Jack glanced around. The entire place sat empty as a bird's nest in December. "Where is everybody?"

"I s'pose at the funeral. There's been too many funerals lately."

"Who…died, if I may ask?" Jack braced himself.

"Oh, somebody from town. You ain't from around here, are you?"

Jack's pounding heart nearly blew right out of his chest. "No, but… who died?" he asked again.

The woman sighed. "Old Doc Moore. He been sick a long time."

A great sigh released from Jack's own lungs.

"We'll surely miss 'im," she went on. "But we've got a new doc now. He's young, straight outta medical school an' smart as a horse's whip, from what I hear. He arrived a while back, bringin' his wife and little girl with him. They bought old Doc Moore's place. Moved right in with him and helped Doc Moore's daughter take care o' him right up to the end. His daughter don't live around here, so she'll be headin' back t' Chicago in the next few days. I hear-tell the new doc and his wife is gonna renovate an' redecorate Doc Moore's old house. It's in near disrepair. Well, listen to me blabbin' away. You want t' sit down an' have a bite t' eat?" She moved her arm in a sweeping motion. "As you can see, you got yer pick o' tables."

"No, thanks. Um, I'm sorry to hear about the doctor, but…well, you wouldn't happen to know anything about Cristina Stiles, would you? And her children?"

"Mrs. Stiles, the one who recently lost 'er husband—an' then 'er house in a fire?"

"Yes."

"Now that was another sad story, wasn't it? I'll tell you, it's been one tragedy after another around here. We had a murder in town a while back, too—right here in this very restaurant. Ripley ain't used to such calamity."

"But about Mrs. Stiles…" Jack was about to lose his patience.

"You know 'er?"

"Yes."

"Did y' know 'er husband?"

"No…yes. Well, no, I didn't."

"He fought for the Rebel forces. This here's a town divided, that's for sure."

"Yes, I've heard that, but Mrs. Stiles—"

She gave her head a despairing shake. "I mean, why *her*, after all she's been through? Hasn't she suffered enough loss?"

"Where is she?" If he'd been speaking to a man, he would have reached across the counter and picked him up by the lapels till he screamed for mercy.

"Oh, I ain't sure. Prob'ly still at the doctor's place. She's bad off, last I heard. Them poor kids."

"Where are the children? Are they all right?"

"Couldn't tell you. All I know is, it was a tragedy all around. I never heard the full story, mind you. I did hear somethin' 'bout her boy pullin' her outta the house though."

Jack started for the door, then stopped and turned. "Where's the doctor's office?"

"End of North Court Street. Big two-story house a block from the Methodist church."

Jack headed out the door just as she hollered, "He might be at the funeral though."

⌣

Cristina lay groggy and exhausted in a room at the Grimshaw residence. Dr. Grimshaw and his wife had been ever so gracious in caring for her ever since the fire and she could never thank Charlotte Garner enough for looking after her children while she recovered. Char and her husband had even insisted that the Stileses move in with their family until they had secured a new home. And plenty of people from the church and town had donated money, clothes, and other necessities to last them till they were back on their feet. Cristina felt overwhelmed by the kindness of others.

Her neighbor, Mr. Trigstead, was tending to her animals in his barns while she was laid up and had waved her off when she tried to reimburse him for their care and feeding. In fact, he offered to buy them as well as her farm and mentioned a price that was more than fair. She told him she'd have to think it over. The thought of giving up her beloved horses saddened her, but she very likely wouldn't have much choice. She'd cried too many times over all her losses, even while thanking the Lord for preserving her life and the lives of her precious children. Nothing on earth—no house, no plot of land, no number of animals—could possibly replace her children. She had yet to write to Jack about the fire. It was the first thing she would do when she regained her strength. She missed him so much.

Not for the first time, Cristina wondered if she should take Mr. Trigstead up on his offer, buy a small vacant lot in town, and build a new house. She was sure she could get a job someplace to support her little family....

A spasm of coughing hit her and out came more of the same black soot she'd been spewing as a result of all the smoke she'd inhaled. The doctor had said she would be dealing with it for days to come, but that the more she coughed, the better it was for her lungs. She'd developed a wheeze, too, which he'd said was normal and would probably clear up once her lungs had fully healed. Had it not been for Elias's quick action in yanking her from the flames, she would most certainly have died.

There came a knock on the door to the parlor, just outside Cristina's room, then the sound of a soft footfall as someone—probably Mrs. Grimshaw—padded down the hall. The door opened with its usual whining creak. "Hello, there," Mrs. Grimshaw said. "I'm sorry, but the doctor is attending a funeral service at the moment. Do you have a pressing need?"

"Um…yes, I have a pressing need. I'm looking for Cristina Stiles and heard I might find her here."

Cristina's ears perked up. It couldn't be! She wondered if she might be hallucinating, as she'd done during and after the fire.

"Oh! Well, yes, she's here, but she's quite ill. May I ask who's calling?"

"Of course, begging your pardon. My name's Jack Fuller," he answered. "I—I'm a friend to Mrs. Stiles."

Cristina tried to sit up, but her sudden movement provoked a coughing spell that muffled any further discussion in the parlor. When at last she regained control of her breathing, it was through watery eyes that she made out a vision standing in her doorway—a blurred vision of a tall figure taking up a large space. She wiped at her wet eyes with the back of her hand. "Jack?" she whispered hoarsely. Ever since the fire, her voice croaked and crackled. "Is—is it *you*?"

"Mrs. Stiles, I'm sorry, he barged right past me," Mrs. Grimshaw apologized, poking her head around Jack's big frame.

Cristina waved her off and gave a raspy gasp. "Am I dreamin'?"

"You're not dreaming, honey," Jack said, his own voice clear, deep, and soothing. He stepped inside the small room, snagged a wooden, high-backed chair, and brought it to her bedside, seemingly oblivious of the doctor's wife. Sitting down, he took Cristina's hand in both of his and brought it to his mouth to kiss. Cristina grinned with a shiver of delight. "You're really here."

"Yes, I really am. I hope you're not upset with me."

"No, no. Just in shock."

"I'll…just…leave you two alone, then," Mrs. Grimshaw muttered quietly. Neither of them acknowledged her comment, although Cristina noticed that, rather than leaving the door open a crack, as she usually did, the kind woman closed it with a gentle click.

"How are you doing?" Jack asked, still holding her hand. "I don't mean to make you talk. I know it must be painful. But…well, when I saw your house—rather, what used to be your house—I have to tell you, I panicked. I thought the worst. It terrified me. Elias and Catherina—where are they? Are they all right?"

"They're fine. They're stayin' with some friends."

"Not Clara?"

She shook her head. "The Garners, a family we met at church. The wife, Charlotte, an' 'er husband, John, are a wonderful couple with three children of their own." Tears sprang to her eyes, much as she willed them not to. "Oh, Jack, I don't know how I can recover from this and start over. I'm seriously considering selling my land an' all my animals t' my neighbor, Mr. Trigstead. Even Starlight and Thunder." She blinked back the tears. "It's all gone, Jack—all of it. We lost everything."

"I know, sweetheart. I'm sorry." He brought her hand to his mouth and gently kissed it once more.

"Clara's come t' see me every day. Poor thing doesn't know what t' do with me. I'm just one disaster after another."

He smiled warmly at her. "I wish I'd been the one taking care of you. Do you know how the fire started?"

"In the chimney, the sheriff said. Thank God Elias wasn't sleepin' in the attic or we all would've died. We had all been sick, so he was lyin' on the floor next t' Catherina's trundle."

"You were all sick?"

She nodded again. "I told you in a letter."

"I never got it. Must be on its way now."

"I thought you weren't musterin' out till November."

"So did I, but the major dismissed me early. That's a story for another time though. Tell me about the fire—if you're able. You're wheezing when you breathe. Are you all right?"

"I'm fine. Even finer now that you're here." For a brief moment, their thirsty eyes just drank in the sight of each other. "The doctor says my voice'll return t' normal in time," she continued, speaking at a whisper. "An' my wheeze is due to my lungs bein' damaged by smoke. He says that'll improve over time, too, but I need to rest, which I hate doin'. I miss my children.

"As for the fire, we were all asleep. Elias woke in the middle o' the night an' decided t' read some more, but when 'e got up t' light the lamp, he heard a strange poppin' noise an' smelled smoke. That's when he discovered the flames in the attic and the smoke pourin' down through a hole in the ceilin'. He snatched up Catherina first, thank God, and laid her outside on the ground, makin' her promise not t' move. By the time he got back inside, the flames had shot down the walls and the house was engulfed in fire and smoke so that he could barely see, but he covered his face with my apron an' had to feel 'is way t' the foot o' my bed. He grabbed me by the ankles an' hauled me outside. It was only by God's grace that he didn't collapse himself. I have a faint memory o' him screamin' my name, but I couldn't help. I don't know how he did it, Jack. He's only ten, but God gave 'im all the strength he needed t' pull me out." At this, her voice clogged with emotion and she couldn't stop the tears from falling.

Jack bent down, gently brushed them away with his fingertips, and kissed her forehead and then both her cheeks. His lips brushed her skin as softly as feather strokes. "Save your voice, honey. I have some things to say now."

37

A bottomless sense of relief had washed over Jack since he'd stepped inside Cristina's sickroom. Not only was she alive, but Elias and Catherina were safe. Deep gratitude filled his being and he praised God for His protective, watchful care over this family he had come to love.

Cristina gazed up at him and he nearly melted into her dark brown eyes. "You can't imagine how much I missed you, Cristina. Every day that went by made me realize even more just what you mean to me. I know we parted on less than good terms, never having had a chance to sort through that argument we'd had the night before I was taken away. Because of that, I didn't know quite how you'd receive me when I returned to Ripley."

"I wanted you t' come back." Though the rawness of her voice made him wince, gladness welled up within him when she uttered those sweet words.

"I'm sorry I was the one who shot him, Cristina. I'm so sorry."

She put two fingers to his mouth. "Shh. No need t' mention it again. I forgave you that mornin' they took you away. I planned t' tell you at breakfast, but I never had the chance. And then, when we started writin' back an' forth, I couldn't tell what you were feelin' or thinkin'. I thought maybe once you got back into the Army and away from me an' the kids, you'd start havin' a few regrets."

"Regrets? No, never. But—I had no idea what you were thinking."

"When I got your letters, I tried t' read into 'em more than was actually there."

He chuckled. "I did the same with yours. That's why I'm here today. No more trying to read between the lines."

"No more," she said, taking a wheezy breath.

"Have you told Elias who shot his father?"

"No, and I won't tell 'im, unless he asks me someday."

"I hope that if he ever does find out, his friendship with me will be strong enough for him to handle that knowledge. I...I want to always be there for him and Catherina...and you." He swallowed hard and watched her face to gauge her expression.

She smiled. "Are you sure about that? We can be a handful."

He chuckled. "I've got big hands." Reaching out, he gently pushed several stray hairs out of her eyes, then ended up playing with a few strands. "I know some would say we haven't known each other long enough, but I feel as though I've known you forever."

"I know what you mean. At first, I felt guilty because my husband had just passed, but, Jack...I started mournin' him the day he left fer the Army. In truth, I think he enlisted outta desperation. He just couldn't handle life in the way most people manage it."

"I'm sorry to hear that, but it does give me a bit of insight into his motives—a possible reason why he did what he did in the end. War can do terrible things to a person's mind."

She gave a solemn nod. "I've learned that. I'm just so glad you survived."

"As am I. It was only by God's grace. I think He had a plan for me that I didn't see coming. A plan that is only now beginning to unfold."

He leaned forward, propping his elbows on the bed, and lowered his face to hers. At his nearness, her pretty lips curved into the tiniest smile, her dimples barely emerging. "I'm going to ask you a question," he whispered. "And you don't have to give me an answer right away. I just want you to think about it."

Her dark eyebrows arched and she gave a wheezy giggle. "You're makin' me nervous."

He moved even closer, so that his lips brushed against hers as he spoke. "No need for nerves, sweetheart. Just hear me out."

"I'm listenin'."

He set himself back just far enough so he could read her eyes. "I love you, Cristina Stiles. What do you think about that?"

She gave a tiny gasp, then bit down on her upper lip, her brown eyes round and shimmery. "What do I think? I think...I love you back, Jack Fuller."

A loud breath of relief whistled out of him. He leaned in again and kissed her, not as thoroughly as he would've liked to because of her precarious health, but he figured there would be time for that later. He released another deep breath. "Now for my question."

"Y' mean, there's more?" She lay there as beautiful as a summer's day, her hands folded on top of the blankets, her bedsheet pulled up to the place where her two topmost buttons had come undone, revealing her creamy throat.

"Indeed. What do you think of Ohio?"

"What do I think of Ohio? That's yer question?"

"Well, not in full." He took both her hands in his and looked at her squarely. "I know that you would miss Clara an awful lot if you were to move with me to Lebanon, but you could visit her by train a couple of times a year. It's not so far as to be out of the question."

"Is that right? And what exactly would prompt me t' move t' Lebanon?"

"Oh, I don't know...changing your name to Cristina Fuller might give you some incentive."

She gave him a smile that sent his pulses racing. "Are you askin' me t' be yer—"

"Yes, I am. Would you, Cristina? Would you do me the honor of being my wife?"

He held his breath while she stared up at him, taking five, six, seven long seconds to answer. At last, she smiled, nodded her head, and whispered in her raspy voice, "Nothin' on earth would thrill me more."

He kissed her again—a little harder and with a little more passion than he should have, seeing as she finally pushed him away so she could get some air. Then she gave a wheezing giggle and clutched her chest. "Oh, my shinin' stars, Jack. Is this how it's gonna be—you stealin' my breath with every kiss?"

He laughed. "You can bet your shining stars, darlin'. For the rest of our lives."

There was a bit of commotion outside the door and Jack tilted his head toward the sound. "Is that who I think it is?"

"I forgot t' mention that Charlotte brings the children t' visit me every afternoon after school."

There came a tentative knock and then the door opened a crack. Mrs. Grimshaw peeked her head inside. "Your children are here with Mrs. Garner." She looked from Cristina to Jack and back again. "What should I tell them?"

Jack swiveled in the chair to face her. "Tell them to come in."

"Jack?" Elias burst right past Mrs. Grimshaw. "Jack?" he repeated. "What—"

"Hello, Elias. I hope you don't mind that I came to visit your mama."

"Mind? No! I'm—happy t' see you again. Are you outta the Army?"

"I am."

"Good." He gave a sheepish grin. "Can you stay? I mean, we don't have a house no more, but we got an empty barn."

"Yes, I'm staying. I'll find a room in town. We have lots of things to talk about, Elias." He gave the boy a friendly pat on the shoulder, wanting to hug him but respecting him enough to give him space. "I'm happy to see you. I think you've grown another inch since I last saw you."

"That's what Maw said." He turned to his sister, who'd been hiding in his shadow. "Look, Cath. It's Jack."

Catherina stepped out from behind her brother, skipped straight into Jack's arms, and immediately broke into tears. "Aww, don't cry, my little lass." He gave her a gentle hug then rested his chin on her head. She pulled back from him and blinked back more tears. "Our house burned down," she said between sobs. "I lost all my toys. But Mama says everything'll work out."

He calmly set her back from him, his hands lightly holding her upper arms. His throat felt achingly raw. "Your mama was exactly right. Everything *will* work out. As for your toys, we can replace them. You, however—you and Elias and your mama—no one can take your place. You're all alive and that's the most important thing." Over her head, he spotted a woman he could only guess was Charlotte Garner and next to her, of course, the doctor's wife. Both women swiped at tear-filled eyes.

"I'm Jack Fuller, by the way," Jack said with a smile. "You must be Charlotte Garner."

"Yes, a pleasure to meet you, though I feel I sort of know you already. Cristina has told me a lot about you."

"Really? It was all nice things, I hope."

She grinned. "Oh, I'd say so." Then she looked past him and winked at Cristina.

Jack directed his gaze to the doctor's wife. "I must apologize for my rush to get past you to reach the woman I love. I didn't even wait to be invited inside."

"Oh, I knew to step aside when I saw the determination in your eyes," she said with a little laugh. "I can see now why it was so important that you came in here."

"Wait." Elias held up his hands. "Did you say y' love Maw?"

Jack searched the boy's face. "I did. Do you mind?"

For a moment, Elias said nothing, just stood in frozen silence, and Jack could tell he had to allow that bit of information to sink in. Soon, Jack found himself holding his breath. If Elias didn't approve, it could complicate matters. Suddenly, the boy's deep brown eyes registered a probing query. "Are you gonna marry her?"

Jack turned and cast Cristina a quick glance, but all she gave him in return was an empty shrug. He was on his own. He regarded the play of emotions on the boy's face and bravely said, "Only with your permission.

After all, you are currently the man of the house." His heart thudded hard against his ribs.

Elias took his time in answering, but at last, he gave a slow nod that turned into a faster one and then a smile formed on his face. "I approve."

Jack turned to Cristina, whose eyes had a misty sheen. He reached over and took her hand. He would remember this moment for the rest of his life. Not only had he managed to steal the heart of a pretty Rebel woman, but he'd lassoed her children's affections, too.

EPILOGUE

Cristina smiled broadly as she listened to her children giggle. Their Grandmother Fuller had stopped by for a quick visit, bringing candy sticks for both of them, a game of checkers for Elias, and a doll for Catherina. Laura Fuller was everything Cristina could have hoped for in a mother-in-law—and in a mother, for that matter—warm and loving, caring and accepting, and generous to a fault. She loved showering her new grandchildren with gifts, despite having been asked by Jack and Cristina to slow down a bit. She knew how much loss they'd suffered and she wanted to make things right for them—never mind that both children were making a fine adjustment to their new surroundings.

Elias and Catherina had even made plenty of friends at their new school before classes concluded in mid-March. They missed their friends from Ripley, of course, but they were resilient and didn't waste much time dwelling on the past. Besides, there was no shortage of chores to do and fun to be had on a farm this size—more animals to tend, more weeds to pull, more eggs to collect, dogs to run and play with, and kittens to cuddle. There were horses to ride, too, including Thunder and Starlight. As a surprise for Cristina, Jack had purchased her horses from Mr. Trigstead and then made arrangements to have them shipped by train to Lebanon. How Cristina's heart thrilled at the sight of them galloping in the vast green pastures with Jack's herd.

More than once, Elias had expressed his approval of having moved to Lebanon. "I miss Ripley," he'd said the other day, "but Jack's home is here and I'd rather be where Jack is." That comment, along with so many other positive remarks from her children, had come as a great reassurance to Cristina. To make matters even sweeter, Catherina had started to call Jack "Daddy." Cristina had asked Elias if this bothered him at all.

"She doesn't remember our real daddy in the way I do," he had responded thoughtfully, "so it's good she thinks o' Jack that way. I think o' him more an' more as my dad, but he'll always be my best friend first."

When Cristina had relayed that conversation to Jack, he'd actually had to brush a tear from his eye. Then he'd drawn Cristina into a warm embrace and thanked her for the privilege of raising her children with her.

Now, as Jack's mother was getting ready to leave, Cristina sent a silent prayer to God once again for so richly blessing her family.

Laura Fuller gathered her belongings slowly, as if reluctant to leave. "I must be on my way," she said. "So many errands to do today."

Catherina ran over to give her grandmother another hug. "You just got here," she whined.

"I know, but I have so much to do in town."

"Can I go with you?"

"Catherina, you mustn't invite yerself along like that," Cristina scolded her softly.

Laura glanced at Cristina, her arm around Catherina's shoulder. "It wouldn't bother me to have the company, if you don't mind my taking her."

"O' course not," Cristina replied.

Laura turned to Elias. "Would you like to join us?"

His face brightened. "Sure!"

"Remember, Jack wants to take you with him this afternoon to gather hay," Cristina reminded him.

"How about I fix them lunch and bring them back after that?" Laura offered. "No later than one, I promise."

"If you're sure they're no bother...."

"How could they possibly be a bother? I love my grandchildren, all six of them."

Cristina smiled to herself. It wouldn't be long till she would have *seven*. She hadn't yet shared the good news with Jack, but she planned to let him in on her little secret today. She could hardly wait to see his excitement.

A few minutes later, she watched out the window as Laura's wagon retreated down the road, with all three of them squeezed together on the buckboard. A year ago, she could never have imagined all that her future held—learning about God and then coming to call Him her Savior; falling in love again, remarrying, and moving to Ohio; having someone to call "Mom"; owning a four-bedroom farmhouse—or being with child again, for goodness' sake!

Everything pointed back to God—all the plans she never saw forming, all the blessings she didn't know existed, and all the joys she wasn't aware awaited her. What a pleasure to serve a living, loving, heavenly Father! And a recent letter from Clara mentioned she'd started going to church on Sundays. Cristina was thrilled beyond measure.

⟋

Jack rode the range with his brother Jesse, rounding up cattle to move them to a new pasture, assisted by their black and white herding dog, Corky. At the gate, Jesse followed the cattle inside, Corky at their heels barking out commands, while Jack circled back around to pick up a few strays that'd lagged behind. While Jack loved getting back to the business of farming—feeling the wind in his face and watching the sun traverse the sky from dawn till dusk—he could hardly wait for those in-between times when he went home for the noon meal or just dropped in because he was close to the house. After almost six months of marriage, what kept him going all day long—whether he was out herding cattle, in the barn milking, tilling the soil, or planting crops—was the knowledge that Cristina would be waiting for him when he got home. He could almost see her now, running down the porch steps and jumping into his arms. He'd whirl her around a few times, then kiss her silly, until Elias stepped outside and said something like, "Eww! Don't you ever stop?"

They had gotten married exactly six weeks after his return to Ripley. Her lungs hadn't healed yet, but Dr. Grimshaw said she shouldn't be discouraged. It would take time, he'd said, perhaps as long as a year. Jack had noticed, though, that with every passing month, the wheeze had faded until it had all but disappeared, and Cristina's voice and energy level had almost returned to normal. The wedding had been a simple ceremony at the Methodist church with only a few friends in attendance. Reverend Wilcox had done the honors, purposely keeping the service brief because Cristina was still recovering. Jack had told his own family not to come. It was, after all, a second marriage for both of them and neither one felt the need for a big party. Besides, Cristina wasn't up for it. Jack's family respected their wishes, but his mother made it clear there would eventually be a party of some sort. She'd held it in April—and invited practically the entire town of Lebanon.

They'd taken a brief honeymoon trip to Ravenswood, leaving the children with the Garners. Jack had always considered himself to be a brave man, but in the hotel room that first night, he'd been almost afraid to touch his wife. Cristina sensed his wariness and assured him that she wouldn't break, so he had taken her to the marriage bed that night—and every night after that for at least the next month…until Cristina finally told him she might have to send notice to Dr. Grimshaw that her husband wasn't letting her have her proper rest.

Jack chuckled at the memory as the house came into view around the bend. He gave a gentle kick to his mount, wanting to get there faster. He didn't see the children playing outside, so he figured Cristina must have given them some indoor chores. Jack had promised to take Elias with him after lunch to help gather hay. They looked forward to spending time together and Jack cherished the bond they were forming. Such a blessing from above. Sometimes he couldn't even contain his emotions when he thought about the way God had handed over this precious family of three into his protective care. What had he done to deserve it? Nothing. But that was God's grace—a special gift, freely given, never earned.

At the house, Jack dismounted and tossed the reins over a post. He would walk the horse out to the barn after lunch for some grain and a fresh drink. Hearing the front door open, he turned, expecting to see his sweet little Cath come running across the porch to leap into his arms. Instead, there stood Cristina, a cheery smile on her dimpled face. If he lived to be a hundred and ten, his heart would always pick up an extra beat at every sight of her. He had loved her almost from the beginning and he would love her with his final breath.

"You're home!" she exclaimed, as if she hadn't just seen him at breakfast mere hours ago. "It's about time." And then she leaped into his arms in much the same way little Cath did. He took a deep breath, loving the soapy smell of her skin and the soft, silky feel of her hair against his cheek. He kissed her soundly, then asked, "Where are the kids?"

"Out with yer mother. She's bringin' 'em back around one."

He raised his eyebrows and grinned. "Is that so? You mean we have the place to ourselves?"

She giggled and touched her finger to his chin. "Yer lunch is ready, Mr. Fuller."

"I think it can wait." He swiftly scooped her up.

She looped her arms around his neck and giggled again. "But I've got some excitin' news t' tell you."

"Your exciting news can wait, my dear. We have an empty house."

She giggled some more and the warm sound enfolded his heart like a sweet embrace.

QUESTIONS FOR GROUP DISCUSSION

1. What was your overall feeling about this book?

2. Which character did you like the most? The least?

3. What are your thoughts about the book's cover? Did it convey enough to you about the contents of the book?

4. Did the storyline seem realistic to you?

5. What portion(s) of the book touched an emotional chord with you?

6. How did you feel about the book's spiritual content? Was it enough or too much?

7. Did you learn anything from reading this book? Did it challenge you in any specific way?

8. Have you read many novels set in the Civil War era? After reading this one, would you seek out more?

9. Would you read another book by this author?

10. Was the pace of the story too fast, too slow, or just right?

11. What feelings did this book evoke in you?

12. Would you recommend this book to others?

ABOUT THE AUTHOR

Born and raised in west Michigan, Sharlene MacLaren attended Spring Arbor University. Upon graduating with an education degree in 1971, she taught second grade for two years, then accepted an invitation to travel internationally for a year with a singing ensemble. After traveling for a year, she returned to her teaching job, then in 1975, she reunited with her childhood sweetheart, and they married that very December. They have raised two lovely daughters, both of whom are now happily married and enjoying their own families. Retired in 2003 after thirty-one years of teaching, Shar loves to read, sing, travel, and spend time with her family—in particular, her adorable grandchildren!

Shar has always enjoyed writing, and her high school classmates eagerly read and passed around her short stories. In the early 2000s, Shar felt God's call upon her heart to take her writing pleasures a step further, so in 2006, she signed a contract with Whitaker House for her first faith-based novel, *Through Every Storm*, thereby launching her professional writing career. With more than twenty published novels now gracing store shelves and being sold online, Shar gives God all the glory.

Shar's novels have won numerous awards. Most recently, *Their Daring Hearts* was named a 2018 Top Pick by *Romantic Times* and her last book, *A Love to Behold*, was voted "Book of the Year" in 2019 by *Interviews & Reviews*.

Shar has done numerous countrywide book signings and has participated in several interviews on television and radio. She loves to speak for community organizations, libraries, church groups, and women's conferences. In her church, she is active in women's ministries, regularly facilitating Bible studies and other events. Shar and her husband, Cecil, live in Spring Lake, Michigan, with their beautiful white collie, Peyton.

Shar loves hearing from her readers. If you wish to contact her as a potential speaker or would simply like to chat with her, please send her an e-mail at SharleneMacLaren@Yahoo.com. She will do her best to answer in a timely manner.

Additional resources:

www.SharleneMacLaren.com

www.instagram.com/sharlenemaclaren

twitter.com/sharzy_lu?lang=en

www.facebook.com/groups/43124814557
(Sharlene MacLaren & Friends)

www.whitakerhouse.com/book-authors/sharlene-maclaren

Welcome to Our House!

We Have a Special Gift for You ...

It is our privilege and pleasure to share in your love of Christian fiction by publishing books that enrich your life and encourage your faith.

To show our appreciation, we invite you to sign up to receive a specially selected **Reader Appreciation Gift**, with our compliments. Just go to the Web address at the bottom of this page.

God bless you as you seek a deeper walk with Him!

WE HAVE A GIFT FOR YOU. VISIT:

whpub.me/fictionthx

WHITAKER
HOUSE